ECLIPSE OF THE BRIGHT MOON

DONALD C. LEE

ECLIPSE OF THE BRIGHT MOON

CamCat
Books

CamCat Publishing, LLC
Brentwood, Tennessee 37027
camcatpublishing.com

Hardcover ISBN 9780744303193
Paperback ISBN 9780744303261
Large-Print Paperback ISBN 9780744303339
eBook ISBN 9780744303285
Audiobook ISBN 9780744303407

Library of Congress Control Number: 2021931133

Cover and book design by Maryann Appel

5   3   1   2   4

*Thanks to Drusilla Campbell for her criticisms
of the earliest draft of this work, and to
Debra Ginsberg and Gail Baker for their editing,
suggestions, and encouragement, and to
Carl Stern for saving the work from a dying computer.*

PART I

APRIL: UPRISING

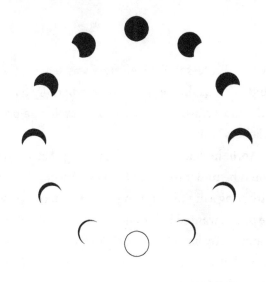

AUTHOR'S PREFACE

APRIL 15, 1989

DENG XIAOPING SAID THAT WHEN YOU OPEN THE windows, the flies come in. In the Spring of 1989, China opened its windows wider than ever before to the fresh breeze of freedom. From Deng's point of view, the flies had come in and needed to be swatted.

One fly had stopped beating its wings today. Hu Yaobang had died, and the government would not announce it for three more days. Then the rumor would brew that he had been swatted. The rumor would be enough to stir up the hurricane of events, the eye of which would sweep across Tiananmen Square in Beijing, and the winds of which would extend out thousands of miles to batter all of China. Eight hundred miles southwest of Beijing, the city of Xi'an, where Professor Dan Norton was teaching American literature and Western history, would be especially hard hit. Dan Norton had almost finished his year as an exchange professor at Shaanxi Teachers University.

In mid-April, he had no way of knowing that in two weeks' time, he would be under threat of Chinese prison, accused by the police of harboring a fugitive and engaging in espionage. Would he do what the police wanted him to do to get himself out of trouble? He would apparently have to choose, just as the Chinese students had to choose between cooperating with corruption, fleeing, or standing up for their values at grave risk.

The dark labyrinth of his tortured soul had led Dan to China to seek redemption. But that is not the heart of the story, only the fictional occasion for its telling. The heart of the story is the actual struggle of the Chinese people against the corruption of their government, which mirrors the history of many such struggles throughout human history. They are stories of fear and hope, cowardice and courage, naïveté and wisdom, selfishness and generosity. Battles for justice are fought and lost time and again; but after many failures, there are often victories, if sometimes not for decades or centuries.

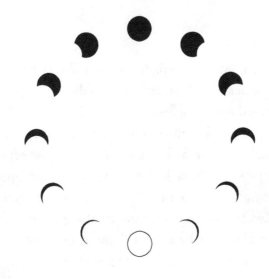

THERE WILL BE BIG TROUBLE

April 18, 1989

THE BLARE OF THE CHINESE NATIONAL ANTHEM from the loudspeakers outside jarred Dan Norton out of his sleep as they did every morning. The communal alarm clock. It had taken him out of his recurring Vietnam nightmare. He pulled the pillow over his ears until the anthem stopped.

Memories of Vietnam exploded in his brain. As a twenty-three-year-old Second Lieutenant forward observer for an artillery battery, he had directed four-deuce mortar shells at a village harboring Viet Cong in 1964. When the Marines moved through the shelled village later in the day, he saw bodies of women and children, gray-haired old people, but no young men, no Viet Cong soldiers. The smell of death and the sickness of guilt and anger burned deeply into his soul. A hundred ghosts from Vietnam tugged at the sleeves of his memory every day.

He lurched down the hall into the bathroom. Cold water on his face helped him feel more human. He poured a glass of water from the pitcher and washed the dark brown taste out of his mouth.

He went back through the living room and opened the balcony door. On the soot-encrusted veranda, he squinted into the new day, the sun shining through the gray smog. Sunlight warmed his cheeks as he looked down at the small, grass- and mud-covered courtyard and the red tile roof of the dining hall. The sweet, suffocating smoke of countless coal fires cooking morning breakfast filled his lungs and made him cough.

Out in the streets, dozens of elderly Chinese citizens would be doing their morning Tai Chi-like calisthenics—all the original spirit of the moves forgotten during years of atheist propaganda. In dozens of kitchens, women would be preparing tea, rice, and sour pickles for breakfast.

He heard the key rattle in the front door and the squeak it made when it opened behind him. He pulled the bathroom door closed. It would be the woman delivering the daily thermos of boiled water for his tea. She never knocked on the door. A minute later as he dressed, he heard the bang of the door closing again.

When he had eaten his breakfast of creamy peach yogurt and baodzes—sticky steamed buns with a dab of almond paste in them—he stepped out the front door and met Tyson Bates, his neighbor on the second floor. Ty lived with his parents who taught conversational English while he studied Chinese language and history here at Shaanxi Teachers University. He stood a lanky, medium height in his cowboy boots, had curly brown hair, gray eyes, a tan face, and a Roman nose. He wore a red checkered shirt, blue jeans, and smelled of Old Spice. They had kept to themselves, and Dan did not know them well yet.

"Did you go on the outing for foreigners yesterday?" Dan asked. "I had to miss it because of a class."

"Skipped it. Once you've seen a dozen Imperial Tombs, the excitement seems to wear off a bit," Ty grinned. "Guess I'm more interested in the living than the dead. It's a drag to spend the party-time of my life in China. They're as repressed here as the folks back in my hometown. They don't know what fun is. I could as well have stayed in Plainfield, Texas."

"Lust and wild parties what you want? You came to the wrong country." Dan smiled. "But I've heard that there are places foreign students go dancing, like at the Highway Institute."

"Parents don't let me go dancing," Ty's shoulders drooped. "Temptations of Satan and all that bull. A Baptist family must be my karmic punishment for a parade of sinful past lives. At least I hope that's the reason. I'd like to know I once had some fun, even if I can't remember it 'cause it was in a past life."

"Christianity and karma?" Dan laughed. "I'm not sure I understand your religious beliefs."

"Me neither." Ty grinned. "Say, I hear you know a lot about Chinese culture. Do you understand the *Tao Te Ching*?"

"A bit." Dan recognized the same search for identity he himself was still struggling with.

"Could you explain what it means when it says, 'When all the world recognizes beauty as beauty, this in itself is ugliness. When all the world recognizes good as good, this in itself is evil'?"

"That has to do with correlative terms." Dan heard voices coming up the staircase. "There can't be ugliness except by contrast with beauty, so ugliness doesn't exist until—"

Ty's parents came charging up the stairs. They were both short, blond, and obese. Mrs. Bates led the way clutching an inch-thick stack of money.

"Aah, payday." Dan pounded the wall with the edge of his fist.

Mrs. Bates came to a sudden halt and stared at Dan, mouth agape, panting.

"Oh, sorry," Dan said. "Didn't mean to startle you. I'm just angry at Wu. I just remembered I'll have to see Wu to get paid. I hate to deal with him."

"Having problems with Wu? Aren't we all?" Mrs. Bates straightened her dress and patted her hair. "What's your problem?"

"Don't mean to bother you about it. But . . . he was supposed to pay for my flight over here. He hasn't reimbursed me yet—after seven months—and I can't afford to buy a ticket home until he pays me what he owes me. Sorry for pounding on the wall."

"I know the feeling," Mr. Bates mumbled.

"We've had the same problem too," Mrs. Bates said. "The man's a liar. Tells you he'll pay for your ticket and doesn't. And you can't buy a foreign flight with Chinese money, and they don't take credit cards in China. So, you need dollars."

"Exactly." Dan felt better to know he wasn't alone. "And the book on teaching in China says we should get ten percent of our pay in dollars each month. But Wu didn't put it in the contract he sent me. He keeps making excuses. I know it may all be a misunderstanding. My friend, Professor Gao Baima, insists that it's just the Chinese system. He says Wu will pay the money when I need it—"

"Don't count on it," Mrs. Bates said.

"Well, Gao told me it's just that in China, everyone has to get permission from his superiors to get anything done. And those superiors have to kowtow to their superiors and present small gifts—"

"Bribes," Mrs. Bates interjected.

"And so on up the ladder. Everyone along the way has the power to say 'no,' but no one has the power to say 'yes' without approval from higher up."

"Right," Mrs. Bates said. "He did the same to us, but we put our foot down, had him rewrite the contract, and he paid us what he owed us."

Dan bit his lip on hearing that they had gotten their money. He had to practice his Buddhist wisdom to control his anger. A few deep breaths.

He needed a walk to clear his head and to consider what to do about Wu. He hadn't walked on the city wall since autumn. He got on a bus for downtown, pushing and shoving with the rest of the crowd to get a place standing in the middle with several bodies pressed against his own. A head taller than most people on the bus, he could breathe above the cloud of garlic fumes.

Dan got off at the Ming Dynasty city wall and climbed the worn stone steps to the top. He walked a half-mile before he could get his frustration for Wu out of his mind. Thinking about history was always a good escape from the grief of worldly troubles. He admired how the wall encircled the center of the city. It was seven miles long with four major gates and ninety-eight defense towers. Above drab contemporary buildings, he could see the blue roof of the ancient Drum Tower, and at the center of the city, the three-story Bell Tower, each story with its own green-tiled roof.

Xi'an had been the capital of China for so much of its history, which was the reason Dan had been eager to teach here. His love of literature and history had drawn him to the ancient heart of

China. Dan had been awed by the army of Terracotta Warriors, just outside the city, that protected the tomb of the Qin Emperor. He had unified China and made Xi'an his capital. To the south, Dan saw the top of the Big Wild Goose Pagoda, where the first Buddhist manuscripts had been brought from India. Xi'an, once called Chang-an, had been the terminus of the Silk Road to the Roman Empire and capital of eleven of China's most important dynasties. All around Dan were imperial tombs and famous temples. Dan had been so excited to be in the center of it.

It depressed him that the luster of its ancient glory had been dimmed by the smog of chemical factories, inefficient toxic fume-spouting "one ox" diesel tractors, yellow smoke from half a million cooking stoves that burned cheap, soft coal, and glacial loess dust kicked up in clouds by busses and trucks.

Dan didn't like the view from the wall to the north of the ugly flat-roofed four to six story concrete socialist style buildings. They hid the shorter, more attractive older gray-brick houses with sloping red-tiled roofs.

The view to the south of grassy slopes plunging into the old water-filled moat was spoiled by the cacophony of trucks, busses and tractors weaving among the hordes of bicyclists on the main street on the other side of the moat. Dan smelled the diesel fumes even on the wall.

Dan thought of one of the many ancient poetic references to the city—Du Fu's *Autumn Meditation*:

". . . Chang-An looks like a chessboard.

Won and lost for a hundred years, sad beyond all telling."

That was an understatement. It had been won and lost for three thousand years. Ironically, Xi'an means "western peace." It seemed lost in its cloud of pollution.

Dan walked another mile, turning the corner toward the north and turned back so he could get to class on time. Halfway back, he met a Japanese student, Yoshiko Sato. She wore a purple and blue silk kimono with three golden chrysanthemums and a matching blue sash. She stood out like a blue morning glory on a lawn of dandelion flowers in the sea of Chinese women with their printed blouses and slacks. Her short, cropped black hair shone with glints of red in the sunlight.

Dan knew from a reference someone had made to her childhood that she must be in her late thirties, but she still looked like a rosy-cheeked, young girl.

Dan had been attracted to Yoshiko's grace and beauty for months. Sometimes she sat with the other Japanese students in the dining hall for foreign guests. Occasionally, she had caught him looking at her. Dan had talked to her and found out that she studied Chinese and interviewed local Buddhist monks for a Japanese Buddhist magazine. He thought a forty-eight-year-old Westerner had no business trying to start a relationship with a younger Japanese student, as much as he might have wanted to. After two failed marriages, he had been avoiding relationships.

Dan was about to turn away, to look over the wall as though he didn't see her, but she glanced at him, and her wide-set brown eyes met his, and she looked down modestly. He couldn't ignore her now. He walked toward her.

"Miss Sato. How are you?" Dan stopped and bowed his head slightly. He spoke in Chinese. "A beautiful day for a walk. You're very dressed up today. What's the special occasion?"

Yoshiko bowed back. "So beautiful. Yes. Professor Norton. I am coming back from taking photos with Buddhist monks at a monastery. How are you?"

He hadn't been out with a woman in five years, since his second divorce. He could ask her out to dinner, but it didn't feel right. "I'll be on the university outing to Hua Ching Hot Spring tomorrow. Will I have the pleasure of seeing you there?" Dan smelled her orange blossom perfume.

Yoshiko blushed. "Hua Ching Hot Spring . . . so beautiful. I wanted to go. But the trip has been canceled."

"Canceled? I didn't know that. Why?"

"The radio reported that Hu Yaobang died . . . three days ago. I just talked to Mr. Wu. He's worried that there will be big trouble." She looked down meekly.

Dan wondered, why cancel the trip? "Hu Yaobang? Former Secretary of the Communist Party? But why would there be trouble?"

"I don't know. I'm so sorry." They both stood silently for a moment.

He considered a restaurant he could ask her to. The Golden Flower Restaurant, but that was way across town. Maybe the Jiaodze Restaurant. Or the . . .

"So nice to see you." She bowed and walked past him.

Dan bowed his head slightly. Her perfume lingered. She was slipping away because he had hesitated. She smiled at a crowd of schoolgirls who giggled at her kimono, hands over mouths. Opportunity lost.

"Sayonara," he mumbled.

HE WHO DIED
SHOULD NOT HAVE

APRIL 20

AS DAN ENTERED THE FOREIGN GUESTS' DINING hall, he thought about the posters he had heard were going up all over campus criticizing the government. That was how other serious political movements had started in China; "big poster" campaigns.

In the hall, bright lavender and chartreuse crepe decorated with paper Easter bunnies, multi-colored eggs, and flowers, a bit bedraggled now, still hung from the white concrete walls. Chinese students had made them for the foreigners. The Chinese loved any excuse for a celebration, even the Western holidays. Now the students would turn their creative energies from Easter decorations to political posters. He hadn't seen any posters yet and wanted to ask someone about them.

Perhaps it was just another Chinese rumor.

The Australian Physics professor, his wife, daughter, and son sat at one table. Dan often joined them, but they were almost finished. The head of a whole fish stared up from a platter. Five Japanese students sat at another table. He remembered Yoshiko's orange blossom perfume. She wasn't there. The strength of his disappointment surprised him.

Beyond the Japanese students, three American students devoured lotus root, pork, and cabbage cooked with star anise and pepper, and peanut chicken with rice. Ty Bates, in his cowboy shirt and boots, drank *qi shui*—what passed as orange soda in China. The other two—freckle-faced Susan, who had had a runny nose and cough for six straight months, probably from the polluted air, and Ed, who looked like Mr. Spock of Star Trek fame except that he was balding in the back—both drank beer. Ty waved for Dan to join them.

Dan asked, "No jiaodzes or noodles today?"

They shook their heads. He loved jiaodzes—steamed or fried dumplings with various meats or vegetables in them, usually pork and cabbage.

The famous Jiaodze Restaurant in downtown Xi'an served two hundred varieties of jiaodzes, each in the shape of its ingredients: pork in the shape of a pig, chicken in the shape of a chicken, cat in the shape of a cat, and so on.

Dan ordered what the students were eating, plus a beer, and sat down with them.

"Your parents aren't eating with us tonight?" he asked Ty.

"They're explaining Christianity to a group of students at the Clock and Watch School. They'll eat there." Ty deftly scooped a ball of rice and cabbage into his mouth with his chopsticks.

"I've never known your parents to miss a meal here," Dan said. "Even after the disaster with the Thanksgiving turkey."

Ed, Susan, and Dan roared with laughter, and even Ty managed one chortle.

Ty's mother had gone to incredible lengths to get a whole turkey and wanted to cook it herself, but the cooks, Ding and Ting, wouldn't let her in the kitchen. Ding threatened to quit over the incident. The turkey arrived alive, so she told them they would have to cure it by hanging it up to let the blood drain, then soak it in saltwater. She gave them elaborate instructions on how to prepare and serve it. Instead of curing it, they slaughtered it, roasted it fresh, sliced it up with the bones cut willy-nilly so every bite was loaded with bone splinters, and served it the Chinese way, with the head and feet on the platter.

"Your mother should learn a bit of Chinese," Susan coughed.

Ty shrugged his shoulders, glum as a hound dog. "It was the toughest, stringiest bird I ever tasted. And the yams, string beans, and potatoes were all cut up and stir-fried with garlic and Peking peppers. That can of cranberry sauce—she had to pay the airline extra for her bag being just over the weight limit because of it— was a pretty lonely reminder of Thanksgiving."

Susan chuckled. "I think Ding and Ting matched that this week with the birthday cake."

"Another episode in her eternal and doomed struggle with the cooks," Ty said.

Mrs. Bates had invited several students for Ty's birthday and had given Ding and Ting the recipe for an American cake. It came out looking like Betty Crocker herself couldn't have done better. Yellow frosting with Ty's name done in blue, spelled correctly and all. Little blue candles Mrs. Bates had brought from home.

"That woman thinks of everything," Dan said.

"Ding and Ting had just about made up for the turkey," Susan said, "until the guests tasted the cake. Someone had put salt in the frosting instead of sugar." Susan laughed and coughed.

"My mother should give up trying to eat like an American while she's in China," Ty said. "She'll never get the cooks to make it her way. They always botch it up."

"The Chinese have developed cooking to a high art for thousands of years. And Ding and Ting are excellent cooks." Dan frowned. "Imagine trying to tell a gourmet French chef he should cook like you do at home. I doubt if the salt in the frosting was a mistake."

They all sat and stared glumly at their plates for a moment.

Dan brought up the issue that he thought would be on everyone's mind.

"I've read about the big poster campaigns, like at the Democracy Wall ten years ago, and now posters are appearing right here in our university." He dipped his chopsticks into his cabbage. "But I haven't seen any posters yet."

"Every major political event in China starts with posters," Ed said. "That's how the pro-democracy demonstrations in '86 to '87 began."

"But they were put down quickly enough," Susan sniffed.

"Tell me what's happening," Ty said. "I haven't seen any posters either."

"Hu Yaobang, the former Communist Party Secretary, died on April 15, and the government didn't announce it until the 18th." Dan had gotten the story from his friend Gao. "He's the one who was ousted for encouraging reform and failing to crack down on the student demonstrations."

"The students' shining hope for justice and fairness in the Government," Susan said, brushing her red hair off her shoulder.

"The Government's delay in reporting the death is enough to make the students suspect that he was poisoned," Dan said, "since he was in good health the last anyone knew."

"Now unsigned posters are appearing in the middle of the night all around the walls of the university," Susan said. "I saw one last night that read: 'He who died shouldn't have; he who hasn't died should have.'"

"Who do they think should have died?" Ty asked. "Do they dare suggest Deng Xiaoping?"

"Or Premier Li Peng," Susan added. "They're both hated for blocking reform."

"Where are the posters?" Ty asked. "I'd like to see them."

"You have to get up before sunrise," Susan said. "Students go around with flashlights to read and copy down the messages to tell the other students because in the morning, the university administrators tear them down. The game has gone on for two nights now."

"Well," Ty said, "that leaves me out. I'm not an early riser. Too many years of milking the cows."

Ed stared at his beer bottle as if it were a crystal ball. "I know how quickly these things can turn against foreigners." His narrow face turned grim. "I almost got killed in Nanjing last semester. That's why I came to Xi'an. Any more of this and I'm out of China."

"What happened to you in Nanjing?" Dan crammed a ball of rice and spicy chicken into his mouth.

Ed scratched his chin. "It's hard to know how it all started. There were a number of African students at Hehai University, where I was studying. The Chinese students thought they were troublemakers. When the administration tried to build a wall around the foreign students' dormitory—you know how this country builds walls around everything—"

"Right," Ty interrupted. "Every factory and other work unit in Xi'an is surrounded by a wall, so the university is walled off from the rest of the city, and you need a blue card to get in. Then, the university classrooms are separated from the university dorms by a wall, and you have to show your blue card to go to class. Then, the foreign guests' compound is separated from the dorms by a wall, and Lao Zhu keeps everyone but—"

Susan laughed. "You'd have thought they'd have learned from the failure of the Great Wall to keep invaders out." She blew her red nose.

"They have created a society of prisons within prisons and claim it's for everyone's protection," Dan said.

"Well, that's exactly why the African students tore down the wall," Ed said.

"Wow," Ty gasped.

"Yes, it made them very angry," Ed said. "When I went to a Christmas dance, there were Chinese students outside that warned me not to go in since there was likely to be trouble. Now I'm not one to loiter under a tree when a lumberjack shouts 'Timber,' so I went to my room and brooded. But I felt like I was leaving my fellow foreign students in a lurch, so I went back to the dance an hour later, and the police had already arrived."

"Noble Ed." Susan smirked.

"I was told that the African students had brought two Chinese women to the dance without proper identification. A brawl had resulted, two Africans and eleven Chinese had been injured, and an African student had killed an elderly Chinese gatekeeper."

"Uh oh," Susan moaned. "That takes it beyond cultural differences to a whole new—"

"It wasn't long before a crowd outside was shouting, 'Down with the black devils' and other racist bull. The next day, Chinese students blocked traffic, confronted police, and chanted anti-African slogans in downtown Nanjing. They wanted the Africans involved punished. It didn't matter that the rumor about the gatekeeper was false."

"You mean, no one was killed?" Ty asked.

Ed shook his head. "Just a rumor. The Africans were grossly rounded up by the police and taken to the train station. There were about a hundred and fifty awaiting transportation. They didn't know to where. Six of us Americans heard they didn't have any food, so we bought lots of baodzes and took them to the train station. There was a crowd of Chinese natives buzzing around like killer bees."

"Jesus," Ty said. "I wouldn't have hung around."

"Just as we started distributing food, a huge crowd arrived. If the police hadn't forced the crowd outside, we might have been killed. We were roughed up by the cops as it was and taken to a guest house two hours outside Nanjing. The compound was surrounded by a hundred cops, and most of us had to sleep on the concrete floor that night. The leaders told me that they were forced to stand outside nude in the frosty air while the police jabbed at their testicles with electric cattle prods."

Susan shook her head as if in disbelief. "The Chinese elementary students seem so bright-eyed, freshly scrubbed, and innocent. What turns some of them into demons?"

"I think it's the legacy of one disappointment after another," Dan said. "The Great Leap Forward, the Cultural Revolution and all. When I was in Hong Kong for Christmas, the papers reported that the rumor was the Nanjing Africans all carried AIDS. The rumor spread to the Hangzhou Agricultural University, where thousands threw rocks at the foreign students' dorms and called Africans by the Chinese words for AIDS, *ai zi*."

Susan laughed. "That's appropriate: 'love child.'"

Dan nodded. "The African students counter-demonstrated, boycotted classes, and kidnapped a school officer."

"A friend of mine in Beijing told me what happened there," Susan said. "Students marched at the Beijing Languages Institute. There was a rumor that an African student had supposedly sexually assaulted a Chinese woman in her dorm room, and she was injured. African students were boycotting classes in protest at what had happened in Nanjing, and Chinese students were boycotting classes in protest of sexual assaults."

"Students will go to any lengths to get out of classes," Dan said dryly.

Susan gave him an exaggerated smile and continued.

"Protesters carried banners that read, 'Hooligans, go home.'"

Dan swallowed a bite of pork. "Well, I read that only one in fifteen hundred Africans has tested HIV positive under China's mandatory testing of foreign students."

"You see how people overreact to rumors?" Ed said. "My original point in telling all this is to show just how hotheaded Chinese citizens can get when riled up by rumors. They can be on a very short fuse."

"They know everything in the government-controlled media is propaganda," Susan said. "All they've got to trust is rumors."

"They've hated 'foreign devils' a long time," Ed said. "They consider a history of Western domination a humiliation to be avenged."

Susan laughed. "When was China occupied by Africans?"

"Or is it that they feel helpless to fight government oppression and turn on easy scapegoats?" Dan asked.

"Either way," Ed grimaced, "I'm leaving if this protest continues. I've had enough."

"No way I'm about to leave," Dan said. "I want to see those posters."

———

Gao Mingyue had had a terrible day avoiding his father who wanted him to go to all the foreign-owned hotels in Xi'an to look for a job. His father was always pushing him to get a job regardless of what Mingyue wanted. They hadn't spoken to each other all day. He would rather go back to driving a truck for the railroad than work as some clerk managing bed linens and dirty laundry. Why had his father bothered to be one of the few parents to pay for his son's education in Economics so he wouldn't have to go where the government sent him if he was going to act just like the government and not give him a choice? He didn't have the influence or connections to get him a good job anyway.

Slouching and dragging his feet, he crossed campus and went to a storage room of the Biology laboratory to make posters with his girlfriend, Song Yingying, a biology student. Seven other students sat on their heels and painted posters on the floor. He nodded at a couple of them he knew. Yingying wielded a large brush to write big characters on an old newspaper: "The People Demand a Free Press." She pushed the hair out of her eyes to look up at Mingyue and left a streak of ink on her forehead. Mingyue laughed and used a wet sheet of paper to rub it off.

"You don't want people to know you've been making posters."

He loved her girlish look and the two short ponytails held by red bows, her pouty lips, and her long eyelashes. He loved her for her proletarian hatred of inequality and injustice. She was no "Shanghai woman" who would refuse to marry a man with less than forty legs. Counting the legs on a man's furniture as a sign of his wealth was bourgeois and reactionary but not uncommon these days. She wasn't a peasant woman either whose parents would "sell" her into marriage for a bride price. Yingying didn't care about wealth, she only cared about justice.

Mingyue had loved Yingying for two years now and hoped they could marry after she graduated this year, if he found a job himself. Although, that didn't look hopeful. Even worse was the prospect of her being assigned a job in another city or the countryside. They would be separated before they had a chance to really be together. The government was so unfair to separate married couples. Love was so difficult in China. An unmarried couple never had a chance to be alone together with holding hands, hugging, and kissing forbidden and with eyes watching everywhere and people eager to report each other.

How that one student had managed to become pregnant—forced to get an abortion and expelled from school—was a mystery to him. He could hardly imagine what it would be like to kiss Yingying, much less what it would feel like to hold her in his arms.

"Have you heard from your friend at Beijing University?" he asked.

"Two faxes." She smiled. "Fifteen hundred students marched in Beijing, another thousand in Nanjing, and others in Shanghai, Wuhan, and Hefei. The government has threatened 'harsh measures.' They say protest will not be tolerated."

"That's what they said in '87 before they did crush the dissent." Mingyue sighed and frowned. "They'll do it. I don't want you to get into trouble."

"When you frown with your bushy eyebrows, you scare me," she said. "Cheer up. We're not going to cave in so easily this time. The students in Beijing have demanded that officially controlled student unions be abandoned and replaced by democratic organizations. They call for free speech, free press, more money for educators, and disclosures by officials and their children of their incomes and bank accounts."

"That's crazy. That's inviting disaster. The government will never agree to any of that. They'll say that's bourgeois reactionary." Some of what the students demanded seemed reasonable to Mingyue. But didn't the Party have the expertise to know what was in the best interest of the people? More than half-educated students probably. "Have you given up Communism? Are you siding with Capitalism? The Party says—"

"We don't care what the Party says. We students are the true communists. We are the leaders of the Revolution. It's the Party that's reactionary now."

"The Party says free press and free speech would unleash reactionary bourgeois forces and challenge the Dictatorship of the Proletariat."

"Don't you see? Wake up!" she said. "Don't let them fool you. They lie."

Mingyue had never experienced this force of her passion directed at him.

He was taken aback. "I know some of them are corrupt, but that doesn't mean . . ." He was confused. ". . . doesn't mean the whole Party . . ."

"The Party leaders are the reactionary element now. They are the new capitalists. Look at how they're getting rich while the people are still poor. You want a dictatorship of the proletariat? We students and workers are the proletariat. We need a free press so we can speak out and oppose the leaders' corruption."

Mingyue slumped into a chair.

He could not deny that the leaders were corrupt. But were they bourgeois reactionaries? He had admired the heroes of the Revolution, the struggle for the victory of the peasants over their oppressors, the feudal landlords. He would be willing to fight for a better world.

But who was right?

Had the Party really betrayed the Revolution?

"Your claims will only make the government even more angry. I don't want you to be hurt."

"We're not giving up." She put her hands on her hips defiantly. "We're sending students out to seek support from local factories and other work units. I've volunteered you. You worked on the railroad before you became a student, didn't you?"

He looked up at her warily, raised one bushy eyebrow, and nodded.

"The Student Coordinating Committee wants you to go to the railroad workers and explain our demands."

He jerked himself to his feet. "I can't. I'm no speaker. I'm not even a student anymore. Get someone else." The other students all looked at him.

"You know what they gripe about," she said. "Just speak to their grievances. They'll listen."

He needed time to think about it. "I'll go talk to Ma and see what he says."

"That hoodlum friend of yours? He has a blue dragon on his hand." She sneered. "No one but criminals wear tattoos in China now."

"He's just high-spirited, like his name, 'Horse.' He stands up to authority. And he still works on the railroad. The perfect man to—"

"Forget him. He's trouble." The anger in her voice surprised him. "Just go to the workers yourself or don't do it at all. I'll talk to them if you're too cowardly."

Cowardly? She called him cowardly in front of other students? He felt his face flush and thought of storming out of the room. But this was no time to worry about saving face. She said she would do it if he didn't. He imagined her talking to a track gang of railroad toughs. They would laugh at her. They might do worse than laugh. He could not let her go there at any cost.

"All right. All right. Shit." Mingyue groaned and rubbed his forehead. "It's crazy. But okay. I'll do it."

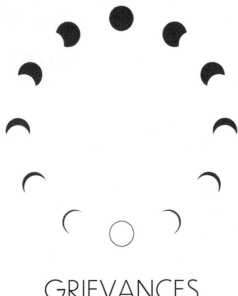

GRIEVANCES

APRIL 21

GAO MINGYUE HAD LONG CRAVED TO DO SOMETHING important like his Revolutionary heroes, but when he stepped off the bus at the train station, his knees trembled. The grasshoppers in his stomach fought each other.

He wanted to ignore Yingying's prejudice and get Ma's help, but he didn't. He entered the railroad yard and walked past men loading a boxcar, wondering what he could say to them. He climbed on a flatcar and spoke to a track gang eating lunch. His voice was stiff and formal and cracked with his first word.

"Comrades . . . I would like to . . . speak to you about recent events. Tomorrow, April 22, there will be a memorial for Hu Yaobang in Xincheng Square in front of the Shaanxi Provincial

Government compound. Many students will be there to listen to a live broadcast of Hu's memorial from Beijing."

The workers glared at him sullenly. One of them asked, "What's that to us? Why should we care what students do? What do we care about what goes on in Beijing? Will it improve our miserable lives?"

Mingyue could taste the pickled cabbage from breakfast. He shuffled his feet. He had to explain the students' demands. What would higher pay for educators or a free press mean to these workers? He swallowed hard and spoke on, like a high wire walker who can't turn back. He hardly knew what he said, but the crowd grew larger and the laughter a bit more hostile.

He saw a man taking pictures of him. Probably a police informer working for the railroad. But that was to be expected. Every nook and cranny of Chinese society had its police informers. Did his heroes Mao Zedong or Zhou Enlai stop rousing the people against injustice early in the communist workers' movement because of a few police informers? The photographer's presence brought out his anger.

With a personal knowledge of the railroad workers' numerous grievances, and a rage that grew from defiance, he spouted a fiery eloquence that surprised him.

"Do the government's new economic policies help you, or a handful of corrupt officials? Isn't your salary staying the same while what you buy gets more expensive, so you seem to have less money each month?" He heard murmurs of agreement. "Is the government making your life better? Or is it just making the bosses' lives better? Is your housing getting better, or is it just decaying? Would you like to change jobs for a better job?"

A man shouted, "Yes!"

"Why can't you? The new policies are increasing unemployment. You may have an 'iron rice bowl,' but will your sons? Do you know anyone whose son can't find a job?" He clenched his fist and waved it over his head. "I myself am 'waiting for a job' two years out of the university."

The mob grew and listened silently. He had to shout now so those at the back could hear. He knew what he was saying was true, not just the propaganda in the media that everyone had to listen to. It was a truth he had kept buried under layers of anger and fear and bitter hopeless disappointment. He knew the railroad workers recognized it for truth, too. He knew now that what he was saying was important. He spoke especially of the corruption of government officials.

"Women have to sleep with their bosses to keep their jobs or to get their husbands promoted." He spat out each word. "And everyone has to give the bosses gifts to curry favor, so the bosses get everything free—free meals at restaurants, free cars, free TV sets, furniture, refrigerators, travel tickets . . ."

These were problems the workers knew all too well, and he could sense that he touched their deepest sentiments. For the first time in his life, he enjoyed speaking to a group. He felt the mob's response to his every word. "Hu Yaobang denounced the corruption and was removed from his position when he supported reform. Of all the top leaders, his was the only son who didn't get rich by abusing the father's power. Hu Yaobang worked for the good of the people, not for his own selfish interest. Hu Yaobang was a true communist." The crowd cheered.

"The other leaders resented and feared him. They say that Hu Yaobang died suddenly. But he was in good health until then. Some people have wondered if his death was natural." He paused.

"Some people have wondered why the government delayed its announcement of his death for several days."

Murmurs arose from the crowd.

He raised his voice. "Hu wanted to end the corruption of the bosses, and the bosses were irritated. How pleased they must be that he is gone. How frightened they must be that the People will be suspicious. But they hope that the People have dead brains and are too cowed, too passive and obedient." He paused, hands on hips, and glowered at them. "Do the People have dead brains?"

The crowd roared in one voice: "No!"

"Are the People cowards?"

"No!"

"Will the People stand up to the bosses for justice?"

"Yes!"

"Will the People demand that the bosses account for their corruption?"

"Yes!"

"Will you join the students at Hu's memorial tomorrow?"

"Yes!"

A worker pushed his way through the crowd. It was his old friend Ma. Ma climbed onto the flatcar, grasped Mingyue's hand, and raised it over his head. "Well said, Comrade Gao."

The workers cheered. Mingyue recognized the blue dragon on the back of his hand. Yingying's wrong, Mingyue thought. He's no criminal. He's for freedom. He'll help us fight against corruption.

<hr />

While he was brushing his teeth, Dan thought of himself from Yoshiko's viewpoint: receding hair, frown wrinkles, the beginning of a beer belly in spite of regular jogging.

He remembered overhearing one of his Chinese students talking about him. "He must have been handsome when he was young." She had meant it to be complimentary, but it wasn't encouraging. "He looks like Harrison Ford," she had said. Hardly. Dan's eyes were closer together, and his sideburns were graying. And how do people in China know about Harrison Ford? Anyway, forty-eight is too old for Yoshiko.

It was stupid to be mooning over a younger woman. Dan supposed it was some midlife crisis kind of thing. She was still of childbearing age, if barely, and he regretted that his fate had kept him from being a father. Dan was an only child and had no children. End of the line. It seemed strange that all his ancestors, human and nonhuman, from the time they had climbed out of the primordial slime, had managed to reproduce. Every one of them, for millions of years. Not one broke the unbroken chain. It could make one proud to be the culmination of all that evolution. But to be the first one to fail. To be the dying ember . . .

All those years of school, then the Marine Corps in Vietnam and grad school. Marrying late to a woman who had said she wanted a child. Abortion. Divorce. Another marriage. Her infidelity. Divorce. Dan thought he would have had a better chance to reproduce if he had been a priest. Anyway, it would be best to forget Yoshiko.

Dan reached for his alarm clock to set it for 4 a.m. so he could go out to see the posters. He hated to have to get up so early when he taught evening classes and went to bed late. But this was a bit of history. He had to see the posters.

There was a knock at the front door. It was 11 p.m. Suddenly very tired, he let in his friend, Gao Baima. The bags under Gao's eyes were even heavier than usual, and he trudged in through the door holding a briefcase and slumped over as if in defeat. Dan saw that he had been using coloring to blacken his hair. Gao walked like a stevedore carrying a heavy sack of coal.

"Mingyue hasn't come home in two days. I think he's making posters. I am his father, but he has no respect. I'm trying to get him a job . . ." He rubbed his forehead. "And now he's making posters. If the police catch him, our whole family will lose face. He'll go to prison." He sagged into the sofa and stared at his shoes.

"You don't approve of the posters?"

"After the Cultural Revolution? That was enough chaos." He shrugged.

Dan decided not to mention where he was going at 4 a.m. "I have some Beijing Beer . . . and some orange juice."

Gao looked up, and his eyes brightened. "Real orange juice? I haven't had orange juice since America. Where did you get it?"

"The Xi'an Hotel past the Little Wild Goose Pagoda. But they only let me buy two individual size cans at a time, since they don't want to run out for their foreign guests. Needless to say, I go once a week. I'll have to take you there to cheer you up. Or better yet, that Japanese-owned hotel where they serve a great chocolate cake a la mode."

"I won't go to a Japanese hotel."

Dan had forgotten for a moment that Gao's parents had been killed by the Japanese in the slaughter in Nanjing during World War II. Maybe a bit of their chocolate cake a la mode would soften your bitterness, he thought. He went to his tiny refrigerator and poured a glass of orange juice for Gao and a glass of beer for himself.

Gao savored the orange juice as if it were a fine wine. "But I didn't come to talk about my son tonight. I came to ask you a favor."

Dan grinned. "It would be my pleasure." Several times, Gao had asked him to order books from the US that he could not get in China.

"I have a nephew in government. He tells me things." Gao blinked several times and looked around the room, everywhere but at Dan. "Things that most people don't know . . . things that I write down hoping they can be made public someday." Gao belched and put his hand over his stomach. He sat silent a moment, grimacing.

"Maybe that orange juice was too much for your ulcer," Dan said. "Can I get you an antacid?"

Gao waved away the suggestion. "It's not the orange juice; it's my son. He's making posters. If he causes trouble . . . and the police come . . . and search my house . . ."

In a land where everyone had to read between the lines, not always accurately, it was not hard for even the unpracticed Dan to see the point.

"Of course. You don't want what you have been writing to be found by the police."

"Yes." Gao belched again.

"Would you like me to keep your material for you until the protests cool down?"

"I don't want to cause you trouble . . ." He looked at his feet, and his cheeks turned red. "But I can't ask anyone else I know to do it."

"You have done so much to help me, it's the least I can do."

Gao pulled an inch-thick manuscript from his briefcase and handed it to Dan.

"Can I read it?" Dan asked.

"Please." Gao put his empty glass on the coffee table. "Something very bad is happening. You know Chinese history. There have been many uprisings and brutal repressions. The situation feels similar to the beginning of the Cultural Revolution."

"That serious?"

"Maybe not. Zhao Ziyang is being weakened by the student reaction. Maybe the government will be unified enough to stop everything now."

"Pardon my ignorance . . . what is Zhao's position?"

Gao raised a bushy eyebrow. "Communist Party Secretary."

"No, I mean, what is his political stance?"

"He wants to listen to students' complaints and end corruption in the government. But two days ago, Deng Xiaoping called for a crackdown. Today, senior leaders sent troops to keep peace in Beijing. It's a power struggle between Zhao's faction and Deng's faction."

"What sort of corruption are you talking about?"

"When the government was planning to develop Hainan Island, before the plan was made public, Deng's son bought up huge amounts of property there. When the government announced the plan publicly, he was able to sell at a high profit and became wealthy."

Dan grinned. "Deng said that to be wealthy is glorious." He knew that Gao, still an old-line communist, disapproved.

"I think that's what you Americans call the insider trading." Gao scowled. "We Chinese were long accustomed to the system of *guanxi*—influential connections—in the old days. But the leaders of the Proletariat should serve the people, not themselves."

"As Pao Chao said, the greatest displeasure of the largest number is the law of nature."

For the first time since he'd arrived, Gao smiled. "From his poem, *The Ruined City*. You always know how to cheer me up with ancient poetry."

"I'll be glad to keep your information. I'll make my own set of notes on what is happening. I should have thought of keeping a journal months ago." Dan looked at his watch. "You should be going now. Lao Zhu locks the gate to the foreign guests' compound every night at midnight. I don't know whether it is more to protect us or keep us prisoners. I'll write down what you told me."

When Professor Gao had gone, Dan sat in the armchair and began reading Gao's document; a litany of injustices. Details of how heads of major state enterprises were engaged in corrupt practices and about political struggles within the leadership and secret imprisonments and assassinations. The most horrifying was the description of the conditions in prisons. Political prisoners were treated as slaves, working in terrible conditions. And in at least one prison, prisoners were executed and their body parts sold on the international market for organ transplants.

Dan found it hard to believe. It sounded like Nazi Germany. He had hoped that mankind had grown beyond such barbarity. No wonder Gao was worried about the papers being found by the police.

Once the shock had subsided, he realized that it was information several American scholars of contemporary China he knew would love to get their hands on. What a coup it would be. Better yet, maybe Dan could publish it himself. But he didn't have the means to corroborate the claims. The scholars would have a better chance to investigate them. The information might not be true.

He would ask Gao if he would like it published in the West. Of course, it couldn't be mailed; all mail in and out of China was read by censors. But it could be carried by hand by a foreigner. Dan couldn't read it all if he was going to get up early. But memories of events flooded his mind, and nervous energy compelled him to put down his thoughts before he forgot them.

He sat at his desk to write. He had some idea of why the students were angry. They gathered from all over the city every Sunday morning in a gazebo at the campus gardens for "English corner." It was a chance to practice speaking English, and they were delighted when Dan was there. A crowd of fifty or a hundred would gather around him and questions that became delicate surprisingly fast:

"Is it true that American students have premarital sex?"

"Yes, some, not all."

"What do you think of the Chinese Communist Party?"

When Dan had tried to be circumspect in answering the latter question, thinking there might be police informers in the crowd and that students could get into trouble, one student said, "Oh, we can say anything we want, we just can't do anything about it."

The students asked questions about American government, politics, discrimination, and religion. They were amazed that American college students could choose their own subjects to study, and they had mixed feelings that the American government did not assign jobs but that American students had to find jobs themselves.

Dan told them, "I would have liked to have been assured of a job when I graduated. So many of my fellow students couldn't find them."

The students' litany of complaints was unending. A Chinese student's education was free, but it was like being in the American military. Room, board, tuition, and a few living expenses all paid for; in return, the students must study what the government decides they will study in accord with the student's aptitude and the needs of the state. One student complained that he wanted to study history but had to study chemistry; another wanted to be a poet but was forced to be a doctor. When they graduated from school, the government assigned them a job, again in accord with the needs of the state. Dan wondered how good a job one would do if he didn't like his work? It sounded inefficient.

Dan was told of one former student who was the head of a government ministry in Lanchow. His wife taught in Xi'an. He had tried for ten years to get transferred to Xi'an to be with his wife, to no avail. They could only see each other once a year for two weeks. This was a common situation in China. It seemed uncaring. Shouldn't the highest need of a workers' state be to make its workers happy? This was the kind of injustice that always raised Dan's blood pressure, and he could feel it getting higher.

The majority of students at Shaanxi Teachers University were from peasant villages. After having tasted the delights of the big city for four years, they would be sent back to their villages to teach for the rest of their lives. They regarded this as a prison sentence, for they would never have a chance to choose for themselves.

Teachers were intellectual workers, and the Communist Party had the attitude that intellectual work was not "real" work, like that of a factory worker. Teachers were poorly paid when compared with manual laborers. In the new economic conditions, where people could run small businesses, a taxi driver in Xi'an made ten times the income of a university professor.

Dan Norton took notes for an hour before he noticed the time. Only three hours until the alarm rang. He stopped writing. He remembered how one of his students had come into his room and casually looked through his drawers and cabinets while he was talking to her. He had been surprised and momentarily angered but suppressed his desire to tell her how rude that was to a Westerner. He didn't know if she was merely curious—because the concept of privacy had no meaning in Chinese culture since Communism— or if some students were assigned to spy on him. He had kept his cool and given her the benefit of the doubt. Cultural differences. Another test of his Buddhist determination to suspend judgment and go with the flow.

But if they found these notes, especially the parts about assassinations, prison slave labor, and selling prisoners' body parts, they might think *he* was a spy. He decided to hide Gao's papers where he hid his precious dollars, passport, and teaching contract—rolled up with rubber bands on top of the bedroom curtain, above the draw string casing, where only a determined thief would find them. He didn't want to rot in a Chinese prison.

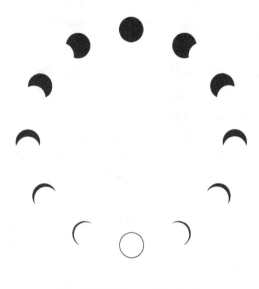

RIOT IN XI'AN

APRIL 22

EARLY IN THE MORNING, MINGYUE JOINED THE railway workers and marched down the main streets of downtown Xi'an to the city center, shouting slogans to the onlookers lining the sidewalks. The workers carried huge red banners that stretched the width of the street with gold characters calling for an end to government corruption. Mingyue marched in the front row, fortified with moral indignation, supported by his friend Ma at his side and hundreds of comrades behind him, buoyed by the carnival atmosphere of a parade. As they entered Xincheng Square, the front row linked arms, and they sang the Internationale. The power of the workers' voices, and Ma's hard muscles against his own, steeled Mingyue's resolve.

They gathered with a huge crowd of students and other workers to listen to the radio broadcast. All the top Communist Party leaders were at Hu's memorial at the Great Hall of the People in Beijing. The eminent Party leaders droned on and on, the loudspeakers on top of telephone poles around the square screeched, and the crowd seethed with mute, restless energy.

When the speeches ended, someone shouted, "Down with corruption," and a chant started up.

"Down with corruption! Down with corruption!"

A man with a cigarette dangling from his lips threw a large beer bottle at a guard patrolling the gold-colored wrought iron gate to the government compound. The bottle shattered at the guard's feet, and he unslung his submachine gun from his shoulder and pointed it above the man's head.

Ma and several young railway workers taunted the guard with insults and mockery. "What? You can't handle a little beer?" Ma stooped over and stuck out his rear end at the guard, waving his hand between his legs. The crowd laughed.

Ranks of policemen with truncheons marched abreast down the street toward them, heels clicking in unison on the pavement. Through a bullhorn, an officer told the protesters to leave, to go home. The lines of policemen stopped and faced the mob.

A man beside Mingyue shouted through a megaphone. "Stand your ground, Comrades."

Another near him shouted, "We've made our point. We can go home now."

"Don't give in now," said the first, "or we're defeated."

The crowd milled in confusion.

Mingyue took the megaphone. "Join us comrade policemen. We workers, students, and peasants are the People. You policemen serve the People. You are the People, too. United, we can end the corruption."

The officer with the bullhorn repeated his command to disperse.

A rock, then another, flew toward the officer. A third stone bounced at his feet and hit him in his shin. He commanded the ranks of policemen to march. The policemen held their truncheons ready to strike and moved forward. As part of the crowd retreated from the police, another part surged toward the government compound. A line of guards blocked the gate.

Workers showered the guards with stones, and the guards retreated. Ma lead the crowd, and it broke through into the compound's courtyard. They threw stones at the six-foot-high plastic red star over the main entrance. One burly railroad worker picked up a shot-put sized stone and heaved it at the star. It cracked, and the crowd cheered.

A dark shadow of premonition flitted through Mingyue's consciousness. The red star had cracked, but it did not break.

Workers behind Mingyue overturned a new, white Toyota van and set it afire. Gasoline fumes and the acrid, black smoke of burning rubber and plastic made him gag and cough. Through the tears in his eyes, he saw police snipers with rifles appear on balconies and rooftops on both sides of the street. Windows in the surrounding buildings tinkled as they shattered. Mingyue did not want this.

The point was to embarrass the government so it would change, not provoke it into anger. He wasn't sure if he was angrier at the government protecting its corrupt leaders with force or at the workers for slipping out of his control. He held up his arms and shouted at the milling crowd.

"Stop! Stop! No violence!"

His voice was lost in the angry shouts around him. Workers swung pipes at policemen, and policemen swung truncheons in return. A young man fell to the street, his head bleeding. Several companions picked him up and carried him away. Mingyue looked at their faces . . . young faces filled with fear.

These were not all workers or even college students, but some were high school or maybe even grammar school students. The children of China were being beaten to protest the leaders' corruption.

Beside Mingyue, a man in a gray Mao cap knocked a policeman down with a crowbar. A shot rang out, and the man crumpled backward to the sidewalk.

Mingyue stared in disbelief at the spreading ooze of blood on the man's chest. He stooped to help the man and looked into his empty, staring eyes. He didn't grasp it right away, then he realized that the man was dead. Mingyue was knocked off his feet by the mob's stampede and sprawled across the dead man's soft, warm belly.

Mingyue heard a loud crack and buzz at the same time that a puff of concrete dust rose from the sidewalk an inch from his hand. His forearm stung. He looked at his arm through the rip in his sleeve and saw blood. A bullet wound. His pride and anger shattered and melted into fear. He pushed himself to his feet and fled east.

His panic did not stop when he left the mob behind and turned south down an unfamiliar back alley. His mouth was dry, and his lungs stung from the half-mile sprint. He stopped only for a moment to leave behind the tattered mantle of leadership of which he had been so proud. His white windbreaker with the red armband of a march organizer was smeared with blood. He ripped it off and threw it into a gutter. His forearm still bled, and he wrapped his handkerchief around it. He ran again until he came to a main shopping street.

His heart raced as he slowed to a walk. He did not want to look like a fleeing thief on a downtown street crowded with shoppers not yet aware of the riot. He passed through the city wall and strode south on Big Wild Goose Temple Boulevard.

Over a mile from the scene of the riot now, busses passed him billowing their normal clouds of dust as if the events across the city existed in another dimension of reality. What had happened already seemed surreal, like a bad dream from which he couldn't wake up.

He wandered three more miles toward home in a zig-zag pattern through back alleys, his heart still racing. People stared at him as he passed. Surely a bloody arm wound could be explained. He had just tripped and fallen on . . . a bicycle . . . no, a truck had grazed him crossing a crowded intersection. The wound stung and throbbed. The blood had dripped on his trousers.

He squatted against the wall outside the Big Wild Goose Pagoda for an hour. Passersby looked at him and walked on. The face of the dead man was clear in his mind. Mingyue knew his speech to the railroad workers had caused it. What did that pagoda stand for? Something about karma and numerous Buddhist hells? Perhaps he was in one of them. He felt sick to his stomach. He leaned against the wall, absorbing the warmth that radiated from the sun-heated bricks, and listened to the pounding in his ears until it stopped.

His mood black as lacquer, he turned down the alleyway to the back gate of the university just as the sun turned red in the dust and smog as it neared the horizon. The dry, dusty-smelling yellow smoke of soft coal cooking fires bellowed out into the narrow brick walled passage from head-high stove pipes and into his face.

He should report to the Student Coordinating Committee what had happened, but he couldn't face the shame of running away. He had not seen his family for three days. Like a nervous dog with his tail between his legs, he trudged toward home. He was two buildings from his family's apartment when he saw a neighbor, Mrs. Zhou. She turned to walk away from him, then stopped and looked all around her. She walked up to him quickly.

"Gao Mingyue." Mrs. Zhou drew her face close to his and spoke softly. "You can't go home. Police are there. I was with your mother. They have photographs of you talking to workers yesterday and using a megaphone in a crowd. There is rioting. You have to hide." Mrs. Zhou turned abruptly and walked away.

Mingyue didn't know which way to turn, but he couldn't stay where he was. He might be recognized by someone less helpful than Mrs. Zhou. Many members of the university community were police informants or leaders in neighborhood committees who spied on other members of the neighborhood, and one didn't always know who they were. But outside his parents' home, he had no means to survive. Could he stay with Ma? He was on the opposite side of the city, and the police would surely be patrolling the railway workers now. He couldn't get to relatives in Nanjing without money.

He stepped into the street corner, communal slit trench toilet to relieve himself and think. The stench of urine on the concrete floor slapped him in the face. Three students he didn't know squatted side by side over the open trough. There was no place to hide in the toilet. He would have to leave before someone recognized him.

When he stepped out into the street again, he heard a familiar voice.

"There he is! Stop him!"

He turned to see Wu Yaoqian, the Foreign Affairs Officer and a known police informer with big ears like radar antennae. Wu pointed at him. The length of an apartment building away, three policemen ran toward Mingyue.

Without thought, he ran away from them. Wrong direction. After two turns, this alleyway would reach a dead end in a storage yard at the outer wall of the university. No hope. He rounded the first corner to the left and ran between the brick walls—the backs of buildings—with no windows and no doors to duck through. He remembered that the next turn to the right would open into the yard where bricks, lumber, stacks of concrete sacks, machines, vehicles, and other building materials were stored. He could hide briefly but they would find him before long.

Beside the wall to the left would be a line of elm trees. Over the eight-foot wall was the foreign teachers' compound, where he had visited Professor Norton once with his father. His father's friend.

Beyond the wall of the foreigners' compound stood the twelve-foot outer wall of the university, too high to climb and planted with glass fragments on top. Mingyue heard footsteps echo in the alley behind him. He turned the second corner and spotted an elm tree ahead of him; its limbs arched over the foreign compound wall. He pulled himself up into the tree, swung his legs over the wall, and slid onto a tile roof. Crouched behind the wall, he pulled his shirt over his nose to muffle his panting breath.

"Search the yard. He must be here somewhere." Mingyue could distinguish the speaker's Sichuan accent. The voice sounded familiar. "Behind the roofing and lumber."

Sheets of corrugated tin crashed to the ground, and stacks of boards tumbled over. Mingyue's foot cramped in its awkward position, but he dared not move it for fear the roof tiles would clatter.

"Look behind those boxes," the Sichuan voice commanded. "In the boxes."

"No one's here, Inspector Song," a second voice responded.

Mingyue's gut tightened. Inspector Song, Yingying's father. They had met twice. So that must be why the police were at his house so fast—he had recognized Mingyue from the photo yesterday. To be arrested by him would ruin his future hopes with her. This quickened his already rapid pulse. Oh, Guanyin, have mercy. Raised as a communist, that spontaneous prayer to the Buddhist Goddess of Mercy surprised him.

"What's over that wall?" the Inspector asked.

"The foreign teachers' compound, Comrade Inspector." It was Wu Yaoqian's high-pitched voice. "If he went that way, he could be out the back gate of the university by now. We can ask Lao Zhu, the foreign compound gatekeeper, if he saw any . . ."

The voices faded away into the distance. Mingyue straightened his cramped foot and pressed it against the wall for a moment until the pain stopped.

The purple sky proclaimed that dusk would soon turn to night. Like his name—Mingyue meaning Bright Moon—the full moon rose bright to the east. His father had once read some foreign poem in which the bright moon had stood for hope, and so his father had named him Bright Moon in the hope of a bright future for his family and China. But Mingyue had not lived up to his name. He couldn't even find a job. And now, hunted by the police, what hope could he be to his family? How could that bright moon mean there was hope for China with police shooting at students and workers?

He saw the moon as the face of an eternal clock that ticked away the moments of each person's destiny, though the hands remained hidden even to the wise. He wished it could warn him of his destiny now. He lay still on the roof and listened to the noises and voices of the policemen searching through the storage yard and wondered if they would come over the wall to search.

He worried that he had not seen Yingying for two days since he had gone to speak with the railroad workers. It now struck him that she was a student criticizing the government and her father was a police inspector chasing one of those critics. He feared for her if her father knew what she was doing.

And now where should he go? He could sleep on the roof all night but the police might come back and search because Lao Zhu said he had not seen Mingyue leave.

But then again, Lao Zhu had other duties and might not have been watching.

When he no longer heard the policemen in the storage yard, he took off his shoes and crawled up the slope of the roof and down the other side, carefully feeling each cool hard curve with his feet so as not to rattle the tiles under him. Smoke rose from the chimney he passed, and he smelled cabbage and pork, anise, and leeks. His stomach reminded him that he had not eaten since breakfast.

Lying on his hungry belly, he looked over the edge. Under the eaves of the roof was a porch. Below him was a pile of cabbages and a stack of coal bricks for cooking. He heard voices, English and Japanese. It must be the foreign guests' dining hall. His family had been invited to Christmas dinner there. They were eating now. He would have to wait until they were finished and until the cooks cleaned up and left or someone might see him.

He saw a clothesline with half a dozen rat skins hanging from it. Mingyue had heard that those cooks caught rats around the foreign guests' dining hall and sold them to puppet makers to make shadow puppets.

He wondered if anyone had heard him on the roof. He lay on the corner of the roof farthest from the kitchen where an overhanging tree branch formed a wall with its leaves. It would protect him from any suspicious eyes below as long as no one looked down from the balconies of the apartment building and as long as the police didn't come back to search.

He wiped sweat from his forehead and lay still, listening as one after another of the foreigners departed and went to their apartments or out the gate of the compound to the foreign students' dormitory.

Lights came on in the apartments one after another. Pots and woks banged in the kitchen.

He heard a female voice from a balcony and tensed. "Look how lovely the moon is tonight." She spoke with an Australian accent. He saw her silhouette. She had her arms on the balcony wall. If she looked down, she would see him.

Mingyue held his breath. His whole body trembled, his stomach muscles tightened, and sweat stung his eyes. He leaned back to hide part of his body behind a tree branch but it was skimpy cover.

"Mummy, I want some lollies." The child's voice was sweet.

"Right-o, Dearie. Cherry or licorice?" The balcony door scraped shut, and Mingyue breathed again. His stomach muscles relaxed. But he couldn't stay on the roof.

He watched a rat run along the ridge of the roof silhouetted against a starry sky. It stopped, sniffed, sat on its haunches, sniffed again, looked at him with shining eyes, and disappeared over the edge. Mingyue had heard that foreigners wouldn't eat rats. He wondered why not? But he was sure that rat would end up on someone's plate soon. Maybe on the foreigners' plates as "pepper chicken," or would the cooks sell the meat to a Chinese restaurant where it would be more appreciated? A few minutes later, the cooks left, laughing and joking about the "long-noses," as they called foreigners.

Mingyue shimmied down a drainpipe. It crackled and suddenly pulled away from the wall until it hung from one long bolt. His hands slipped from the sweat, and he fell six feet onto the concrete porch. The strain of the impact hurt his groin and made his arm wound ache even more.

He crept in the shadows along the blue and red brick wall of the apartment building and approached Lao Zhu's front door at the base of the stairs. Had the police talked to him yet? Were they still there? A sheet to keep flies out hung across the doorway. He heard the voices of Lao Zhu's family and saw their shadows on the sheet. No sign of the police. He stepped as quietly as he could past the doorway, up the stairs to the second floor. He stood in front of Professor Norton's door wondering if he dared ring the bell, if he could trust a foreigner, if he could trust anyone now that he was an outcast.

Maybe it was the loss of blood that made him so dizzy and weak. His fingertip met the moonlight shadow of his hand. He rang the bell.

Professor Norton opened the door and smiled. His hazel eyes widened. "Mingyue! You're bleeding!"

Mingyue looked at his blood-spattered shoes. His voice, barely above a whisper, cracked.

"Professor Norton. May I speak with you?"

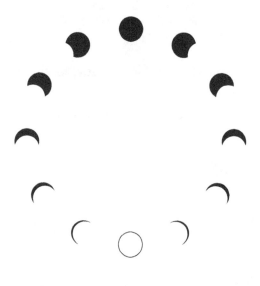

ILLEGAL GUEST

APRIL 23

GAO MINGYUE LOOKED OUT PROFESSOR NORTON'S window at the moon, careful to stay back in the dark where no one would see him from outside. Memories of yesterday's events fluttered around him like the shadows of demons and hungry ghosts. Now it was a full twenty-four hours that he had put the kind American professor in danger. Surely the police would be back to search the building. Yet his stomach churned at the thought of fleeing for he would likely be seen. Perhaps after the moon set, he could go to his friend in the Muslim Quarter.

But that was halfway across the city. A long walk in a city under martial law where the police were looking for him. And the moon wouldn't set now until after dawn.

What of his mother, father, and brother when the police broke into their apartment? Had they been harmed? He couldn't bear to think of his mother suffering from a kidney ailment in prison. Professor Norton would return soon from teaching his evening class. Perhaps he would have news. How his arm wound stung. At least the gash was shallow. He struggled to keep it still so the wound would not bleed more. The bandages were soaked. His memories stung as well.

He thought of the man who had been killed in the riot; a riot stirred up by Mingyue's speech. The man had died in the prime of his life. His ghost would have cause to be angry. Mingyue shivered.

He thought of how he had run away—a leader abandoning his comrades.

He remembered his embarrassment as Professor Norton welcomed him and helped clean his wound . . . without asking too many questions. He was sure the professor didn't really want him in his home, but he seemed friendly enough—too accepting to believe. Did the professor understand the danger he put himself in or was he naïve?

Mingyue was roused from his thoughts by voices. Out the window he saw Professor Norton and a half-dozen people walking toward the foreign teachers' compound. His stomach tensed. They stopped at the gate and talked another five minutes. When the others departed, Professor Norton came upstairs. Mingyue's stomach muscles relaxed. He sat in a chair away from the window. Professor Norton turned on the light and entered the room.

"I was worried that those people would come upstairs with you," Mingyue said.

"A group of students always escorts me home. They ask me questions they were too shy to ask in class." Dan Norton took off his jacket and tie and threw them over a chair. "Your father told me—"

"My father?" Mingyue leaped up and paced across the room. He dreaded to hear the news. "Is my family . . . is . . ."

"I visited them. Your family is all well. They weren't arrested. But your father fears for you, and I feel terrible not telling him where you are."

"You must not tell him." Mingyue slumped onto the couch. "If he doesn't know, he won't need to lie to the police. He's not a good liar."

"That's one of the things I like about him." Dan smiled and went to the refrigerator for a beer.

"What do you want me to get you when I shop tomorrow? I'm sure you're tired of my breakfast food. That's all I'm used to keeping in the refrigerator."

Mingyue didn't want to burden the professor anymore. Surely the man must realize the seriousness of the situation. He seemed too casual.

Maybe he had reported Mingyue to the police already.

"With beer, too, I've eaten well, thank you. But I don't want to put you in any more danger. I will go across the city to a friend tonight." He started to rise from his seat.

"No." Dan put out his hand, fingers up as if to hold Mingyue on the couch. "You'd better not leave. Didn't you watch the news on television? Jesus, the whole goddamn city is under martial law and a curfew. Yesterday's riots continued today. Students have called on workers to strike. Vehicles and buildings were burned, stores looted, and they claim eighteen were arrested and over a hundred policemen were injured. And you want to stroll across the city after curfew?"

"Oh shit!" Mingyue leaped to his feet. "Did they say who those they killed were?"

"The government denies anyone was killed," Dan said. "But of course, they didn't even mention that any students or workers were hurt. Judging by the media, only helpless incredibly restrained policemen were the innocent victims."

"They don't think the lives of anyone who opposes them have any value." Mingyue slumped back into the couch. "They must think of us as disposable objects."

"They don't want people to know so they deny it, but rumors are that six civilians and two policemen have been killed. The officials are lying bastards." Mingyue could hear the anger in Dan's voice.

"You side with the students against the government?" Mingyue was surprised that anyone as old as his father would understand.

"I was a grad student at Berkeley in the sixties. I know how brutal the police can be. I watched the Oakland Riot Squad crack nonviolent anti-war protesters' heads."

Mingyue wasn't sure he understood. If he did, it was new to him that such things went on in America too.

Dan's voice grew louder and a bit menacing. "I hated their guts. If I'd had a machine gun . . . But no. That's old history, old anger I haven't let go." He paced back and forth. "I can't stand injustice. Especially if it's perpetrated by the police who are supposed to uphold justice. It puts me in a rage." He looked at Mingyue. "Of course I'll root for the students; for justice and democracy. But I'm trying to be a good Buddhist and let go of my anger. Look, Mingyue, I know you don't want to be here, and I sure as hell would rather you not have to be, but there's nothing we can do about that now. We don't have much of a damn choice at the moment. So, let's just dig in our heels and think about the next move when the situation changes."

Mingyue rubbed his forehead and moaned. The situation was worse than he had feared. But at least the American was not naïve. "Does anyone know I'm here?"

"No one. I don't know if I can keep your father from coming here because he . . . wants me to help him with . . . some work. If he comes, hide under my bed. Oh . . . the History Cochairman, Du, may come this evening to bring me copies of some material for my class."

Mingyue's nostrils flared. "Don't trust him. He got where he is by lying about his colleagues during the Cultural Revolution."

Dan laughed nervously and thought, *et tu*, Du. "Du too? I thought I liked him. In any case, if anyone comes, take your blankets and pillow off the couch and hide under my bed."

As Mingyue watched television, Dan opened his journal and stared at the pages. He was too tired to think. After Mingyue came, he could not sleep for hours. Just as he had finally started dozing, the alarm rang at 4 a.m. He had forgotten to turn it off. Too tired to get up but still he couldn't sleep until after sunrise. Then he had had his anxiety dream again and had awakened with a pounding heart.

Now he needed to write all these events down. According to the government, it had been the worst violence in Xi'an since the Cultural Revolution. There had been riots in Changsha, too. And Beijing students had stormed Party headquarters calling for an end to dictatorship. But Dan couldn't concentrate. He was too tired to write.

Dan thought about May 4 coming soon. It would be the 70th anniversary of China's first student uprising which had called for democracy. Seventy years and they still didn't have democracy. But Chinese memory runs deep. Perhaps it would all blow up on May 4.

Dan put aside the journal and tended to his guest's wound. He hoped he did the right thing, wiping the wound with alcohol and using bandages that were much too small. It did not seem to be deep, but he feared it needed the care of a doctor. He wanted to bring one, but Mingyue said that any Chinese doctor would turn him in to the police. The patient's right to privacy did not apply in China; Dan was scared for him.

He was a bit scared for himself, too. He had gotten up early and wiped up the blood in front of his door. He hoped no one saw it. He also checked to make sure there were no spots on the stairs. Harboring a fugitive in China was risky, but some things had to be done. Dan's friends had always said he was too driven by moral duty. But he thought the life of a coward wasn't worth living. Then again, he would have much preferred not to have been drawn into this mess.

The blood, the violence took him back to Vietnam. That day, he'd called in artillery on the Viet Cong village and found only civilian bodies. In his gut, he had felt sure there were no Viet Cong soldiers in the village. He'd watched it for days. But his head had told him that surely the intelligence people knew more than he did about it. He was just an inexperienced Lieutenant, too rational to argue with his commanding officer on the basis of a gut feeling. When would he learn to trust his gut as much as his head?

He had carried a little, almond-eyed girl in his arms to the corpsman. She had held his finger tightly and looked up at him with trust. But she had died before he could lay her down on the stretcher. She held on to his finger and stared into his eyes, pleading even in death. His stomach had never quite unknotted from that one. He could still feel her grip on his hand. He knew it wasn't his fault exactly. He had been only one factor in a huge nexus of causes. But he knew he had to make up for it somehow.

China wasn't Vietnam, and the Chinese had killed his father in the Korean War. Another complex nexus of causes. Dan's need had nothing to do with avenging a wrong. He had to restore a balance in himself. Karma. Teaching, keeping a journal, and protecting Gao's son were a necessary part of the retribution. In his heart, it was compassion for Mingyue, while his head told him it was a matter of justice. His head and heart agreed for a change. He was sure he was doing the right thing for Gao's son . . . he knew he was.

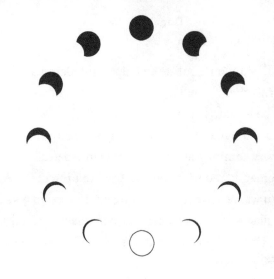

UNWELCOME VISITORS

APRIL 25

DAN HAD ACTED CALMLY WITH MINGYUE—MARINE Corps bravado and all that—but his recurring anxiety dream had come back, this time in a version from his early Marine Corps days. In the dream, he was in officer training, and there was going to be a rifle inspection in a few minutes. He looked for his rifle and couldn't find it until he finally saw it laying in the mud. There was no way he could clean it in time for the inspection. He had awakened with his heart racing.

It might seem obvious why the dream, but this time it wasn't that he was afraid of the police, though perhaps he should be. Rather it was that he was not sure he had made the right decisions about how to protect Mingyue. Should he find a doctor? Should he tell Gao? Should he enlist the help of the Bates family? Even if he could trust them, would it be better not to endanger them? He wanted to be loyal to his only friend, Gao Baima, who had invited him to China and mentored him through so many difficulties with the university administration; Wu Yaoqian especially.

Dan remembered when he had tried to protect the American student Wu wanted to expel for riding her ten-speed bike through outlying villages. She had been warned they were off-limits to foreigners. Dan had no legitimate defense. Gao had interceded as Wu's old friend.

But Dan knew that Gao could not protect him now. He knew full well what it meant to harbor a political fugitive in China. American citizenship would be no protection. He could end up in prison, being tortured as an American spy, and maybe even die without anyone knowing what had happened to him. And the U.S. government could not help him.

Dan worried that Mingyue's wound hadn't completely scabbed over yet and kept oozing. It had been hell getting large bandages and a bit of medical information without, Dan hoped, rousing suspicion. His temperature was up but not alarmingly high.

The doorbell rang. "Shit." Dan tensed and waved his hand for Mingyue to hide. Mingyue moved to the bedroom half of the apartment, separated from the living room only by curtains that formed one whole wall.

"Hope it's not Gao or Wu . . ." Dan muttered to himself. "Or that nosy student that spies on me. Did we remove all evidence of Mingyue?"

Mingyue drew the curtains shut as Dan looked around the apartment and walked weak-kneed to the door and opened it. It was a student, one of the class monitors.

"The copies of Chapter Seventeen you wanted for class, Professor Norton."

Dan took the papers and closed the door. Chinese students could not buy foreign texts, so Dan was having his History text copied for class at his own expense. No copyright laws in China to prevent it. He wiped the sweat from his brow, and Mingyue came back out. It was time for Dan to go to class.

Dan returned to his apartment after class. Mingyue was washing a bowl and a pot he had used to make soup for himself. Dan took a big bottle of Beijing Beer out of the refrigerator.

"Want some?" he asked Mingyue.

"Yes, please." Mingyue dried his hands on a towel.

Dan poured two glasses of beer, took them to the living room, and set them on the coffee table. He collapsed into the armchair, and Mingyue sat stiffly on the edge of the couch.

"Good news," Dan said. "The riots have ended, and martial law has been lifted." He raised his beer toward Mingyue and took a long draught.

Mingyue's shoulders relaxed perceptibly, and he took a sip of his beer. "Then I can go to—"

The doorbell rang. Mingyue moved quickly into the bedroom and drew the curtains shut. Dan opened the front door.

Wu Yaoqian, the foreign affairs officer, stood there, his ears standing out like a koala's. A man Dan did not know stood behind him—a red scar on his cheek and his deep-set eyes squinting.

"Professor Norton," Wu said, "this is Inspector Song of the Xi'an Police Department. We must speak with you."

A shot of adrenaline jolted Dan's body. "Oh, Xi'an Police Department." He spoke loud enough for Mingyue to hear. "Please come in."

Wu lead the way into the living room as Dan shut the door behind his guests.

"Wu Yaoqian, Inspector . . . Song, is it? Please, seat yourselves. Is this a call of duty or may I offer you drinks? I have orangeade, of course, and Beijing or Tsingtao beer and a Chinese white wine; rather good I think." He showed the men to the couch.

The Inspector shook his head, but Wu said, "Tsingtao beer," in his high-pitched voice that made him sound as girlish as his small chin made him look.

The Inspector casually surveyed the room, including the closed curtains.

Dan went to the refrigerator and poured a glass of beer. He set it in front of Wu and sat in his armchair.

"What can I do for you?"

He saw that the Inspector's deep-set eyes were squinting at the three mostly full beer glasses upon the table. Dan had not thought to remove Mingyue's glass. It was as if he had been climbing a teetering ladder and a step had given way under his foot, leaving him dangling.

"Oh! How absentminded of me. I must have poured myself two glasses."

The Inspector's nostrils flared, and he squinted at Dan. Dan was sure the Inspector didn't believe him.

He listened to his heart pound in the long silence. How stupid he had been. He realized he shouldn't even have mentioned it. His thoughts couldn't focus on what needed to be said next. He wanted to break eye contact with the Inspector and look away. He wanted to swallow.

But he dared not.

"Do you mind if I smoke?" the Inspector asked.

Dan was so relieved that, though he did mind, he shook his head and cleared his throat.

"Not at all." He went to his desk for an ashtray. His hands trembled as he picked it up. The Inspector took a cigarette from a pack of Marlboros and lighted up. So cowboy country comes to the land of lotus purity, Dan thought. He must know some foreigner who has access to the Friendship Store. Wouldn't it be ironic if the Chinese addiction to the cancer stick were the cement of Sino-American peace? A bit of sarcasm and his hand stopped shaking.

The Inspector drew on his cigarette and leaned back in the couch. He let out the smoke in a ring, then leaned forward. He spoke slowly in clear English, working the wrinkles in his forehead.

"I suppose you are aware that renegade hoodlums have caused turmoil in our city."

Dan sipped his beer and looked the Inspector in the eye. With effort he avoided looking at the third glass. "Yes, I'm aware of the riots."

"One of those hoodlums ran through the foreign teachers' compound three days ago. He tore a drainpipe loose and left blood on the concrete below it." The Inspector squinted at Dan. "We found drops of blood in front of Lao Zhu's door."

Dan looked into his beer as he swirled it in his glass.

"We want to warn all foreigners to keep their doors and windows locked," the Inspector said. "We will also have Lao Zhu lock the gate to the compound at 10 p.m. as long as the disturbances last. It is for the protection of our foreign guests, of course."

He was glad the inspector had not asked him if he had seen or heard anything of the "hoodlum" that night for he was not a good liar. He was eager to shift the conversation.

"Some of my colleagues and monitors come after ten to bring me course materials. It will be inconvenient for them . . ."

"—And perhaps students come in the evening to discuss course material." The Inspector drew on his cigarette.

"Yes. That too," Dan thought he saw the bedroom curtain ripple.

"It is the policy of the Chinese Government that female students do not go alone to male teachers' apartments. It violates our moral principles. You Westerners do not have high sexual standards. Perhaps the university is being lax . . ."

"No. No." Wu, who was responsible for enforcing the policy, shot upright in his seat sloshing some of his beer into his lap and squeaked in Chinese. "No. Lao Zhu watches. That is not allowed."

The Inspector stared at Wu as if he were some species of beetle that had wandered across the floor. The red scar on his cheek made him look cruel. He stubbed out his cigarette in the ashtray and leaned back in the couch. "I hear that many students go to visit your neighbors the Bates family night after night."

Dan wondered why the conversation had taken this turn. What was really on the Inspector's mind?

"We have known for a long time that they are Christian missionaries and try to convert our students. If they conduct secret religious services, that is forbidden by our government policy."

Dan had guessed the Bates family were missionaries, but he knew nothing of any secret services.

"I don't know. I'm not a Christian, so I've never been invited to their apartment," Dan said. The Inspector's hard look softened into an almost smile; whether pleased or cynical, Dan couldn't tell. "I've hardly spoken with them since the death of Hu Yaobang." Dan found himself looking at Mingyue's glass and quickly looked up at the Inspector.

"Ah. Hu Yaobang." The Inspector looked sharply at Dan and smirked. "A sorry business that has caused much trouble." Wu jerked upright in one spasm.

Dan wasn't sure what to say. Sometimes the Chinese were terribly indirect, then at times, unexpectedly direct. He decided on discreet neutrality and recited a poem in Chinese.

"... a giant corpse only feeds more vultures. Perhaps it is only for this that heroes and aspirants achieve fame and merit."

Wu Yaoqian looked at Dan and then at the Inspector with the pained expression of a lost child. A grin spread slowly across the Inspector's face, making his scar disappear in a dimple. The conversation was carried on in Chinese from that point on.

"You know our poet, Juan Chi," the Inspector said. "He is one of my favorites. But another poet of the same time period may also be appropriate to the occasion: 'The life of man is like a shadow play which must in the end return to nothingness.'"

"That was Tao Chien," Dan said, "from 'Two Poems on Returning to Dwell in the Country.' One of my favorites is his 'Written while Drunk'! 'The mountain air is fine at evening of the day and flying birds return together homewards. Within these things there is a hint of Truth, but when I start to tell it, I cannot find the words.'"

The Inspector's smile melted, and the corners of his mouth drooped. "You remind me of my childhood home in the mountains of Sichuan. There you could see the mountains to the north, the Tsinling Shan. Here, those mountains are hidden by smoke and dust."

The Inspector sank deeper into the couch, and his eyes looked far off in time and place. Suddenly he rose to his feet, carefully surveyed the room, and strode toward the door without another word. Wu leaped from his seat like a startled quail and followed. Dan escorted them out and shut the door behind them, puzzled why a police inspector would waste his time on such a visit. That was the foreign affair officer's job. He hadn't shown any sign of suspecting that a fugitive was hiding there, unless looking at an extra glass of beer could be construed as suspicion.

Dan watched the two men exit the front gate from his window before he called Mingyue out from under the bed.

"Did you hear what they said, Mingyue?"

Mingyue sat back down on the couch and sipped his beer. His voice shook. "I met Inspector Song a few times since I know his daughter, Yingying. She was a student in my class." Mingyue swallowed hard and kicked at the rug with the heel of his shoe. "I love her. Now, have I made her father my enemy? He thinks I'm just a renegade hoodlum."

Dan reached out to put his hand on Mingyue's shoulder out of sympathy but withdrew it, remembering the Chinese taboo on touching.

"Martial law has ended," Mingyue said. "I should leave now."

"Don't be foolish. Where will you go?"

"I have a friend in the Muslim Quarter."

"Do you think they suspect you are hiding here, Mingyue? And why was Wu so nervous?"

"If they did, then why didn't they just have the apartment searched? Wu Yaoqian knows that my father is your friend. I never should have come here and put you in danger."

"You might as well finish that beer before you go." Dan knew he needed another beer.

DOG MEAT

APRIL 28

DAN HADN'T BEEN AWARE OF THE KNOT IN HIS NECK until it began to relax and hurt three days after Mingyue's departure. He massaged his neck the best he could by himself.

The university provided the foreign guests a minibus for a weekly shopping tour downtown. Dan rarely went but decided to go this week so he could find a notebook small enough to keep in his pocket. He would continue his journal on it and keep it in his pocket where snoopers wouldn't find it. He saw Yoshiko near the back of the bus sitting with a Japanese student and was ashamed of his pang of envy. But he couldn't stop being aware of her voice as they chatted in Japanese.

Dan sat with Ty Bates across the aisle from his parents.

"Political events are really brewing," Ty said. "The students in Beijing are thumbing their noses at the government's threat to crack down and are calling Deng and Li Peng tyrants. They established student unions independent of the government and elected their own leaders."

"It's a taste of democracy," Dan said. "Hope it doesn't turn sour."

"Are you getting nervous?" Ty asked. "Ed told me he's getting his ticket to the good old US of A tomorrow. Some Japanese students are discussing leaving too."

Dan hoped it wasn't Yoshiko talking about leaving. "Fred Jackson, that student from Cincinnati, has left already. Fred's parents heard about the turmoil and sent him a ticket."

"I expect that was just an excuse to save embarrassment," Ty said. "He never did adjust to conditions here . . . with up to ten students to a room in the dorms."

"Why go now? I think the situation's calming down," Dan said.

Ty asked, "With 150,000 people in Tiananmen Square criticizing government corruption and shouting, 'Down with Dictatorship'?"

"But the government has done nothing for days. When soldiers and police surrounded the square, marchers shouted 'People love the peoples' police; the peoples' police love the people.'" Dan chuckled. "Berkeley students should have tried that in the sixties. I can hear it now: 'People love the peoples' pigs; the peoples' pigs love the people.'"

"Not sure that would have been in the right spirit," Ty laughed. "I hear the students smashed soda bottles on the ground after finding out Deng Xiaoping's son is involved in shady business deals because Xiaoping sounds like 'small bottle' in Chinese."

"But the government has agreed conditionally to dialogue with the students. There's hope yet," Dan said.

"Except no one knows what the conditions will be," Ty said and stood up. "Oops, I'm getting off here."

The bus stopped, and Ty got off. Dan nodded to Mr. and Mrs. Bates who remained seated. Mrs. Bates liked to go to the Friendship Store, where foreigners, for FEC—Foreign Exchange Currency—could buy foreign goods not available to the Chinese.

"Well, you've been a stranger," Mrs. Bates said. "It's good to get out now that those dreadful riots are over. Going to the Friendship Store?"

"You're going there again?" Dan asked.

"We go every week if we can," Mrs. Bates smiled. "You can't get decent crackers and biscuits in the Chinese stores. I can't stand those horrid moon cakes."

She doesn't seem to like anything Chinese, Dan thought. "I've asked the driver to leave me off in the middle of town."

"Has Wu Yaoqian reimbursed you yet?"

Dan shook his head.

"He manages to give us six kinds of grief, too," she said. "We had to fight with him to get those wretched drapes changed and to replace the ugly, old sofa. Now there's a leak in the ceiling right above our toilet. When we sit there, it drips on our heads. I hate to think of the Australian couple sitting on theirs upstairs at the same time and . . ."

Dan wanted to laugh at the picture that arose in his mind of the Australians sitting upstairs on their toilet as a couple and Mrs. Bates downstairs getting dribbled on.

It reminded him of the cartoon about Reagan's "trickle-down theory" of economics: it pictured a three-story outhouse, each story directly over the one below with the one on top marked "upper class," the next one "middle class," and the one on the bottom "lower class."

Mrs. Bates caught her breath. ". . . well, I don't know if what drips on us is just water. We bought a rain cap for the occasion."

Dan was now trying to stifle a guffaw with partial success, though his throat tightened and sounded like a leaky steam pipe. He was glad he didn't live under the Bateses' apartment.

She continued. "Wu says he ordered a plumber, but it's been two weeks now. He doesn't seem to remember it's his job to take care of our needs."

"I think the Chinese are extremely generous hosts, especially given their standard of living. They give their guests the best of everything. My colleagues and students constantly embarrass me with gifts. Like last winter when an English professor I hardly knew, Su, came to my door with a package of fresh meat. He assured me it was a special meat that would keep me healthy and warm in the winter. I tried to convince him I didn't cook for myself, but he insisted I take it. He said the Chinese had to take care of their foreign friends. I probably committed a grave breach of etiquette when I gave it to Gao. Gao said he was sure he knew what it was, and it was very expensive. It wasn't until a month later that I heard that the Chinese believe dog meat keeps one healthy and warm in the winter."

"Oh, how disgusting." Mrs. Bates recoiled from Dan.

"Of course there are few dogs in the city," Dan said. "They're even rare in the countryside, so Su had made a great sacrifice to get it for me."

"If there are few dogs in the city," Mrs. Bates asked, "why are the sidewalks covered with dog droppings?"

"That's not dogs," Dan answered. "That's from children. Young children don't wear diapers. They have slits in their pants and squat in the streets."

Mrs. Bates turned pale. "I didn't know . . ."

"Sorry," Dan said. "My point was about generosity. Wu takes us sightseeing and provides this van for shopping. Imagine any American university doing that for its foreign guests." Dan couldn't believe he was defending Wu. It was his curse to see both sides of an issue and have to give the man his credit even if he did despise him.

"Well, Wu owes us special consideration after all we've done for . . ." She blushed and changed the subject. "What are you shopping for?"

"The usual hopeless search for orange juice, cheese, and chocolate," Dan said, wondering what special consideration it was that Wu owed them. "If worse comes to worse, I'll settle for presents for family back home. Silk maybe. It's easy to mail."

"Chocolate, cheese, and orange juice?" Mr. Bates asked. "Good luck. They don't even have them at the Friendship Store. And I wouldn't send any presents through the mail. They're likely to be stolen by the censors."

Dan got off in front of the big government department store. He stood a moment trying to decide between the government store and the free market across the street. Yoshiko stepped off the bus behind him and went into the department store. Without thinking, he followed her in.

Bored saleswomen stood behind rows of wooden counters ignoring the customers. Pots, pans, woks, thick woolen orange blankets, and towels hung from the walls. Dan looked at pretty blue and gold silk slippers, flowered yellow cotton blouses, and green down vests all in Chinese sizes too small for relatives back home. He was jostled by a short, stocky woman exuding garlic fumes as he picked up a pair of red and gold brocade shoes that smelled like diesel fuel, whether from the glue or a disinfectant, he didn't know. When he asked a passing saleswoman about a pocket-sized notebook, he got the usual disinterested refrain, *méiyŏu*, "not have."

Dan watched Yoshiko investigate a blouse, then disappear behind a row of tall carved cabinets. He tried to turn his attention back to shopping even though he longed to talk to her.

At the cash register, one employee was showing a customer a set of flowered towels while half a dozen customers shouted and jostled for her attention. Behind the counter, three other employees filed their nails, combed their hair, and chatted. It was the typical situation in state-run businesses. The employees had "iron rice bowls," which meant they could not be fired. They had grievances with their bosses and no power over work conditions except to ignore their customers.

Dan saw three pretty plastic combs with multi-colored luminescent flowers and gold sparkles in the showcase. They would be light enough to carry back home for nieces. But Dan would have to push and shove and shout for attention to get waited on. They probably weren't to an American teenager's taste anyway.

He gave up on the combs and decided to hazard the free market across the street, where petty vendors hawked their wares with enthusiasm. Dan hated to go there because it was the opposite of being ignored in the state stores; it was pressure tactics. Vendors shoved their wares under your nose and tried to bargain even if you ignored them.

As he walked toward the exit, he caught a glimpse of Yoshiko leaving the store ahead of him. He walked outside and saw her talking to a man with a black coat and a blue Mao cap. He couldn't believe he caught himself wondering if he was her lover. He had no cause for such stupid jealousy.

As he crossed the street, he dodged a man on a three-wheeled bicycle with an eight-foot stack of cabbages on the cart behind him and almost ran in front of a straw-hatted, barefoot peasant pulling a tank of sewage gathered from city latrines to fertilize the fields somewhere out of the city. Yoshiko had distracted him dangerously. He had to keep his wits on the crowded city streets.

He crossed the street and quickly ducked into a tiny street stall selling blouses. He bought three silk blouses for his nieces and hurried back across the street before any other vendors could accost him with bracelets and watches and such.

In front of the department store he saw that a taxi had stopped for Yoshiko and her companion. As Yoshiko got in, the man took off his coat and hat to reveal the bald head and saffron robes of a Buddhist monk. Dan had known that she interviewed Chinese monks for a Japanese Buddhist magazine. It was her main purpose for being here. In spite of feeling foolish about his presumptuous jealousy, he still envied the monk.

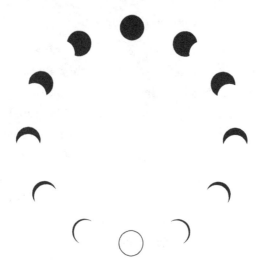

SATANIC BARGAIN

APRIL 29

DAN SMELLED THE PEPPER PORK AS HE ENTERED THE dining room for lunch. He looked around the room for Yoshiko, but she wasn't there. Perhaps she had eaten earlier. The Easter decorations still hanging from the ceiling looked bedraggled.

He sat at a large round table with the Bateses and several other foreigners.

The foreign guests had been taken to the Xi'an Opera the night before and were discussing it around a circular table with a huge lazy Susan heaped with pepper pork and a variety of vegetables and rice.

"Years ago, I saw *The White Haired Girl* at the Beijing Opera, back when they were doing only the communist operas allowed by Mao's wife," said Howard, the Australian chemist. "A bit maudlin. I'm glad they've gone back to the classics."

"History and tragedy, loyalty and courage, love and pathos," said Jim, the Canadian geologist. "It had everything you get in Western opera: story and music, set design and costumes, in addition to the sword fight with backflips. Magnificent coordination. All that in colorful costumes and singing at the same time—"

"Singing?" Mrs. Bates interjected. "Screeching you mean. I would have fallen asleep but my hair was standing on end from all that clanging of gongs. It sounded like cats fighting in a cupboard full of pots and pans."

The picture of Mrs. Bates with her hair standing on end made Dan want to laugh, but he suppressed the urge.

"I'll have to admit," the Canadian chuckled, "there's something to what you say. Of course, I don't even like the screeching in most Western operas." He put his hand to his chest and emitted a high-pitched sound like a dying donkey which gave way to a coughing fit.

When Ty's parents and the others had left to teach class, Ty and Dan sat finishing their meal together.

"Would you mind if I have a sip or two of your beer?" Ty asked. "Now that my parents are gone . . . I've heard about how a few hairs of the dog that bit you—"

Dan lifted his eyebrows a few times and pushed his beer bottle toward Ty. "I thought you didn't drink."

Ty's laugh was a series of suppressed snorts. "After the opera, I went to a party with a few Japanese and American students. They were drinking Mao Tai. In a foolish moment of comradeship, I tossed a whole glassful into my mouth and swallowed. First alcoholic drink in my life."

"Mao Tai is a bit strong for a beginner."

"My head exploded in slow motion, and I breathed fire like a dragon. The others roared with laughter. Everything shone in a holy light for a while, so I had a few more." Ty poured himself half a glass of beer and sipped it. He grimaced and wiped his mouth with his sleeve.

"I presume your parents don't know."

Ty shook his head and scowled. "Ouch." He rubbed his forehead. "I've been reading Marx. I like the bit about throwing off one's chains and all. I've been cooped up in Plainfield Texas, all my life until now."

"Where's Plainfield?"

"It's near Muleshoe, Needmore, and Circle Back. You don't know how those factory-farm chickens feel until you've been cooped up in Plainfield with no room to scratch your itches. Have you ever been to West Texas?"

Dan nodded. "Drove through once. Miles and miles of nothing but miles and miles. Plenty of room to scratch itches as far as I could see. Miles and miles . . . a tired old joke . . . you must have heard it before."

"Yep, but it's true. In Plainfield, the days all have seventy-two hours. The main forms of entertainment are watching the mosquitoes bite your arm in the summer and in the winter, gossiping about who fell asleep in church last week."

"I lived in a town like that in South Carolina," Dan said, "except we had swamps where we could play with the water moccasins, coral snakes, copper heads, and alligators."

"I forgot to mention the rattlesnake roundup and feast. Highlight of the year." Ty laughed. "Still, I think it's time to fly the coop, taste the taste of life like other people taste it, at least until they lasso me and drag me back to Plainfield. I need some sins to repent and memories to keep me warm on those cold winter Sundays when the preacher drones on and on." He sipped the beer again. "Is everything alcoholic this bitter?"

Dan shrugged and picked up the book at Ty's elbow. "What's this you're reading? Bogdanov's *Empiriomonism*?"

"Song Yingying wanted me to read it and discuss it with her." Ty sipped on the beer again. "She's my Chinese tutor. Some visiting teacher, a Marxist from Australia, gave it to her last year."

"Lenin criticized Bogdanov," Dan said. "I don't think it would count as orthodox Marxism in China."

"I suspect that's why she treasures it so," Ty said. "Forbidden fruit and all that. Like beer to an American teenager." He lifted his beer in a mock toast to Dan and sipped a bit more.

"Have you read it?"

"I was trying to this morning, but listen to this."

"Must I?"

"Here." Ty opened the book at random and read where his eyes happened to fall. "We, discarding metaphysical 'things in themselves' as empty fetishes, place in their stead 'empirical substitution!' This substitution, which originates in each man's recognition of the psyche of others, presupposes that the 'basis' of the phenomena of physical experiences consists of . . ." Dan yawned.

"I'm sure it's all perfectly true. I understand all the individual words all right," Ty said, "but my brain can't fit them together; it's not the sort of thing to foist on someone experiencing his first hangover."

"Why are you even trying to read it?"

"Have you seen her, with her cute little ponytails tied with big pink ribbons that make her look like a twelve-year old? Curves that would intimidate a race car driver? With her pouty lips and butterfly eyelashes, she's a knockout." Ty twirled the lazy Susan.

"In short, you're falling for her."

"When she was teaching me Chinese conversation yesterday, I was trying to compose the sentence 'I want to ride your horse.' But I gave the word horse the wrong tone and it came out 'I want to ride your mother.' Yingying turned red and laughed, and I didn't realize what I had said until an hour later. My feeling was more than embarrassment, it was desperation."

"I hate to tell you this, but she has a boyfriend," Dan said. "You know him. Gao Mingyue, Professor Gao's son."

Ty's shoulders drooped. "Guess we can't win them all, can we?" He rose from the table. "Well, I've got to get to class."

———

Song Yingying waited for the bus in the hot sun under a clear sky on Chang'anlu, the wide boulevard in front of the university. She had heard nothing of Mingyue since he had gone off to stir up the workers. Perhaps he didn't like her anymore. She could understand if he wasn't attracted to a girl with small ears and a girlish look. But maybe he had been hurt. Her friends said that he had been a brilliant orator. He had disappeared during the riot and had not been heard from since. She had visited several hospitals and not found him. If he were in prison, one might never know. And she was the one who had convinced him to go. For several days now she had been sick with fear and guilt and did not know what more to do.

She pushed and shoved with everyone else getting on the bus. It was the same everywhere. People pushed and shoved to buy stamps at the post office or to get attention at the department store ever since the Cultural Revolution when politeness was denounced as bourgeois. A young man jerked his elbow into the gray-haired old lady's chest in front of Yingying on the bus steps, and the old lady stumbled back, off balance. Yingying caught her and fell back on her rump. The old lady sprawled on top of her. They lay gasping for breath. Other people rushed past them onto the bus, which rolled away, three people hanging out the door, leaving the two women coughing in a cloud of noxious fumes and dust.

The old lady rolled over and stood, trembling. *"Xie xie, xie xie,"* the old lady thanked her and bowed her head several times. "Are you hurt?"

"I'm fine." Yingying stood up. She looked at her arm and saw that her sleeve was torn and her elbow scraped. Her rump felt bruised and stung, and she trembled. She wished she could push the rude young man off the bus. She was not sure if she was angrier at missing the bus or at her vulnerability or at the stupidity of the idea that politeness is bourgeois. The old lady might have been badly hurt. There was no respect for elders anymore, she thought. It was another error of the Cultural Revolution, but who would dare criticize it and risk being denounced as bourgeois? Just because the Bourgeoisie practiced Confucian politeness and the Proletariat were rude and from the communist point of view the Bourgeoisie is bad, doesn't mean being rude is good. Couldn't everyone see such thinking was stupid? Perhaps it was a government scheme for population control, to kill off the elderly, or a Darwinian scheme for the survival of the rudest.

She had heard Professor Norton's lecture on Thoreau when he said that Marx was right that, through history, many of the laws had been made in the interests of the ruling class, but Marx was wrong to proclaim that all ethics was a matter of class interests. Some moral principles are universal; they are the principles appropriate to a future classless society, and therefore, to all societies. People would be happier in a polite classless society than a rude one. Yingying agreed. People could be polite in a classless society. Would she dare raise this as an issue at the next student organizing committee meeting? She waited for the next bus.

When she stopped shaking, she wiped the tears from her eyes and blew her nose. It had been a bad day, worrying about Mingyue and falling at the bus stop. Now, for the first time in two weeks, she would have to face her father, who as a policeman, would surely disapprove of her work against the government even if he had always opposed corruption.

The second bus had been too crowded to get on, and she had to wait for the third. When she arrived home, she washed her scraped elbow, changed her blouse, and had her mother put Tiger Balm on the cuts on her fanny.

She still felt a bit shaky. Her anger at the young man who had pushed the old lady welled up again.

After eating, while her mother and sister were washing dishes, her father lit a cigarette and settled into a corner of the couch.

"I have something you might like to see," he said.

He pulled three pictures from his pocket and laid them on the coffee table in front of him. She sat on the couch beside him and looked at them. The first was of Mingyue in the railroad yard talking to the workers. The second was a line of marchers on a downtown street with banners. Mingyue was clearly discernible in the middle of the front row. The third was of Mingyue using a megaphone.

Yingying's breathing became short and shallow.

"We're looking for all the leaders of the riots for questioning." He blew a cloud of smoke toward the ceiling and did not look at her.

Questioning? You mean torture, she thought. Are you asking me to betray him? In that instant her lifetime relationship with her father flipped into another dimension. It was like seeing photograph negatives for the first time. The hair rose on her arms. In a burst of adrenaline and clarity, she realized that he had become more and more formal and had been distant and official with her for some time already. She had not felt the warmth of love she had known as a child, and she had not been consciously aware of it until now. He had never been outright cold like this before with her. There was a threat in his eyes. She slid away from him to the end of the couch and crossed her arms tightly.

"Did you find him . . . Father?" The last word stuck in her throat. He had begun to feel less like a father to her and more like a professional policeman, a defender of the government.

"I know where he is. I have seen him in a foreigner's apartment building with a telescope."

He was not in a hospital, but he might soon be in prison and tortured. She shivered. "Then why don't you arrest him?" Her fear was more for Mingyue than for herself.

"My own daughter is on the Student Organizing Committee." He scowled at her and looked away again.

Her heart skipped a beat.

"I've been wondering what to do about that, too," he said.

"We are struggling against corruption, father. I thought you would approve. You've always complained of high-level corruption and injustice. I can't believe you support it." Her voice shook. She had seldom argued with her father, but she was struggling for all that was meaningful in her life now: Mingyue, justice, her father that she had always loved so much. She had to get it all clear in her mind.

"My job is to prevent crime. Any kind of crime. We can't allow riots where people are killed—"

"Killed?" she asked. "The government denies that anyone was killed. Are the rumors true then?"

He frowned. "There is a power struggle at high levels of government that will decide whether the corruption ends or not. Student interference may only give the forces of reaction an excuse for violence."

"There would be no power struggle if we had not raised the issues." Her pulse pounded in her ears.

"Not so. The forces in the struggle are using you. I want you to stop involving yourself in student politics. Get off the committee. Your activity could harm the whole family."

"Harm your career, you mean." The outburst frightened her because she half believed it. He squinted at her. The cheek around the scar reddened.

She knew that he was right that his job was the foundation of the family's security and prosperity. She felt guilty, confused, and betrayed. She remembered how he had been forced to arrest old friends during the Cultural Revolution. Perhaps he was not the hero of integrity and courage she had always imagined him.

"You're waiting to see which side of the power struggle wins. You want to be on the winning side." She couldn't believe she had said that. She must be losing control. She didn't mean it. It had slipped out.

He glowered at her. His scarred cheek twitched. "You force me to bargain with you. Well then, I'll do it. If you and he end your political activity, I'll bury Mingyue's file where the police department will forget about it. I'll tell you where he is. You go to him and convince him to stop. If he refuses, you must end your relationship with him. If you refuse, you will never see him again anyway because he will be in prison."

"Father." Her tone was more disappointment and disgust than anger. "How could you?" But as she sat in silence and glowered at him, her anger grew again until she feared she would throw something at her father. The lamp, a plate . . .

She picked up her coat and heard the threat and despair in his voice.

"So, you refuse."

She walked out the door and slammed it. Her stomach shook from both fear and anger. She could not let Mingyue be arrested. He had to flee. She wished she knew where his Muslim friend lived. He might be the foreigner her father mentioned, since he thought of Chinese Muslims as foreigners. He might be there, and she could warn him. But she didn't know.

She hardly knew what she was doing. In a daze of fear, hurt, and anger, she took a bus back to the university. She could not face her roommates. She needed to be by herself. She went into an empty classroom and stared at the wall. Could her father really be bribing her? It was more like blackmail. She could not believe her father would threaten her like that. And she couldn't just let Mingyue go. And how could she just turn her back on her fellow students and the fight for democracy? She didn't know what to do.

THE MOON
AND THE MANURE

APRIL 29

GAO BAIMA MET DAN AFTER HIS EVENING CLASS AT the door of the lecture hall. They walked together in the dark under trees rustling and swaying in the waning breeze of a storm. Lights from the windows of the student dorms ahead glistened in the puddles on the sidewalk. Dan caught a faint whiff of roses that lined the pathway, as if they rejoiced at being liberated by the rain from their normal prison of dust and soot. Crowds of students and teachers emerged from the science building and the library chattering and laughing.

"The speech you gave to assembled faculty in November, 'Freedom and Democracy in American Literature,'" Gao said, "will be published this month in *Shaanxi Literary Quarterly*."

"That's our publication, since you translated it into Chinese." Dan smiled. "Thank you. But I wonder if publishing it now is a bit dangerous."

"They were planning to publish it next fall, but they put it in Spring edition on purpose," Gao said. "If someone from China had written it, the government could punish him, but they can't punish what a foreigner writes."

A rather pointed gesture of defiance, Dan thought. "But they could object to you translating it and the Quarterly publishing it."

"Well," Gao said, "it is true that your March speech did make some people angry when you criticized Lenin and Stalin—when you said that they perverted the democratic doctrine of Marx and Engels into a dictatorial one which created a new oppressor class, the Communist Party. Your sponsors are being punished. Professor Chen had been planning to do research at George Washington University next year. He has been told that he will not be allowed to go abroad. And Professor Yao's appointment as Cochair of Political Science Department has been canceled."

"Shit." Dan winced. "Perhaps I shouldn't meddle in Chinese politics. I never would have given that speech if I'd known it would cause . . ." Stop, Dan told himself. Don't be disingenuous.

"I think it is a necessary cost of struggle for freedom of speech," Gao said. "I am sure they would choose to do it all over again if they had the choice."

"Still, it would be more just if I were the one to be punished," Dan said. Actually, it would be an honor to be sent home early for defending freedom and democracy, not to mention saving further hassle with Wu about airfare. "I'm not used to my words being a matter of life and death. In America, a talk like that would have stimulated a few yawns and been quickly forgotten."

And what of Mingyue? Dan had meddled in a Chinese internal affair. Nothing could be more offensive to the Chinese government.

Gao walked with his hands crossed behind him and fell silent. Dan dreaded bringing up the subject of Mingyue again. He hated to deceive his friend, but he was sure it was for his son's safety . . . and the family's.

"When will your son be coming home? Have you heard from him?"

The corners of Gao's mouth drooped like a clown's. "I've heard nothing. If he is in prison . . ." He gulped.

Dan wanted to tell him that his son was with a friend, but even that would give away too much. With a jolt, Dan realized that Mingyue might not have made it to his friend's; he might have been picked up by the police on the way.

Gao handed Dan his latest installment of political notes, they said goodnight, and Dan walked back toward his apartment down shrub-lined sidewalks past the bland concrete five-story buildings where the faculty lived. Normally he preferred an irregular Romantic aesthetic, like Japanese gardens, to the classical geometric patterns that prevailed in modern China. But the garden with sidewalks going off at orderly right angles fit his mood tonight after a week of chaos.

Dan looked up as the clouds parted and showed a half moon. He was reminded of the many Chinese poems about the moon. From the Buddhist point of view, Dan thought, the moon is no more beautiful, intrinsically, than a pile of horse manure. At least the manure is warm and full of life, while the moon is a cold barren rock. That's not to put down the moon. The wise Buddhist takes joy in both of them.

Because the whole campus was being dug up for the installation of steam pipes, Dan had to be careful not to step into ditches in the dark. Piles of dirt had covered half the sidewalk for months, and rain was melting them into a slippery, inch-thick layer of ooze over the rest of the concrete. He braced himself for each step, as if he were on ice skates. He stepped into a deep layer of muck, and his shoe was sucked off. He balanced on one foot to put it back on and walked home with the laces dragging in mud. He had been pulled back into chaos.

Dan laughed at himself. He knew that life is a paradox . . . a series of jokes on us. If one could just laugh like a Tibetan Buddhist monk, one would never be disappointed. The picture of himself slipping in the mud next and falling on his rear end made him smile. He could enjoy both the moon and the mud . . . the manure.

When he walked into his living room, his neck and shoulders tensed. Something was not right, but he didn't know what. He examined the bedroom, bathroom, and kitchen. No one was in the apartment, but there was a smell that shouldn't be there. Some of the notes he had been taking on his desk for his class earlier in the day were out of order.

Perhaps he had been careless in his hurry to get to class. Or perhaps not. He recognized the smell of cigarette smoke in the air. A grim suspicion flitted through the dark recesses of his mind like a bat, and he felt shaky.

He pushed the chair under the window to add Gao's notes to his stash. His hand groped on top of the ledge above the curtains. To his relief, his money was all there and his passport. But the notes on the events in China were gone, along with his teaching contract. Why the teaching contract too? Wu? He felt like he had just received a ticking package in the mail. His knees were suddenly weak, and he felt unsteady on his chair. He saw the cigarette butt in the ashtray.

"Horse manure," he mumbled. His visitor had left a deliberate calling card. "It's the manure. Inspector Song."

After sleepless hours of tossing and turning, Dan had finally fallen asleep when the doorbell rang. The police? He flipped on the light, and his clock read 3 a.m. The gate would be locked. The doorbell rang again.

Dan opened the door and saw it was Mingyue hanging his head like a naughty boy. A jolt of adrenaline surged through Dan's body. Dan pulled him in and locked the door before he dared speak a word.

"My friend only let me stay a few nights," Mingyue said. "I've been wandering the streets hiding in the shadows and didn't know where to go. I climbed the wall again."

"Oh God!" The nightmare was starting again. Dan hated it. But he had to do his duty to his friend and the cause of democracy. "I think you're as safe here as anywhere. The police have already been here and not found you. They won't come again." At least not for you, he thought.

THE BIRD

APRIL 30

YINGYING HAD LAIN AWAKE MUCH OF THE NIGHT worrying that her rejection of her father's proposal had condemned Mingyue to prison. In a dream, she and Mingyue were imprisoned in a bird cage, and her father had smashed the cage down with his boots so that they were being crushed inside it. She awoke breathing hard and soaked in sweat.

When she was very young, several of the old men of the village took their birds in cages for a walk every morning, meeting under a tree near her house. They hung the cages in a tree, sat on benches, and chatted while the birds sang to each other. She would often go out to talk to the birds. Her father noticed her interest and gave her a beautiful yellow canary for her birthday.

She loved to hear it sing and fed it faithfully. Soon after that, owning pet birds was one of the things that was declared bourgeois. The Red Guards broke into her neighbor's house and confiscated a wooden statue of Confucius, an altar, several bookcases full of Western and Confucian books, Western musical records, and a bird in its cage. All these, and similar things from other houses, were taken to the center of the village and put on a pile. All the people of the village were gathered to hear the owners denounced until they confessed their bourgeois pollution.

The pile of goods was set on fire. A woman, a leader of the Red Guards, picked up the bird cage. Her voice resounded in Yingying's memory, as full of self-righteous confidence as a lion tamer in a circus and as loud as the clashing cymbals in the opera. She lifted the cage over her head with a sneer and flung it on the fire. Yingying watched in terror as the bird hopped around the cage, beat its wings on the bars, and squawked, its feathers in flames, until she could no longer see it through the smoke. Yingying cried, but her father shook her and made her stop. That frightened her even more for she feared her father as well as the Red Guard. He had betrayed her.

At that moment, a hardness grew somewhere in her chest as her innocence went up in smoke; her body felt hollow and numb and helpless, and a cold hatred was born in her heart. She hoped the Red Guard leader would burn for a century on hot coals when she returned to whatever hell she was the queen of.

When they got home, her father had explained that it was too dangerous to have a bird, and they would have to get rid of Yingying's. She imagined him throwing it on the fire, and she screamed and hugged the cage. The bird flapped against the bars in panic. Her father opened the window of the room, then pried the cage from Yingying's arms and opened the cage door. The bird fluttered frantically around its accustomed home and settled on the perch, as if it didn't understand what the open door meant. Her father held the whimpering child gently and stroked her hair. Yingying watched the bird and sucked her thumb.

After a moment, the bird flew out the door and landed on the windowsill. It hopped back and forth on the window ledge. Yingying called to the bird, broke loose from her father's arms, and ran to grab it. It flew out of her reach out the window, circling, and landed on a tree limb. Yingying's happiness went out the window with it. She called desperately for the bird to come back.

"Think if you really want him to come back," her father said softly. "There will be no more bird seed to buy in the store and he will be hungry. Then the Red Guards will come and take him to be burned. But if he flies away, he will be free to travel to the ends of the world. He will be master of Heaven. Perhaps he will meet friends and even a wife and have little children who will make people happy with their songs. Perhaps someday you can choose to be free like him, if you want."

Now Yingying wished that the bird would fly away to Heaven. She watched, trembling, as the bird walked back and forth on the tree limb, as if unsure which choice to make. As if unsure of his new freedom and his new world.

"Fly away, little bird," she whispered.

Finally, the bird flew over the neighbor's rooftop, and Yingying's heart soared after him. It was her love of the bird that had led her to become a biology student so she could study birds. She hadn't realized that biology was mainly a preparation to study agriculture or medicine. She wasn't excited about domestic ducks and chickens.

Her father had understood then. Had he now forgotten the wisdom of his youth? Had his heart become stone? Well, she thought bitterly, he was wrong anyway. A canary would not have survived long in a cold North China winter. Stupid man. And she had believed him.

She did not go to her classes and instead took the bus downtown to the City Police Department. The huge red star over the doorway was cracked, and she remembered what she had heard, that Mingyue and his followers had damaged it. She smirked for an instant, then turned her face into a steel mask. The guard recognized her as the Inspector's daughter and let her in. When she strode down the hall to her father's office, all heads turned to watch her. She banged open her father's door and charged in like a field marshal about to launch an attack of a dozen armies. She slammed the door shut behind her. Her father raised his eyes from the papers on his desk.

"I'll stop my political activity and never see Mingyue again." She realized that her anger might be heard in the hall and lowered her voice. "And you bury his file. But you must be the one to tell him. I'll not be the one to force him to choose between me and the fight for justice and freedom. If I saw him again, I could not say goodbye." Her shoulders sagged like sails when the wind dies, and she looked away from her father.

Inspector Song lit a cigarette and took two long puffs before he answered. "Agreed."

She glared at him as he leaned back in his chair—his face as expressionless as hers—stared at the ceiling, and inhaled another long draw of smoke. She turned to leave, then turned back to him.

"Don't ever expect me to speak to you again . . ." She started to say "father" but couldn't. She sneered and spat out the word.

". . . Inspector. I'll visit mother and little sister when you are at work. When I graduate, I won't need your *guanxi* to get a job. The government can send me to the borders of China—to Harbin, Tibet, or Hainan for all I care. The farther away from here, the better."

She turned and strode out the door without looking back.

A CHASM

APRIL 30

HALF-DEFLATED FROM A MOSTLY SLEEPLESS NIGHT of worry about Mingyue's return and the missing papers paired with his recurring anxiety dream, Dan dragged himself on to the university minibus for the bi-weekly excursion for foreign guests arranged by the Foreign Affairs Office.

Approximately twice a month since October, there had been trips to prehistoric sites, imperial tombs of various dynasties, the terra-cotta warrior museum, and famous temples. There was so much of historical interest to see around Xi'an that Dan hadn't yet taken in half of it. Of all the places one might teach in China, surely Xi'an had the most to offer anyone interested in history, but Dan didn't have his heart in it today. He had gone in order to keep up the appearance of normalcy in his life, in spite of the danger of another visit from the police. If he missed the trip, Wu would wonder why and would come snooping around in Dan's apartment to see if he was sick. Dan did not want to take the chance of Mingyue being caught.

The bus was almost filled. Ed, Ty Bates and his parents, the Australian physicist's family, a Canadian geologist staying only a month, a Russian student, and several American and Japanese students crowded in. There were only two seats left when Dan got on last. The bus began moving and he lurched into the seat beside Yoshiko.

"Do you mind if I sit here?"

She shook her head and smiled. "One cannot protest what fate has decided." She had her hair in a Chinese style, straight down and cut across sharply at mid neck and wore a Chinese blouse and pants, but she still exuded a graceful style and shy reserve that immediately separated her from Chinese women and their proletarian directness.

"I've forgotten where we are going today," he said. "Is it far?"

"Not far." She glanced at him, then looked down at her lap. "Just south of the city. It is Xingjiao Temple. Very exciting."

"A Buddhist temple, isn't it?" God, she's beautiful, he thought. Her lips are so delicate.

"Oh, yes. Very important. It has a pagoda of Xuan Zhang and brochures say 'many ancient utmost precious scriptures written on bamboo strips.' The abbot will show us. Not many people can see them."

"Xuan Zhang? Isn't he the one memorialized in the great novel, *Monkey*? He brought back translations of manuscripts from India. I thought he lived in the Big Wild Goose Pagoda Temple when he returned. It's so close to the university that I jog by it and think of him sometimes. I imagine Monkey climbing to the top of the pagoda like King Kong on the Empire State Building." Dan had an image of the Inspector climbing up to the top of his curtains. Why did he look there? Was it so obvious?

Yoshiko laughed. "Yes. He lived there."

"Do you know the story of *Monkey*?" Here he was, finally sitting with Yoshiko, and he couldn't get the Inspector out of his mind. Why did the Inspector come into the apartment in the first place? Did he suspect that Mingyue was there? Dan had gone over these questions a hundred times.

"It is one of my favorites. My father has the first edition of Gakutei translation and some prints of the story by Hokusai."

"Ah. Then you were raised in a cultured family," Dan said. "How fortunate. I was not. My father was a military officer."

"It was my love of the story that made me want to study where Xuan Zhang lived," Yoshiko said. "Kukai brought the Dharma to Japan from here, too."

"I'm pleased that the Chinese government has restored so many monasteries and has proclaimed religious freedom," Dan said. "Ten years ago, it was only a few elderly ladies who dared to light incense and kowtow in the temples because Marxism proclaimed religion to be the opiate of the masses." He knew he must be making a fool of himself by stating the obvious. She knew all of this.

"I've spoken with the priests at several temples," Yoshiko said. "You know that the Chinese government has allowed temples to be reopened for mainly economic reasons. Thousands of Japanese tourists visit those temples and provides China with much needed hard foreign currency for foreign exchange."

"So, the kowtow of religion has become the cash cow of the masses. Sorry. That was a stupid joke; you won't know what I meant."

Yoshiko looked at Dan as if he had suddenly started speaking in tongues. "And the government decided that allowing priests to maintain the temples and support themselves by selling souvenirs would be cheaper than paying museum caretakers. Buddhist and Taoist temples are reopened, but no Confucian temples are yet."

He did not want to mix her up in his messy life. Bad timing. "Of course. Confucianism was hierarchical and preserved class division, whereas Buddhism rejected the Hindu caste system and is essentially classless."

Yoshiko looked up at Dan, and he almost lost the thread of the discussion. "But Taoism traditionally criticizes government," she said. "Isn't that dangerous to Communism?"

"The selection of religious leaders is under government control," he said. "For instance, the Catholic Church here is not under Rome's control but under a Chinese archbishop approved by the government. I'm sure they control the Taoists too."

"And the Tibetan Buddhists are not under the Dalai Lama," she added, "but under the Panchen Lama chosen by the Chinese." She paused and grinned. "So. Cash cow of the masses. I understand." She giggled.

She was beautiful, informed, and bright, too.

Dan felt Yoshiko's warm arm against his and his thoughts about religion ceased. They both fell into silence—his now awkward and self-conscious. The two-lane highway was crowded with trucks, busses, horse carts, slow fume-spewing "one-ox" tractors pulling wagons filled with people, bicyclists, and pedestrians. Peasants had spread their spring wheat grains to dry on the highway, and the vehicles just drove right over them. Dan wondered if it would crush and foul the wheat. It gave him a new appreciation of the concept of multiple use.

Why did the Inspector pick out the notes, he wondered? What would he do when he read them?

In the seat behind him, Ty Bates' mother complained about the narrow seats, the bumpy road, the diesel fumes coming in the window, and how the cooks always made her eggs over easy hard as rubber. How trivial all that seemed in the face of his own troubles. Would police be waiting for him?

The bus turned off the main highway and climbed a narrow winding road up the side of a steep hill overlooking a flat valley of wheat fields. The high mountains across the valley floated at the top of a sea of smog. A small five-tiered pagoda stood on the edge of the hill like a sentinel guarding the valley. It looked ancient with bushes growing here and there from the side of its brick walls. Around three sides of the pagoda clustered old blue-brick buildings of the monastery with blue and brown tiled roofs. The buildings were small scale and intimate. Beyond them, across a field of golden flowers, amidst pine trees, stood the two-story building with roof corners curved up where the guests were taken.

Yoshiko stood under a willow tree, looking out at the mountains floating on mist. Dan saw a tear in the corner of her eye.

"One yen for your thoughts, Yoshiko."

"That mountain arches perfectly, like a courtesan's eyebrow," she said. "It's so beautiful, I wish I could die so it's the last thing I see."

"A very Japanese sentiment." Dan laughed. "I always thought beauty made life worth living."

"It is best to die in the fullness of happiness, like spring blossoms."

Yes, he thought. Why not choose the moment of one's death instead of leaving it to meaningless random chance? While Yoshiko hadn't mentioned it directly, there was a melancholy tone to her words that led his thoughts to Sartre, who said suicide was a person's greatest freedom. Round out one's life with a triumphant "hurrah!" instead of shrinking in fear. Choose when to finish the masterpiece with one last stroke of the paintbrush. He did understand, all too well, and a deep pang of sorrow made him one with Yoshiko.

"Where in Japan do you live?" He thought he might work up the courage to ask her out after all.

"Nagasaki."

"Oh. Did your family . . . suffer from . . . the war?"

"My grandparents died in the bomb. And my mother died a few years ago from the radiation." She had no trace of emotion in her voice.

He felt his cheeks flush. "Then you are kind even to speak to an American like me."

"Buddhists carry no resentment. I understand the nexus of causes that . . . It would be foolish to be angry. It would only make me suffer more." She looked at him. "But my grandparents were strong nationalists. Perhaps their ghosts . . . would be angry if . . ." She looked down a moment in silence, then walked on to catch up with the rest of the group entering a building.

If she went out with me, he thought, finishing hers. He kicked a stone. The cloudless sky seemed to have gotten smoggier and darker.

The bald abbot glowed with pride and smiled broadly as he showed the guests the precious Beiye scriptures written on bamboo strips by an Indian Buddhist monk. He served the guests tea and answered questions. Dan would normally have a dozen questions. But he sat silent. His thoughts were on Mingyue, the missing papers, and Yoshiko. She asked several good questions. He was taken by her intelligence. But the atomic bomb had opened up a chasm between them.

When the group boarded the bus for the return trip, Dan dared not sit next to Yoshiko again. She was already sitting with another Japanese student and chatting.

Dan sat with Spock-eared Ed.

"I don't know what I'm still doing here." Ed's voice sounded despondent. "I must be a masochist."

"Just what I'm beginning to feel myself," Dan said, wishing he could explain why to a sympathetic ear.

"Say," Ed said, "could I ask you for some help arranging with Wu to leave? I can't seem to get him to understand what I want."

"Wu's the last person I'm likely to be any help with, but I'd be glad to give it a try." Dealing with Wu wasn't what Dan needed on top of everything else, but he'd make the effort.

Ed settled into a nap in spite of the swaying and bumping of the bus down the winding road. Dan brooded on the documents missing in his room and fell into a dark pit of gloom. He wondered how he was going to tell his friend Gao that they were gone. To what use would they be put? Blackmail? And he wondered what he was doing falling in hopeless love when he had put himself into such a stupid position—in possibly serious trouble? The bus seemed to be hurling itself down to some grim disaster.

THREAT

APRIL 30

DAN CAME HOME FROM HIS EVENING CLASS, OPENED a beer, and sat at his desk to read a paper one of his students—a high school English teacher—had written in totally incompetent English. Mingyue was curled up on the couch reading Dan's text on world history when the doorbell rang.

Mingyue scrambled to hide under Dan's bed. Dan looked around to see if there was any evidence of Mingyue's presence, then went to the door.

It was Inspector Song. Dan looked to see if there were any other policemen. His heart raced.

"You've come alone? Time for the showdown at OK Corral and my pistols are empty."

"You have pistols?" The Inspector squinted at him. "Forbidden in—"

"Stupid joke." Dan grimaced. "It's a pleasure to see you again," he said sarcastically.

"Not a pleasure," the Inspector said. He walked directly to the sofa and plunked himself down. "Distasteful business. Several issues. Let me be direct. No poetry this time. May I smoke?"

"Go ahead." Dan sat. His armpits were damp already. He was sure it was the Inspector who had taken the papers. The cigarette he was lighting had the same odor he had noticed lingering in the air on the night he discovered them gone.

"Wu Yaoqian pays you monthly," the Inspector said, exhaling smoke. "Do you have any complaints?"

This line of questioning was a curious surprise and not at all what Dan had expected. He wondered why the Inspector had asked.

"Complaints? What do you mean?"

"Dollars? FEC?" The Inspector scratched his neck, wrinkled his forehead, pursed his lips, and looked at him impassively as if he expected a confession. He inhaled and puffed out a perfect smoke ring.

"But I don't want to bore you with my petty—"

"No, please tell me. How many dollars does he give you?"

Without saying a word, just raising his eyebrows at appropriate moments, the Inspector got the story out of Dan about Wu not reimbursing him for his airline ticket, and not telling him that he could get ten percent of his pay in dollars. By the end of the story, the Inspector's eyes were half shut as if he were about to go to sleep. His cigarette dangled loosely from his fingers and threatened to fall on the rug.

"I see." The Inspector opened his eyes. "Why didn't you report this to the authorities?" Ashes floated to the floor.

"I thought Wu was the authority." Dan knew that the Inspector knew that Wu was a police informer and so had *guanxi* with the police. He shrugged his shoulders. "I decided to be patient."

"A prudent virtue." The Inspector took a last draw from his cigarette and stubbed it out in the ashtray Dan now kept permanently on the coffee table. "As for the next item of business . . ." The Inspector pulled a bundle of papers from an inner jacket pocket. Dan recognized them as his missing notes. The sudden threat took away his breath a moment. The Inspector coughed a dry, smoky cough. "I searched your apartment for Gao Mingyue and found these. There is information here about what goes on in Chinese government that is not available to the general public. A foreigner with such information might be considered by the government authorities . . . how shall I say . . . to be engaged in espionage. There is enough fear in higher Party circles about foreigners corrupting Chinese students with Western bourgeois ideas. This would not help calm those fears. It would be unwise to continue such writing for the sake of the university's ability to continue inviting foreign scholars, as well as your own safety." He put the papers back into his pocket.

Sweat stung Dan's eyes. He wished he could read between the lines. The Inspector's threat had been so restrained. Did the Inspector want a bribe? Was he keeping the papers for blackmail? "Did you take my teaching contract too?"

The Inspector continued. "Another issue. I saw Gao Mingyue in your apartment through the window. Not only could you be arrested for espionage but also for harboring a fugitive. Very serious crimes. You might not have to worry about airline tickets home."

The Inspector with his red cheek scar and deep squinting eyes looked menacing and cruel. Dan's fist tightened into a ball, and his shoulder muscles strained.

"Perhaps I should call the American Embassy." His breaths became short and rapid. "Why did you take my contract?"

"The first time I came to arrest him, he was gone." The Inspector raised his voice and spoke slowly and clearly. "I know that Gao Mingyue is here again. Listen carefully, Gao. I will bury your file and you can go home. The price is that you are to end all political activity and you are never to see my daughter again. Yingying has agreed to give up political activity and never see you again either."

A loud moan of protest emanated from the bedroom.

"Just go home to your family and find a job. If you do not, your file will come back to life; we will hunt you down, and you will go to prison." Inspector Song rose from the couch and went to the door. "Remember, no political activity. Do not see my daughter. Do you understand me, Gao Mingyue?"

There was no answer.

"You are very fortunate to have this choice, and you will not have it much longer if you do not answer." Song's voice echoed in the apartment. "Do you understand me?"

Mingyue's voice was small. "Yes, Inspector Song."

Song dropped his voice and looked Dan in the eye. "You'd better make sure he does what I said if you don't want to go to prison, too." He left and slammed the door behind him.

Mingyue wanted to stay hidden like a wounded cat, but he dragged himself from under the bed and slunk into the living room. Dan

Norton stood by the door, rigid as a terra-cotta warrior, his face drained of blood. Mingyue slumped onto the couch, folded his hands on his lap, and hung his head. He belched from the nauseating acid ball of regret in his stomach.

He rocked in his seat and hardly noticed when the professor sat in the armchair facing him, silent.

Mingyue's voice shook as he spoke. "I don't want to stop my political activity. I may have gotten into it to please Yingying, but now it's not just for Yingying. It's important to help the workers; to end the corruption. And if I stop, I'll never see her again. But if I don't stop, I'll go to prison. Either way I'll never see her again. Curse her father." He was sick at the prospect of never seeing Yingying again. "I have to see her. I can't just let her go." He held his knees and rocked. "I can't just think of myself. I'm putting you and my family in danger. On the other hand, should I put the safety of a handful of people ahead of justice for the Chinese People? Isn't that being selfish? A bad communist? Shit." He held his stomach. "I'm getting my father's ulcer."

He rocked and rocked until he became aware of his companion's silent stare. He had to get out of Professor Norton's apartment. He saw no alternative but to accept the Inspector's terms.

His voice quivered when he thanked Professor Norton for providing refuge for so many days, begged his forgiveness for putting him in danger, and promised that he would give up Yingying and political activity, half believing it. The professor shook his hand with a strong grip, gave him a smile with eyes that conveyed equal measures of compassion and resignation, and muttered so softly Mingyue hardly understood him.

"Don't worry, it was ... It will all work out for the ..."

The professor stood speechless in the front doorway as Mingyue walked down the stairs, feeling as if his legs would collapse under him. The two hundred yards to his parent's apartment seemed like miles. His promise to the professor sat bitter in his mouth. Could he keep such a promise? He had to see Yingying. In secret, so no one would know.

When he walked in his own door, his little brother, a university student, smiled and shouted, "Mingyue's home!" They walked into the kitchen. Tears welled up in his mother's eyes. Mingyue told them what had happened.

"You have endangered Professor Norton?" Gao Baima entered the kitchen and scowled. "Very bad . . . Very bad. Because of you, the family has lost face, son." His voice fell to a sorrowful tone. "How will I get you a job? Who will want to hire a troublemaker? All our neighbors know that you led the protest that turned into a riot. Vehicles and buildings were destroyed, and people were killed. Don't you see you were a fool? You must admit it." Mingyue had been away from his father's tyranny for a week and was jolted by the force of his father's scorn. He was already on the verge of giving in to the Inspector. Did he have to be humiliated by his father, too?

"I was struggling for justice for the Chinese workers. You've always been a good communist. You should understand that." This strong pang of loyalty to the workers, if unfamiliar, came out of a true belief. Mingyue surprised himself at his newfound strength.

"The People have had enough Cultural Revolution. They're tired of chaos and—"

Mingyue stood with his hands on his hips. "The People are tired of government corruption and yearn for more freedom, Father."

Gao Baima's face turned scarlet, and his voice grew louder. "Many people are tired of this disrespect for elders since the Cultural Revolution. I would not have dared to argue with my father. Is that what you call freedom? You must learn responsibility to your family. You must apologize."

Mingyue stood three inches taller than his father. He folded his arms across his chest. "You told me that the Americans and French fought for their freedom from the feudal aristocracy and it took many years. You told me that the Russians and we Chinese fought for freedom from the bourgeoisie. You've taught me that change will come. Don't we have to keep fighting for our freedom from bourgeois leaders posing as communists, too?"

Gao Baima's veins stood out at his temples. He shook his finger in his son's face.

"Yes, there is corruption, but the freedoms the students demand are bourgeois freedoms. You don't know how things were before the Revolution. They're much better now. I didn't teach you to put your family in danger for bourgeois freedoms. You must apologize now to each of us." He paused, and the two stood motionless and tense, glowering at each other. "Apologize now or leave this family . . . forever."

Mrs. Gao pulled at her husband's arm, her face contorted with fear. Gao pushed her away and raised his arm in a threat to hit her with his backhand. Mingyue's little brother backed out of the room. Mingyue grabbed his father's arm and held it rigid. They glared into each other's eyes.

Through his anger Mingyue felt the guilt he had carried ever since he had run away from his fellow workers and students during the riot, leaving them to face the bullets without him. He thought of himself as a coward for fleeing and a failure for letting the workers get out of control. He had thoughtlessly put Professor Norton and his own family in danger. And now he was threatening his father. It was all wrong. It was his fault. In anguish, he fell to his knees and clutched his father's ankles, head bowed. He began shaking.

He choked and had a hard time forcing out each word. A weight pressed against his chest.

"I apologize . . . to you, father. I apologize to you, mother. I apologize to . . . you, little brother. I was so proud to be a leader . . . But I was a fool."

A wave of grief swept over him, and he sobbed. But a small voice inside that loud grief told him in disgust that he had given in to his father once more, and his apology was all a lie.

PART II
MAY:
STRUGGLE

MAY DAY

MAY 1

DAN'S ANXIETY DREAM WAS BACK IN FULL FORCE.
He awoke with his heart racing and remembered that in his dream,
he had been enjoying a picnic at the beach. A wave came and
scattered his basket, plates, and food over the sand. As he tried to
pick them up, he saw a huge tidal wave coming. He was running
from it when he awoke.

He remembered that his safety depended on Mingyue's
choice. If Mingyue accepted the Inspector's bargain and gave up
political activity and Yingying, his file would be buried and there
would be no charges of harboring a fugitive.

The Inspector expected him to pressure Mingyue. After all,
that was how a totalitarian society worked. Everyone controlled

everyone else out of fear. Was that the blackmail Dan was supposed to pay to keep the papers a secret?

Maybe there was information in those papers the Inspector wanted to use for his own power games. Dan was not about to play his game and pressure Mingyue. His choice would have to be his own. But Dan had no confidence that a man in love would give up his lover that easily. He knew he had to practice his Buddhist ability to let go of anger and fear . . . not cling.

But espionage! Harboring a fugitive!

There was no reason anymore not to pressure Wu. It was long past time for any more polite patience. He had tried going with the flow for too many months, and it had not worked. It was time to get his money back. It was time to get out of Xi'an and out of the Inspector's reach.

Dan walked through the faculty housing area between rows of five-story, gray concrete apartment buildings. He didn't see many people. May Day. It was not likely that Wu would be in his office on a big holiday. The sky was grayer than usual. It looked like it was going to rain.

Dan walked through the gate where one had had to show their blue card at the beginning of the year. There was no guard there anymore. A sign of the increasing openness of the society. He climbed the stairs and went into the white Administration building. Wu's office was empty.

Mayday . . . Mayday . . . He didn't know where he was going next . . . but he knew he was going down in flames.

Dan walked through the university rose garden to calm his anxiety.

Mayday. It was a call for help, but there was no one to help. Gao was no help now with his son in trouble. Wu's job was to help.

The Inspector's job was to help. And they were what Dan needed help against.

Mayday. The marvelous irony of it. A call for help. But also, the pagan day of rebirth . . . Spring . . . the maypole . . . fertility. And change. Dan needed something to change for the better. He needed a rebirth. Fat chance.

Mayday. The communists had made it the day of Revolution, Dan thought. But they have forgotten yin and yang; everything changes to its opposite.

The moon waxes and wanes and waxes again. The cycle of Revolution doesn't end with Communism. Now the students were trying to bring about another Revolution in the cycle, challenging the old corrupt leaders.

Dan did not really want to go home. He wanted to be part of this. Something special was happening. He did not want to miss it. A big moment in Chinese history.

Dan came to the gazebo just as a light drizzle began. He sat on the bench inside.

He thought of Hegel's dialectic: history as God's urge toward freedom. In Marx's hands, God died, and Hegel's dialectic of freedom had become Stalin's unfreedom. Then what happened? Another turn of the cycle: glasnost. The Chinese adopt capitalist economics, and the students struggle for freedom. The Bates family wants to convert all the Chinese to Christianity. And God's going to rise from His coffin. Another turn of the dialectic. And Dan was in the middle of it.

Dan's anger began to fade. He would even have laughed at himself but his head ached. He watched drops of water drip from the roof and rubbed his forehead. The drizzle stopped, and Dan walked again.

A dozen students passed Dan carrying a rolled up red banner and signs. They laughed and joked, on their way to a demonstration. They were lighthearted. The Revolution should be joyous, Dan thought. He would have to learn to be more lighthearted. He would just have to learn to go on fighting, but never forget, as Buddha said, it's all an illusion.

Laugh at it while fighting the good fight for justice. Laugh at himself, but never stop doing his best. He just had to learn to play the game joyously, win or lose.

Dan decided he would have to look at Wu and the Inspector like bulls in a bullring. They challenge the matador to do his best, to temper his soul. One had to face the abyss of his fate and steel his nerve.

He would go to the Inspector and get his contract back or ask him to force Wu to give him a proper contract.

Dan took the bus downtown. It was not crowded because the normal Mayday parades had been canceled due to the protests. Most Chinese were home with their families. Dan strode into the Police Headquarters demanding, in Chinese, to see Inspector Song.

He was told to wait. Dan waited. And waited.

Finally, a policeman walked down the hall to Dan. "You American Professor Nar Tun?"

"Yes, Norton. I have to see Inspector Song," Dan said in Chinese.

"Inspector Song can't see you. He's very busy."

"Please tell him I have to get my teaching contract back," Dan said. "I need it in a dispute with Wu . . . the Foreign Affairs Officer of—"

"We can't give you the contract" The policeman shook his head. "We have to keep it as evidence."

"Evidence of what?"

The policeman glowered at Dan. "Inspector Song gives you good advice: China is very dangerous now for foreigners. You go home to America and the Inspector will not give you any more problems."

"That's what I'm trying to . . ." He switched to English. "Shit!"

Dan turned and strode toward the door.

ANXIETY

MAY 3

IT HAD BEEN TWO DAYS, AND NOTHING HAD COME of Dan's visit to Inspector Song. He'd left copies of the relevant pages about contracts from the *Manual on Teaching in China* in Wu's office when Wu was out. He received no response. Life at the university hovered on the edge of normalcy. Half of Dan's students, mostly teachers, were coming to his classes, and half were involved in political organizing. The government hadn't acted, and Dan, like most of China, was sleepwalking in a semi-conscious state of numb anxiety. Most people went about their daily business as if nothing were unusual; as if acting normally would make the world normal. Dan went to Gao's for the latest news. Gao's ulcer had flared up, and he couldn't work or eat.

"I'm so grateful that you protected my son," Gao said. "Mingyue told me that an inspector threatened you. I don't know how to repay you. Not only for hiding him, but . . ." Gao cleared his throat, "for having information that could get you . . . It's my fault."

"No need for blame. I wanted to help." Dan's laugh was strained. "What is Inspector Song likely to do?"

Gao shook his head and wiped his face. "I shouldn't have given you those papers."

"What's done is done." Dan shrugged. "You were doing what's right for China."

"I'm afraid." Gao sighed. "According to BBC, 6000 students marched in Shanghai, demanding democracy and freedom of the press. Beijing students threatened to march again tomorrow, May 4—the anniversary of the first democracy movement—unless the government recognizes their independent unions."

"I think it's great," Dan said. "There's a glimmer of hope in China now." He saw the absurdity of trying to cheer Gao up when it was his own neck in the noose.

"They ask too much," Gao said. "It will provoke the government. They want Deng Xiaoping and Li Peng to resign. They want elected leaders and independent judiciary—a legal system willing to punish officials as well as ordinary people."

"That's all fair," Dan said. "The beginning of real democracy."

"Unrealistic. When have leaders ever given up their power peacefully?" Gao slumped into a chair. "Who has the guns? Not the students."

"Gandhi ended British rule with nonviolent protests," Dan replied, knowing it was wishful thinking.

"Chinese leaders are not British," Gao said.

While Dan and Gao sat in the living room talking, Mingyue came in the door and looked through a stack of music tapes.

"There is my lazy son," Gao said. "He just mopes around the apartment and won't speak to me. He won't look for a job like the Inspector told him to. He may yet be arrested, and the whole family will lose face again."

Mingyue walked out without looking at either of them or speaking a word. Dan heard a door slam.

When Dan got home from Gao's, he was eager to begin a new journal. He had to record his thoughts. He wouldn't let fear of prison defeat him. Totalitarianism and injustice had to be fought by memory, like Anne Frank's Diary and Solzhenitsyn's *Gulag Archipelago*. He would remember what Gao and he had written before and write that and more.

It took several hours for Dan to write an outline of as much as he could remember from the papers the Inspector had taken. He had a good memory. To hell with the Inspector, Dan thought. Damn the torpedoes. Full steam ahead.

─────────

Yingying didn't go to class. She hadn't eaten or gotten out of bed since she came back to the university after the confrontation with her father. She had even been too depressed to take off her street clothes or shoes. She hated her father and the government he worked for.

Her five roommates brought her baodzes and a cup of tea, but she lay on her side facing the wall and wouldn't speak to them. She couldn't tell anyone the bargain she had made. When her roommates had all gone to class, she finally let loose the flood of tears that had built up behind the dam of her anger. She felt as if the two men she had loved in her life, her father and Mingyue, had both died. They were as good as dead to her. She would never see them again.

Why did women in China have to suffer so, she wondered? She remembered that Western women were different. She and several of her classmates had invited Professor Norton to the rooftop of a classroom building where they would not be overheard by informers, and they had asked him questions about the women's liberation movement in America. She had been surprised to learn that American women wanted to escape the role of housewives and take more responsible jobs with pay equal to men's. Chinese women would be glad to be able to stay at home to raise their children while their husbands worked. Chinese women had to work a full day as hard as their husbands for equally low pay, then go home and do another full day of work as housewives and mothers.

One of Yingying's classmates had said she had heard that some women lived together as lovers in America. The Chinese government claimed that homosexuals did not exist in China since homosexuality was a result of the breakdown of society under Capitalism. She did not know what to make of Professor Norton's statement that studies showed 10% of people in every society were homosexuals. It didn't make sense biologically. But she wondered about two of her classmates after that.

It seemed strange that many American women gave up being married and having children to pursue careers. Was that because they were homosexual? Not having a family was incomprehensible in China. Chinese families pressured their children to marry and have children. Having a son was necessary because, since a daughter would join her husband's family, only a son would provide for his parents when they were old. There was no social security in China other than a son. So, unmarried daughters were only a burden to a family under the "one child" policy.

Yingying had no brothers. Perhaps that was why her parents were cold to her. But it wasn't her fault she was a woman. She had not been given a choice. Maybe they should kill all the girl children in China, she thought bitterly, and see how Chinese society ground to a halt then.

She wiped the tears off her cheeks, went to the window, and watched crowds of students, some going to and from classes, some carrying posters for a demonstration. She wanted to go to the demonstration. She wanted to be part of the force changing China.

She saw a flash of yellow come toward the window, and for an instant, thought her beloved bird had come back home to her. Her moment of joy and hope dissolved when she saw that it was a piece of trash blowing in the wind. She flopped back into bed.

Ting Lili, a leading member of the Student Coordinating Committee, strode into the room. Ting was one of those women known as a dragon lady—physically attractive with a loud voice and a commanding presence that always sapped Yingying's will to resist her. The last person she ever wanted to see. Lili sounded the clarion call to action.

"Time to get up, Comrade Song. Do you know what is happening? Students all over China are pressuring the government for reform."

Yingying rolled over to face Lili, who wore blue jeans, a white blouse, and a blue Mao cap with a big red star. Lili reminded her of the Red Guard leader who had flung the bird cage into the flames. She suddenly hated her.

"Strangely enough, they've added inflation to their set of issues," Yingying sneered. "Inflation is the result of the very economic liberalization the students wanted. I don't suppose many people will notice the inconsistency."

Yingying sat up on the edge of her bed, wiped her nose, and sipped her cold tea. Lili wanted to get her involved, and she wanted to be involved, but she had to protect Mingyue.

"That the government has done nothing to stop us for two weeks shows how weak they are," Lili said, hands on hips, her feet planted on the floor like a Sumo wrestler. "They already agreed to speak with the Beijing student leaders. We must pressure them more, and they will crumble."

"Good," Yingying said. "I wish the old religious ideas were true and the government leaders all had souls and the lowest Buddhist Hell really existed for them to all go to." And you too, she thought.

The dragon lady smiled. "We are organizing major strikes and demonstrations all over the city. We need you to go to the medical school and recruit medical students for first-aid work. The people need you."

"You don't understand. I can't."

"Why?"

Yingying felt now that she would lose face with the students on top of everything else. Lili would enjoy destroying her. She had the sudden urge to get up and go to the toilet.

"I can't!"

She ran out of the room sobbing.

"Coward!" Lili shouted after her. The sound of her voice echoed down the concrete corridor.

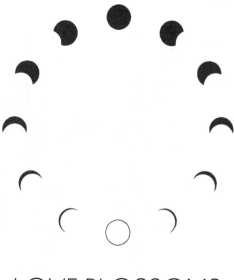

LOVE BLOSSOMS

MAY 5

THERE HAD BEEN A BIG MARCH ON MAY 4TH, BUT nothing dramatic had happened, probably because so many students went home for the holiday. Dan began to relax a bit because with the decline of student unrest, it would be less likely that Mingyue would be sucked back into political activity and Dan would apparently be off the hook with the Inspector. Maybe the whole thing would blow over and the students would go back to their studies and Dan's classes would be back to normal. Wu certainly seemed to act as if all were normal, scheduling a bus trip for foreign guests to Louguantai.

Dan waited outside the bus door. The bus was filling up, and Yoshiko was not there. He was determined that he would sit with her. He tapped his foot and craned his neck in both directions. The driver said he had to leave now. Dan climbed aboard and sat with Ty. Yoshiko arrived just as the driver started up the engine. Her eyes met Dan's, and she lurched into a seat as the bus moved forward. She sat with another Japanese student two rows ahead of Dan across the aisle.

Dan's left knee began to bounce as if he had a nervous disorder. He stopped it. "God, I'm all out of kilter. Like China. I need to get back into balance." He looked at Ty. "You're quiet today."

"I've been thinking . . . about qi and things. Qi gong might help you get back in balance."

They talked about how Louguantai had been an astronomical observatory already 3,000 years ago and was the place Laozi reputedly wrote the *Tao Te Ching* and founded Taoism 2,500 years ago. And where a famous qi gong master was helping to heal cancer patients who had been pronounced incurable by Western medicine. Ty wanted to study qi gong.

Dan had a hard time concentrating on the conversation. He was too aware of Yoshiko talking with the other man ahead of him. He had to admit to himself he was jealous.

The bus pulled into the parking lot at the base of the foothills. Dan and Ty strolled on the road up the hill to the Taoist temple complex. Dan watched Yoshiko's graceful steps ahead of him. At the temple complex, Taoist monks wore black robes, long scraggly beards unheard of on other Chinese and what to Dan looked like tall, black cooks' hats. Ty went to the healing area to learn about qi gong while Dan wandered to the main temple compound. Among the cluster of buildings, Dan found the "Platform for Imparting Taoism," a temple on a raised platform of gray brick—modest in size with dark brown carved wooden panels, red pillars, and a tile roof richly populated with a variety of gargoyles to protect it from evil spirits. It was, Dan thought, an appropriate monument to Laozi who had, according to tradition, founded Taoism at that exact place.

Dozens of visitors swarmed into the compound's courtyard and into several buildings to light incense and get their fortunes read. Behind the temple, people hiked to and fro on the trail up the mountain. At the base of a steep hill crouched the humble brick and gray tile buildings where the monks lived.

Dan climbed the worn, gray stone steps of the main temple, flowing with the crowd of Chinese.

At a turn in the steps he faced a niche containing an altar with burning incense before a statue of a goddess he didn't know. A black-robed monk sat beside the altar with his black cook's hat. On the table before him lay a much-fingered book and cups full of inscribed bamboo strips. A fortune teller. Dan remembered the book on Tang Dynasty linked verses he had submitted for publication before leaving for China. Would it be accepted? Of course, he didn't believe in fortune telling, but he did it for the experience so he could tell his Chinese literature students back in America about it—so he told himself. The fortune teller held out the cup of bamboo strips toward Dan.

"Pick one."

Dan did. The monk looked at the markings and opened his book.

"Supreme success. You will succeed before the full moon," the fortune teller said.

Well, that would be easy to confirm or disprove. He wanted to believe, but the full moon was only a few days away. Unlikely. The answer cheered him up anyway. He walked into the main temple.

Yoshiko paid another fortune teller by a statue of Kuan Yin, the Goddess of Mercy. She turned away from him, smiling.

"You got a good fortune?" Dan asked.

"I'm too shy. I must be bold to get what I want."

"What do you want?"

She looked down and laughed.

On the ride back to Xi'an, Dan was surprised and pleased when Yoshiko sat next to him. Dan saw the packages in her carrying bag.

"You bought souvenirs at Louguantai?"

"Presents for my family," she said. "Temple rubbings."

"Oh, I didn't see them for sale, but I suppose I have enough already. I bought some in Beijing and Hangzhou."

"You have temple rubbings?"

"Buddhist rubbings of Bodhisattvas. One of Kuan Yin and others, they didn't know who at the stores. The communist clerks are so ignorant of their ancient religious traditions. Four long scrolls of the eight immortals, some in the clouds and some descending to earth. And forty prints and paintings of horses, mountains, waterfalls . . . that sort of thing. For friends and family when I get home." Dan smiled. "You should come up and see my rubbings some time."

"I'd love to."

Dan laughed. "I was joking. That was an old movie line: 'Come up and see my etchings sometime.'"

"You were joking? You don't want me to see them?" She looked down and frowned.

"Oh, yes. I want you to see them. I meant . . ." He blushed and didn't know how to explain the joke. He decided it was better left unexplained. "Yes, I do want you to see them. Please come whenever it's convenient."

"I'll come tonight after supper," she said, smiling.

"I have class until 9:00." Dan wondered what had closed the chasm between them.

"I'll come at 9:30."

"You show me yours, and I'll show you mine." He didn't realize what he was saying until he had said it and his ears started to burn.

"Yes," she said. "I'll show you mine tonight."

Dan arrived at his apartment after class to find mail outside the door. One letter announced that his book had been accepted for publication. His scientific skepticism told him that one coincidence did not prove anything. But some part of him wanted to believe that he knew all along that the fortune had to be true. And the good luck would not stop there. He spread his best two dozen paintings, prints, and rubbings on the floor for Yoshiko's perusal, and opened a bottle of wine to celebrate the acceptance of the book manuscript. She arrived at 9:30 promptly and floated through the doorway like a refreshing breeze wafting orange blossom scent.

"A book of mine on linked-poetry has been accepted for publication," he said. "I've opened a bottle of wine to celebrate. Will you join me?"

"Yes, please. I love link poetry. Congratulations." She bowed slightly and sat on the couch.

He poured her a glass. "I asked a fortune teller at Louguantai about it, and he assured me of supreme success before the full moon. Here it is a few days before the full moon."

"Did you know the fortune teller you asked represented the Goddess of Literature?"

"No." The hair rose on the back of his neck. The probability of two such coincidences . . . "How did you know which fortune teller I went to?"

Yoshiko smiled bashfully. "I saw you climbing the temple stairs and was curious which fortune teller you would ask." She took some rubbings out of a bag, then saw the pictures on the floor.

"Oh, how beautiful! I like that one." She pointed at an ancient scroll of mountains and waterfalls. "And the tiny house with people drinking wine by the lake. I feel I'm there." She drank a sip from her glass and looked over the other works. "And this one of the immortals in the clouds. I want to fly with them. These are quality works." She drank again and blushed as her eyes fell upon a print. "This couple in the garden with a lantern ... lovers meeting at night under a moon ... it reminds me of *The Tale of Genji*."

"Where Genji climbs over the fence into his lover's garden?"

"Yes. I studied French at Sophia University in Tokyo. My favorite is Proust ... tales of mistresses ..." She blushed and looked at Dan.

Dan blushed too, feeling uneasy about where his thoughts were drifting. He picked up another picture. "What do you think of this picture of the Little Wild Goose Pagoda with the road toward it lined with blossoming trees under a moon? Not great art, but I thought I might add a fragment of a poem by Li Ch'ing Chao ... 'vacantly dreaming of Ch'ang-an, how the road goes up to the old capital. Please tell them: spring is fine this year.'"

"Oh, I know that one." Yoshiko's eyes sparkled. She continued it. "'Have pity! Spring, like all men living, will soon grow old.'"

"Yes, that's it," Dan said. "Your Chinese is excellent. I would write the poem myself, but my calligraphy is terrible."

"I could write it for you," Yoshiko said. "I've been told my Running Hand style is very good."

"I would love to have you write it." Dan grinned. "I'm so glad you didn't suggest grass characters; I can never read them." He handed her two pictures. "I want you to have this one that reminds you of Genji."

Their eyes met for a long breathless moment. Her eyes, flecked with gold, blinked. Her red lips quivered.

"The fortune teller at Louguantai told me my parents' ghosts would not be angry if . . . But I am very shy." She looked away. "I want to . . ."

She hung her head and her shoulders drooped. Dan looked at the wisp of black hair that hung down the back of her white neck and dared not hope what she meant. She turned to look at him again. "I want to stay with you tonight."

Dan swallowed. "I think you said . . . something I wish for more than anything . . ."

Her laugh was all silver bells and bird calls.

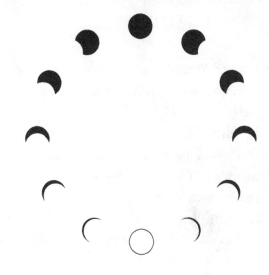

HUA CHING HOT SPRING

MAY 7

DAN AND YOSHIKO HAD SPENT TWO NIGHTS together now. Dan's heart had been reawakened from a long slumber. Yoshiko went from the dining hall after dinner to Dan's apartment and from Dan's to breakfast in the dining hall. That way she would not have to go through the gate late at night where Lao Zhu, the gate keeper, would stop her. It seemed strange for two adults to have to act like teenagers hiding their activities from their parents. That was life in a totalitarian state.

Today, because of the holidays, Wu had rescheduled the long-postponed excursion to Hua Ching Hot Spring. Yoshiko, Ed, the Bates family, and several other foreign students were going. Dan had invited Gao along, too. He sat next to Gao when they boarded the bus since he and Yoshiko had agreed not to sit together so as not to draw attention to their relationship. Yoshiko sat with Wu, to Dan's disgust.

During the thirty-mile ride, Gao and Dan talked politics.

"I know there was a big march on May 4 in Beijing," Dan said. "Tens of thousands in Tiananmen Square, but it doesn't sound like anything has happened since then."

"Zhao Ziyang, the Secretary of the Communist Party, calmed the situation," Gao said. "He claimed publicly that dialogue with the students was desirable. A student poster even said, 'We firmly support the correct leadership of the Communist Party.'"

"Sounds to me like they may be saying the present leadership is not correct." Dan grinned.

"No, they support Zhao." Gao frowned as if he had just understood the ambiguity. "At least it counters the government claim that students are trying to overthrow the Party."

"Then it seems that dialogue may be possible now," Dan said.

Gao shrugged. "Except that Deng Xiaoping and Li Peng do not agree with Zhao."

When they got off the bus at the hot spring, Dan admired Yoshiko. She wore tight designer jeans and a silk blouse with a picture of a swan emerging from tall green reeds. Elegant, Dan thought, and symbolic. She's the swan. The brown background matched the color of her eyes. He wanted to take her arm and bask in her radiance. But they had agreed not to be obvious.

Dan walked into the reception room with Gao. A thirty-foot silver and light blue silk rug filled the center of the room. Upon it stood a teak table carved in tortoise and crane longevity motifs. An incense fragrance filled the room. Ceiling beams painted with red, baby blue, and light green floral patterns and golden dragons lightened the mahogany walled room. Dan admired the elaborate painting of a phoenix flying upward on a twelve-foot-tall screen. This was the world of ancient emperors that Dan had dwelt in with his imagination for over twenty years. He had read about it, studied the language, and taught its literature. Now he could feel the polished teak wood with his hand, feast his eyes, and fill his lungs with the incense. It was a step back in time from the drab industrial Xi'an of the twentieth century.

Dan and Gao stepped through the full moon shaped door onto a garden path beside a pond lined with willows. Beyond the pond lay the cloud shadowed bulk of Li Mountain like the back of a water buffalo. Puffy clouds rolled behind the mountain. In the pond, clusters of lotus pads reached up their pink flowers through a blanket of mist. A row of nine dragon-headed gargoyles disgorged steaming water from their mouths into the pond along a marble wall. Overhead, clusters of plum blossoms dropped petals like confetti. Looking wistfully into the water, Yoshiko walked gracefully ahead of Dan.

"Nine Dragon Hot Spring," Gao remarked, bringing Dan back from his romantic reverie. "It was very important in Chinese history."

"Because of the 'Xi'an Incident' when Chiang Kai-Shek was captured by the communists when he was found hiding in a cave here in the nude in midwinter?" Dan asked.

"That too," Gao said. "But the last Tang emperor, Xuanzong, liked to stay here with his favorite concubine, Yang Guifei. It destroyed China's greatest dynasty."

A white marble platform shaped like a boat seemed to float at the edge of the pond. Its six foot high dragon head prow appeared to move through the white clouds reflected in the mirror smooth water.

"It's beautiful," Dan said. "How could dwelling in such beauty destroy a dynasty?" He couldn't recall this bit of history.

In the middle of the boat stood a pavilion on red columns. A lacy gold banister encircled it, and a green-tiled two-tiered roof capped it. The lower roof was square and golden dragons surmounted its upturned corners, guardians against evil spirits. The roof corners were curved up, Dan knew, because the Chinese thought evil spirits traveled only in straight lines and couldn't get into the building along the curved roof corners. The upper roof was circular, capped by a huge golden lotus like Buddha's topknot. It was the very architecture Dan loved. And there was Yoshiko, standing on the prow of the boat like a goddess.

"The Tang Dynasty, according to some, was a high point of Chinese culture," Gao said. "The emperor fell in love with his concubine and spent so much time with her here at Huaqing Palace Hot Spring that he neglected his imperial duties, and his court became very worried."

Dan watched Yoshiko looking into the waters of the pond and could imagine how the emperor felt. "A good setting for a love story."

"Good for love, but bad for China," Gao said. "Various ministers tried to turn him away from her with no success. The situation in the nation deteriorated so much that a band of rebels became stronger and stronger, and finally threatened the Imperial Palace itself."

Dan remembered that Yoshiko loved tales of mistresses. He would have to remember to tell her this one.

"The ministers dragged the concubine before the emperor, gave him a knife, and demanded that he kill her so he could turn his mind back to his duties."

"Couldn't they just abduct her and say she was kidnapped by the bandits?" Dan asked. "That might have turned his attention to his duties."

"No one would dare. The emperor, as divinely appointed mediator between heaven and earth, had to be the one to solve the problem," Gao said. "But he refused to kill her. The concubine called him a coward, grabbed the knife, and killed herself. She has been a model heroine to the Chinese ever since. But her brave deed was too late to prevent the rebels' victory. The emperor fled to Sichuan, and the brilliant Tang Dynasty ended."

Gao hung his head looking slightly sadder than usual. Dan thought that Yoshiko would love the story. Its tragic ending was perfect for the Japanese temperament. Of course, she probably already knew it.

"The Tang Dynasty was very important," Gao said. "Open to the West like now. It was the time of the Silk Road to the Roman Empire."

The Bates family walked to the side of the pond. Chinese heads turned.

"Chinese people are all so thin," Gao said. "They never see fat people. But how appropriate for this place. The Tang Dynasty was the only time in Chinese history when being fat was fashionable in China."

"You're right." Dan remembered the ceramic figurines of fat people in the Qianling Mausoleum. "Even the horses were portrayed as fat; I love the ceramic horses. You can always tell a Tang Dynasty ceramic horse because it's fat."

"But now it's not so rare in the big cities," Gao said. "With the 'one-child' policy, only-children are spoiled. They eat hamburgers and pizza and Kentucky fried chicken, and we've begun to see fat children in Beijing and Shanghai."

"They eat pizza?" Dan laughed. "I thought the Chinese hated cheese."

"I didn't like cheese until I tasted a pepperoni pizza," Gao chuckled. "There's an American-owned hotel in Xi'an that serves pizzas now. Wu took me to the opening this year."

"My birthday's coming up soon," Dan said. "Let's go there for pizza and chocolate cake and get fat."

Dan looked at his watch. It was the time Wu had scheduled the group to hike. Maybe he and Yoshiko could walk up the mountain together, and he could share the courtesan story with her. That wouldn't be too obvious.

"Are you ready to climb Li Mountain?" Dan asked. "Let's go to the top and lean our backs against the sky."

"Will those Japanese students go too?" Gao asked.

Dan nodded.

"I was a child in Nanjing during the war," Gao said. "My memories of Japanese atrocities are too bitter to . . ." He frowned. "I couldn't bear to walk near them. You go ahead. I've lived in Xi'an twenty years and never had a chance to use the hot spring. I want to bathe in a hot tub. I'll meet you at the bus."

As Dan walked to join the hikers, he thought how sad that Gao would not accept Yoshiko. He remembered that his own father had been badly wounded by the Japanese during World War II and killed by the Chinese in the Korean War. Dan didn't hold any grudges. It wasn't anything personal.

Dan had laughed when the Japanese and American students at the university had thrown a Pearl Harbor Day party and joked about "getting bombed together," "flying high" on beer, and "getting shot down" when the American boys had come on to the Japanese girls and vice versa.

Wu led the way, and the group began to climb the path through a valley of elm, pine, and underbrush. Yoshiko seemed to avoid looking at Dan and walked and chatted with Ty. Two other Japanese students followed, and Dan walked with Ed.

"I asked Professor Gao to talk with Wu about reimbursing part of your unused tuition," Dan said. "I don't know how it's going to work out."

"I really appreciate what you're doing," Ed said. "I'll be sad to leave. I really do like this place."

Ed's sentiments echoed Dan's own. Dan fell behind Ed and walked beside the Russian student. Dozens of Chinese families passed them up and down the path. Dan knew it was Yoshiko's orange blossom perfume he smelled. Dan was chagrined to realize that he envied Ty.

He and Yoshiko had agreed to keep their relationship a secret, but she was doing too good a job of it. She seemed to be flirting with Ty. Perhaps she was enjoying her acting. He wanted desperately to be the one walking with her, to share the romance of the day. He wanted their eyes to meet in a knowing look at least, but they didn't.

Dan knew he was being absurd. An old fool. He tried to divert his attention to the beauty of the landscape. The trail overlooked a dark green pine clad slope on the other side of the valley. Much of the trail was a steep stone stairway, laid with intensive labor over the centuries, and harder to climb than dirt trails back home. It wound through the cool afternoon shadow of the mountain, but Dan was sweating. Trees grew thicker.

He fell behind the Russian. A Chinese couple with a young son charged past Dan going up. He became aware that he was the old man of the group and was out of shape.

It took two hours to reach the nose of a ridge where they had a view. They were not sure how much farther it was to the top of the mountain and decided to turn around. The ridge was littered with trash, reeked of garbage and excrement, and the view of the Wei Valley to the north was obscured by smog from the factories of Xi'an. Even the nearby tomb of the Qin emperor and the Terracotta Warrior Museum hid in the haze. With Yoshiko still flirting with Ty, and apparently oblivious of Dan and Dan feeling his age and smelling garbage, the day had turned sour.

Dan just wanted to flee in disgust. He hurtled in a fast walk down the trail and was back at the hot spring long before the rest of the group. He watched dying blossoms falling into the pond for awhile. They no longer seemed beautiful, just tragic.

Dan climbed into the minibus and sat with Gao. Bright sunshine streamed in the window where Yoshiko sat with Ty. How fitting that the two old men sat together on the gloomy side of the bus.

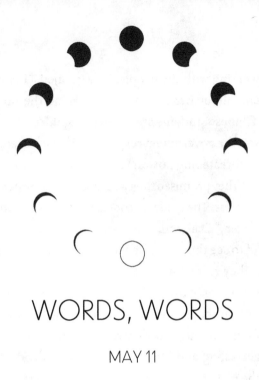

WORDS, WORDS

MAY 11

DAN WENT TO LUNCH IN THE CAFETERIA AND GOT himself a bowl of chicken, leeks, and noodles.

He sat with the three American students, who were in the middle of a conversation. Dan noticed that Ty was not in his usual cowboy outfit.

He must have bought clothes in a Chinese store.

"Did you hear about the petition?" Ty asked, and Dan shook his head. "2000 Chinese journalists signed a petition seeking more freedom of the press and delivered it to the government."

"Gutsy," Dan said. "Probably fruitless, but definitely gutsy."

"Thousands of Beijing students are protesting censorship. Police even cleared the way, and the students chanted 'Thank you, police, for working with the people.'" Ty grinned. "I remembered what you said about Berkeley students calling the police 'pigs.' Maybe the Chinese students are getting it right."

"So how is the government responding?" Dan asked. "Continuing to make threatening noises?"

"Surprise! They promised they would allow more open reporting of corruption cases. The students consider it a major victory."

"A small step," Dan said. "But a step."

"I'm glad to see them standing up for democracy," Susan said.

"But are they ready for democracy?" Ed asked. "They have no tradition of freedom of the individual. Do they even know what it means? After four thousand years of kowtowing to authority, they don't know squat about individual responsibility."

"I predict a long and bloody struggle for individual rights in the face of the need for government control," Dan said.

"Jesus," Ty said. "We're still in the middle of that struggle back home."

In your own family, Dan thought. He slurped a spoonful of noodles.

"And we've got no end of individualism in America," Ty said.

"And not much responsibility," Susan added.

"But the Chinese have that tradition of obedience to the Emperor," Ed said. "And now the Communist Party."

"Actually," Dan said, "the Chinese don't have much tradition of loyalty to the state. Unlike the Japanese who believe their Emperors to be directly descended from Amaterasu, the sun goddess, and therefore, irreplaceable. If the Chinese Emperor doesn't follow the Mandate of Heaven to preserve harmony in the society, it's time for a new Emperor. That's why the Chinese have had uprising after uprising and dynasty after dynasty."

"But that's ancient history," Ty said. "Under communism, all that feudal thinking—"

"No," Susan cut in. "The peasants, at least, still think that way. When Mao, Zhou Enlai, Marshal What's-his-name—Chu, was it—and a lot of other communist leaders all died about the same time, there were floods and earthquakes and other natural disasters showing the displeasure of Heaven. The peasants just considered it the fall of another dynasty. Now Deng's the new Emperor."

"I suspect the government sees the problem from a completely different angle than we do," Dan said. "According to Sun Yat-sen, the Chinese people have as much cohesion as a bucket of sand. China might fall apart like a dry sand castle without the control the Communist Party provides. The Party's like the wetness that holds the sand together. Those grains of sand have always been the family, the central focus of Chinese values."

"Until the Cultural Revolution got family members to turn on each other," Ed said.

Dan thought of Gao, trying to hold his family together in spite of the forces tearing it apart.

Susan looked at her watch and stood up. "I've got to get to class."

"Me too." Ed jumped to his feet. "But I want to thank you, Professor Norton, for your help."

"Has Wu come through with the cash?"

The corners of Ed's mouth drooped. "Not yet. But he's working on it." Ed and Susan walked out the door.

"I'll bet." Dan's tone was ironic.

"What's all that about?" Ty asked.

"Oh, you know . . . Ed's trying to leave for home," Dan said.

"What's Wu got to do with it? He can get his own plane out."

"Ed wants a prorated share of his room, board, and tuition back. I tried to help. A lot of help I'm likely to be. I can't even get my own money back. But I got Professor Gao to intercede, he's Wu's friend, and to my surprise, Wu agreed."

Ty's tone was sarcastic. "Wahoo. Victory."

"Yeah, yeah. It's been a week and a half and Wuhoo the Yahoo hasn't coughed up the cash yet. And probably never will. He's just saving face by seeming to agree."

"So Ed's hanging around? He must not be that worried."

"He had prepaid plane tickets from Beijing home, but so many people are trying to get out, he may not be able to get a flight right away, and he needs the cash in case he has to stay in Beijing awhile."

"God help him if it depends on Wu." Ty finished his chi-shui. "Speaking of God, I'm reading the *Tao Te Ching*."

"God? Tao? I'm not sure there's a connection." Dan always turned to the *Tao Te Ching* when he was troubled. It put things in perspective. It was like looking at his own life through the reverse end of a telescope. Made it seem small and abstract. It was a good time to discuss it so he could forget the sword of Damocles the Inspector dangled over his own neck.

"What does the first verse mean? 'Tao can be talked about, but not the Eternal Tao. Names can be named, but not the Eternal Name.' Can't we even speak the word 'God?'"

"Words set limits; they define, and to define is to limit. Can we use limited words to designate the Unlimited?" Dan asked. "Even ordinary things are much more than our limited definitions make them seem. Tao is no thing, for things are limited, differentiated from other things. But Tao is not nothing. Perhaps it's like a Zen koan, a paradox, meant to push your understanding beyond the limits of ordinary language." Dan recognized the light of understanding in Ty's eyes. "What do your parents think of your dabbling in Chinese philosophy?"

"Please don't tell them. They want me to learn Chinese so we can convert the Chinese to Christianity. But if they knew I was reading the *Tao Te Ching*, they'd consider it intercourse with the devil—not that they have any idea what's in it. I'd sooner go to the Communist Party Headquarters and try to hawk *Bibles* than have my parents find out what I've been reading." Ty rubbed his knuckles, and they turned red. "For eighteen years I thought they knew God personally, but..."

"I won't mention a thing." A good kid at heart, Dan thought. Like a lotus poking its pure bud above the mud and slime of the world.

Dan worked all afternoon to prepare for his classes, but he was too anxious to concentrate. Had Mingyue given up politics? Could he? Should he?

After teaching Asian literature for fifteen years, it was refreshing to teach American literature, except that the Chinese students had no access to books, and he had to make extensive copies of readings from his own texts. He loaned out several novels he had brought to each student one at a time. Hemingway and Mark Twain were the Chinese students' favorites.

It was the History of Western Civilization class that took most of his effort. He wasn't trained as a history teacher, while most of his students were themselves history teachers in universities or high schools. Likely, it wasn't the history that interested them but the Socratic teaching method with question and answer. Ironically, they hardly ever asked questions because it would imply that the teacher had not taught well and he would lose face. Now, though, only a handful of students were showing up because of political events.

Tonight it would be conversational English. This class was exclusively for the elite of the university faculty: the President of the University, a world famous mathematician, the Chairs of the Physics, Chemistry, and Political Science departments, and other leading members who were likely to go to international conferences and had to know how to speak everyday English. Dan taught things like how to use knives and forks and table manners in general, such as that belching is not polite in the West nor is throwing one's bones on the floor as they do in Chinese restaurants.

He had many sessions on idioms, like when the Physics Chair asked, "What is happy hour? Aren't Americans happy at other times?"

Or, what are boomboxes? They had been told that some Americans like to walk around in the city listening to music with a boombox on their shoulders. But the previous year, an Australian teacher had told them that a boombox in Australia was a toilet. The picture of an American walking around listening to the noises coming from a toilet perched on his shoulder conjured up raucous laughter, except for the Political Science Chair, Professor Ha, who thought everyone should still be learning Russian, not English, and who always sat with his arms folded tightly across his chest and a frown on his face, as if defying the world trying to make him laugh.

Dan walked to class. He decided tonight's class would be about race relations in America. Just when his mind seemed finally to be focused on the topic, he saw Inspector Song enter the Administration Building. Dan's thoughts scattered like gunshot-startled ducks. What was the Inspector up to? Shit. He couldn't do anything heavy like race relations. He wouldn't be able to concentrate.

He had noticed that his students used the word "shit" a lot in their English speech, so when he walked into the classroom he announced, "These are the words one does not use in polite company."

He wrote on the blackboard all the swear words and vulgar expressions he could think of—shit, fuck, asshole, bitch . . . on and on until he filled one whole board. He wanted to shout them at Inspector Song. Then on a second blackboard, he put numerous variations of the same word: dick, peter, cock, dong, schlong, pecker, willie, meat, prick . . . and so on. That provoked lively discussion, especially since Dan didn't know the Chinese translation for most of the words, and he had to explain in embarrassing detail or draw pictures on the blackboard, which drew crowds of students to the doorway.

These eminent faculty members argued merrily over the best Chinese equivalents. Students drifted into the room and lined the back wall to listen.

The Political Science Chair, Professor Ha, looked at Dan as if he were something that ought to be complained about to the secret police and asked, "If these words are not polite, how can a doctor talk to his patients about these things?"

Dan laughed. He could always count on Professor Ha, his class clown, to throw him a screwball. Dan had to think a moment.

"The Germanic-based Anglo-Saxon words are generally considered vulgar, but one can use the Latin-based French forms: excretion, intercourse, anus, penis . . . and so forth." He wrote them next to their vulgar equivalents. "When you're angry, it wouldn't give as much satisfaction to say the word 'excretion' as it would to say 'shit.' Words like 'shit' and 'fuck' have an explosive quality that expresses anger well."

Various professors mumbled "excrete" and "shit" like serious wine tasters seeing how the words felt on their tongues. Professor Ha lowered his brows and folded his arms tighter. "They mean exactly the same thing, but one is polite, and the other is not? Absurd."

"Well," Dan said, "the French-speaking Normans conquered the Germanic-speaking Anglo-Saxons. The conqueror's language is considered polite; the language of the vanquished is vulgar. It is the same reason that the names of the foods we eat, beef and pork for instance, come from the French words, while the names of the animals they came from, cow and swine, are Germanic words. The conquered Anglo-Saxon peasants raised the food, while the conquering French nobles only ate the food."

"Ah." Professor Ha put his hands on his knees, elbows akimbo, and leaned forward. "That's a good Marxian explanation of the origin of vulgarity." Ha even raised his eyebrows as if the lead weights were taken off of them.

Dan laughed. It was simple philology, not Marxism, but if it made Ha happy, why disabuse him and put the weights back on his eyebrows?

"I'd wondered if your arms were sewn into that cross-arm defiance. Guess you can move them after all."

Dan felt like a cowboy firmly back in the saddle of his own horse again after a week in jail. But not for long. When he walked out the door of the classroom building, there sat the Inspector on a bench, smoking and squinting at Dan. Dan wondered if the creep was watching him. Was that meant as a threat? Why else would he be hanging around the university?

After a sleepless night, Yingying huddled in her bed, her back to her roommates as if she were asleep. She couldn't face them. After they left, she dragged herself out of bed. It was too late for breakfast or for her first class. If she hurried, she could make it to her second class, but she did not have the energy. It was like slogging through mud just to walk outside. Her anger at her father had turned into depression.

She sat on a bench in front of the library and studied the fifteen-foot-high monolith laced with Swiss-cheese-like holes that was the artistic centerpiece of the campus. The stone represented the yang, and the holes represented the yin in all things.

Normally she could imagine that it was part of a mountain landscape, and she could see herself wandering through valleys and caves, surrounded by trees and waterfalls. It had never failed to cheer her up. But it didn't cheer her up today. The stone was just a clod, and the gray sky seemed dimmer than usual. She wondered what Mingyue was doing and if he felt miserable too? Who could she ask about him? Who could tell her where he was and if he was safe?

At lunch, she didn't want to sit with her friends. But that was no problem; they were avoiding her. She saw Little Mei walking toward her. Their eyes met, and Little Mei wrinkled her nostrils like she smelled something foul. She turned and walked away. Another friend, already eating, saw her coming and turned her back to her. They didn't understand, and she couldn't tell them about a deal with a policeman, even if he was her own father. She had to clench her teeth tight to suppress the tears.

In her afternoon class on invertebrates, her classmates snubbed her. She could hardly concentrate on the lecture. After class, she went into the gardens and sat on a bench to study. The open book swam before her eyes, and she could not focus her mind on it. She wanted to go home to her mother, but her father would be off work by the time she got there.

She had never been so alone. She stood rigid in the path, jostled by passing students. Why had she lost her father, Mingyue, her friends? It was not fair to be punished for struggling for justice. Her head was a balloon about to explode, and if it popped, the whole world would cease to exist.

She had to know how he was. She would talk to his father. That was it. Why hadn't she thought of it sooner? His class must have just ended. She ran down the garden path, scratching her arms on roses as she dodged groups of students, and stopped in front of his classroom. She rubbed her arm, and the sticky blood smeared on her palm. Professor Gao emerged from the classroom, carried along by a stream of students.

"Professor Gao . . . wait . . . how are you?" She pushed through the students toward him. "How is your—"

Gao's eyes narrowed, and his upper lip twisted into a snarl.

"Too dangerous. I cannot talk to you. You stay away from my son. Don't you ever try to see him, or I'll report you to the police." He walked away from her.

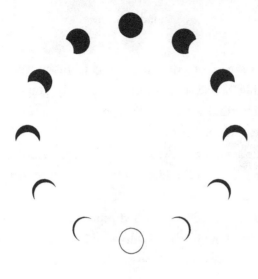

HUNGER STRIKES

MAY 14

MINGYUE AND HIS FATHER HAD SPOKEN VERY LITTLE in the two weeks since he had come home. Mingyue brooded. His leadership of the railroad workers had failed. The government denied that anyone had been killed during the riots in Xi'an in April, and Mingyue knew they lied. But he had no proof. He did not even know the dead man's name.

Mingyue remembered what his father had done once when Mingyue was a small boy during the Cultural Revolution. His mother had been singing an old folk song while she chopped vegetables.

"You seem happy today," his father said to her. "I haven't heard you sing for years."

"I had a marvelous dream last night," his mother said. "We lived in a big house and were wealthy. My grandparents and parents and brother were still alive, and we had a feast with all my family there. I was so happy."

Mingyue's father frowned. "It's bourgeois to want to be wealthy. You cling to the ideas of the old culture. I thought you were a good communist."

Later that week, Mr. Gao had reported his wife to the Red Guards. They bound her hands, dragged her out of the house, and had her stand before a mocking crowd in a dunce cap and recant her bourgeois desires in a public humiliation. Mingyue trembled in disbelief as his father stood there without protest and just watched. He had never heard his mother sing since that day. And Mingyue had learned not to share his dreams. The irony was that now, Deng Xiaoping claimed that to be rich was glorious.

Mingyue had feared and hated his father because of that betrayal. If he could betray his wife for a dream, then no one in the family was safe. Now, his father had done it to him—demanded that he renounce something he should not have renounced—if not in public, at least before his family. His father had betrayed him as he had betrayed his mother. Mingyue had buried his anger under fear all these years. It was the anger that grew now, burning away the fear.

Gao Baima invited Dan Norton to his home for supper. Mingyue looked at the small living room as if through the eyes of the guest. It contained a couch, a dining room table, chairs, a coffee table, end tables, a beautifully carved teak cabinet full of knickknacks—terra-cotta warriors, soapstone goddesses, Tang Dynasty-style, ceramic horses—a television set, and the video player Gao had brought back from the States. Surely enough legs to please even a Shanghai woman, Mingyue thought. He wondered where his father got the money for it all on a Chinese professor's salary of thirty dollars a month. It had never occurred to him that his father might be involved in something shady. But Wu, a known police informant, had long been his friend. And Mingyue had never made the connection . . . until now.

The family had saved the last few jiaodzes to be stuffed so that Professor Norton could take part in the ritual too. Gao showed Dan how to put in the pork and cabbage and press the edges of the dough together. Mingyue handed Dan a glass of Beijing beer. The rest of the family was in the kitchen, from which the odors of anise, leeks, and peppers wafted.

Dan folded a jiaodze awkwardly. He made his too big and lopsided. He had put too much pork and cabbage inside the dough. And when he pinched the edges closed, he made big, uneven rims, not the thin aesthetic scallops Gao and Mingyue made. Mingyue wanted to help Dan.

"If you hold it like this with one—"

"Don't you presume to correct your elders," his father said sharply, and he glowered under his bushy black eyebrows.

"But I only wanted to help." It seemed unfair. Mingyue choked back his conflicting desires to restrain himself in front of the guest and to not lash out. He wondered why he put up with this shit.

"Don't anyone else eat my monstrosities after they're cooked," Dan said. "Let me pay for my own clumsiness."

They sat silently, and Dan stuffed and folded one jiaodze in the time it took Gao to fold four.

Mingyue wondered why his father was allowed to go to America when so many others weren't? He was not even a member of the Party. How could he afford to bring back the stereo system?

Gao finally broke the awkward silence. "Yesterday, Zhao begged the leadership to open government and stop corruption. He even called for investigation of his own two sons. They're making big money by using their family *guanxi*. Economic liberalization is causing inflation. It hurts some people while others get rich."

Mingyue thought how his father had no *guanxi* except Wu. Maybe they were ...

"That's been true in capitalist countries, too," Dan said. "It's a kind of Social Darwinism; the survival of the most corrupt."

"Most people don't like to live that way. People get hurt," Gao said. "But no one knows what to do about it. It's *guantuo*, official profiteering, they hate the most."

Mingyue was struck by the irony of his father criticizing corruption.

"Same thing in America, but there, the corruption is in both government and business." Dan made a lumpy jiaodze, and it split, ruined. "So give me an example, and I'll put it in my notes."

"Well," Gao rubbed a drop of water on the split, carefully pulling together the two edges of the dough, and salvaged it. "This is widely known. Fuel is very scarce and the price is fixed, so people have to buy coal laced with rocks just to get any fuel at all. Some people in the coal-mining regions get wealthy selling the rocks to the adulterators."

Mingyue took the jiaodzes the three of them had made into the kitchen for his mother to fry. His mother and brother laughed at the ones Dan had made. But Mingyue couldn't laugh. He listened to the conversation and fumed. They were hypocrites. All talk; but they wouldn't do anything about it. And Mingyue couldn't do anything.

"We have something similar in America," Dan said. "Some products are mostly packaging. The packagers get wealthy and create tons of trash to pollute the environment to boot. At least rocks aren't polluting."

Gao shrugged his shoulders. "I think there is hope for China. A politburo meeting endorsed Zhao's moderate line. They agreed to talk to students, to take limited steps toward democracy, and to make faster economic and political change. Deng apparently backed Zhao and said that his call for a crackdown on students was because Beijing officials gave him bad information."

"Then the students really are winning," Dan smiled. "That's the first time I've heard a Chinese official admit to being misinformed."

"They may have won a battle," Gao frowned, "but I doubt that the war is over. Deng will not give up his power that easily and lose face. I'm sure he's working behind the scenes."

Mingyue entered carrying a platter heaped with jiaodzes; some steamed and some fried. His head swam with confusion and anger at his father. If the students were winning, why did he have to give in?

Gao continued. "But it is a step forward for China that the People's Daily published a long article calling for more democracy, human rights, and government by balance of powers."

"That's an official organ of the government talking?" Dan raised his eyebrows.

Gao sighed. "It's the first time in history the Chinese press has been in favor of human rights."

Mingyue glowered at his father. How could he speak of human rights after silencing his own son? Mingyue spoke in a quiet poisoned voice. "Two thousand students in Beijing began hunger strikes yesterday. The government can suppress violence, but what can it do against self-sacrifice?" Mingyue sneered bitterly. He would not be silent.

Gao's eyes opened wide for a moment, then he frowned at his son. Mingyue continued. "They said they would strike until Soviet leader Gorbachev's arrival tomorrow for the first Sino-Soviet summit in thirty years."

"Gorbachev?" Dan asked. "What's he got to do with it?"

"Gorbachev is the students' champion of democracy," Mingyue said louder, more confident.

"Not Americans because Marxism has anti-capitalist concepts to resist 'bourgeois liberalization' and 'Westernization,' but there are no concepts to resist communist 'glasnost.' The leaders don't know how to answer it."

"That is ironic." Dan laughed. "For a Soviet leader to be a champion of democracy."

"Besides," Gao said, "many Western reporters will be here for the summit. The leaders want to make a good impression. They won't crack down on the students while Gorbachev is here. They want the summit to be the center of attention, not the struggle with the students. But it worries me that protests in support of Zhou may weaken him." Gao's calm voice belied the warning scowl he shot at his son that seemed to say, "That's why you must leave politics alone." "Hard-liners will have an excuse for repression."

Of course his father would play it safe. He had always given in to the government. Mingyue wanted to join the protests.

His mother and brother came into the room with plates heaped with food; lotus root, shredded pepper and peanut pork, cabbage cooked with star anise, a whole fish, leeks, and a sweet wine. Mingyue's reaction to the feast was disgust. All this food while the students were on a hunger strike to save China. They were doing something, while his father went on eating as if it were all academic.

The talk turned to lighter topics, such as how all the sidewalks were covered with mud from the rain because piles of dirt from the ditches for the steam pipes had sat on the sidewalks untouched for three months; how doctors had diagnosed Mrs. Gao's back pain as curable kidney problems; and how the quarrel with Mr. Gao's neighbor over the noise his radio made was escalating.

Mingyue sat silent and sullen. He felt Dan's questioning eyes upon him. The cold heavy chain that bound Dan's fate to Mingyue's weighed heavily between them.

As Mingyue lay in bed, he thought about how he had given in to Inspector Song and his father. He always gave in to his father.

Now the student pressure on the government was growing and successful. The media were reporting more. Maybe his actions were not a failure. The riots of a few were transformed into a peaceful mass movement of many. Students, faculty, workers, peasants, even government workers, had joined the demonstrations. And now students were beginning hunger strikes. Nonviolent. He had given in too soon. Maybe the error his father had forced him to confess was not an error. Maybe it was not an error to struggle for freedom and against corruption, even if it did endanger the family. His grandfather had struggled against the corrupt landlords and the Japanese invaders. Hadn't that endangered the family? Perhaps danger was necessary to win a worthwhile future for the family.

He had been a coward twice: once when he abandoned his companions and his leadership during the riot, and now again when he backed down from a just cause, from his conviction that the government was corrupt and the people must struggle for freedom and justice.

He had kowtowed to the Inspector and traded his love for Yingying and the cause of justice to have his file buried. But a buried file could always be dug up again. Its stench would ooze up from the grave like that of a rotten carcass to remind him that it could be used against him at any time the rest of his life to force him to do things he shouldn't do. He had been corrupted by the very corruption he had set out to fight. He had told his father he was a fool; only now did he realize what a fool he had really been. He didn't deserve her love. A tear rolled down his cheek. He didn't deserve to live. He'd lost Yingying. He'd lost face with the students. He had no freedom because he had been handcuffed by a bargain. What more did he have to lose?

He remembered the hunger strike. Perhaps he could redeem his cowardice, even face the student committee again, if he proposed to them that Xi'an students join Beijing students in the hunger strike. Let Inspector Song arrest him. He no longer feared arrest; he welcomed it. He needed it to regain his self-respect. Better to be a hero in prison than an unemployable, loveless, faceless walking corpse as he had been the last two weeks. And he wouldn't be in prison long if the students won the battle.

He resolved that he would be the first hunger striker in Xi'an. Like the Beijing students, he would vow not to eat again until the government gave in to the demands for justice. He would be a leader once again, not a quitter. Not a coward.

"Mingyue, you're safe. That's a relief," said his friend, Yen Pingchung, as they met crossing campus. "We feared you might be dead or in prison."

"Have I lost face with the students?"

"Lost face? You led the railway workers in the demonstration. They say your speeches were inspiring. Everyone knows you've been a fugitive from the corrupt government. The police are looking for you. You're a hero."

Sure, I'm China's bright hope for the future just like my name, Bright Moon, Mingyue thought, ironically. If so, China's lost. "I have to speak with the committee. I have a proposal."

"We will be organizing a demonstration in support of the Beijing students tonight. They began hunger strikes last week, you know."

Fifty students had gathered in a classroom. Mingyue sat beside Yen Pingchung and Ting Lili in front of the room. As he looked over the students, his anger at his father gave way to fear. It was no small thing to pledge a hunger strike. He would be arrested. Did he dare? He wiped the sweat of his palms on his trouser leg.

Pingchung spoke:

"The Committee proposes that we organize a demonstration of students from all Xi'an universities. We must get workers to join us to support Beijing students' demands. We will march again and again until the corruption of the sons of high government officials ends. We demand more democracy, freedom of job choice, speech, and the press, and more money for teachers."

The students cheered. Mingyue held up his hands to quiet them and spoke in a quiet quavering voice. "We must support their demands and add one of our own: that our provincial government talk with us about the deaths in April. I know someone died." He looked at the floor and lowered his voice to a practically a whisper. "I saw him. I touched him."

People in the back of the room asked people in front to explain what he had said. The bare concrete walls of the room echoed their murmurs like whispers of ghosts.

Mingyue wondered who of the students in the room were the inevitable government spies. Was he too cowardly to speak of the hunger strike? Yen Pingchung explained what had been said to the whole room and endorsed Mingyue's proposal. The students cheered again.

The dragon lady, Ting Lili, stood, hands on hips like a lion tamer about to crack her whip, and they fell silent.

"It will take days to organize the whole city. We don't have the time. We must act now. I propose that we announce a demonstration in front of the University Administration Building tomorrow and demand the support of the President and faculty."

Some students cheered wildly. Another shouted, "Tomorrow is too soon to organize. Some of us do go to our classes, unlike others I know."

Ting glowered at him. "Some of us care more for the good of the Chinese people than our personal careers, unlike others I know. We should stop going to classes. If each of us tells five classmates, everyone on campus will know by tomorrow evening, after classes are over. We will meet in front of the Administration Building at sundown." Her last sentence was delivered as a self-evident command.

Mingyue stood to speak, and the room fell quiet. His voice grew stronger now.

"I support both proposals. We can demonstrate here tomorrow and in the whole city in a few days. We can attack on several fronts at once. I intend to go to the Bell Tower tomorrow—since it is at the center of Xi'an and close to government office buildings—and join the Beijing students in a hunger strike. I will fast to death or until the government meets our demands. I hope some of you will join me."

The students were silent for a moment, then talked excitedly among themselves. Two students rose to speak.

"I'll fast with you for one day."

"I'll get friends at the Foreign Language Institute to join us."

Others rose to pledge their support with recruiting, partial fasts, or periodic sitting. He was committed now. He would have to do it or he would lose face. Of course he would probably be arrested before he even got to the Bell Tower. His stomach trembled.

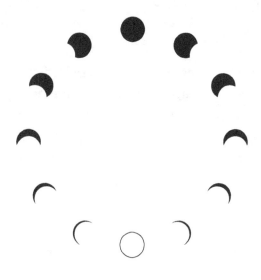

AT THE BELL TOWER

MAY 16

YOSHIKO LEFT DAN'S APARTMENT IN TIME TO GO TO breakfast, and he savored the orange blossom perfume she left on his pillow. They had discussed the political situation and agreed in their support for the Chinese students. And they had discussed how famous Chinese poetry often contained disguised political themes. A meeting of minds on politics and poetry was crucial to their relationship. It had been a perfect night, and he longed to see her again as soon as possible.

It was absurd though. He was under threat from the Chinese police. He was too old for her. He was American, and she was Japanese. Or at least half Japanese. She had told him her father was Chinese. Her father had been brought to Japan as a prisoner

of war. It seemed to be a source of embarrassment. She had even
suggested that no one in Japan wanted to marry her because of
it. Perhaps he had gone too far to hint that he would be happy to
marry her. That he would love for her to have his child. He didn't
want to scare her away. But he couldn't deny his feelings in spite
of the hopeless absurdity. He didn't want to be, but he was in love
with her.

Dan wasn't sure he understood their cultural differences, for
all of his studies of Asia. He couldn't grasp at a gut level how she
could be so shy in public and so bold when she offered herself to
him in private.

How unashamed she was sexually. But when he mentioned
marriage and children, he couldn't read any reaction. He didn't
know what she felt, and it left him in a limbo of anxiety.

He went to his friend Gao's apartment to ask him to copy
some readings for his students. Gao Baima opened his door with a
worried expression on his face, as usual.

"Come in. Sit." Gao swallowed. "I have bad news. Very bad.
Can I get you beer or *qi shui?*"

"*Qi shui,* please." Dan sat on the couch. It could be macroscopic
or personal. From Gao's tone, Dan dreaded that it would be all too
personal.

Gao returned with two glasses of *qi shui* and handed one to
Dan. "My son, Mingyue, has gone to join the hunger strike. Now
he'll be arrested. And he puts you in danger again."

Dan rocked back on his seat and spilled *qi shui* on his shirt.
The image of the Inspector smoking his cigarette, eyes squinted,
threatening arrest for harboring a fugitive and espionage rose
before his eyes. He wiped his shirt with his handkerchief, and Gao
brought him a wet towel from the kitchen.

"If Mingyue is arrested, I'll probably be arrested too," Dan said. "I think I need to contact the American Embassy, though, I'm not sure they could help much. It's not like they could get me a lawyer. If one is arrested, one is presumed guilty, and a trial is only to decide on the sentence." He felt chilled.

"First he told me he was giving up all political activity," Gao groaned. "And now suddenly, he tells me that he must fight corruption and hypocrisy. He looked at me with an anger I have never seen in his eyes, as if . . . and for the first time in my life, I feared him. He said, 'You told me to apologize or leave this family. I withdraw my apology. I was not in error. I will leave the family . . . forever.' Oh, how I regret that I said those words." Gao put his face in his hands, and his chest heaved. He held his stomach.

Dan's own stomach began to flip over. "I must get to a telephone. I have the Embassy number in my desk drawer. Maybe they can do something. I've got to go."

"They'll kill all the protesters . . ." Gao looked at the window across the room, as if he were watching something outside. The deep bags under his eyes seemed to get heavier. "That's all they know how to do; kill. Like the sparrows." He belched.

"You have to take care of your ulcer," Dan said. "What sparrows?"

"They'll kill us like they killed the all sparrows." Gao put his head back into his hands. ". . . like we killed all the sparrows."

"Ah." Dan remembered the story Gao had told him a few months ago. It was about a series of big government campaigns. When the bureaucrats decided that flies spread disease, they mobilized the Chinese people in a campaign against flies. They issued every Chinese person a flyswatter, and on a certain day, had every one in China swat every fly in sight. The result was a great success; the fly population was decimated. Dan had seen very few flies in China, even years after the campaign.

The government next had the idea that growing grass in the city takes too much water. They ordered that all the grass in Beijing be dug up. The next year, they had terrible dust storms and had to plant the grass again. It was the kind of ironic justice Dan loved.

The government then decided that crop yields would be improved if the sparrow population could be decreased, because sparrows ate too much grain. Again, they mobilized the Chinese people. The government ordered that everyone in China make noise to scare the sparrows to death. On the appointed day, Gao went to his roof top and beat on a wok with a big spoon. Others went into the fields. They lit firecrackers, pounded drums, blew whistles, beat on pots and pans, shouted; anything to make noise for hours. A billion people made noise like the trumpet at Jericho, and the sparrows came tumbling down. The birds were so frightened that they flew in circles for hours until they were exhausted and died. Almost all the sparrows in China were killed.

The next year, the government expected a great harvest of grain. But it was a disaster. They had a plague of insects that ate all the crops, and thousands of people starved. The government bureaucrats had made a gross error. They didn't listen to their scientists or peasants. Sparrows don't eat crops, they eat insects.

"They'll kill all the protesters," Gao moaned. "They'll kill my son." He jaw muscles bulged from clenching his teeth.

Dan remembered that Mao had been willing to risk a nuclear war. The loss of a few hundred million Chinese was nothing to him, because the remaining few hundred million could celebrate a great victory. What was the death of a few million flies, or sparrows, or students in the face of historical destiny? Dan knew he himself was but a sparrow tossed on the winds of history. Would God, or even Yoshiko, mourn when he fell, exhausted?

Dan's nervous stomach settled. It was like it had been in Vietnam. Dan had been scared of dying in combat ever since all the World War II John Wayne movies he had seen as a child. He always identified with the Marines who died on the beaches. He always imagined the worst and dreaded it. But when the mortar shells began to fall all around him, and he had to call the corpsmen for his wounded, the world became surreal like he was outside himself at a distance, watching a movie instead of his own life, and he lost his fear.

Now worry about Gao and Mingyue and the Chinese trying to win their freedoms made him strangely unconcerned for himself. The web of his fate had spun far beyond his control. And he had a battle plan now. He would call the Embassy as soon as he got back to the apartment.

Dan struggled to think of something comforting to say to his friend.

"Young people Mingyue's age dramatize," he said. "When his anger cools, he'll realize how much he loves his family and come back. Meanwhile, the police will probably ignore hunger strikers for a while. After all, they haven't done anything since the riots ended." The tension in Gao's jaw seemed to relax a bit.

Dan went back to his apartment to call the American Embassy. In five tries, he got a busy signal each time. He drummed his fingers on the desk until his fingers hurt. He went to eat, as much out of frustration as of hunger. He hoped to join Yoshiko for lunch, but she was not in the dining hall. All in all, it had been a shitty day so far. He bought a bowl of spicy noodles and cabbage and sat with Ty Bates.

"A Qi Gong master contacted me," Ty said. "He invited us to learn Qi Gong with him. I'm going to a group session from six to seven tonight. Do you want to come too?"

"I'd love to, but I teach class then." Dan twirled his noodles with his chopsticks and looked at them as if he were a tea leaf reader.

"Do you know Han Shan, the 'Cold Mountain' poems?" Ty asked.

"Not well." Dan barely heard the question. His mind was on Yoshiko, the Embassy, Inspector Song. He picked up a bite of cabbage and noodles with his chopsticks and stuffed them into his mouth.

"Han Shan—Cold Mountain—seems to have been the name of both a recluse and the mountain he lived on," Ty said. "His poems really speak to me: 'Go tell families with silverware and cars, what's the use of all that noise and money?' I like that. I suppose 'cars' is a translation of 'chariots,' and I didn't know ancient Chinese had silverware. I suppose it's a loose translation. But anyway, Christianity has taught me from my youth to reject material things, and I've been surrounded by hypocrites. I can't stand the hypocrisy. Han Shan appeals to me more and more." He took a bite of spicy pork and rice on his chopsticks.

"Oh. Of course. I know Han Shan," Dan's attention returned to the dining hall. "I remember a line that struck me. 'Today I'm back at Cold Mountain: I'll sleep by the creek and purify my ears.' Purify my ears. Beautiful. I wonder where I need to sleep to purify my thoughts. Sorry. I'm a bit distracted."

"I suppose I should purify my stomach and stop eating all this meat." Ty pushed away his plate. "I'm tempted to join the Beijing hunger strikers, both for political support and to purify my body with a fast for a few days."

Dan's whole body jumped as if his knee had been hit by a doctor. Ty had reminded him of Mingyue's return to political activity and the danger to himself.

"I hope you're not serious. The Chinese government would neither appreciate nor tolerate foreign interference in their internal affairs. They're already worried about the corrupting influence of foreign bourgeois ideas." Dan knew he was talking about himself. He began to wolf down his noodles so he could get back to the telephone.

"I'm serious," Ty said. "But only tempted . . . Oh Jesus . . ."

Dan saw Ty's mother come through the door.

"Please don't tell her that we talk about Chinese religion."

"Or that you hate hypocrisy."

Ty blushed.

Mrs. Bates came to Ty and Dan and sat in a chair, puffing.

"Have you been paid yet?" She asked Dan.

"Payday again? I always forget," Dan said. "Good. I've got to squeeze some dollars out of him. Two more months and—"

"Well, we asked Wu for dollars as usual, but he didn't have any," she said. "Claims it's because of the political troubles."

Dan leapt to his feet. "He's lying. It's an excuse."

"I'm sure he's lying." Mrs. Bates sagged in her chair. "But everything is so upset around here. Probably time for us all to leave."

Mr. Bates came up to the table. "Wu asked me to give you your pay." He handed Dan a stack of Yuan. "He said he was too busy to wait for you today."

"Yeah, yeah." Dan scowled. "He probably just can't face me."

Yingying had been steaming in anger at her father for eleven days; going to classes but not hearing the lectures, unable to do any homework or sleep. She wondered if she had made a mistake giving in to her father's bargain. She was alienated from her fellow students who snubbed her, but that was nothing compared to how much she loved Mingyue and missed him. Could she live without him the rest of her life?

Yingying crouched on the grass and leaned her back against the sun-heated brick wall of her dormitory building, plucking aimlessly at blades of grass. Her mind was a dark fog. It was a hot and sunny day, but she felt cold. A flock of birds alighted in a tree and chirped at each other.

How could they be so happy when she was so miserable? They didn't have to make political bargains with fathers. They were free. She saw Ting Lili walking toward her—the last person she needed to see in her black mood. The birds all flew off, but there was nowhere for Yingying to retreat.

"I don't suppose you intend to join the demonstration tonight, do you?" Lili stood with her arms folded and glowered at Yingying. "Siding with the administration, are you?"

Yingying looked at the grass as if studying a bug. "You must hate me as much as I hate you."

"But I think you'll be interested to know that Gao Mingyue has begun a hunger strike to the death at the Bell Tower."

Yingying looked up at Lili, trying to comprehend this news. Lili smirked like she had scored a blow for justice, spun around, and strode off. Yingying felt as if she had been struck.

She called after Lili. "Where are you going? To spread more misery elsewhere on campus?"

If Mingyue died in a hunger strike to the death, it would be her death. She couldn't let him. She stood and swayed, dizzy. She had to stop him. But no, he wouldn't die. It would be as bad as if he did, though. He would be arrested and sent to prison. She sat back on the grass and plucked leaves and threw them angrily.

How could my father do this to me, she wondered. I was a fearless student leader, and he turned me into a frightened, defeated coward. Just because he threatened Mingyue. Was it that easy to puncture my determination?

After a gloomy moment, she realized that she had been freed from her father's curse. If Mingyue had broken the agreement, then she was no longer bound by it either; she didn't have to give up political activity. She could see Mingyue. It felt as if a hundred pound sack of rice had been lifted from her back.

She went to the dining hall and had her first good meal in days. She thought about what to do and decided that she had to join Mingyue. If he were arrested, she would probably never see him again. She had to explain that she had only agreed to her father's terms out of love for him. She would beg his forgiveness and convince him to give up his hunger strike. But if he wouldn't stop, she would be at his side until the police dragged them off.

Yingying took the bus to the Bell Tower where a small group of about twenty students had gathered with blankets to sit on and signs announcing their demands for an end to corruption, higher pay for teachers, the right to choose their own union leaders, and for the Xi'an government to admit that they had killed students during the riots. Busses and trucks rolled by kicking up dust and spewing diesel fumes. Pedestrians passed by and stared at the students as if they were monkeys in a zoo. She saw Mingyue in the midst of the strikers, sitting with his eyes shut as if meditating. His heavy eyebrows and broad forehead bore a frown. His powerful square jaw had a determined set. His thin body and fragile arm bones made him look like he had already fasted for a week, even though it had only been two days. He wouldn't survive a fast for long.

"He has not eaten for two days," a student told her. "He drinks only water. Several other students have joined him for a day or two, but they take fruit juice. We've asked students from the medical school to monitor their health."

"I'll join him." Yingying surprised herself with her decision. "I'll drink only water." The student shrugged his shoulders and nodded.

She sat beside Mingyue. He opened his eyes and looked at her.

"All is well now," he said with tears in his eyes.

———   ———   ———

Dan tried to call the Embassy several times more and got busy signals until it was time for his class. When he finished teaching and left his classroom, he was accompanied by a dozen of his students who told him that a student demonstration had been called that evening in front of the Administration Building. They wanted to protect him on his way home since there was no other route than by the demonstration. He asked them if he would really need protection, especially since he sympathized with the students. They said the protection would not be against students but against the police.

For a time, he and his students mingled with the crowd of several hundred to listen to the speeches. The student speakers cited instances of corruption, such as that children of high cadres who were terrible students were given the best jobs, while honors students were sent to remote rural areas.

One student told of how a foreign charity had given Xi'an a fully equipped ambulance, but officials of the Xi'an Municipal

Foreign Affairs department sold the vehicle and used the money to buy apartments for themselves.

Another student reported that the Soviet leader, Gorbachev, had said that a Chinese uprising was necessary as part of the painful process of healthy worldwide upheaval in communist countries. He claimed that economic change was impossible without political reform. He saw the student uprising in China as a very serious turning point in the development of world socialism. The students cheered to that.

There were no police present. After an hour of listening to speeches, the crowd grew restless for action. At the suggestion of the dragon lady, Ting, the students marched to the faculty apartment buildings and called for faculty support, weaving in a long line through the faculty apartment compound. Dan and his "protectors" followed them. The demonstration reminded him of his radical days as a student at Berkeley. He felt young and exhilarated. Better to be in danger here, supporting the forces of justice, than in danger in Vietnam for no good reason at all.

Swarms of chanting students poured between the drab concrete, four-story apartment buildings. Most of the faculty cowered, silent, behind their doors. A few came to their balconies and waved their support at the students. The march ended in front of the President's apartment, where the students chanted for an hour. The President did not appear.

Dan thought of the protesters in other universities around the city and in every major city and provincial capital and of the million people in Beijing, all struggling for justice and democracy. He wondered what political struggles must be raging behind the closed doors of government and the army. Who would win? He thought of Mingyue at the Bell Tower, glad that Mingyue was doing what he had to, in spite of the danger to himself. He would have to visit the boy tomorrow and express his support.

Dan went home, wishing that Yoshiko would come to him again. He hadn't seen her since morning and had longed for her all day. Perhaps she was waiting for him.

But she wasn't.

He thought it might be late enough that he could get through to the Embassy. He laid a pencil and pad of paper in front of him and phoned. The university operator succeeded in getting him through to Beijing. A recorded voice answered in English recommending that all American citizens leave China as soon as possible. Applications for visas were not being taken at this time. "For further help, our normal business hours are—" Dan slammed the phone onto its cradle. They were probably all at happy hour being happy, he thought. That was what he needed, a few good stiff drinks.

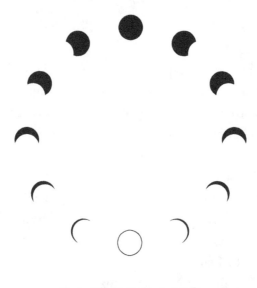

BAD BREAKS

MAY 18

DAN KEPT TRYING TO GET THROUGH TO THE US Embassy all morning and, between confusion with the university operator, phone lines to Beijing being tied up, and busy signals, it was driving him crazy.

Yoshiko had not shown up at his apartment or the dining hall for two days now.

Dan puzzled over her absence. Was she avoiding him? He missed her to distraction.

Dan dressed in his green and white jogging outfit and went out for a run. A crowd of university students was gathered in front of the administration building. He saw Ed at the back of the crowd and stopped beside him.

"What's going on?" Dan asked.

"The students are demanding that the truth be told about the killings in April," Ed said. "Rumors are that all the victims were students."

"The government's still denying that anyone died?" Dan asked.

"Right. But look." Ed pointed at the front of the building.

Dan looked and saw a row of funeral wreaths on stands. "Who are they for?"

"Unnamed," Ed said. "No one knows who the students were."

"Parents were probably warned by the government not to say anything," Dan said. "Why are you still hanging around? I thought you were on your way home by now."

"I'm still trying to get what Wu owes me, but I should probably forget that and just go. Things are heating up again. Demonstrations all over China. A million people demonstrated in Beijing yesterday. Zhao Ziyang lost to Deng Xiaoping in the politburo and Deng pronounced martial law in Beijing. The proverbial you-know-what is heading straight for the fan right now, and here I am begging Wu for pennies."

"You're right that we should get out of here," Dan said. "I've been trying to get through to the American Embassy."

"The only good news is that General Xu of the Thirty-Eighth Amy in Beijing refused to enforce martial law," Ed said.

"I doubt that's good news," Dan said. "When generals start disobeying orders, things are really getting dangerous."

Students cheered as several of them unrolled a banner that read, "Stupid Old People Should Resign Quickly."

"That reminds me of the slogan in the '60s, 'Don't trust anyone over thirty,'" Dan said. Dan waved goodbye to Ed and continued his run, torn between hope for the students' cause and fear for its outcome. He ran out of the university gate and by the Army factory and then through fields of spring wheat, where five peasants hoeing in a row looked up to stare at him passing.

The muddy road became spotted with almost impassable ponds in the middle of an ancient village. A huge pig crossed in front of him and splashed into one of the puddles in the road. The pig stopped and looked at him as if it dared him to come into its private wallow.

Dan turned around and ran the mile back toward the Big Wild Goose Pagoda, past the Japanese hotel. He wanted to go into the hotel restaurant to look for Yoshiko, but he was too sweaty and smelly. Maybe he would meet her walking. He knew he was acting like a teenager. And he had the same frustrated longing he'd had then.

He ran another mile back to the university. The lawn by the student dorm was being "mowed." China couldn't afford lawn mowers, but they had lots of cheap hand labor. Students formed a line shoulder to shoulder the width of the lawn on their knees and plucked the grass, blade by blade, by hand. They were part way across the lawn. Before them lay a field of uncut grass; behind them, a lawn smooth as a golf course putting green.

Dan envisioned half the billion Chinese lined up weaponless and marching across Beijing. They could mow down their government in a day, like a plague of locusts. But of course, they were too disorganized. Dan ran out of his way by the foreign student dorm on the chance of seeing Yoshiko.

When he arrived back at the foreigners' compound, Mr. and Mrs. Bates were standing by the street looking glum.

Mrs. Bates spewed her words out like a broken water pipe. "We're waiting for the university car. Ty's in the hospital. He was riding his bicycle back from the sit ins at the Bell Tower when he hit an open manhole and flipped into a truck. His arm is shattered."

Dan knew exactly how this could happen. Peasants stole manhole covers to make plowshares. It was especially dangerous to bicycle or even walk across an ill-lighted street after dark in Xi'an.

"Lucky he wasn't killed," Dan said. "Are you aware that Chinese hospitals have no nursing care?"

"Oh my God!" Mrs. Bates' voice quivered.

"If patients want to eat, their families have to feed them. If they need sheets changed, the families have to wash and change them, and so on."

Her face went pale. "We didn't know. We'll have to take sheets and buy him something to eat on the way. What else do we need to know? Is the medical care reliable?"

Dan could have told Mrs. Bates plenty of stories about Chinese medicine. When Dan was on a US-China People's Friendship Association trip in 1979, just after the fall of the Gang of Four, he had Peking duck in Beijing. Chinese cooks cut up the meat, bones and all. He got a sliver of duck bone between his gum and tooth and couldn't get it out. The tour group moved on to Kunming and was visiting a factory commune where they make silver filigree out in a rural area. Dan mentioned to someone in his tour group that the duck bone was bothering him, and that person mentioned it to the tour leader who whisked him into the barefoot doctor's dental chair before he could protest. Barefoot doctors were given minimal medical training and sent to the countryside where medical care had been non-existent. The dentist pulled out the bone. That seemed to go well. She kept working on Dan's teeth with a drill. When she was done, Dan asked what she had been doing.

"I filed down your eyeteeth," she said, without so much as blinking. "They were too long."

They didn't seem to fit the Chinese standard on her dental chart. When Dan got home, American dentists were horrified at the damage.

The past winter, Dan had had a sore throat and a hundred and four degree fever and had been taken to a local hospital. He stood in a long line of people being seen by a doctor who sat in the middle of a huge auditorium-like room at a children's school desk. The doctor looked at peoples' throats one after the other with the same metal tongue depressor; he dipped it in the same glass of alcohol after each use, since they don't have autoclaves for sterilization.

Dan offered the doctor a clean pair of chopsticks, but the man glared at him and shook his head. Dan, aware of the line of thirty people behind him, gave in and opened his mouth to the metal tongue depressor.

"Tonsillitis," the doctor said.

What confidence he still had in this doctor seriously deflated. "I can't have tonsillitis. I had my tonsils out when I was six years old."

The doctor made a dry sucking noise with his mouth. "Well, those American doctors didn't do a very good job," he said, probing deeper into Dan's throat and peering from under a bushy eyebrow. "There's still part of it left, and it's swollen."

The doctor prescribed Terramycin and snake bile. Dan was given six vials of snake bile where one should be taken a day. He was cured immediately. His fever was gone in an hour, and he felt like jogging by the end of the first day. The snake bile was clear and tasteless. Was it the bile or the Terramycin that cured him? Dan didn't know. He thought it was an interesting experience of

Chinese culture. But he didn't expect that Mrs. Bates would be equally enthusiastic about snake bile.

He was reminded of what a visiting American doctor had told him earlier in the year. A group of American doctors had been visiting Chinese hospitals, and this doctor had been housed in the apartment above Dan's for a few days. He had told Dan of how the group of doctors was being bussed to an Imperial tomb and came upon a traffic accident. A truck full of peasants had overturned, and the American doctors saw over a dozen injured and bleeding Chinese needing aid.

The doctors asked to be let off the bus to go help but were told it was not the foreigners' business, the tour was behind schedule, and Chinese doctors would be quite capable of taking care of the injured. The driver would not open the door. Stuck in traffic, the bus did not move. The doctors watched, helpless and horrified, as bleeding people with broken bones protruding from their bodies, were lifted like sacks of coal, screaming from pain and fear, and thrown onto the back of a truck.

He wouldn't tell her these stories. He wouldn't talk about the lung diseases. He wouldn't mention that twenty percent of the Chinese population had hepatitis—over two hundred million people—and that there were several hepatitis hospitals near the university where clusters of patients went to the curbside kiosks to eat noodles cooked on braziers.

When one patient finished with his bowl and chop sticks, they were sloshed in a tub of gray water with bits of noodle and cabbage floating in it—not too hot for the vendor to immerse his hand in—and were used to serve the next person. Dan had tried to discourage American students from eating there, but they liked to go native.

"We were just thinking about leaving China," Mrs. Bates said. "But now ..."

"Jesus, you're trapped in China too," Dan said, realizing too late that the use of that particular swear word was probably highly offensive to the Bateses. "What hospital is he in?"

"The Eighth Army," Ty's father said.

"Good. It's the best in the city. I have class most evenings, but I can help daytimes."

"I doubt if you'll have class tonight," Mr. Bates said. "Most of the students in the university are on strike. There are more than a hundred students on hunger strike at the Bell Tower from universities all over town."

"I know," Dan said. He only had one undergraduate student and a few school teachers and faculty members left in his classes. "My class last night turned into a vigorous political discussion."

"Mine too," Mr. Bates said.

"And lots of the faculty signed posters and petitions in support of the students who—"

Mrs. Bates jerked her husband's arm. "How can you talk politics when your son is in a hospital with a broken arm?"

When Dan entered his apartment, intending to call the Embassy again, he found a note that had been slid under the door, along with the picture Yoshiko said she would write the poem on. He read the note:

"Very sorry I must leaving Xi'an. I go back to Japan. Situation too dangerous for foreigners. Many students leaving. I hope you go home safely too. I dreamed to be your mistress. But we had eleven perfect nights. You understand the Buddhist idea that clinging causes suffering. We must let go now. I will

always treasure our perfect time together. Now nothing can spoil it. Yoshiko."

"No!" Dan's heart screamed. He wanted to cry but couldn't. He had to stop her. But where was she now? He ran out of the apartment and arrived breathless at the foreign women student's dorm. Susan sat on the concrete step in front of the door, reading.

"Is Yoshiko Sato here?" Dan asked.

Susan squinted through her red eyebrows at him with her head cocked to the side. "She went to the airport this morning."

"Oh damn! I have to stop her. I'll get a cab." He turned toward the university main gate and felt his pocket for his wallet. He had enough cash.

"Her plane will have left by now," she said. "Even if it was delayed for hours, it will have left by now."

"Maybe not. With all the chaos . . ." He turned back toward Susan. "They wouldn't let me into the waiting room without a ticket, would they? But I could call the airport. Which flight did she take? Beijing? Shanghai?"

Susan shrugged.

His shoulders sagged. "They wouldn't tell me at the airport, would they? And Wu wouldn't tell me. Damn."

Dan walked back to his apartment in a slouch, dragging his feet. He hoped her flight was canceled. Maybe she would come back. If this were a movie, he would go to the airport through hell and high water, and she would be waiting for him. But she had chosen to go. He collapsed into his armchair and hung his head on his chest.

It seemed all so futile. He picked up the picture she had left and read the fragment of the poem about Chang'an she had written on the picture. It was a beautiful running hand style and perfectly placed to add to the beauty of the painting.

On the back, she had written another poem fragment by Li Yu: "One dream that scarcely outlasts the burning of a candle, or a petal's fall, and then we go."

That scorched his heart as if the candle in the poem had dripped wax on it. But he would treasure her gift—even the pain of it. It had been perfect. She had said it was best to die when one chose; perhaps it was best to end perfection when one chose rather than watch it wither. Should he ask for more?

The poem reminded him of another line in a poem by Li Yu: "The past is only to be regretted." He knew it was a very un-Buddhist idea—the ultimate in clinging. He should just let go.

Another fragment by Li Yu finally brought the tears: "Scissors do not sever, nor reason unravel, the pain of separation. It lodges in the heart with a taste of its own."

At the Bell Tower, Mingyue looked up at the moon and stars overhead. Bright moon, his name sake.

Now in his fourth day of fasting, his hunger-pangs were easing. He had never been so happy and so miserable. Happy because Yingying slept beside him on the concrete sidewalk for a third night in a row.

He was a hero, a leader among the hunger strikers, and they seemed to be gaining support throughout the city as students were gaining support all over China, even from the Army. There were more than a hundred who had joined him from several universities; some fasting, and some just sitting in. And people passing by waved and held up the "V" sign of support.

But he was miserable too now that his anger at his father had cooled a bit, and he did not want to be estranged from him. The government might not back down soon, if ever. He did not want to die. He did not want Yingying to die. He wanted her to stop the fast, or at least take fruit juice. But she wouldn't. He began to despair of his own courage again; he knew he had not really expected to have to die for his cause. He had presumed he would be arrested. But there were no police anywhere to be seen. Perhaps they were waiting to see who would win the power struggle in Beijing. He would lose face if he quit. He would have to fast until the government gave in . . . or he died.

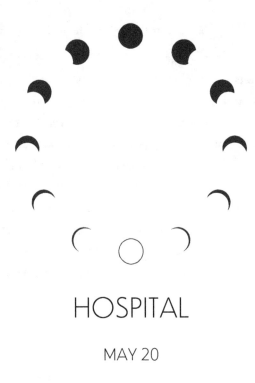

HOSPITAL

MAY 20

DAN WAS UPSET OVER YOSHIKO'S DEPARTURE AND the fact that he got nothing but busy signals at the US Embassy; except the one time he was put through and accidentally cut off by the university operator. He decided to get out of his apartment. He went to the Eighth Army Hospital to visit Ty, taking with him a box of pork and cabbage jiaodzes, rice, pepper chicken, chopsticks, and a cup accompanied by a pot of tea wrapped in a towel to keep warm.

The university minivan driver drove Dan to the hospital. Dan had given the driver a carton of Camel cigarettes, one of those little presents or bribes that were necessary to grease the wheels in China. Maybe one should just think of them as tips. It made the driver eager to please which depressed Dan. It was the only time in his life he had given bribes. It made him feel dirty, like he was helping to perpetuate the very corruption the students were fighting against. At least cancer sticks had a certain ironic element of revenge to them. Like Dan was plunging in a dagger and the driver was thanking him for it. Not a good Buddhist sentiment.

Dan had the unnerving thought that that might be the reason Wu hadn't given him his money: Dan hadn't given him presents. Well, he sure wasn't going to give Wu any bribes now.

But that seemed too trivial a reason. Still, the thought nagged at him and strengthened his resentment of the driver's cigarettes all the more.

Dan and the driver wound their way down the bleak concrete halls with white paint peeling from the walls, where patients waiting to see a doctor lay on the bare cement floor in various states of misery surrounded by squatting family members. Ty shared his room with half a dozen men on rusting steel army beds. Dan smelled urine.

Bare light bulbs hung from the ceiling. The patient next to Ty with his leg in traction snored like an angry bear. Ty's right arm was in a cast to the shoulder, and his gray eyes had black swollen rings as if someone had beaten him. He looked like a raccoon. When his eyes met Dan's, Ty's mouth stretched into an attempted grin.

"Your mother sent me with a care package." Dan smiled, hoping the physical smile would dispel his black psychological cloud. He got a chair from the other side of the room. "I hope the food and tea aren't too cold. Can you feed yourself?"

"I'm so hungry, I could inhale it." Ty laughed and winced. Using his left hand, he stuffed his mouth with a jiaodze. "Ow . . . it hurts my arm to move."

Dan poured tea and held the cup to Ty's lips while Ty sipped it.

"Maybe I can feed you rice with the chopsticks. Lie still. Have you heard the prognosis yet?"

"The upper arm bone is broken clear through and shattered; about two dozen fragments according to the x-rays. Jesus it hurts. It feels like I just hit my elbow on the funny bone. Ha ha, very funny; God played a nasty joke on me."

"Peasants, so I heard."

"Sometimes I don't think I can stand it without passing out."

Dan sucked air through his teeth. "Are they giving you painkillers?"

"They've given me acupuncture, and at least it stopped me from wanting to scream. The doctors say they need to put in a steel rod to connect the bones. My parents want to fly me back to the States for the operation. Can you imagine having to choose between an operation in a Chinese hospital that doesn't even have anesthetics except for acupuncture . . ."

"Or proper sterilization of instruments," Dan added.

"Or a long hard trip back to the States in agony with your arm being jostled as you're loaded into the baggage compartment?"

"A slight exaggeration." The sunniness of Ty's personality, able to joke even under such duress, cast a beam of light into Dan's inner gloom. "But from what I hear, foreigners in great numbers are fleeing Beijing, so I don't know how easy it would be to get a flight out. They might take a medical emergency first. How about Hong Kong? It would be a shorter trip, and they have top quality medical care there."

"I don't know if my mother would trust any Chinese doctor. She asked to have me put in a private room, and the doctor laughed as if she had just done a pratfall." Ty grimaced, closed his eyes, and moaned. "I wish I could turn on my side. My back is so tired of this position. I've been trying to do as much Qi Gong meditation as I can, and it helps a lot, even if I can't get into the right sitting position. I just visualize it."

Dan shoveled a chopstick load of sticky rice and chicken into Ty's mouth and poured another cup of tea. "I guess that means you went to the Qi Gong master?" Dan asked.

"It was great." Ty swallowed and took another sip of tea. He described what had happened. It was a sitting meditation with visualization and long, slow breathing. Ty had felt intense heat all through his body, and his sweat was so profuse that it stung his eyes, dripped down his face, and soaked his clothing. At the end, he felt as if his legs were lead weights sinking into the ground.

"I don't know that that's healthy." Dan worried for Ty.

"The master said it was all a very good reaction; the sweating was expelling toxins, and the heavy legs were a strong connection with the earth. Well, I *was* raised on a farm. I certainly felt great afterward. The master said I was a very promising student. Now I regret that I'll have to leave. I really wanted to study with him."

Dan was both incredulous and envious. "I've done a Zen meditation for ten years, and nothing like that ever happened to me."

"Qi Gong has the most powerful meditation technique." Ty ate another jiaodze. "I guess I'm missing all the excitement. Have you been to the Bell Tower?"

"Not yet." Dan's anxiety returned with the need to get to a telephone. "I plan to go downtown this afternoon to watch the big demonstration. They expect a hundred thousand."

"Don't get caught between the marchers and the police."

Dan thought of Mingyue and the Inspector. "I'm already caught between them," he said. But he did not explain.

Dan went back to his apartment and called the American Embassy again. He finally got through to someone above the receptionist and explained his problem about being under threat of arrest because of the papers critical of the government.

The voice at the other end of the line moaned. "So give the papers back to your friend."

"They've been confiscated by the police."

"Look," the voice was of an adult chastising a child, "if they didn't arrest you at the time, they're probably not going to. The Chinese are a bit busy with other problems right now, and I doubt that they want to add an international stir to the stew. If they do arrest you, call us. Meanwhile, I suggest you leave the country as soon as possible. That would solve the problem from both the Chinese point of view and from ours."

Dan paused a long moment. He wanted to say, "There's a complication," but he didn't see that mention of hiding a fugitive or that a bargain had been made and broken or that he had no money would help. The Embassy did not loan money.

"Thanks." He could hear the cynicism in his own voice. "I'll call you when I'm put in prison." He hung up. They both knew that the Chinese don't allow phone calls from prison.

The Embassy advice was simply go home. But Dan didn't want to go home. He wrestled with himself. It would be safer to go home. Shouldn't he just cut his losses and run? It wasn't like he expected Yoshiko to return if things calmed down. Or that he had made such great lectures for the next two months that his Chinese students would be deprived of something special if he left early. It wasn't that anyone would think him a coward if he left now. It wasn't even that he would be stranded without dollars from Wu. It occurred to him for the first time that he could fly or take a train to Shenzhen on his Chinese *yuan*, cross the border to Hong Kong, and use his credit cards for a ticket home. None of that was a real reason for staying.

He really didn't want to leave because history was in the making, and he wanted to experience it, to be a witness, to be part of it, not hear about it from a distance. He wanted to live it, not just study it as a scholar. Dan was no daredevil; he had no need for danger. But leaving would be like walking out of a five act play after the first act and going home to read about it. He wanted to be there recording it. And if he could play a small part, and smuggle Gao's papers out, he would be serving history, like the Soviet dissidents struggling against Communism and Latin American dissidents fighting against right-wing dictatorships. Foolish? Maybe but necessary for his self-respect.

On the other hand, he wanted justice from Wu too. He wanted him to honor his agreement so Dan wouldn't feel powerless in Wu's corrupt world. His previous confrontations hadn't produced results. He'd have to do something much more dramatic. All his Marine Corps nature had wanted to attack, but he had forced himself to practice *Wu Wei*, Taoist actionless action, letting go of one's ego, flowing with the situation. It had seemed appropriate to try to be Eastern in an Eastern culture. Now he was disgusted with himself. What do you do when floating with the situation leads you to the top of a waterfall?

The crowd sitting in around the Bell Tower in the center of Xi'an had grown so much that students crouching on their heels or lying down on blankets were bumping elbows and pushing against each other with the slightest twist to stretch cramped muscles or turn over. The stench of bodies unwashed for five days and newcomers' garlic breath mixed with the odors of tobacco smoke and rotting banana peels and dirty wool blankets wet by the morning showers and urine from the pool on the floor of the overwhelmed public slit-trench toilet.

Yingying worried that Mingyue was getting weaker and weaker. He drank small amounts of water but refused even fruit juice. He had not eaten for six days now, and she for four. He staggered when he stood and needed help to walk to the toilet to relieve himself, which was not often. She held his head in her lap and would have been happy to sit that way with him for hours, on the hard concrete in the shade of the Bell Tower, if he weren't dying.

But he was dying. This man she had chosen to be the father of her children was about to extinguish himself, of his own choice, like a candle flame that has burnt too fast, leaving the wax in a big wasted pool. Her own determination was plagued with doubts. Was justice so important if they would have no children to make the sacrifice for? Was justice even as important as just holding him and rocking slightly like a mother comforting her child? Oh, how she would like to be able to make sense of it all. Was it her eyes, or was the day darker than usual, in spite of the cloudless sky, as if candles were going out all over China?

She snuffed up the tears in her nose and wiped the moisture off her cheek. Remembering her father's and mother's coldness brought back that anger that hardened her again. Yes, a pity to end life so soon, but she would do it, too. This corrupt world was too ugly, not worth living in; too cruel for this self-pity.

Nearby, several students from the technical university listened avidly to the radio and made reports over a loudspeaker system they had rigged all around the Bell Tower.

"Zhao Ziyang joined the students in Tiananmen Square yesterday," they announced. "Deng Xiaoping, backed by Premier Li Peng and President Yang Shangkun proclaimed martial law in Beijing today over the strong objections of Zhao Ziyang."

The crowd boiled with a variety of moans, hisses, and hoots. The tensions of anger and fear were as palpable as electric static before a lightning discharge. Yingying heard shouts. "All they want is power and wealth; they don't care about the people," and, "Tyrants!"

The speakers continued. "The Army was called into Beijing but turned away by the people. Soldiers and tanks converged on the city, but steelworkers, grandmothers, children, and students surrounded the troop convoys and formed human barricades to stop them. Busses were placed across the roads to stop the tanks." The crowd around the Bell Tower cheered, jeered at the government leaders, and laughed. Two students slapped each other's backs in self-congratulation.

A hunger striker near Yingying shouted, "A government that uses the people's army against the people is doomed to fall." Those nearby who heard him clapped their hands.

The loudspeaker continued. "Beijing is on general strike. Over one thousand are sitting in here in Xi'an, and we are supported by over a hundred thousand teachers, government workers, peasants, industrial workers, middle school and university students." The shouting and clapping was so loud, it hurt Yingying's ears like firecrackers in New Year.

Medical students went through the crowd offering juice, buns, fruit, and water. Most of the crowd sitting in took at least juice. A medic tried to coax Mingyue to drink juice, but Mingyue didn't speak, put his hand over his mouth, closed his eyes, and lay still. The student took his pulse, shook his head, shrugged, and left. The medic's attitude didn't reassure Yingying.

"I don't want to see you die," she said softly into his ear. "Please take juice. I will too."

He opened his eyes and looked at her with a pained expression, his voice weak and shaky. "I don't want to die either, but that is what makes my death a meaningful sacrifice. It's not easy to leave you. I've never felt so close to anyone. Thank you for being with me."

He closed his eyes and lay still on her lap. She nearly cried, but her grief sat in her chest and clawed to get out.

She remembered that when Professor Norton had talked about a Stoic philosopher, he had said, "What a person is willing to die for tells a lot about that person." He had asked, "What are you willing to die for? We each have to die someday. Doesn't it make sense to make our death meaningful?"

Yingying didn't want to die. She didn't want Mingyue to die. His moment of tenderness had made life worth living again. The world wasn't all ugly. They were young and had most of their lives yet before them.

She remembered how when she was younger, she had been drawn to ancient romantic tales of women who died to save their lovers. Those books had been burned during the Cultural Revolution.

The communists praised women who sacrificed themselves for the People. But the "People" was an abstract idea. If the People were a lot of corrupt individuals cheating each other, why should anyone want to die for them?

Was she sacrificing herself because she hated those people who had burned the books and the birds, destroyed romance, and cheated each other? Was it because those were the people her father served—and she was angry at her father? It made no sense to die out of anger. She wanted to jump to her feet. She had to get out of there. She had to get Mingyue out of there. But the sudden burst of strength drained away, and she couldn't move.

DECEIVED

MAY 20

YINGYING WAS DRAWN OUT OF HER THOUGHTS back to the Bell Tower when the speakers made another announcement.

"There are two hundred thousand people on hunger strike in Beijing, and the Politburo said that it would not tolerate chaos. The police have clubbed Beijing demonstrators." The crowd groaned and murmured angrily. "Zhao Ziyang apologized to the students on TV for the show of force and the slow pace of government response to their demands. Li Peng blamed Zhao on TV for spreading chaos and damaging China's international standing." Laughter rose from the crowd. "Beijing Mayor, Chen Xitong, said soldiers were authorized to take any measures necessary to restore order. Li Peng also blamed students for endangering public health with hunger strikes and sit ins." Strikers around Yingying guffawed and began to chant, "Down with Chen Xitong . . . Down with Li Peng." Yingying joined them and heard Mingyue's weak voice beside her. She wondered if, for all the bravado, others in the crowd were so frightened as she was that the government would react with brutal force in Xi'an soon.

Crowds grew on both sides of the major streets around the Bell Tower in anticipation of the demonstration. Students moved through the hunger strikers passing out glasses of juice and pieces of fruit and baodzes to whoever wanted them. Yingying's head spun with dizziness. For three days, most of her thoughts had been of food. Her mother had never been regarded a good cook, but Yingying longed to go home for her mother's leek and dumpling soup.

Mingyue urged her to eat. "Why should you starve? Eat until I'm arrested. You can start a hunger strike after that. Then your father will arrest you and send you home."

"You're not making sense. Hunger is affecting your mind. And my father would probably let me rot in prison after what I said to him just to teach me a lesson,"

"Regret is worse than hunger. I regret putting my family and Professor Norton in danger. I regret making you suffer. You should eat so I don't suffer your pain too."

"As I suffer yours?" Yingying buried her face in her hands. "If you have nothing but regret, why don't you stop? Why don't you go home?"

"Maybe you won't understand. I feel free. All my life I have thought what the Party thought and done what the Party wanted. I did what my father wanted. Now I am thinking what I want to think and doing what I think is right. Not what my father thinks, not what the Party thinks, not even what the students and workers think; but what I think. I feel free. My body may be hungry. They may put me in prison. But I am free, for the first time, and I won't give that up."

She understood. She hadn't understood it until now, but she felt that way too. She had decided to stay with him. Not her father, not the Party, and not even the students had decided. It was her choice—frightening—but now it had to be, no matter the consequences.

"I do understand." She smiled at him. "Close your eyes. Save your energy."

Yingying wanted to take a baodze and an apple, but she shook her head and took only water. What was hunger compared to the threat of clubs and bullets? But no police or soldiers had been seen for days.

The loudspeakers blared. "We have just heard that the Shaanxi government finally admits that someone was killed in April." The crowd cheered, and Yingying, too, clapped. The Provincial Government had given in to a student demand. Her hopes rose. Maybe the sacrifice was meaningful after all.

The cheering and singing grew louder as the marchers drew nearer, carrying street-wide red and gold banners proclaiming student demands. The rows of marchers filled the street from curb to curb, stirring up clouds of dust like busses. They kept coming, wave after wave, singing, flashing "V" signs. Various industrial work units carried banners identifying themselves, and they represented the major industries in the city. Peasants, teachers, students, and even government workers carried signs against corruption, row after row, column after column. The marchers and hunger strikers cheered each other. The whole center of the city pulsed with an energy of repressed discontent seeking for expression. A million private grudges and resentments lurked like hungry ghosts in the shadows of men's memories. What could the People's Army and People's Police dare to do against the anger of the People?

The shadow of the Bell Tower had shifted away from Mingyue and Yingying, and thousands of pairs of lungs sucked the air. Yingying felt suffocated in the growing press of unwashed bodies sweating in the hot sun.

When the chemical workers had passed, a fellow student nudged Yingying.

"Here come the Shaanxi Teachers University faculty. Mingyue's parents are marching with them."

"Where are they?" Yingying asked.

"His father is the one carrying the sign that says, 'Shaanxi Teachers University faculty support their students,' in English. His mother has stopped marching and is looking at the hunger strikers."

Yingying recognized his father. "Mingyue, wake up." She shook him gently. "You have to see this."

His eyes opened part way.

"Your parents are marching in support of the students."

He strained to sit up and looked at the marchers passing by. His mother left the street and picked her way through the mass of squatting hunger strikers, stepping over many who lay still, looking right and left. She went in the wrong direction, away from Mingyue.

"Help me stand," Mingyue said.

Yingying helped him up and pointed in the direction of his mother. He leaned on Yingying. His father caught up with his wife and pulled on her arm. She shook him off and plunged into the crowd in Mingyue's direction. Mingyue waved. His mother cried out, "Mingyue!"

He collapsed back into a squatting position on his heels. His mother wove her way through the hunger strikers and kneeled beside him. Yingying backed away from her, dizzy from the effort. She had never met his mother before and thought now was not the time; it would only add confusion to the already strained reunion. She would just be one of the crowd. She watched.

Mrs. Gao was short and stout with a broad face and narrow Mongolian eyes. Mingyue had told her that his mother was from Northern Shaanxi Province. Mr. Gao was short and thin with rounder eyes and thick bushy brows, like Mingyue's.

"You look so weak." His mother's face was distorted with fear and grief. She buried her face in his chest. "You must come home now. You've done enough."

He wrapped an arm around her, and his voice cracked. "No, mother."

His father, Gao Baima, stood behind his wife and looked down at his son. "We faculty support the students against corruption now."

Father and son looked at each other with sad eyes that spoke unspoken regrets and hurts. Yingying guessed that the professor wanted to say, "I support you, son. I'm proud of you," but couldn't. Professor Gao took his wife gently under the arm and pulled her to her feet. She clung to Mingyue's hand.

"Command him to come home," she screeched at her husband. "He's your son."

"Don't try to keep him from doing what he must do." He pulled her back toward the marchers. "We've fallen far behind the university faculty already." She wiped her eyes and blew her nose on a handkerchief as they rejoined the demonstration. Yingying wondered how Mingyue must feel, but he laid his head on her lap again and closed his eyes, frowning only slightly.

"I should have introduced you to my mother."

"When this is all over."

Marchers flowed past for another hour. Yingying held Mingyue up, and they sang the Chinese National Anthem and cheered as the supporters streamed by.

The loudspeakers made another announcement. "Li Peng says that student strikes are counter-productive. Zhao Ziyang has offered to resign as Secretary of the Communist Party. The Party has not yet acted on his offer." The crowd of hunger strikers moaned in unison, and their angry murmurs sounded like the growls of a great dragon about to awaken.

One striker near Yingying said to his neighbor, "He has fallen from power."

The crowd began chanting, "We support Zhao Ziyang. We support Zhao Ziyang." The chant spread to the marchers and those watching from the sidewalks. "We support Zhao Ziyang. We support Zhao Ziyang."

When the last marchers had passed and the watching crowd dispersed, leaving behind their debris of cigarette butts and food wrappings, the hunger strikers were left to their dull waiting, discussing the day's events, medical attentions, and sleeping. The afternoon shadows of the Bell Tower and lotus shaped street lamps were long when the single police van pulled up in front of the Bell Tower, and the strikers grew silent and craned their heads to see what might happen. A police officer stepped from the van and announced through a bullhorn, "The Beijing government has made the concessions the Beijing students demanded. The Beijing students' hunger strike has just ended. You can all go home now. All your demands have now been met."

The thousand hunger strikers around the Bell Tower met the announcement with mute disbelief. The police officer repeated himself several times, and the van drove away.

The students on the loudspeaker said that a radio report confirmed that the Beijing students had indeed ended their strike. The crowd cheered and sang a song of victory together. Yingying overheard one of the students who had been listening to the radio wonder to his friends if it was true since he hadn't heard anything on the air from Beijing about government concessions. His friends argued that the Beijing students wouldn't have ended their strike, and the Shaanxi government wouldn't have given in to the local student demands to admit that someone had been killed in April if the Beijing government hadn't already made the other concessions.

Yingying wondered if they should be so willing to believe a corrupt government. But the hunger strikers were already beginning to disperse. In spite of her doubts, she felt energized by the apparent victory. The sky, even so close to dusk, seemed brighter again. She breathed deeper.

Mingyue finally agreed to drink peach juice, and they both sipped it slowly. They soon had stomach aches and lay down again. Yingying held his head on her lap. It struck her that she had her man back again. They wouldn't die. The reprieve had come just in time. They could have both justice and life. Tears of relief rolled down her cheek.

"We won," Mingyue mumbled, eyes closed. "The people stood up for justice and won."

"You stood for justice and won." She grinned at him. "You forced the government to admit it lied about the deaths in April. It was your idea and your leadership. I'm proud of you."

Mingyue opened his eyes and looked at her. "We won. I would not have had the courage without you at my side. I've never been so happy." He reached up and held his hand on her cheek a moment, then dropped it by his side. "I'm so weak."

Almost all the students had left, and the trash of fruit peels, plastic bags, protest placards, empty water bottles and cigarette butts littered the sidewalk like debris from a battlefield. Yingying worried how she and Mingyue would get home. They were too weak to walk the four miles back to the university. And they would not be able to push and shove their way onto a crowded bus. She had never taken a taxi cab before. It would be outrageously expensive, and they were rare except at the airport and tourist hotels. Also, she had only enough in her pocket for bus fare. No, a taxi was out of the question. Mingyue leaned on her as she helped him to the curb to cross the street. She leaned on him as much as he on her. They were both exhausted, and she had no idea how they would get home. Wait until after the evening rush hour, perhaps. When an empty cab came by, she hailed it down on an impulse.

"Where you want to go?" The driver stared forward at the street.

"The Teachers University," Yingying said, wondering if she could borrow the fare from a classmate.

"Wrong way. I work the Golden Flower Hotel and airport for tourists. More money." The driver leered at her and shoved his gear shift into first.

"Are there still tourists in Xi'an?" She didn't like her own mocking tone.

The cab lurched forward twenty feet and stopped. The driver stuck his head out the window. "What's wrong with your friend?" Mingyue was doubled over holding his stomach. The cab backed up, and the driver looked Mingyue up and down.

"Hunger striker. No food or juice for six days."

The driver peered at Yingying. "You too?"

She nodded. "Four days."

"Get in."

They arrived outside the dorms.

Yingying was frightened when the driver told her the price of the ride. She helped Mingyue stand, and he swayed. She said she had to go inside to get some money. The driver laughed and waved her away.

"We workers support your cause." He drove off

Yingying held Mingyue's arm as they climbed the stairs to his parent's apartment. Mingyue's mother opened the door and gasped.

"Mingyue! Mingyue!" Her voice quivered, and she grasped his arm and pulled him in the door, leaving Yingying standing outside in the shadows. "My son." She reached to pull the door shut.

Mingyue staggered back against the door and held it open. "Mother, this is Yingying. She helped me home. She's a hunger striker too."

Mrs. Gao looked at Yingying with a side glance that seemed to ask the question, is she just a fellow hunger striker or something more to him?

"Yes," his mother said. "You come in too. I'll get you both some soup. Maybe *baodzes*. Nothing too heavy or spicy for people coming off a fast." She seated Mingyue and Yingying on the couch and bustled into the kitchen.

Mingyue's father sat in an armchair tapping his hand on the arm and looked at the couple without expression. "The Inspector will come to arrest you."

Mingyue shifted his position in his seat several times and stared at his hands. Yingying wondered how Professor Gao could be so cold.

Just like her own father. The atmosphere seemed as oppressive as at the Bell Tower.

"We heard on the local radio that the strike had ended," Mrs. Gao said. "We hoped you would be home tonight. Don't eat too fast, or it will make you sick."

They turned on the television while Mingyue and Yingying ate. The newscasters said that over a million demonstrators had marched in Beijing, three hundred thousand in Xi'an, a quarter million in Shanghai, and thousands in every provincial capital.

The TV cameras showed pictures of a copy of the Statue of Liberty that had been made by Shanghai protesters and of helicopters flying over Beijing announcing martial law to thick crowds of people below.

"I think the people are winning," Mr. Gao said. "Surely the government will give in now and change its ways."

The television reported that Zhao Ziyang had disappeared, and his whereabouts were unknown. The rest of the Politburo was determined to stop the violence.

"What violence?" Mrs. Gao asked. "The demonstrations have been peaceful. The government wants an excuse to act."

The local news also said that martial law was expected in Xi'an tomorrow.

"They have threatened much and done nothing for weeks," said Mrs. Gao. "Who will believe them?"

"At least your family supports the students," Yingying said quietly in Mingyue's ear. "You're lucky. My father . . . running dog of the regime . . ."

Yingying felt a strange mixture of fear, anger, and hope about the political situation. She didn't know what to feel about the unresolved tension between Mingyue and his father.

Mingyue said he was feeling stronger and would walk Yingying back to her student dormitory.

"No. You're too weak yet," she said. "I should walk you to the medical ward for a checkup. We can both get one."

"No. It's too late. I have to talk to you." He walked her down the stairs leaning his arm on the wall with each step. "I want to hold you in my arms," he said. "I'll miss you tonight, after four nights side by side."

"We'd be reported." She backed away from him, wanting more than ever to rush into his embrace. "I have to go. You need to talk to your father."

"I want to tell my parents that I love you and am going to marry you," Mingyue said.

"Shouldn't you ask me first?" she laughed.

He pulled her into the shadows of a locked doorway and held her in his arms. "Will you marry me?"

Her heart raced and she hugged him tightly, dizzy and weak-kneed. "Yes."

Their lips almost met when passing eyes startled her. She jerked back and pushed him away. Perhaps in the new openness they wouldn't be reported. It had almost been their first kiss. Her lips tingled. He crumpled onto the bottom stair. She worried that she had pushed him too hard.

"Are you all right?"

He grunted. The passerby was a classmate. She stopped and turned to Yingying.

"Have you heard? Eleven students have immolated themselves in Xi'an, and three hundred in Beijing. The hunger strikes in Beijing are growing larger in spite of martial law."

Mingyue leaped to his feet and swayed like a palm tree in a storm. Even in the dim porch light, Yingying saw that his face was red.

"The hunger strikes are continuing in Beijing?" He staggered. His eyes were as big as jade pi disks, and his mouth hung open.

The classmate nodded. Mingyue collapsed back onto the stairs and held his head between his hands as if to keep it from exploding. His voice trembled. "The government lied to us. They tricked us . . . again. The people will be twice as angry now."

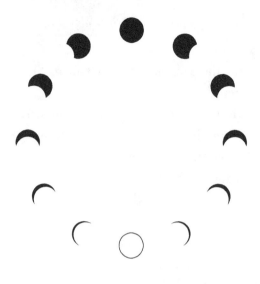

MAJOR DECISIONS

MAY 22

THE CHEERFUL OLD COBBLER SQUATTED ON THE sidewalk outside the university and cut up old truck tires to make shoe soles. He'd done a good job repairing Dan's shoes, even if they did feel a bit weird at first being an inch thicker than before. What the well-attired man wears in China, Dan thought. Now maybe I can burn rubber and make a fast getaway when they come to arrest me. He grinned at his bad puns.

Dan stopped at a small university sundries store. After eight months of looking everywhere for decent chocolate, finding one kind with a texture of sand held together by a thin coating of something brown resembling mud, then another that had the consistency of wax and no taste, he had finally found a chocolate bar that tasted like chocolate. Given Yoshiko's departure and the threat of arrest, Dan needed something to cheer him up after cutting back on his beer intake. But chocolate as an alcohol substitute was still an addiction.

The store only had five bars and would not be likely to have any more for months. The saleswoman refused to sell them all to Dan, since then she wouldn't have any for her other customers. Dan knew that, unlike in a capitalist store, the point in a communist store seemed not to be to sell but to show one's power over the customer. The saleswoman would get her salary whether she sold anything or not. Perhaps she was proud to have something of quality in stock for a change. But as a chocoholic, he persisted in arguing with her until she sold him three bars. He stepped out the door with the hard-won fruits of his victory in his pocket, wondering how the government would react to the demonstrations he had watched two days before, when he saw a taxicab with Ty in it pass through the front gate of the university. It couldn't be. He blinked and looked again. He was sure it was Ty, by himself. The cab disappeared around the corner.

Dan wondered what Ty was doing out of the hospital. Had Dan seen a cast on Ty's arm in the cab? He didn't think so. He hurried across campus to the foreign guests' compound and ran up the stairs. The door to the Bates' apartment stood open, and loud voices came from within. The flab on Mrs. Bates' arms quivered as she flapped them like a bird stuck in mud.

"But I saw the x-ray," Mrs. Bates shouted, her round face drained of blood and white as a full moon. "The bone was shattered."

Mr. Bates waved to Dan to come in. His jowls stood like sentries on either side of a massive jaw holding up a pudgy nose. With his gothic-arched eyebrows, it was a face that could frighten a congregation into weeping for Jesus. Ty stood in the living room with no cast.

"Believe me, I'm cured," Ty said. "The Qi Gong master visited me last night and projected his *qi* into my arm. I could feel it healing. Afterward, I took off the cast. Look, I can move it. No pain." He raised his arm over his head, held it out to the side, and flexed his muscle. "This morning, the doctors took another x-ray and said the bone is completely healed with no sign of a break."

"It's that out-of-date Chinese x-ray machine," Mr. Bates said. His bad breath reached out to Dan halfway across the room. "The pictures were probably inaccurate the first time."

"Or mixed up with someone else's," Dan added.

"You just had a bad sprain," Mr. Bates said.

"I know the bone was shattered, and I know the master healed it," Ty said. "If Jesus could heal . . . and the Bible says that many others could too in his day . . . it was not unusual—"

"Do you dare compare Jesus with some Chinese, voodoo, witch doctor con artist?" Mrs. Bates stepped back from her son with eyes the size of half-dollars, looking as if her son had just sprouted a pair of horns and cloven hooves. "It must be the devil's work."

"Voodoo? I think you have the wrong continent," Dan said. Then again, he suspected all paganism probably looked the same to her.

"The devil's work? Is the devil a healer? Is healing evil? I can't doubt the pain I felt. I can't doubt the soothing warmth I felt and the tingling, like worms burrowing through my arm as the master healed it. I think I can tell good from evil. Why can't you believe that my experience is as valid as . . . But what good would it do to argue with you about the *Bible*?" He slumped.

Mrs. Bates folded her hands in prayer, closed her eyes, and bowed her head. "Dear Lord, protect my son from this evil. Help him to repent his sinful thoughts . . ." Her prayer softened to a mumble. Mr. Bates joined in with his lower-pitched rumble.

At first it seemed a gentle form of coercion, but Dan realized it had the threat of Hell behind it.

"Hey, I thought you'd be happy," Ty said, "that I was no longer in pain . . . that I was healed. Or maybe you'll be more pleased to consider how much money this is going to save you. You always did care more about money than about my life. Money and faith; faith and money." His face contorted with grief and anger for a brief instant, and he banged both fists down on the table. "I don't need any more of your bullshit!"

His parents looked up from their prayers, mouths agape.

"If you don't like what I've said so far, get a load of this. I can't take any more of your hypocritical God-talk—all fear and hate. What's that to do with God? I'm leaving the church and going to study with a Chi Gong master."

Wow, Dan thought. Now that's a breakthrough.

His parents stood like portraits of a couple hit by cattle prods as he walked out the front door.

—————

Mingyue and Yingying had rested two nights from their ordeal. Now they had the gazebo in the university garden to themselves, and they sat side by side and argued about what they should do next. Yingying wanted to go back and begin the hunger strike again. She would join the strike to the death. She was angrier at the government and her father than she'd ever been. They were the same thing to her, emotionally.

"They've shoved their torches into the beehive," she shouted, "and the bees will be angry and sting them!"

"Not if the smoke is strong enough to quell them," Mingyue retorted coolly. "The government made fools of us with their lie. We were naïve. Who would take our strike seriously the second time? Besides, now we've eaten. We will be starting all over again, and our previous effort was for nothing, We must admit that we've failed."

"That's what they're counting on," she said. "That we will be discouraged and give up. But I'm sure more people will have been angered by such a blatant lie. It proves the government's corruption and undemocratic nature. It proves that they deceive and manipulate the people. Even more will be willing to join us now."

"The government is corrupt and undemocratic? Will that surprise anyone? I've thought about it while I was fasting," he said. "If the strike goes on long enough so that lives are in danger, they only have to tie us down and feed us intravenously with sugar solution. No one will be allowed to die unless they want us to die. They have more information and brute force than we do, and it will be their choice whether or not to let us die, depending on whether it will benefit them or not. I don't want to give them that choice."

"Have you become cowardly after your earlier bravery?" She sneered and turned her back on him.

"Wisdom is what you get by learning from your foolishness. I hope I have learned something."

That was too much for her. He had gone mushy like rotten fruit. "I'll do what has to be done myself. You can hide in fear if you want." She faced him again and glowered, spitting some of her rage at him. "Coward!"

"I have in mind a more dramatic and final action that can't be co-opted so easily." He spoke gently, sadly. "I want to keep the choice to die, and when, in my own hands. You told me what Professor Norton said about Jean-Paul Sartre. That suicide is the ultimate act of freedom. I'll make it a freedom they can't steal from me."

Yingying was frightened by his resigned tone of voice. "What are you saying? Suicide?" Mingyue slumped. Yingying wanted to shake him. She stood up, hands on hips, and faced him. "What do you mean? You're not making sense."

"Maybe I shouldn't tell you. I don't want you involved."

"Who sat with you at the hunger strike? How can I not be involved? You tell me."

He looked away from her. "I'm going to immolate myself tomorrow."

Yingying gasped, terrified. She didn't want to lose him so soon. She didn't want him to suffer. "In the hunger strike, I didn't really expect us to die. It was to force the government to change, for our future, for our children. We won't have any children if you die."

"I don't want to leave you." He choked. "It's the fear of losing you that's the pain. So I'll get it over with fast. No time for regret."

"You'll leave me with all the regret." But she had called him a coward, and now it was she who was cowardly. She couldn't have it both ways. And he was right, a hunger strike was a threat that might or might not reach its terrible and unthinkable conclusion. One hoped the enemy would give in and one could bask in the glory of victory. It was a gamble with death. But immolation did not depend on the enemy's reaction. It was a self-contained, self-controlled act of refusal. It was so . . . final.

Her anger turned to guilt for having doubted him. She should have remembered that her classmate, Lili, had called her a coward when she wasn't. She took his hand in hers and fell silent for a long time. She trembled as she remembered ancient heroines who had killed themselves.

"I'll do it, too, as long as we can die together. We'll find our personal freedom in the struggle for the freedom of the people. We'll be heroes of the people. That will give our lives meaning." She pressed her body against his and leaned her head on his shoulder.

"I'd rather if you could live . . . so you could tell people about me. Then my sacrifice would live in the future. If we both die, we may be forgotten."

"I couldn't be happy without you. The students will remember us. They'll tell their children about us as heroic lovers." She sobbed, feeling his hot tears flow down her cheek and mingle with her own. "Tonight will be our last night. Let's at least spend it together."

Mingyue and Yingying searched the university construction storage yard and found a can of kerosene and hid it behind a bush. Since it would raise suspicions if they carried the can across half the city to the Bell Tower, they decided that they would perform the drama on the staircase in front of the University Administration Building.

They ate in the student dining hall with several other students from the coordinating committee and asked for the latest news about the immolations.

"The rumors of people immolating themselves in Xi'an are false," a student leader said. "But we hear that two hundred tried in Beijing, and eleven succeeded."

"Is it so difficult to immolate oneself that so many failed?" Mingyue asked.

"Firemen sprayed them," the student said.

"Then one must not announce one's intentions publicly ahead of time," Mingyue said. "But someone here in Xi'an should do it in support of the Beijing students." He looked at Yingying.

She was overcome with grief at the thought of what would happen tomorrow and ran outside and waited for Mingyue under a tree. She hugged the tree and cried. She didn't want to let go of life. She didn't want to let go of Mingyue. It was not so much fear of dying, or of the pain, but of ending a love with Mingyue that had only just begun and in normal times would have gone on for a lifetime. It was a Chinese curse: "May you be born in interesting times."

She wished that she had a soul and that the ancient tales of lovers living on as ghosts were true. But her communist education had mocked the ancient superstitions. Communism said nothing about the death of an individual. The individual was nothing; the working class was everything. What is the working class but a community of working individuals? If the individual is nothing, then so is the group of individuals. Was it enough to die for the working class? She had doubts about what she had pledged to do out of love and anger. She shivered in the heat of the evening, as if all her *qi* were dispersing into the universe already, liberated into the greater flow of energy. That wasn't what she wanted.

Mingyue walked with her, hand in hand, in spite of peoples' stares as they passed. It was all right for boys to walk hand in hand with boys or girls with girls, but it was taboo for men and women to show signs of affection in public. It was their last night together, let someone report them, it wouldn't matter. Yingying felt a thrill to defy the taboo. Her courage came back. Even more scandalous, she had taken a blanket from her bed, and Mingyue carried it under his arm. She had lost all fear. Now they would both be leaders and heroes.

They went back to the storage yard where they had seen a truck loaded with sand. They climbed up on the truck and dug a nest in the dune. The night would be warm enough that they could lie on the blanket and look up at the stars. It was a rare clear night. Yingying had never seen the stars so bright. They lay close to each other, silent.

She looked at his face, watching the sky, and smelled a vague hint of soap on his skin. She remembered how the odors of his unwashed body had repelled and, at the same time, excited her. She brushed her hand through his thick black hair.

The thought that it was their last night together overwhelmed her. She rolled over on to him and kissed him hard on the lips. Defiantly. But after all those years of repression, she expected something marvelous. It didn't feel special at all. Just his hard teeth against her hard teeth. In disappointment and resignation, she let go of the tension, and so did Mingyue.

They held their lips together, soft now, moving slightly, exploring. She felt his tongue on her upper lip and pulled away, repulsed. He looked puzzled and hurt.

Her lips throbbed. She licked their moistness and lost her repulsion. She probed his lips with her tongue. The whole world condensed to two pairs of lips and two tongues. Their breath became one.

She felt suffocated. She was breathing fast. She pulled back from his lips and put her cheek to his. They lay still and she felt her ear warm to his fast breaths. She dared to pull his hand to her breast. He rubbed it softly, and the nipple rose hard to his touch. He rubbed faster until his touch pinched her and she drew away. It all seemed to be going wrong.

She sobbed and bathed him in her tears. He held her gently.

"Perhaps we should just lie arm in arm and go to sleep," she said.

He nodded and looked down as if he had been defeated. They lay still awhile, and she almost fell asleep, but her arm began to tingle under his head from the circulation being cut off by his weight. She pulled her arm from under him and he looked at her with sad eyes. She rolled over against him and kissed him tenderly, aware again that this was their last night.

Unfamiliar sensations tingled in the depths of her belly. A flow of *qi* between them? A hollow hunger she had never known. She knew it was forbidden. But should the normal taboos stop her when she was about to die for the people?

She opened Mingyue's shirt and lay her cheek on his chest. She caressed his chest muscles and felt their tension. She kissed the sweat on his neck. His brown eyes were wide, and he looked frightened . . . confused. But he looked into her eyes, and his expression softened.

"It is a sad joy," she said, "that in choosing death, we have come alive."

"I was just thinking something similar," he replied. "As our time for love is a thousand-fold shortened, my love for you is a thousand times as intense."

The words thrilled her as they resonated with her own feeling. "Our chosen fate is a merciful cruelty," she said.

His eyes were her eyes now; his thoughts hers. Perhaps the myths were true—their souls touched.

He moved his hand down her back, across her hip, down her leg, up to her belly, and ever so slowly, as if he expected her to stop him, along the skin under her slacks, further down. Waves of *qi* flowed from his hand to her belly and up and down her body. She unbuttoned the buttons, clumsy in her hurry. She pulled her slacks down and off her feet. Mingyue stripped off his own.

They lay back down, but the urgency was gone. They lay still again, trembling.

She felt his leg muscles against hers, and the tingle came back stronger. She put his hand back on her belly. He slid his fingers gently into her pubic hair. It took time for him to explore, for it was unknown territory to her as well as to him—the fluids and unfamiliar scents. She closed her eyes and gave in to her need. *Qi* energy flowed between them, binding them as one pulsating form. Excitement expanded to fill her whole consciousness. He opened the hidden gate to regions of delight she had not imagined. He moved deep inside her, into the mysterious craving at the center of her being.

Now he was where he belonged; he had come home to her.

It was a blur of unfamiliar tingling, tension, shivering, sweating, panting, moaning, joy. She stifled her screams lest the outside world interfere. The pent up passion she knew for the first time spilled over its dam . . . again and again, late into the night . . . until, the reservoir spent, blissful sleep claimed them arm in arm, as if their plan for tomorrow were but an abstraction.

IMMOLATION

MAY 23

DAN HEARD A KNOCK AT THE DOOR. WHEN HE opened it, Mr. and Mrs. Bates stood on the doormat staring at him. It was the first time in the many months they had been in Xi'an that they had come to Dan's apartment. They greeted each other, awkwardly and uneasily. Mr. Bates wiped his feet as if he had walked through mud crossing the breezeway from his own apartment.

Dan ushered them into the living room.

Mr. Bates, short and three feet from port to starboard, sidled into Dan's armchair, snug as a swollen foot crammed into a tight shoe. Mrs. Bates occupied most of the sofa.

"Can I get you anything to drink? I have *qi shui*."

Mrs. Bates wrinkled her nose and shook her head.

"That's all the Chinese ever serve. If I have any more *qi shui*, I think I'll burst."

The picture in his mind of Mrs. Bates bursting in his living room made Dan want to laugh. It would certainly add a badly needed splash of color. There was an awkward silence.

"Did you hear about the Russian student?" Mrs. Bates blurted. "Boris something-or-other-ski was sent home because of an affair with a Chinese student? I told my husband this was no place to bring our son. The evil influences. Those godless Russians and Chinese . . ."

Dan wondered if she included him on her list of the godless. "Yes. It's just as objectionable to the Chinese as it is to you."

"But they have such different values," Mrs. Bates said. "Did you hear that a Chinese woman told the Australian couple that they should have tied a board to their daughter Kimberly's head when she was a baby, like the Chinese do, to make it flat in back? Then she wouldn't have such an ugly, round head. She actually said it. 'Ugly!' Right there in front of the child. That poor beautiful child's feelings . . . can you imagine what she would look like, with her long blond hair and . . ."

Dan was sure the couple had come about their son. He leaned forward and cleared his throat. "How's Ty?"

"That's what we came to ask you," Mr. Bates said. "Do you know where he went? He didn't come home last night, and . . . with a broken arm and all that . . . He's never done anything like that before. We're worried." Dan shook his head.

"We've reported it to Wu Yaoqian," Mrs. Bates said, "but he says one night away is nothing to be concerned about. The man just doesn't want to be bothered."

"I suppose he's a bit busy, what with the student demonstrations, sending so many foreigners home, being a police informant and what not." Dan wondered what he was doing, appearing to defend Wu, even if ironically. "No, I don't know where Ty went."

Mrs. Bates raised her eyebrows and cast him the kind of look that suggested he had passed gas, and she was trying to appear to ignore it. Her self-righteousness irritated him.

"He is of legal age to make his own decisions, of course."

Mrs. Bates puffed up like an indignant blowfish. "We're a close family—"

Dan regretted his gratuitous dig. "I'm sorry I'm not much help. You could go downtown and report it to the police yourself. They'd probably like a diversion from wondering when the political fan is going to blow the excrement their way."

"We've already done it," Mr. Bates said, red in the face, "and got the same response as from Mr. Wu." He stood up.

Dan escorted them out the door. It must be my antipathy to the arrogance of dogma, Dan thought. I can't respect a religion based on *schadenfreude*—taking joy in other people's suffering. They gloat that they are going to Heaven while everyone else will be condemned to eternal Hell by their petty all-too-human vengeful God. But I shouldn't have been so flippant with their justifiable concern for a son. I've let the strain of events get to me. I won't let it get under my skin again.

After lunch, Dan sat with Gao in the gazebo in the university gardens. A tree in front of them rained purple blossoms Dan didn't recognize.

"Look, Gao," Dan said. "With the new openness of the press, a lot of what was in your notes has been made public. I don't think it can be called espionage anymore."

"No one will dare talk about the prisons or organ harvesting yet." Gao slouched on the bench. "And how long will the press be free? Deng Xiaoping has already stripped Zhao Ziyang of his powers and only left him with the empty title of Party Secretary."

"Then I suppose the power struggle is over and the students have lost," Dan said. "But I don't understand how Deng has so much power. His only official title is Head of the Military Commission, while I thought Party Secretary was the highest position."

"Power in China is not in titles," Gao shook his head. "It's in connections. Zhao has support of two of the five members of Standing Committee of Politburo, and Zhao and Deng are struggling for vote of another member."

"That would give Zhao a majority," Dan said. "So it's not hopeless after all."

"I don't know," Gao said. "Most people don't like Deng and Li Peng and many people support the students. The People's Daily supports Zhao over Deng. Many soldiers and top military leaders support the students. So maybe Deng doesn't control the Army. Even the National People's Congress is gathering support to stop martial law."

"And they're usually a rubber stamp organization for Deng," Dan said. "So maybe things are going Zhao's way."

"It's too early to tell." Gao sighed. "Each of the top leaders has powerful connections in the Army. Family loyalties are still more important in China than ideology, even after all those years of Communism."

"That's scary. I knew morality had been thrown out the window by Marxism. And I could understand genuine disagreement about what's best for China. But you're saying what's best for China is irrelevant? You mean China's fate depends on which families just happen to have the strongest connections?" My fate, he thought.

Gao nodded. "Some Army commanders say they will not act against the patriotic students. Others say they must keep the public order."

"They disguise selfish interests in abstract platitudes." It had never been so clear to Dan that ideals are so often just a façade for deeper motives.

"Tanks and trucks full of soldiers are moving toward Beijing. Thousands of troops are moving into the city by way of subway tunnels," Gao said.

Dan shivered at the image that arose in his mind of thousands of rats with submachine guns strapped to their backs scurrying through sewer tunnels toward Tiananmen Square. His skin tingled like it once had just before a nearby lightning strike. It was like a great meaningless force of nature building up; like a heartless, mindless hurricane or a flood that would sweep all innocent life away, as had happened time after time throughout Chinese history. But it was directed by minds, the minds of men driven by lust for power, greed, maybe fear. And the students, the cream of Chinese society and its best hope for the decent future, were at risk.

***

Yingying's dream of floating on a cloud with Mingyue shattered. She awoke to the first hint of dawn. The dull metallic gray overcast brought her back to fear; to the social reality of harsh injustice and their angry defiance. She knew what it was to burn herself. She had often burned her fingers cooking. And once, she had spilled hot cooking oil on her leg. That had peeled her skin and hurt for months. But this pain would not last for months. Seconds? A minute or two? Could she even imagine what it would be for that agony to spread all over her body, for even a few minutes?

But students had done it in Beijing, monks in Vietnam. Could she and Mingyue have really decided to immolate themselves? It seemed so unlikely, so abstract, and so unreal. Having loved as they had loved was like being thrown into a fantasy world. She had been cast as the heroine of a Chinese Opera and Mingyue as the hero; a world she had always longed for when her life seemed bitter and meaningless. Reality sometimes seemed unlivable; only the poetic was worth living. Here beside her lay the delicious forbidden lover. Out there lurked the cruel deniers of love, of self-worth, of life, the enemy who must be defied at the risk of all that was precious, or all that was precious would surely be lost. The Opera must end in the ennobling tragedy that raised the heroine above the mundane. She must play the heroine with courage. She must conquer fear with the repressed noble sentiments that bubbled up from her memory.

Mingyue stirred.

"Unfair morning! Let the sweet night return that was ours alone," she whispered in his ear. "How quickly the dreaded dawn came, this dawn that announces our dusk. I wish that the night had never ended. Dawn whisks us to our eternal night that separates us forever."

"I'm sorry I put you in this situation," Mingyue muttered. "You go home. I'll do it myself. I love you too much to want you to waste your life as I have wasted mine."

"No." She caressed his cheek. "We will just go to another deep sleep, arm in arm. For if death is but an eternal unknowing sleep, we'll never know separation. For I could never again be able to stand separation from you. Separation is a death we never need to know. We won't know anything but today together. And if the old tales are true, we'll tumble through space, locked arm in arm, as ghosts forever."

She lay beside him, his warm arm wrapped around her neck, her hand on his slow heartbeat. This was it, the whole middle of their love—what most couples spend forty or fifty years working out—in an eternal instant. It was appreciation as much as grief that made the tears flow and tickle her ears. She wanted it to go on and on, perfect like this; the slow rhythm of his breathing, the roar of the morning traffic beyond the wall, the silence that absorbed that roar in the peacefulness of the storage yard, the firmness of the sand under the blanket, the cool morning air. But immolation or not, it would come to an end.

Every life is an empty illusion, a dream that ends tragically with death. What does it matter when? This moment would have to be enough for the body, whose every moment is only the now; immolation would fulfill the spirit.

The mere decision to do it had burned away her anger at her father and brought her peace with the world. And now that Mingyue would be taken from her, by their own choice, how he had become a part of her. Their oneness became real in the shadow of total loss.

They ate at the student dorms, keeping away from the other students. Yingying felt numb and mechanical, and the ordinary activity of students making posters, leaving campus to join the daily demonstrations with the expectation that they had a future, expected to be alive tomorrow, could smile and joke, all seemed unreal to her, as if she were watching it in a movie. How could they be happy when the world was so dim? She wondered how many of them would remember her or care what she had done a year from now. For her, there was no year from now.

Mingyue's voice seemed for a moment to come from a long distance away. It startled her.

"I want you to live," he said quietly, so no one could overhear. "For one to die will be as good as two. And you can make them remember me. Will you live to keep my memory alive? To make sure the government does not hide the truth?"

"Are you discouraged so quickly? So quickly you want to separate us? What kind of life would a life of grief be . . . without you?" she asked. "We will die together. We can write letters to our friends, parents, government leaders, explaining why we did it. If we die arm in arm in a crowd of students, they will not forget."

She didn't want to be separated from him. But she wasn't just doing it for him. She was also being a bit selfish; she wanted to be a hero too.

Mingyue nodded, resignation and regret in his eyes. But not just for himself. She knew it was also for her. It made her love him all the more.

First they went to Yingying's room. It was forbidden, but no one stopped them. They made a small poster saying, "We support student demands." Then they went to the post office and bought paper, stamps, and envelopes and spent the rest of the morning writing letters, explaining the reasons for student anger and for their action, to Deng Xiaoping, Li Peng, their families, and a dozen friends.

The government defies the will of the people and has lost the Mandate of Heaven. We sacrifice ourselves for the common good. May the flames that consume our bodies purify your heart and call you to action in harmony with the needs of the Chinese people. Remember us, and our death will not be in vain.

After they mailed the letters, they walked hand in hand. He carried the can of kerosene and she, the poster. Eyes turned, but no one stopped them. They propped the poster up on the cement steps of the Administration Building and sat down. Mingyue took a box of matches from his pocket, put it beside the poster, and unscrewed the cap on the kerosene can. Yingying sat beside him and held his arm.

Two dozen students gathered around Mingyue and Yingying to watch at a discreet distance. A student Yingying recognized from the coordinating committee ran up to them. Mingyue held the can up to pour the liquid death over his head.

"Stop!" The student shouted and cringed back from them. Mingyue lowered the can. "The rumors are false," the student said. "No one has immolated himself, either here or in Beijing."

Mingyue sat unmoving for a few moments. Yingying wondered if he would change his mind.

"There will be immolations now," Mingyue spoke calmly. "Xi'an will lead the way to justice and democracy."

"Then wait until I find a camera," the student said. "The government will deny it ever happened if we don't have proof." He ran off toward the student dormitories.

Mingyue paused. He spoke to the crowd in general. "Someone may come and try to stop us if we wait."

He lifted the can again and tipped it. Yingying wrapped her arms around him. The gathering students jostled each other stepping back. The cold liquid splashed on her head, and she shut her stinging eyes. The strong smell made her dizzy and nauseous. Mingyue kept pouring, and the cold soaked into her clothing. It will not be cold for long, she thought, and shivered. He poured the liquid over his own shoulders and legs.

A loud crackling sound, like the fake thunder in the opera, and Mingyue's sudden lurch forward startled her, and her eyes opened in spite of the intense stinging. The can bounced down the stairs spilling its contents and students tripped over each other to get out of the way. She turned to see her father wipe kerosene off his shoe with a handkerchief. He stuffed the handkerchief into his pocket. Kerosene soaked one trouser leg.

"Come with me, you two hoodlums. You're under arrest." He grabbed Mingyue and Yingying each by an arm and pulled them through the main door of the Administration Building.

"You stupid children!" The Inspector shouted. "What do you think you're doing? You could ruin everything. This struggle is for adults. I've done everything I could to keep you two out of trouble, and you keep going right back to it. Well get this through your thick skulls. You're fools if you're under the romantic illusion that your self-immolation would change anything." He pushed Mingyue and Yingying into a small office and closed the door behind them. "The government controls the media. Troops have occupied the offices of the People's Daily, Xinhua News Agency, and the Central TV Station. Openness in reporting has just ended, and the people would not even hear of your sacrifice."

He lighted a cigarette and looked at them with a smirk. Yingying shivered under her father's stare, her eyes teared in agony, and she gagged on the kerosene fumes.

"I heard that Deng Xiaoping was on his way to visit relatives in Wuhan," the Inspector said. "The trip was supposed to be a secret.

But students surrounded the train at Wuhan bridge and won't let Deng off. Now that could change things. Unified action, not isolated individual action. The students must have been told by someone high in the government. You see, it's a complex game of chess, and players who act on their own don't count."

He paced the room and puffed at his cigarette like a runaway railroad locomotive. Yingying was puzzled. Was her father saying what she thought he was saying? Perhaps he could tell that the tide had turned against Deng now, and he wanted to position himself on the winning team. It did not please her that he might be on her side now; it would just mean the forces for freedom and justice would be corrupted.

"You would be more effective alive and working with the student organizing committee," he said. "You can tell them you were under arrest and warned to give up your political activity. But continue it, of course. We could exchange useful information from time to time."

So that's it. Now he wants us to spy for the government, she thought. She looked at Mingyue. He just stared wide-eyed at his feet, as if he were already dead. His clothing dripped kerosene onto the floor. Kerosene dripped from her father's pants leg. She too was soaked, and the fumes made her cough.

"I think you'd better put out that cigarette, father, or all three of us may yet go up in flames."

She laughed hysterically.

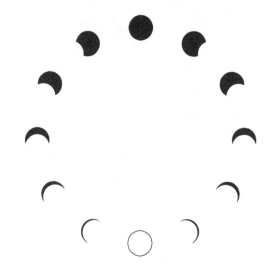

BELLY OF THE DRAGON

MAY 29

DAN FELT SORRY FOR MR. AND MRS. BATES, EVEN IF he didn't like them. They had informed the police. Of course, with the student unrest, Dan was sure the police were too busy to concern themselves about one missing son. On the other hand, the Chinese were always good hosts and paid special attention to the problems of foreigners. If the squeaky wheel always gets the grease, Mrs. Bates would get lots of grease. There was probably not much that Dan could do to help; they would find more comfort in Jesus.

And then, what should he do about the Inspector's threat? Should he squeeze his money out of Wu and leave or just stay calm and let things run their course? After all, tensions were easing in China. Forty people had been injured in a rock and brick throwing brawl between soldiers and peasants, but the army had withdrawn from three locations on the outskirts of Beijing and top military leaders openly criticized martial law. More people went to work in Beijing as barricades came down and some public bus lines were running again. Zhao Ziyang was reported to have returned to his office, and his support seemed to be increasing as pro-democracy demonstrations had spread to Shenzhen on the border with Hong Kong.

Dan saw that a letter had been slid under his front door and picked it up. From Japan. Yoshiko had only been gone for nine days and had already sent a letter. He tore it open. It was in Chinese.

Dear Professor Norton:

On the airplane I realized that I did not leave only because of political unrest. I must tell you my true feelings. Please excuse a long story.

My father was Chinese, orphaned by a flood. He became a Buddhist monk, and his temple was destroyed by the Japanese during the war. He joined Mao's army in the mountains of southern China and pulled a cannon like an ox through mud and over snowy mountain passes and through desert for three thousand miles during the Long March. In northern China he was wounded and captured by the Japanese. As a prisoner he was made a servant of a high Japanese officer who was a Buddhist. When the officer found out that my father had been a monk, they became friends. The officer took my father to Nagasaki when the Japanese retreated. My father became a Buddhist scholar and married a Japanese woman. He would be scorned as a traitor in China, and is scorned as Chinese in Japan.

I love you and I wish we could be together. But you suggested marriage and a child. When I remember the discrimination I felt as a child, I would not want my own child to suffer so. It is bad enough that northern Japanese look down upon southern Japanese and that all Japanese look down upon a half-Chinese girl. Then how much more would they mistreat a child who is mixed Japanese, Chinese, and Western. I cannot impose such a life upon a child just for my selfish love.

I hope you will understand and forgive me.
Yoshiko

He deceived himself with hope for a moment. She could go with him to America. Not that there was a lesser amount of racism in America. But it couldn't be as bad. There had to be a solution. Why did he have to spoil it by suggesting marriage?

Gao might not forgive the Japanese for the rape of Nanjing, but discrimination could be overcome by time. On the other hand, Dan remembered that he held a grudge against Mr. and Mrs. Bates, not only for being fundamentalists and prejudiced themselves, but (he could hardly admit it to himself) for being obese and Texans. He was not prejudice-free himself. He could understand not wanting to bring a child into a judgmental world. No, he should remember that they had had a perfect time and should not be greedy for more.

He could remember the scent of her orange blossom perfume on his pillow. Tears weighed heavily in his chest.

It was time to go home. Without any more hope that Yoshiko would come back, and with his students on strike, he had no more purpose for being here. He was marking time and losing his enthusiasm for being in China. He would have to face Wu again. And not let him off the hook this time. Camp on his doorstep if necessary.

Dan strode toward Wu's office in the Administration Building with his jaws clenched and his hands in fists. He was going to get his airline ticket refund if he had to sell Wu's blood to pay for them. A hundred yards from the front stairway, he saw Wu walk rapidly down the stairs and turn away through a crowd of students coming out of the Science Building and toward the front gate of the university.

Dan quickened his pace and followed. He was beyond caring that Wu would "lose face" if confronted in a crowd. Let him try to take revenge.

Wu walked through the corner of the formal garden and out the front gate. For a moment, Dan lost sight of him. When Dan got outside the gate, Wu wasn't in the crowd getting on the bus. He looked up and down the street and saw Wu walking south, toward the edge of the city.

After a long block of shop fronts and apartment buildings, Wu turned down a narrow alley and into the doorway of a dilapidated brick building that looked abandoned. Dan followed him down the alley. When he reached the doorway, he saw a beefy man in a trench coat with the collar turned up and a pork pie hat pulled down over his eyes, like a villain out of a film noir, who leaned against the wall in the shadows beside the doorway holding a cigarette. The man squinted at him from under the brim of his hat with the hint of a snarl on his broad flat face and slowly raised his cigarette to his mouth, watching Dan as a tiger contemplates a deer. Dan saw a blue dragon tattoo on the back of his hand. Dan remembered that he had seen the same tattoo on another man's hand in Wu's office.

"What you want?" the man asked. He put one hand in his pocket and blew smoke at Dan.

"I need to speak to Wu," Dan said in Chinese. "That man who just went in there."

"No can enter." The man stood straight, flicked his cigarette on the ground, and squinted at Dan.

"Then please call him out here," Dan said.

"He very busy. You leave." The man stepped closer and leaned toward Dan.

"Will he be out soon?" Dan asked. "I'll just wait here. I have to see him."

"You should not stick your long nose where it does not belong." The man pulled out a switchblade knife and flicked it open inches from Dan's face. "Go back to hell, foreign devil. Or I will enjoy cutting your nose down to Chinese size."

"You really should learn some bourgeois politeness." Dan grabbed the knife-hand, spun around a full turn while lifting the man's hand over his head, and twisted the man's arm up hard behind his back. The man groaned in pain and dropped the knife. Dan kicked the knife down the alley.

"There was no need to be rude, punk," Dan said. "The next time you pull a knife on me, I'll break your neck."

He slammed the man's head into the brick wall, and the man slumped to the ground, unconscious. He felt the man's pulse to make sure he was still alive. Dan brushed his hands against each other and walked away, shaking. He hadn't been sure he still had the moves or the strength. It seemed that Wu must be dealing with some criminal tong with the blue dragon insignia. Probably using Dan's money. When he went home, he honed one edge of a heavy brass buckle to a razor sharpness. It was an old Marine Corps trick for when Marines went on liberty in dangerous foreign countries. One could swing a heavy sharp-edged belt buckle like a mace against attackers with knives. His father had used it once in Nicaragua.

Carrying weapons was illegal in most countries, so one had to make it as little obvious as possible, sharp edge on the bottom. He didn't want to be caught by Blue Dragon gang members empty-handed.

Honing the belt edge calmed him. When he began to think rationally again, he realized that he had made a whole new set of enemies. Stupid mistake. He should have left at first warning.

Gao Baima came to Dan's apartment after Dan's evening class. They drank beer.

"Well, it turns out that the rumor was false," Gao said.

"Which one this time?" Dan leaned back in his chair and closed his eyes, tired. He could not forget that Gao was Wu's friend. And Wu was dealing with criminals. Should he trust Gao?

"Deng Xiaoping was not on the train that was stopped in Wuhan," Gao said. "I don't even know if a train was stopped at all. The rumors are as inaccurate as ever."

"And the government does nothing." No, he could not say anything about a tong. Gao might already know. He might tell Wu. He might even be in on it. After all, he always defended Wu. And Gao was the only person in China he had thought he could count on. His friend. Ha.

"They do nothing because the power struggle has not been resolved. Even the students are tired of the strike; the Beijing students proposed ending their occupation of Tiananmen Square, but non-Beijing students resisted, and the sit in continues." Gao sipped his beer.

Dan decided he had no choice now but to flow with the situation. Yoshiko was not coming back. Students were on strike and not going to class. He wanted to get out of the Inspector's line of fire, and now the Blue Dragon was a danger. It would be wise to get out of Xi'an. He had no dollars to get home, but he had lots of Chinese Yuan he had not spent. Gao's students were on strike too.

"Look, I have an idea." Dan could feel his pulse beat faster. "Neither of us has classes now. How would you like to take a trip with me? I've wanted to go to Dunhuang to see the Mogao Caves and the hanging monastery at Tienshui before I go home. Now would be a good time."

"I can't travel." Gao scowled. "No money."

"I have lots of *Yuan*," Dan said. "They pay me much more than Chinese professors, and I haven't spent it. I'll pay your way."

Gao's cheeks turned red, and he looked away. "No. No. Too generous. I couldn't."

"You can earn it by being my tour guide. Make the arrangements. Plane tickets, hotel reservations and all that."

Gao raised his bushy eyebrows. Dan knew he wanted to do it but was embarrassed. "No," Gao said. "Wu must make arrangements, or he lose face. It's his job."

Wu again, like a constant recurring nightmare. But what if it did not involve dollars and if Gao were the intermediary? Even if Wu were a criminal, he wouldn't cheat his friend Gao would he? Unless he was in on it too. But Gao was Dan's only connection. He had to trust him that far.

"I can't deal with Wu," Dan said. "Makes me angry every time I talk to him. You work with him. Make arrangements to see the

Buddhist cave art in Dunhuang, maybe the Yellow Hat Tibetan monastery; what's it called? Xiahe, near Lanzhou. And we could take a train to Tienshui to see the Buddhist monastery hanging from the side of a cliff"

Gao stopped him. "Bandits hold up that train."

Dan laughed. "Every time? I'll take the risk if you're game."

Gao sat silently rubbing his neck. "The university is on strike, and I have no classes . . . I'll see what I can do."

Dan had him. He smiled. It would be a great way to end the year.

Yingying went to see her mother when she knew her father would be at work. Yingying's grandfather had been a Shanghai banker before the Revolution.

Her family had been sent to the countryside for "re-education" after the communists took over China in 1949. Her grandfather had died in an accident when a backyard iron smelter exploded during the Great Leap Forward.

Her grandmother, a pampered daughter of the big city with bound feet, had died of a heart attack, falling behind the line of peasants while they were planting rice, so no one noticed her sinking into the mud, face down, until lunch break, when her daughter, Yingying's mother, found one bare crippled foot sticking up out of the ooze. She had grown up a streetwise orphan of the Commune and had been hardened by years in the paddies planting rice.

When Yingying came in the door, she said, "You should respect your father. It's his hard and dangerous work that puts rice in our bowls."

"You, too, think I should give up the man I love and the struggle for justice?" Yingying sneered. "For what? A future of heaping rice bowls and empty lives?"

"You don't know what an empty rice bowl is like. I do. We have a good life now. Don't you spoil it for us."

"Life could be even better without government corruption. 'Peoples' Republic!' It's a joke. 'Bosses Republic of China' would be more like it."

"You're a student," her mother snarled. "You've had the luxury to be idealistic. Your father has to be practical. The halls of bureaucracy twist and turn like snake holes. He has to deal with greedy, powerful, vengeful men. He has to be a snake charmer."

"I should have known I wouldn't get any support from you, either."

Yingying knew her mother would sacrifice her own life to protect her; but she had come to the wrong place for sympathy. Mingyue had been too depressed and uncommunicative to give her the warmth she needed, and her mother was so cold. Yingying had always been bitter about that. She would have to go back and bury her grief in student political activity.

She knew her mother was right, of course; Yingying did not know what her father had to deal with in his job. And he couldn't tell her. Still, she was not ready to trust him again.

"I'll just take care of myself. No one else will." She walked out of the house and slammed the front door.

———

Mingyue was plunged into a hell of despair, anger, and self-loathing that even Yingying could not soothe. He might as well have died. He lived with his parents as if they were prison wardens.

He seldom spoke and could not laugh. Humor had drained from his world. He gave up all hope of ever communicating with his father.

The students regarded Mingyue and Yingying as heroes, but Mingyue bore their praises like scourges. He had failed to control the railway workers and had abandoned them. He had not carried through the hunger strike. And he had been thwarted in his attempt to immolate himself. What could be more pitiful and incompetent than a person who can't even kill himself? He was as out of control of his life as a shadow puppet. He needed a victory to regain his self-respect.

Yingying served on the planning committee and as liaison between Shaanxi Teachers University and the watch and clock school and the cadres school nearby. Mingyue performed menial tasks for the student organizing committee: making signs for demonstrations and carrying messages to workers and peasant groups, while he waited and watched for the chance to do something bigger, something more meaningful, something that would outweigh all his failures.

He decided. He would go to Beijing and join the protesters in Tiananmen Square. That was the center of the action; the belly of the dragon that was awakening China.

PART III
JUNE: CRACKDOWN

TRAVEL

JUNE 2

GAO BAIMA HAD TO DEAL WITH WU YAOQIAN; DAN wouldn't have been able to control his temper any more. He thought he knew the feeling that all Chinese must feel in their daily lives; confronted with bureaucratic stubbornness, incompetence, and corruption; the feeling of being violated, manipulated and helpless.

Gao had served as Dan's intermediary with Wu to get airline tickets and hotel reservations in Dunhuang to see the Mogao Caves, then in Lanzhou to see the Tibetan monastery, then train tickets to Tienshui to see the hanging monastery and then back to Xi'an. It would be a marvelous finishing touch to a year in China. But for three frustrating days, Dan had talked to Gao, and Gao had talked to Wu, and nothing was done. Finally, Wu announced that airline and train tickets must be bought at point of origin in China, so Dan would have to give him extra money to send someone to Dunhuang and Lanzhou to buy the return tickets.

Gao had assured him it was true that tickets could only be bought at point of origin in China.

"Why didn't Wu say that in the first place and save three days of hassle?" Dan shouted. "Saving face? I'll never understand that man."

"It's the way things are done." Gao mumbled.

"Absurd. It's a rip-off. Besides, we don't have enough time. We have to be there tomorrow for the hotel. We can buy our own bugging return tickets."

Dan was ready to take his chances and just pay as they went, but Gao had a better idea. He called a former student of his who worked in the Gansu Provincial government. Dunhuang and Lanzhou were both in Gansu Province. Within hours, Gao reported that all arrangements had been made and tickets would be waiting for them.

⌐·− ⌐·− ⌐·−

Mingyue had no money for a train ticket, but as a former railway worker, he knew ways to hide on a freight train. He knew the code that marked railroad cars by destination. Early in the morning, in the Xi'an railway yard, Ma helped Mingyue elude workers and guards and find a freight train destined for Beijing. While Ma offered guards cigarettes and joked with them to distract them, Mingyue searched the length of the train for a place to hitch a ride.

Cars carrying coal and iron ore were open on the top, and he might be seen. Box car doors stood open, but he saw two workers moving from one car to another locking doors. He didn't want to be locked into a boxcar for days. One could die before they unlocked it. He only had food and water for two days, and it could be very hot in late spring. He hid under the boxcar when workers passed him closing doors. Too late now to climb into a boxcar even if he changed his mind.

A tarp hung loose at the corner of the next car, a flatcar, and he crawled under it. He mumbled thanks to the careless worker who had not secured it properly. In the pitch dark, he crawled across the splintered wooden floor, feeling ahead of him until he came to cold steel; the side of a vehicle; cold, greasy tractor treads. Beyond that, rubber tires. Further exploration lead him to the deduction that it was a military half-track vehicle, and there were two vehicles on the car. Military reinforcements going to Beijing. A good sign that the journey would be swift.

The irony struck Mingyue that the vehicles were likely on the way to stop the very students he was going to join, and they might shoot at him. It might be a worthwhile contribution to the student cause if he could loosen the chains and let the vehicles roll off the train. But the chains were thick and padlocked. And people could be hurt. Not a good idea.

One of the vehicles had its front window rolled down, and Mingyue crawled in and stretched out on the driver's seat. The sun beat down on the black tarp, and sweat dripped into his eyes. Pinprick holes in the tarp let in slivers of light that made motes of dust dance. The train began to move, and Mingyue breathed a sigh of relief and fell asleep listening to the soothing *clack clack* of the wheels on the track.

Mingyue woke with a start when the train screeched and bumped. He listened. The train lurched backward. No light came through the tarp. Night. His shirt clung to his skin from sweat. He knew that part of the train was going to Kaifeng and Shanghai. It must be that they were in Zhengzhou, east of Xi'an, and the train was being divided. Part would go north to Beijing and part to Kaifeng and beyond.

The train lurched forward again and stopped. In a moment of panic, he wondered if he was on the right part of the train. He didn't want to end up in Shanghai. But of course, the military shipment must be bound for Beijing.

He gathered his food and water into his sack and crawled to the loose end of the tarp. He might have time to look outside and investigate. Voices nearby made him stop.

"Someone didn't tie this tarp down."

Mingyue heard the scraping of the rope on the tarp. The canvas pressed down on his back. His fear jolted him as if the man had hit him. He was trapped. He wanted to shout for them to let him out. But he would surely be arrested. He thought better of it. There must be some other way. But if he waited until the tarp was undone, which could be days, he would also be arrested, or might be dead. No, it was safer to be arrested now. He shouted for help. But the men were gone, and the train began moving again.

Maybe he could cut a hole in the tarp. He had no knife, but there must be something sharp in the vehicles. Survival seemed more important than getting to Beijing now. Mingyue searched everywhere; under the vehicles, in the drivers' compartments, under the seats. He could not find anything sharp.

He could not open the rear doors of the vehicles because they were held shut by the tarp. In the map pocket of the second vehicle, he found a heavy wrench. No sharp edges, but he could break the windows, and that would give him sharp edges. It was only now that he had a solution that he became aware of the extent of his panic. His hands shook.

The train rolled along at full speed. No one would hear the window shatter. He struck the side window. It was thick reinforced glass, and it did not shatter. He hit it another dozen blows with all his strength. It broke. He felt carefully in the dark until he found a shard with one smooth edge he could hold; a big enough piece to hold like a knife. He poked at the canvas but could not penetrate it. He ripped at the tarp like a cat trying to claw its way out of a cloth bag.

"Aaagh!" The glass slipped against his palm and cut it. He sucked the blood, not sure in the dark how bad the cut was. He took a clean shirt from the food bag and wrapped it around his hand and lay on the floor panting and trembling.

He took a few deep breaths and stopped panting. He went back to work on the canvas, this time slowly and rhythmically sawing on the tarp until it gave. An hour of effort resulted in a u-shape cut. He could crawl out.

The cool night dried the sweat on his brow. He looked out at the stars and relaxed. Lights of passing towns disappeared into the dark, and the rhythmic throbbing pain in his hand lulled him to sleep.

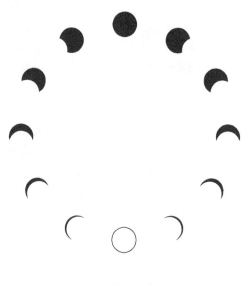

UNEASY CALM

JUNE 3

DAN SAT BY THE WINDOW ON THE LEFT SIDE OF THE plane with Gao next to him. The nineteen-thousand-foot peak of the Kilien Shan rose snow-capped out of the khaki brown Gobi Desert patched with bits of agricultural green. Somewhere farther back in those white mountain ridges between brown valleys, Dan knew there was a twenty-thousand-foot peak in the Humboldt Range, but he couldn't distinguish it from the dozens of other high peaks. He pointed out to Gao the westernmost end of the Great Wall.

"Well, here we are going away from Beijing while Ed must be in Beijing by now," Dan said. "He flew there yesterday."

"Not a good time to be in Beijing," Gao said, looking a bit green from the turbulence. "The government is beginning to crackdown.

The army took over radio and TV stations and newspapers, so the news doesn't even mention the protests anymore."

"The whole movement is dying without a whimper." Dan hung his head.

"BBC says that students built a goddess of democracy like the Statue of Liberty," Gao muttered. "But the government says it must come down. It is 'bourgeois liberalization' and an abomination in a square devoted to heroes of the revolution."

Dan liked the irony. "That's a clever insult to hurl when everyone can see that the Party's economic program is just that, bourgeois liberalization."

"News programs call for the students to give up," Gao said. "Zhao Ziyang is under house arrest. Workers are being arrested. One was the leader of an unauthorized labor union. Others were members of a motorcycle gang that warned people of troop movements."

"Strange how they're arresting workers but not students," Dan mused.

"It shows how much the government fears losing control of the workers. It is a communist proverb that 'intellectuals may strike for three years without effect, but if workers strike for three days, the government will fall.'"

"Some workers are protesting," Dan said. "Let us hope the rest join them in a three-day strike." Dan couldn't tell if Gao's look was disagreement or fear.

"I think a few leaders will be arrested and life will be back to normal soon," Gao said. "Students will return to classes when we get back to Xi'an. Perhaps we chose a good time for a trip, as long as it was away from Beijing."

Dan and Gao arrived in Dunhuang and took a taxi into town. Between the airport and town, the landscape stretched flat, barren, sandy-colored, hardpan dirt to the distant wrinkled, brown mountains. It reminded Dan of the Mojave Desert in California until he saw a man riding a short-legged two-humped camel followed by a woman on foot with a scarf over her head and face. Muslim country. Where had China gone?

———

Mingyue awoke as the gray twilight showed that the train was coming into the outskirts of a big city. His hand stung, and the undershirt was soaked with blood. He feared to unwrap it and look at the damage. And he was hungry. He saw a sign that said "Beijing."

He would have to get off before the train stopped. He realized what he must do first. He did what he could to trash the vehicles and make them useless for attacking students. He opened the hoods and pulled wires and hoses. The spark plugs went into the oil intake. He took a long drink of water and put the remainder of it, along with dirt clods off the wheels, into the gas tanks. He smashed more windows with the wrench, causing fresh blood stains on the undershirt. The slowing rhythm of the *clack clack* of the train wheels warned him to get out, and he jumped off the train as it slowed.

Three railroad workers saw him walking down the tracks and shouted at him. One of them came toward him, and he turned and ran between parked box cars until his lungs hurt. He looked back and couldn't see anyone. He explored the huge unfamiliar freight yard until he found his way to a cross street and merged into the traffic of hand drawn carts, bicycles, pedestrians, and trucks. He flowed with the river of humanity, past barricades of old vehicles and junk, into the center of the city.

Along the way to Tiananmen Square, he bought food and water. It was late afternoon of June 3 when he entered the great square, big enough to hold a million people but crowded with a sea of tents, posters, banners, empty bottles, plastic bags, pieces of paper, and piles of rotten garbage. People walked, stood, squatted, lay down, talked, read, sewed, and cooked on Bunsen burners. His nose was assaulted by the familiar odors of feces, urine, garbage, and dirty clothing mixed with those of cooking garlic and cabbage. On one side of the square stood the pinstripe columns of the Great Hall of the people dominated by the picture of Mao. The statue of the goddess of liberty faced it holding her torch of freedom in defiance. In the middle stood the Heroes' Monument. Beyond that crouched Mao's tomb. He had seen pictures, but those had not prepared him for how immense it was.

Mingyue had never been to Beijing, and he thrilled with awe, but his feet ached from the long walk through the city. He stood and looked about him, unsure what to do. A woman wearing thick glasses and a red arm band introduced herself as a monitor from National Tsing Hua University. She noticed his cut hand and, without prying as to its cause, poured alcohol on the wound from her first aid kit. The pain of the stinging made him dizzy. She wrapped a gauze bandage around two fingers and the palm.

"Where can I join the hunger strikers?" he asked.

"The hunger strike has ended," she said. "We are just sitting in now. You can join us."

She checked that he had food and drink and showed him where he was welcome to sleep on the concrete between two tents.

A student with a camera chatted with Mingyue. "TV crews aren't allowed to come here anymore, so I'm taking pictures to sell to the foreign media. Good money."

"What do you think the government will do?" Mingyue asked.

"Don't worry. The Thirty-Eighth Army is protecting us. The government has to give in if the army doesn't support it."

At sunset, Mingyue stretched out on his back on the hard concrete with his jacket under his head and watched the stars appear slowly in the darkening sky. He listened to the babble of voices around him—students discussing the political situation, a couple quarreling about whether to continue the sit in or leave, radio news that he couldn't make out. He had survived the train ride. He had made it to Beijing and was at the calm eye of the political hurricane.

He had to do this. He had to be part of the struggle. But now that he had come all this way, if the hunger strike was over, what did he need to do? He was too tired to think. He could decide tomorrow.

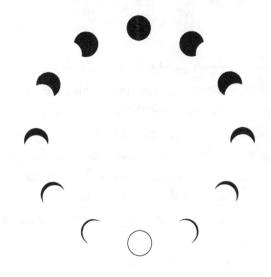

DUNHUANG: A STORM

JUNE 4

THE SKY WAS PERFECTLY BLUE, AND THE AIR CALM when Dan and Gao had breakfast in the hotel dining room. But the forecast was for unsettled weather. Just as they were about to get into the minivan for the drive to the Mogao Caves, a black cloud spraying lightning bolts moved toward the town from the direction of Beijing. It seemed as if the gods were angry, as if evil forces had been unleashed in the east. A virga of gray rain fell from the bottom of the cloud but did not reach the thirsty earth. Under the cloud, low to the ground, a yellow-tan, turban-shaped presence billowed. It rolled into town like a thick fog bank. The moving river of air turned brown with sand and soil. Willow branches no longer hung down but flapped straight out to the side like banners. Pieces of trash blew down the street like little race cars. Dan could not see ten feet in front of him. Grains of sand hit his cheek like miniature machine-gun bullets and stung. The minivan driver motioned Dan and Gao away, and they half-ran and half-floated on the wind, like people caught in a flash flood, back into the hotel lobby.

An hour later, Dan watched the cloud retreat, held up by the full arch of a double rainbow. The sky had turned blue again, and the bone-dry town gleamed as if it had been scoured clean. Dan and Gao took the minivan across flat desert into the low-wrinkled, brown hills toward the caves, stopping for a camel ride on the way.

Dan had tried to coax Gao to take a camel ride in vain. Dan went by himself. The beast did not seem to like his foreign accent. Or perhaps it was the tentative way he tugged on the reins. Dan was wary that it might spit at him. But now he was comfortable with this two-hump Bactrian, and the camel had settled down from obstreperous to merely comic, like a snooty dowager with its thick fur coat and big feet.

Dan had ridden a one-hump Dromedary in Morocco. Riding a Dromedary was like being on top of a mountain peak in an earthquake where the mountain swayed and one's head felt light from the high-altitude shortage of oxygen. The Bactrian camel was shorter and slower and felt more earthly; one sat securely and snugly between the humps. Maybe if he could not get tickets home from Wu, he could ride a camel to Pakistan and use credit cards from there.

Dan rode around Crescent Moon Spring, shaped like Mother Earth's grin, a six hundred-foot long sparkle of blue water, reflecting the perfectly blue sky overhead, enfolded by a narrow strip of green, and surrounded by the towering hundred-foot white sand dunes of Singing Sand Mountain on every side. It was said that a heavenly steed rose from the lake during the early Han Dynasty, and the Moon-goddess once came here by mistake. The sun burned Dan's eyes glaring off the bright sand.

After the camel ride, the minivan continued along a valley bottom, the west side of which became a steep cliff with caves. Four hundred and ninety-two surviving caves—there were originally over a thousand during the Tang Dynasty—and all carved with statues and painted with both religious and secular scenes over ten centuries. "Incredible," Dan enthused. And the eighty-five-foot-tall Buddha. All this on the Silk Road between the Takla Makan and the Gobi, with the Jade Pass, the frontier garrison of Song Dynasty poetry just to the west. Dan was living his favorite poetry. It was the kind of place that made him understand how Lawrence of Arabia could want to don his Arab robes and jeweled scimitar, poke his camel in the ribs, and bounce away from civilization with a war whoop.

Dan came out of his dream world when he noticed the expression on Gao's face. He looked like he had eaten one too many sour plums. "You look worried, my friend. More worried than usual."

"I listened to the BBC radio while you were riding the camel," Gao mumbled. "You know how the demonstrations were decreasing; crowds in Tiananmen Square were getting smaller?"

"Right. The whole situation was calming down. I presumed it was grinding to a halt."

"A speeding police van killed three bicyclists, and people got upset again. Angry crowds beat up soldiers and confiscated weapons from military busses. I fear more confrontation. Today, the army took control of Beijing, and workers are resisting with pipes and firebombs. It's so violent. I don't know what will happen."

Gao's shoulders dropped, and he stared at his shoes. Dan listened to the heavy silence of the sand dunes.

"They should stop." Gao held his stomach. Dan was not sure any more whether he meant the students or the government.

"The government won't listen to why they're angry," Dan said. "They'll just react to the violence. Anger breeds anger. Violence breeds violence." Dan knew as he said it that his philosophizing could not cut away Gao's ulcer pain and palpable depression.

Back in Dunhuang, Dan and Gao went to the hotel restaurant, and it was the first time Dan had ever seen Gao drunk. After a couple of large bottles of beer and a five course dinner, Dan ordered a bottle of Maotai.

When Gao had finished off half of it, he ordered four more cups for four men at the next table from his old home, Nanjing, and started to recite a poem by Wei Chuang. "'All hail the bounty of our mentor and host.'" Gao raised his cup to Dan, and the neighbors raised their cups too. "'We must all sigh that springtime's span is short, so don't protest when the golden cups are filled. Whenever you come by wine, then laugh and shout. After all, how long does a man's life last?'" The neighbors downed their Maotai and applauded and laughed merrily. Gao staggered and sat back into his seat unsteadily.

"Well recited," Dan said. "Just the right amount of drunken slurring."

The longest day of the year was not far off, and even at the end of the long dinner, the sun was only now setting. Dan and Gao staggered into their room, and Dan stood on the balcony to face the blood red sun in the clear desert sky. He remembered another fragment of the Wei Chuang poem. "'With knotted heart, I watch the fading sunset, and think of you, of you, who cannot know.'"

When he had gotten on the airplane in Xi'an, thinking of Yoshiko, he wondered if the plane could lift off carrying such a weigh of sorrow as was in his heart. He wondered if Yoshiko might have watched the same sunset earlier and thought of him.

Dan went back into the room, and Gao turned off the radio. Gao rubbed his forehead and bit his lip.

"Something very bad has happened. Very bad." He scowled like someone befouled by a passing pigeon.

"What happened?"

Gao hung his head in silence.

"Something on the radio? Beijing?"

Gao cleared his throat, like he was trying to speak, but he didn't . . . or couldn't. When his ulcer began biting, he could make Alfred Hitchcock look like a comedian by comparison. Since Gao had always looked worried since Dan had known him, usually about his son, Dan couldn't tell if he was any more worried than usual.

"So . . . what happened?"

"Very bad for China. But maybe it's just rumors." Gao shook his head. "Who knows what's true? Chinese radio and BBC don't agree."

"Well, what did they say?"

"Can't trust the media. Go to sleep."

In spite of all his drink, Dan could not sleep. Why would Gao not just tell him?

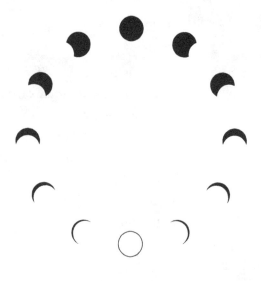

XI'AN: BAD NEWS

JUNE 4

YINGYING SEARCHED EVERYWHERE FOR MINGYUE. She dared to go to his family's apartment to ask for him. Mrs. Gao answered the door, eyes wide with fear. She was as frantic and puzzled by his absence as Yingying. He had left no message and told no one what he was doing. He had just disappeared. For two days now, no one had seen him. Had he been arrested? If so, one might never hear from him again. Yingying wrestled with the idea of going to her father. Mingyue's safety had to be more important than her pride, her anger, her disgust, her fear. But she could not face him, not yet. She would wait. Mingyue might turn up.

She went to three local hospitals and found nothing to allay her fears. She went back to Mrs. Gao who told her the radio hinted at something important happening in Beijing, but it was unclear what. Transportation all over the country was being disrupted.

"And my husband is in Dunhuang," Mrs. Gao said. "I warned him not to go, but he doesn't listen to me. I tried to phone. Left a message at his hotel but couldn't talk to him. I don't know if he got the message. The phones are busy. Planes aren't flying. Trains are . . ." She buried her face in her hands.

Yingying left and talked to fellow students at the gazebo. BBC had reported that the Army had moved into Tiananmen Square and that hundreds of students had been shot.

She gasped. "Hundreds?"

"Maybe thousands," a student replied. "No one is sure yet. The government is not reporting it. According to witnesses, it was a massacre."

Yingying slumped onto a bench. She had no energy to stand. "We can't let them do such things."

Shocked by the news and futile in her efforts to find Mingyue, she needed to do something to channel her frustration. She needed action, any action in a group of comrades to combat her anxiety and helplessness. She joined the river of students that flowed out onto Nandajie and marched toward the center of the city chanting, "Down with Deng Xiaoping; down with Li Peng." They merged with a river of workers, and Yingying saw Ma. She squirmed her way through the crowd and tugged at his sleeve.

"Where's Mingyue?"

He looked at her. "I sent someone to tell you. Didn't he find you? Mingyue's in Beijing. He went to join the demonstrators at Tiananmen Square."

She staggered back. "Mingyue . . . in Tian . . . ?" She choked. "Where they're shooting . . . hundreds . . ."

She turned and ran toward the university. Her legs were heavy, like running under water. Like in a nightmare.

How could he . . . ? Why didn't he tell her? Was he . . . ? Was he . . . ?

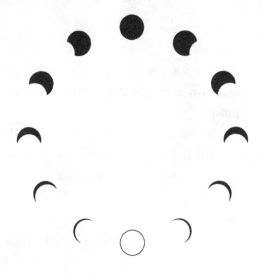

BEIJING: BLOOD

JUNE 4

MINGYUE HAD ONLY SLEPT AN HOUR WHEN HE WAS awakened by loud voices near him. He had to pee, and his hand stung, but he was so tired, he just wanted to go back to sleep. He turned over to shield his eyes from the bright floodlights that illuminated the square.

"We have to get her to the hospital." The voice drew Mingyue's attention to the tent beside him.

"Roll her onto the stretcher."

A head popped up out of the tent, and Mingyue recognized the monitor who had bandaged him the day before. She looked at him.

"You!" She beckoned him with her hand. "You're strong enough to help. We need to get this woman to a hospital. She was already weak from the hunger strike, then someone gave her bad food. Diarrhea for two days. She didn't drink enough water. She has almost no pulse."

The monitor stepped out of the tent. A man behind her backed out the tent flap dragging a stretcher with a woman on it. The woman's eyes were shut, and she moaned.

"Grab the other end," the monitor commanded.

"But my hand—"

"The People must work together or we will fail." The monitor turned on her heels and strode away from Mingyue, leaving no doubt about what he would do. The man holding the stretcher looked at Mingyue with pleading eyes.

"What time is it?" Mingyue asked.

"About midnight."

"Shit." Mingyue yawned and wondered if he would get any sleep tonight. He picked up the other end of the stretcher. It stung his cut hand. "Where do we go?"

"I'll lead. Tongren Hospital. It's a long way. Ambulances can't get through."

"Stop at the first toilet along the way."

The man picked his way among sleepers, tents, protest signs, and piles of garbage, and Mingyue followed. It took ten minutes just to get to the street at the edge of the square, and Mingyue's hands were already tired. His cut hand burned in agony. They came to a street corner lined with trees.

"I have to stop a moment," Mingyue said.

They put down their burden, and Mingyue relieved himself against a tree. His bandage was red with fresh blood. He would have someone look at it at the hospital, if he could even make it that far. The uniform *thunk, thunk, thunk* of boots tapped out a rhythm. The sound came from the street they were about to enter and grew louder.

Soldiers marched at double time.

They came into view, helmets shining in the glow of the floodlights. A long column of men—rifles and automatic weapons held diagonally across their chests; faces carved in granite, expressionless.

They jogged past Mingyue, with exaggerated high steps, and the column split, half the men turning right, half left, along the edge of the square. When several hundred had gone by, they stopped and turned to face the square, backs to Mingyue.

Adrenaline rushed through Mingyue's body, and the hair rose on the back of his neck. He wanted to run through the square, shouting the alarm. But the soldiers stood between him and the protesters. Loudspeakers ordered people to clear the streets. Mingyue watched protesters crawl out of their tents. Some scurried away from the troops. Some hurried toward the troops, pleading with them. One couple climbed back into their tent, as if to be out of sight was to be safe.

The soldiers loaded their weapons, fidgeted with their safeties, shifted from foot to foot, and waited.

A man ran by Mingyue and shouted, "Get away from here. They're going to shoot."

"The People's Army would not shoot the people," Mingyue's companion said.

The running man stopped. "They've already started shooting people along Chang'an Boulevard. At that bridge that the people blockaded with busses, they shot students, workers, women, children. I saw them kill a pregnant woman kneeling beside her wounded husband and an old gray-haired grandmother who

Donald C. Lee

leaned on a cane and shook her fists at them. And they shot a lot of university students at the old Democracy Wall. They act like Japanese invaders, not Chinese. Not the People's Army." He spat on the ground. "And they're on the way here. But the people are fighting back. They set the busses and some military trucks on fire. They've killed soldiers, too. I have to warn the student leaders." He ran off.

Mingyue wondered if the midnight air had suddenly chilled.

A heavy rumble came from the street behind Mingyue. He turned to see a column of tanks roll toward the square. The lead tank drove straight forward, straight into the square, straight toward the tent Mingyue had seen the couple retreat into. When it was close to the tent, the man put out his head and waved at the tank. Screams rose from the crowd. The tank rolled straight on, rumbled on the concrete, and spewed its clouds of diesel fumes. The man tried to lift himself out of the tent, but the tank tread rolled over his head with a loud metallic "crack."

Mingyue stood stunned as the tank ground over the tent leaving it flat and shredded and splotched with red.

Bile rose in Mingyue's throat. He wished he had a weapon to shoot at the soldiers.

"Let's go." His companion picked up his end of the stretcher.

Mingyue, jarred out of his paralysis, grabbed his end and followed. Part of him wanted to go back and fight, but he knew it was his duty to carry the stretcher. And part of him was glad for an excuse to flee. He followed his burden as if it would guide him out of Hell.

Volleys of gunfire echoed in the distance. He was not sure if the sounds came from Tiananmen Square or other parts of the city. Ironic, the "Square of Heavenly Peace."

They passed through crowds of frightened and angry residents who poured into the streets from surrounding buildings and ran through the dimly lit streets. Some carried stones and bottles, and some wore hard hats and carried pipes, crowbars, and big wrenches.

Mingyue's arms and hands cramped, and his bandage dripped blood. He felt that if he were to drop his burden, he would lose his grip on everything of value to him.

The "crack" of the man's head echoed in his ears with the machine-gun fire.

They had to take a long route to avoid soldiers and rested more and more often. It took the rest of the night—it seemed an eternity—to get to the hospital.

The girl on the stretcher had stopped moaning.

They limped into the emergency entrance at first light.

Ambulances arrived in convoys. The hospital was already filled with the wounded and dying. People lying and sitting lined the walls of the corridors. Blood lay in pools.

Mingyue and his companion found the triage area and set the stretcher in front of a nurse. An Army officer with a dozen soldiers barged into the room.

"None but soldiers are to be treated, and no one is to leave the hospital," he said, hands on hips. "The Army has taken charge." He looked at the woman on the stretcher Mingyue had carried. "Student." He sneered. "Get her out of the way." He motioned to Mingyue and his companion to move her against the wall. "She is to receive no treatment."

"But she'll die." The words escaped Mingyue's lips before he thought.

The officer drew his pistol from its holster and glowered at Mingyue. "Are you a student? Let's see your blue card."

"Worker, waiting for a job." His voice quivered and broke. He fumbled in his pocket for his identity card. His hand trembled and burned. The sticky bandage dripped red on his pants legs. The card would show that he was from Xi'an and had no business being in Beijing.

Maybe he could smear enough blood on the card so the soldier could not read it. He held the card out to the soldier with his bloody hand, inconspicuously pressing his bandage against it.

The soldier took the card and rubbed it to clean it off. Mingyue's shoulders slumped. The soldier scowled. "What's this?" He held the card closer to his face. "I can't read it."

A doctor burst into the room followed by eight colleagues. "Nurse, we need a supply of blood bags and needles. We'll have to go into the community to find blood donors."

"No one leaves the hospital," the officer said. He waved his pistol at the doctors.

The doctor looked at him with his lip curled up. "This is a medical matter, not a military one. There are dozens of patients that need blood desperately."

The doctor took boxes of needles, plastic tubes, cotton swabs, and blood bags and began to distribute them to his colleagues. "The rest of what you need is in the—"

The sentence was cut off by the blast from the officer's pistol.

The officer shot each of the nine doctors, one after the other. Their blood splashed on Mingyue's shirt. Mingyue, his companion, and the nurse just stared, mouths agape.

The dead doctors lay on the floor in slowly spreading pools of blood.

Mingyue wanted to escape, but the door was blocked by soldiers. One soldier held his rifle to Mingyue's head. He growled,

"Come with me, student." Mingyue's hatred mixed with his fear, and he thought of grabbing the rifle.

The nurse held Mingyue and his companion by the elbows. "I'll need these men's blood to save the lives of our glorious soldiers who are wounded. You," she pointed at Mingyue, "sit at that desk and roll up your sleeve."

She shoved Mingyue roughly into a seat. The soldier scowled at the nurse.

He lowered his rifle.

The officer ordered his men to carry the bodies and stretcher patients out of the room. The nurse set up the blood bags, hands shaking, and inserted the needles into Mingyue and his companion. The soldiers carried out four of the bodies. While the blood bag slowly filled with blood, the nurse swabbed Mingyue's hand with alcohol and re-wrapped the bandage.

"I'll see if I can get any blood out of those doctors, too." She choked. "Even my husband." She stared, teeth gritted, at a corpse on the floor. Her hands dangled helplessly at her side. "Maybe I won't even bother to check the soldiers' blood types . . . but no, it's not their fault . . ."

"I think you just saved my life," Mingyue said.

"And mine," his companion added. "I'm an international trade law student."

The nurse sighed and whispered, "We're dealing with crazy men. An ambulance driver trying to bring several wounded students into the crowded emergency room told some soldiers to get out of the way and they shot him. A student lying in the corridor with a stomach wound—who died moments later—told me that the elite Fifteenth Paratroopers marched into the square and shot hundreds of students without warning. Tanks of the

Twenty-Seventh Army ran over tents with people still huddled in them."

"We saw it as we left the square." Mingyue's voice shook. "Why? It's a nightmare."

"Local soldiers from Beijing cooperated with the students. But a patient told me that he had tried to talk to the soldiers of the Twenty-Seventh Army and explain to them what was happening. The soldiers were from some southern region and couldn't even understand Mandarin."

"Ignorant peasants?" The law student asked. "But why so angry?"

"It may have been a form of madness." She glanced at the door as if afraid the soldiers would overhear her. "I had to do a blood test on a wounded soldier and found high levels of amphetamines in his blood. When I asked him if he had taken drugs, he denied it but said that the soldiers had been told that the counter-revolutionary hoodlums in Tiananmen Square had lots of diseases because of the unsanitary conditions, and the soldiers had been given injections before they went in."

"They were all doped up? The role of the Army is to serve the People, not slaughter them," Mingyue said. "Criminal."

"In a country still without law," the law student said, "'criminal' is whatever the Party says it is."

"You'll have to leave now since your bags are full, before the soldiers come back for you." The nurse pulled out the needles, put bandages on the wounds, and directed them out by way of a less-used corridor. "Hurry. Drink water when you get a chance."

Mingyue, dizzy and weak, his hand burning, staggered after his companion down the corridor, past scurrying doctors and moaning patients lying in the corridor unattended. He wondered if he should go back to the square and fight. How could he fight well-armed, drug-crazed peasants without a weapon? Hunger strikes and sit ins and demonstrations only work against leaders who care about public opinion. Martyrdom and self-sacrifice would only be laughed at by leaders willing to slaughter unarmed students.

One patient asked Mingyue for a drink of water—a young woman with her leg wrapped in a blood-soaked cloth. His law student companion continued on and disappeared around a corner. Mingyue remembered that he had passed thermoses of water and cups. He went back and drank a cup full, then poured a cup for the woman. He heard the *thunk thunk* of several boots down the hall coming closer.

Military boots. He swayed, dizzy. Was it worth his life to help her?

He ran back to the woman and knelt to help her drink as the beat of the boots grew louder, closer. He held the cup to the woman's lips and mumbled a prayer for the first time in his life. "Dear grandmother." He had never honored his ancestors. "I'll clean your grave at the next Spring Festival if you help me get to the railroad yard . . . and home . . ."

A soldier shouted. "You there. What are you doing?"

Mingyue jerked his head around.

Down the hall, a nurse was bandaging a student's arm. The soldier raised his rifle and smashed the butt into the nurse's face. She sprawled on the floor. The soldier smashed the butt onto the student's arm. Mingyue turned and ran down the corridor as the student's screams echoed off the walls.

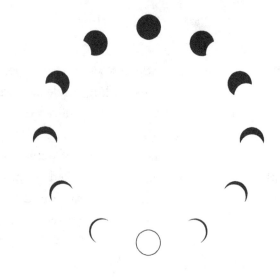

LANZHOU: BARRICADES

JUNE 5

THE FLIGHT TO LANZHOU BOUNCED AND PITCHED, as roughly as any Dan had experienced, and that included the one from Louisville to Chicago that had left mashed potatoes, gravy, and peas dripping from the ceiling of the airplane.

When the plane bucked and yawed again, Gao turned green, took the "sanitary bag" out of the pocket in front of him, and clutched it to his chest. Dan insisted that he would feel better if he sat by the window seat and kept his eyes on the horizon.

Gao refused twice, but holding the bag open in front of his mouth, he agreed to switch seats. The move allowed the color of his face to slowly restore itself to normal. Dan kept his eyes on the horizon too. Gao refused to tell him what had happened in

Beijing because Gao didn't believe the reports. But whatever it was, it must be bad.

"I think the gods are very angry," Dan said. He was sweating a lot.

Dan thought of the ancient religious idea of synchronicity. It was as if yesterday's sand storm and today's turbulence reflected the political turmoil radiating out from Beijing. Or was it the other way around? "As above, so below," what occurs on the macroscopic plane is mirrored in the microcosm. That idea is found in Renaissance books on alchemy as well as in the Chinese *I Ching*.

He remembered the flight from Beijing to Xi'an at New Year when the plane had landed in a blinding snowstorm, and he had known that the Xi'an airport had no radar. That was scarier. The thought did not comfort him.

When the plane landed at Lanzhou airport, he thought his ordeal was over, but it had just begun. The airport was an angry beehive of people swarming in panic. Half the people were trying to get flights out of Lanzhou . . . and couldn't. The other half had just landed and were trying to get ground transportation into Lanzhou . . . and couldn't. Gao Baima made numerous inquiries and was told that busses were not running. The city had shut down. Airlines had shut down.

Dan and Gao had hotel reservations in downtown Lanzhou, but there was no way to get there. They overheard that the hotels at the airport were all full. Dan could envision sleeping on the concrete floor in the airport lounge, which would be unpleasant even if it were clean.

Gao spent an hour talking to everyone he could, making inquiries and finally found a burly bus driver willing to go to the city for a bit of extra money. A crowd rushed the bus like a pack of bulldogs when the butcher has dropped a steak. People pushed and shoved with heavy suitcases, and Dan was not sure he would come out of the fray with all his arms and legs intact, but being a bit bigger than the others—something of an advantage when the society has thrown politeness overboard—he plowed ahead and drew Gao along in his wake.

Was he losing his politeness too? It was all being rubbed away. They got a seat together.

Once aboard the bus, riding through green farms in a river valley nestled between dry, brown mountains, everything seemed normal again, and Dan relaxed and sighed with relief

Dan saw the city in the distance, stretched along the great Yellow River in a valley between mountain ranges. They crossed a bridge over the river at the south end of the city. The driver stopped the bus at the edge of the city and said everyone would have to walk from there. Women screamed in his face, and men shook their fists, but he ignored their pleas and just motioned them out. People seemed to give up the fight, and almost everyone had left when Dan tried to speak in his best Chinese.

"Could you tell us how far it is to the Hotel Lanzhou?"

The driver lowered his heavy eyebrows and gave Dan a look that made his bones melt. He gave in to the inevitable and stumbled off the bus. Gao asked a fellow passenger and was told that their hotel was miles away at the north end of the city, and they would have to walk.

They followed the other passengers through the barricades that had been strung across the street. People could walk through, but no vehicles were allowed through by the student guards. There were no busses or taxis inside the barricades. No vehicles of any sort were allowed to move in the city under the threat of destruction.

Dan and Gao lugged their suitcases across a wide square barren of trees. The bright sun in the clear sky drew sweat to soak Dan's shirt. The square was not only devoid of vehicles but almost empty of people. Only a few people walked here and there to keep it from looking like a surrealistic painting of the time after a nuclear holocaust. A city of over half a million, dead and silent. One could smell the fresh air and see the mountains, perhaps because the factories had stopped and traffic disappeared. Dan was sure that few people had ever had the privilege of seeing Lanzhou like this. Even the people of Lanzhou were missing it, whether from fear or because they were huddled around their TVs and radios. Dan and Gao walked blocks and blocks without seeing police, soldiers, students, shoppers, or workers. Perhaps Dan would hear the rumble of tanks or hear the click of marching boots at any moment. Even the birds seemed to be afraid to sing.

They traversed most of the length of that hot urban desert, down the middle of a wide, empty, major boulevard, stopping only to sit on their suitcases to rest and mop their brows every mile or so. It took two and a half hours to get to their hotel. When they entered the hotel lobby, stooped and sweat-soaked, they dragged their tongues on the ground as if they had just come out of the Gobi. A ten-foot statue of a temple-guardian god, in armor and holding a flaming sword, scowled at Dan with mouth corners drawn down, baring animal teeth, as if Dan emitted an odor that offended the god's nose. Actually, Dan noticed that he offended his own nose. But the hotel staff seemed pleased to greet new guests.

Dan and Gao showered and changed clothes and hungrily slurped down a bowl of beef and noodles accompanied by lots of *qi shui* and beer. Dan relaxed into the comfort one feels when an aching body rests after a long hike.

At sunset, a demonstration of thousands paraded by the hotel. Dan waved the V-sign and the demonstrators waved Vs back. Gao asked people for details about what was happening. He was told that in Beijing yesterday, seven thousand people had been massacred. Dan's brief moment of comfort evaporated.

Elements of the Thirty-Eighth Army from Beijing had supported Zhao Ziyang and refused to advance on the city. The Twenty-Seventh Army from Hebei Province, supporting Deng Xiaoping and President Yang Shangkun, was purportedly responsible for the massacre.

The two armies were reported to be fighting each other on the outskirts of Beijing. There were also battles between protesters and the Twenty-Seventh Army. Military vehicles had been burned and more civilians killed.

Students had captured weapons from the military. One soldier who had killed a child was hanged and burned by an angry mob. The government claimed that over a thousand soldiers had been killed or wounded. The whole city of Lanzhou too was blockaded by angry students and workers.

"Seven thousand people killed?" Dan asked. "Did I hear you right?"

"Seven thousand," Gao nodded, his face an emotionless mask, "and many more wounded."

"Jesus! Unbelievable!" Dan shook his head. "When students were beaten in Berkeley and Chicago, and two killed at Kent State, it was a national crisis. I wonder what Americans would do if their government killed seven thousand. It's almost beyond comprehension."

"What did people do when dozens of striking American workers were killed by strike-breaking police earlier in the century?" Gao asked, eyebrows raised.

"Nothing." Dan blushed. "That's why I was sympathetic to Marxism for much of my life. I thought it stood for democracy and justice."

Gao nodded and mumbled. "I, too, admired the Marxists' concern for the poor."

"And now?"

Gao did not answer.

Gao asked about train tickets to Tienshui. All the trains were being commandeered by students trying to get to Beijing to join the battle there. No passenger trains would be going to Xi'an. The bus tour to the Tibetan monastery was also canceled. Gao spent the evening trying to get more information and to find out how to get back to Xi'an. There was no apparent way. Then Gao got the phone message from his wife that had been relayed from Dunhuang saying that his son was missing and couldn't be found. Gao stood stunned and swaying as if bitten by a poisonous snake.

"Oh, my god," Dan muttered. "They've begun arresting student leaders, and he's been arrested." Gao ran from one member of the hotel staff to another pleading that he'd have to get back to Xi'an. They shrugged their shoulders.

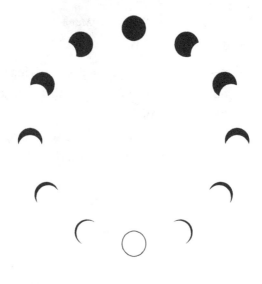

XI'AN: PLANS

JUNE 5

YINGYING MET WITH REPRESENTATIVES OF THE Student Coordinating Committees from several Xi'an universities.

"More riots today," a student leader said. "Students and workers arrested. What should we do?"

"We have to consider," a student said, "that there are two armies here in Xi'an. One, on the eastern edge of the city, is local, from Shaanxi Province. I think they will be sympathetic and restrain themselves.

"The other, on the southwestern edge of the city, and thus closer to the university, is from Jiangsu Province. No one knows what they intend to do. We have barricades, but they could not stand against determined army action. Tanks would roll over our barricades like a pile of chopsticks. We could have a massacre to rival Beijing's right here in Xi'an."

Another student said, "I have a fax from my cousin in Chengdu. He says that police attacked demonstrators there and 300 to 400 people have been killed and over a thousand wounded. Police used concussion grenades, truncheons, knives, and electric cattle prods as well as guns. Hospitals were ordered not to accept wounded students, and several hospital employees were arrested for disobeying orders. Today—right now—police are preventing ambulances from functioning. The dead include children and the elderly. So it's not only Beijing where people are being massacred, and Chen is right that it could happen here too. We must be cautious."

A third student spoke out angrily. "Don't let that frighten us and keep us from acting. My committee is communicating with other universities. Thousands of students have blocked intersections in Shanghai and Changsha, and demonstrated in Guangzhou, Shenyang, and Changchun. In Beijing, the workers support the students. And in Wuhan, which is a primary Army communications center where even Deng himself had to go to get approval for martial law, students and steelworkers have blocked one end of the Changjiang Bridge, holding off police and troops at the other end. It's the only bridge across the Yangtze River for hundreds of miles in either direction. Wuhan University students voted to continue boycotting classes by nineteen hundred and thirty votes to seventy. The people working together will prevail, and we must be the leaders."

There were cheers and laughter.

A fourth student said, "I agree with Li. Students are confronting soldiers and getting on trains in Nanjing, Guangzhou, and Changsha to go to Beijing and support the students there."

Chen said, "At five p.m. yesterday, loudspeakers in Xi'an's central square played the Internationale which shows that we have the support of someone in the local government." Students cheered. "But the government in Beijing moved more troops into the city yesterday and predicted a long battle against the 'dregs of society.'" People moaned.

A voice at the back of the room said, "It's the leaders who are the dregs of society."

Another student rose from his chair. "The riots here are already beyond our control, and there has been damage to buildings and vehicles. The armies will not restrain themselves for long."

Yingying stood to be recognized. "I propose that we send student representatives to speak with the army leaders. Maybe we can convince them to remain patient."

"A good idea," the chairman said. "Are you willing to lead a delegation?"

Yingying blushed. She did not consider herself a strong enough personality to confront high military officers. "It would be wise of the committee to choose a stronger speaker, like Comrade Ting."

"Too abrasive," someone said.

The committee members just stared at her, unblinking like a covey of big black birds. She felt her proletarian enthusiasm to better the world begin to wither. The chairman grunted like a goat with an upset stomach. Someone had to do the job.

She stuck out her chin and nodded. "Yes."

<hr />

Mingyue hopped aboard an overnight freight train directed back to Xi'an. He went through hours of sleepless black depression, hearing the "crack" of the man's crushed head and seeing the shredded tent, seeing the doctors fall dead as they were shot, remembering the smell of death in the hospital that he had hardly noticed at the time. But even before the train arrived home, his helplessness had turned to rage. He fumed. He thought that Inspector Song was right. Demonstrations and riots would not change anything. The deaths of seven thousand students in Beijing wouldn't change anything. The Army would decide the outcome of the struggle, because they controlled the weapons.

Like Mao said, power grows out of the barrel of a gun. Only if students were armed would their voice be heard. They had already been through military training, so what they needed was the weapons.

Mingyue decided he was going to get the weapons from the Army's own armory.

Mingyue thought of his old buddy, Ma—Horse. Besides the railroad, they had done military service together. The man had done guard duty at the armory. If anyone knew how to get in and get out weapons, it would be Horse.

When the train arrived in Xi'an, Mingyue didn't go home. He went to Horse's apartment in the northern part of the city. It was after work hours. Horse lived with his wife, mother, and father, so Mingyue walked with him in a park.

"What a mess your clothes are." Ma laughed, a high-pitched, stifled laugh like a horse's whinny. "You stink, you know."

"I just arrived from Beijing in a shipment of chemical fertilizer."

"No wonder you stink." Ma suddenly looked grim. "Were you at the square?"

Mingyue nodded. Horse looked at him with admiration. "Do you think the people will succeed in changing the government for the better?" Mingyue asked.

Horse grinned. "To me, the demonstrations like are big parties; you get drunk enough to say a few things that have been bothering you, then you go home to your same old life again. The government has no reason to listen to the people because the people have no power."

"Just what I think. Because we have no weapons." Mingyue studied Horse's face. "But if we had weapons, they would have to listen."

"*If* we had weapons." Horse whinnied. "That's a big if."

"There's an armory full of them."

Mingyue saw the light go on in Horse's eyes. He squinted at Mingyue. "Are you suggesting what I think you're suggesting?"

Mingyue nodded. "If the people had those weapons, the Army would be more reluctant to act with impunity."

"Are you asking me to join you in taking them?"

Mingyue nodded.

"You're a bolder lad than I ever thought you were." Horse slapped Mingyue on the back. "A marvelous idea. Great fun too." His eyes sparkled. "What is your plan?"

Mingyue shrugged his shoulders. "I don't . . . I'm working on it."

Horse snorted. "You came to me because I know the armory from the inside."

His expression turned grim again, and he scratched his chin and studied the ground, silent for some time. Mingyue tried to ignore the nagging feeling. There was something about Ma's blue dragon tattoo that worried him, but he did not know what.

"I know how to get in," Ma said. "It's not carefully guarded. And I helped install the bars on the windows. The windows are high, close to the roof overhang, and will be open in hot weather.

One could reach the bolts that hold the bars inside . . . standing on the wall . . . if one is careful not to break the window and make noise." He looked at Mingyue. "It could be done. But we will have to select our companions well. I know three railway workers I can trust. We will need several more if we are going to be able to carry away weapons and ammunition and provide our own security to get away safely and quickly."

"I think I know a few students and former students I can trust. We can wear masks."

"When I was young," Horse said, "my family lived in a cave in the ruins of the Han Dynasty city walls in Xi'an's northwest suburbs. I know an old abandoned cave hidden by thick bushes where we could hide the weapons. And you were a truck driver for the railroad. We can 'borrow' a truck from the yards, and you can be our driver."

Mingyue was pleased that they had so quickly made a plan. The most difficult part would be to select and recruit a few more trustworthy conspirators. Mingyue smiled. This plan could turn the tide in the students' favor. He mustn't go home now, or his parents would get in the way and keep him from doing anything.

"Could you put me up for a few days?"

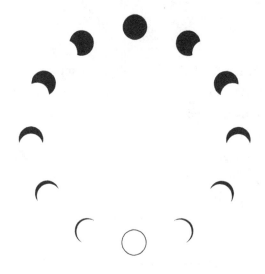

XI'AN: COMRADE GENERAL

JUNE 6

WANTING TO GO DIRECTLY TO THE TOP, YINGYING went to the Shaanxi Army Headquarters with four fellow students. She asked to speak to the commanding general. The soldiers laughed and relayed her request to a junior officer. The students followed a soldier into a concrete room with one bare light bulb and three wooden chairs. A guard was posted at the door. Two of the students sat on the concrete floor against a wall and huddled their knees to their chest, as if they wanted to return as close as possible to the fetal position. Yingying sat rigid on her chair feeling like a prisoner. An hour passed, and nothing happened.

Yingying knew Chinese bureaucracy. The fact that they had not been turned away yet was a hopeful sign. No one at a lower level could decide anything positive, but they could make a negative decision. Her request must be going up the chain of command, and there was no knowing how long it would take to get to the top. It could be months. Hours passed, and no one had the heart to talk.

Two of the students fell asleep like cut flowers wilting without water. Yingying felt more encouraged because they had not been turned away yet.

She thought about the destruction the riots were causing in Xi'an and the people who'd been arrested. Even a foreigner, an American from her university, whom she'd taught Chinese and whose parents taught English, had been arrested and beaten today while he was meditating in the middle of the street in front of a barricade. Would a general be restrained if that continued? Generals like order, not chaos.

After four hours, a junior officer burst into the room and one of the sleeping students rose like a quail flushed by a bird dog. "The General will see the student leader," the officer said. "The rest of you wait here."

Yingying rose from her chair in spite of her rubbery legs, steeled her jaw, and followed the officer outside past several barracks and a fountain containing a twenty-foot high monolith. She was led into a three-story, concrete building and down a barren hallway. The officer knocked on a half-open door.

"The student leader, as you commanded, Comrade General."

"Enter." The voice was gravely and cold.

Yingying straightened her back and strode through the door. The General looked at her from a stuffed armchair. He was stocky and bull necked and exuded a presence of strength and authority. His face was stony. She was intimidated but driven on by the anger at her father and her disgust at the whole corrupt edifice of Chinese society.

He pointed to a chair across a small black lacquer table with intricately carved legs. On the table was a pot of tea and two cups. He poured Yingying tea as she sat. She felt alone without the support of her fellow students. Her teacup shook in her hand as she took it from the General and held it with both hands to steady it. She wondered who would speak first and tried to read the thoughts in the General's impassive eyes.

"Which university do you represent?" the General asked.

"Shaanxi Teachers University," Yingying replied, and took a sip of tea.

"The lead university," he said. "Where you go, the other universities will follow." They sat silently as they both sipped tea and stared at each other. Like a moth, she circled the flame of her destiny erratically. "The stone in your fountain is one of the most beautiful I have seen," Yingying lied.

A glint sparkled in the General's eye, though the rest of his face remained expressionless. "I picked it myself. I am pleased that you recognize good taste in the ancient art."

"I am surprised that a man of yang would recognize the importance of so much yin." Her hand stopped shaking.

"The proper balance of yin and yang is as important in the military art as in medicine and cooking."

"What does the General think of the actions of the students this month, and the reaction of the Government in Beijing? Were they a proper mixture of yin and yang?"

The General's laugh sounded like a tank rolling across a steel bridge. "You are blunt. A good proletarian characteristic," he said. His hard face softened. "My own grandchildren are university students. We admire the students' desire for freedom and justice. But the power struggle is over, and Deng Xiaoping has won. We cannot tolerate chaos. You students must learn patience. My men do not want to shoot students, who are in many cases their own children. But we may have to move soon to restore order." He leapt to his feet, and Yingying spilled tea on her lap. "The students will do well to get out of our way when we do move." He pounded the desk with his fist. "You see, I know the commander of the Jiangsu Army. He will not be as restrained as I. I will have to move into the city before he does to save lives and spare the city unnecessary destruction. If the students slow me down, they will suffer the consequences."

The General strode from the room. Yingying sat in her chair, stunned. Her cup chattered on her saucer and she set it on the desk. She was confused, for it was not clear if the General had threatened the students, or if he had offered a bargain. If the students would cooperate with him, if they would not impede the local army, they would not be harmed. And was the General right about the Jiangsu Army, or was it a ruse? Should the students try to slow down the Jiangsu army, or would that just create more danger of it reacting violently? She would have to tell the students what the General had said and hope that clearer heads would know what to do.

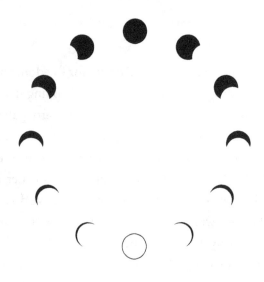

LANZHOU: ESCAPE

JUNE 6

FOR SEVERAL HOURS IN THE MORNING, GAO MADE frantic and fruitless attempts to call his wife in Xi'an—the train station, the airport, the former student at the Gansu provincial travel bureau who had helped him get travel tickets and hotel accommodations—all to no avail. Phone lines were tied up, the train station had shut down, and his former student was busy with important government work.

Gao couldn't eat breakfast. His ulcer was acting up again. He was told he had to wait. Dan tried to apologize for getting him into this mess. There was no light at the end of the tunnel and nothing to be done. Dan and Gao went out into the streets of Lanzhou to find out as much as possible about the situation.

Crowds of people gathered at major intersections, where loudspeakers constantly broadcasted the news from BBC and Voice of America. Several small groups of demonstrators paraded down the major streets chanting and singing, carrying signs with messages like, "Slash Deng Xiaoping" and "Slash Li Peng." Dan and Gao walked the few blocks to Lanzhou University where professors chanted, "We support our students" and "Wake up, Chinese people." Gao talked with Lanzhou University professors and found out that student delegations had been sent to local factories to talk to the workers; others went to blockade all the entrances to the city. The military and police were nowhere in evidence; they were likely waiting for orders from higher up.

Reports were that six people were killed and six injured in Shanghai when a train plowed into students blocking a rail line. Angry crowds had set eight of the train's cars ablaze and overturned busses to block intersections.

When the loudspeakers announced that Li Peng was dead, shot by a policeman whose son had died in the massacre, the city shook with the uproar of applause and celebration. People marched joyously flashing V signs, smiling, and chanting, "Death to Deng Xiaoping."

Dan and Gao went back to their hotel to ask if there was any way to return to Xi'an. The clerk said that he would recommend that they remain in the hotel a few more days until the situation settled. He was sure that if the army moved into the city, foreign guests would be safe in the hotel. When Gao insisted that he had to get back to Xi'an because his son was in trouble, the clerk looked around him nervously and in a low voice said that if they were willing to risk the danger, they could go to the airport in a minivan which had to deliver some foreign guests' luggage. The driver was very familiar with the city and would try unpaved back alleys instead of the blockaded main streets.

"The students have said they would kill anyone in a moving vehicle," Gao said to Dan. "I can't ask you to endanger your life." His eyes pleaded and belied his words.

"We have to choose." Dan knew Gao's choice, but he had to make the consequences clear to them both. "We can stay here in the hotel and wait until transportation is available again. Who knows how long that will be? The army may sweep through the city and meet resistance. No one would be safe from stray bullets. Still, the hotel is likely to be safer than—"

"No." Gao's voice had a frantic edge. "They told me a tourist hotel was burned down in Chengdu today when protesters tried to take refuge there, and soldiers pursued them into the hotel. It might be a bloodbath, and we could be caught in the crossfire."

"Or we could try to get through Lanzhou to the airport," Dan shrugged his shoulders, "and see if we can get back to Xi'an where there could also be a bloodbath. But at least you could be with your family. I vote for leaving. We have to search for Mingyue."

"And you could make arrangements to leave China," Gao said. "Yes, I think that would be best for both of us." He looked relieved.

Dan and Gao sat in the seat behind the driver, who hunched forward like a buzzard waiting for something to die. Beside him, the navigator cracked nervous jokes in an accent Dan could not understand. Gao frowned and snorted in a weak attempt to show that he shared the man's humor. They set out after dark riding down muddy alleys where they jolted through deep pot holes and ponds at the risk of being stuck in the mud, breaking a spine, or worse, an axle. Gao hunched down in his seat like a turtle pulling into his shell while Dan craned his neck to look in all directions.

First they tried the shortest route to the northern bridge. As they crept from a side alley to the edge of the main road to the north, they could see the road wind along the side of a cliff beside the Yellow River. A police car ahead of them crept to the first bend in the road, stopped for a moment, then quickly backed up, turned around, and sped toward them.

"We can't go that way," the navigator said. "We'll have to try the central bridge."

They followed the police car down the main street toward the mountains and away from the river, hoping to go around the eastern edge of the city even though their ultimate destination was to the west. The street was wide and deserted. The navigator joked that with the moon rising over the mountain, it was a beautiful night to die. They came to a huge steel mill, silhouetted dark against the moon. The police car ahead of them stopped. Their headlights showed a line of forklifts parked shoulder to shoulder across the road stretching from the factory's brick wall on one side to the walls of the apartment buildings on the other.

"The steel workers have lined up their forklifts to stop tanks," the navigator said. "We can't get through here. We'll have to go back the way we came and try the only other route I know. Much longer."

Dan couldn't see anyone guarding the barricade, but he guessed people behind the barricade could see the vehicles. It was a cool night, but sweat formed on his forehead. The driver backed the minivan up, turned around, and went down another long series of rutted and pothole littered back alleys, bumping and grinding slowly forward. In one deep puddle, the van fishtailed and settled into the mud like a frog in its pond. The driver spun the wheels, and the van edged forward a foot.

"We'll have to get out and push," Dan said.

"No problem," the navigator said in English and laughed. It was the universal refrain Dan had heard in Mexico and Morocco and the Philippines and everywhere else in the world where people knew very little English and had to have a lot of patience. He laughed too and relaxed the tension in his stomach. The driver gunned the motor, and the wheels spun faster. Gao slunk further down into his seat. The van gave a sudden lurch and bumped forward again. They kept their lights out when crossing paved streets so as not to draw attention.

After two hours of increasing backache from the bouncing, they came to the main street crossing the central bridge. It seemed totally dark and empty. They turned on to it and crept forward in first gear. The safety of the other side of the river was only a couple hundred yards ahead of them as they entered the bridge. No sign of a blockade. No people.

Moonlight glistened off the river, and all was silent but for the chug of the van's engine as the driver leaned forward to peer ahead into the gloom without the aid of headlights.

A man stepped out of the shadows and motioned for the driver to stop. He came to the driver's window.

"Are you crazy?" the man asked. "Haven't you heard? The other end of the bridge is blockaded. You'll be killed if you go any farther. Turn around and get out of here as fast as you can."

Dan heard a murmur of angry voices coming closer and saw a dozen figures ahead, moving toward them through the web of shadows cast by the bridge girders. The face of a boy, perhaps fifteen years old, loomed out of the dark at Dan's side of the van. His face was a grotesque mask of anger and hatred, and he carried a crowbar. He peered at Dan.

The boy reached toward the door handle. Dan pushed down the lock. The boy shook the handle, then raised his crowbar and smashed the window. Shards of glass sprayed Dan, and he jerked his head away so fast, he sprained his neck. The boy reached his hand inside the van to unlock the door.

"Stop him! Hit him!" Gao shouted from a shapeless mass on the car floor.

Dan pressed the boy's hand down on the fragments of glass in the door frame and moved it across the glass. The boy pulled away his arm spurting blood, his expression turned to horror and pain.

The driver slammed his gears into reverse, left rubber backing up thirty yards, slammed the gears into low, and did a quick U-turn. Dan braced himself, sure that the van would roll. The beams of several flashlights illuminated the van and several voices shouted to stop. A brick hit the roof.

The driver accelerated the van like a drag racer a half mile down the road. The navigator pointed toward another side road, and the van swayed and bumped hard as it swerved onto the road. Every pothole jarred Dan's sprained neck. Again they were stuck in a mud puddle, and it looked like they would have to get out and push. Faces peered out at them from a lighted apartment building, then the lights went out. After a bit of rocking the van with their bodies, it found traction again.

It was another hour of agonizing back roads before they reached the southern bridge and crossed safely. The picture of the boy's horror and pain would not leave Dan's thoughts.

He was on the boy's side against government corruption, for democracy. Why did he have to hurt the boy? Did he cut a vein or artery? Would the boy die? He felt sick to his stomach. His only contribution to the cause of liberty was to hurt one of its champions. But he had had to defend himself. Would the boy ever understand?

Dan remembered the Vietnam village, blood spurting from a woman's arm. From the fire Dan had called in. He didn't want to hurt the innocent again—just a boy—but it was beyond his power to help. Guilt mixed with helplessness. He looked at Gao.

"I didn't want to do that."

Gao looked down. "I know."

The drive that had taken an hour coming from the airport had taken four and a half hours to get back.

At the airport, Gao was told that no Chinese were allowed to fly. Only foreigners could get tickets. Dan talked to a group of American oil men who had been advising the Chinese on a drilling project west of Xining. They wanted out of China as soon as possible.

He didn't tell them his story of escape from the city. He thought at first it was out of consideration. He didn't want to alarm them any more than they were already alarmed. But he realized it was as much out of shame at hurting the boy; he had wanted to hurt the boy out of his own fear. Maybe he could have just held his arm from opening the door.

Dan felt strangely calm. Since his flight from death on the Yellow River bridge, he had lost his fear; he only felt depressed about what he had had to do to the boy.

"I'll get you a ticket," Gao said. "You can leave in the morning."

"I'm not going to leave you stuck here for God knows how long by yourself and with no money. We have to find Mingyue. I said I'd pay your way. I'm not leaving until you leave."

"No, you'd better leave while you can." Gao's tone was resigned. Hopeless. "The situation might get worse."

Dan thought of all those movies he had seen of refugees trying to get out of Germany, or Nazi-held Greece, or China and other such places during World War II. The ones who left immediately survived, and the ones who delayed didn't. But surely this wasn't as serious. Then he thought of the forklifts positioned to stop tanks. It was serious. But he had to get Gao back to his family first. He had gotten him into this mess. They would be okay as long as his money held out.

"No," Dan said. "Let's see if we can get a hotel room here for the night. We'll go back to Xi'an together."

They found a drab hotel room of bare concrete walls that echoed the voices of every guest in the hallway. But a scrub in the locker-room style communal shower felt refreshing. Gao spent half the night on the phone trying to contact the former student who had the high government post in Lanzhou.

He couldn't get through. His former student was busy still with pressing government concerns. Dan couldn't sleep most of the night; hearing the arrival of every new guest, kept awake by the pain in his sprained neck, thinking how selfish he had been to take Gao on the trip, and haunted by the boy's face.

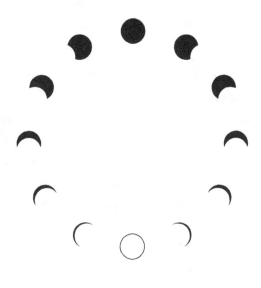

THE ARMORY

JUNE 7

GAO SPENT THE MORNING AT THE LANZHOU AIRPORT trying to telephone his former student, without success. It was still possible for foreigners and high-level Chinese cadres and military personnel to fly, but not for ordinary Chinese, in spite of all Dan's pleading with airport administrators. Dan did not want to leave his friend stranded, so he would not go without him. He could see Gao's worry for his family in his eyes. He felt guilty for having dragged Gao away from his home at such a crucial time.

Seven thousand dead in Beijing. Lanzhou was a powder keg waiting to blow. There must be conflict in other cities. Like Xi'an. Thousands of students on trains going to Beijing. For another slaughter? The country's whole transportation system was shut down to normal travel. How long would food last in the cities? In Lanzhou airport? Dan figured his Yuan would only last another week.

Gao finally got through to the former student in the early afternoon. He got immediate special permission to fly and they had plane tickets for Xi'an by evening.

"I thought you always complained that you had no *guanxi*," Dan said as they waited for the plane to take off. "Now that's what I call *guanxi*—we call it 'pull' in America."

"I was his teacher," Gao said. "We Chinese honor our teachers."

"It's true," Dan replied. "I've never felt such gratitude from my students as here. Even putting dunce caps on their teachers during the Cultural Revolution hasn't totally destroyed respect for them." Dan thought of his American students who would address a professor while chewing gum and say, "Hi, Doc." No Chinese student would be so crass. "America has created a more classless society than China. American democracy means equal disrespect for all except rock stars and athletes. The dumbing down of America; a true Cultural Revolution. That's not to say there aren't great economic and power differences in both countries. But there is less consciousness of them in America. Almost everyone thinks he's middle-class. Not so in China. But there is equal alienation, cynicism, and destruction of values. Shit, I've become a cynic, too. Me, the former Berkeley idealist. Ha! The lover of Chinese poetry. I'm a frustrated romantic."

When the plane landed in Xi'an and they were in a taxi on their way back to the university, they saw the streets littered with the debris from demonstrations and riots: remnants of furniture, a broken sawhorse, tires, rocks and chunks of concrete, burned vehicles, broken windows.

Dan asked the taxi driver, "Were the demonstrations violent here?"

"More damage was done in Xi'an than any other city but Beijing."

"From his tone of voice, I think he's bragging," Dan said to Gao in English.

Almost as soon as Dan put his suitcase down in his bedroom, one of his students, Lu, came to his apartment to talk to him. Lu said he was angry at his government and frightened for his life. There had been a brief ray of hope for a life of freer choice, but now, the privileges of a few and the despair of the many would continue. Lu had been empowered with a voice for two months; now its loss was worse than if he had never experienced it. He felt more helpless since he knew what it was to hope. He told Dan that the university had announced that it would close a month early.

"Most of the students are from peasant families—conservative and frightened of authority by nature," Lu said. "The government wants to disperse the students back to the villages to confine the movement."

Lu was planning to go to distant relatives in the countryside to escape persecution. He feared there would be a civil war.

Dan went to Gao's for news. Gao sat in an armchair looking like a puppet whose strings had been cut. Gao's wife told Dan between sobs that Mingyue had gone to Beijing, and they didn't know what had become of him. Dan knew there was no way to console the family. He went home in a blue funk.

Dan's usefulness at the university (he realized that he was probably deluding himself that he had any) had come to an end. Dan would meet with his class tonight for the last time to say goodbye. He regretted that he had not gotten to twentieth-century history or American literature. But what meaning did that have when Mingyue was missing? How could one find him in Beijing? What meaning did his courses have when seven thousand students with all their new ideas and aspirations had been slaughtered? A whole generation of hope.

He turned on the radio to listen to BBC news. The English news had been stopped. He turned on the television and saw pictures of a train burning in Shanghai and an army convoy burning in Beijing. The commentary was pro-government, pro-soldiers, anti-student, anti-hooligan, and blamed foreign bourgeois corruption for the troubles. Dan thought of his own lectures that had been critical of Stalinism and Leninism. To them, he was a foreign bourgeois corrupter. His ideas helped stimulate the desire for freedom . . . and the slaughter. He had come to help the Chinese progress. Big help he had been. He was now a target of the government and had no way to duck but to leave as soon as possible. He had to find Wu.

Dan had just begun unpacking when Mr. Bates came to his door. Mr. Bates looked shrunken; a bit deflated like a balloon the day after the party and his skin more wrinkled. He wore a rumpled red tie, and the armpits of his white shirt showed sweat stains. Black bags under his eyes attested sleeplessness.

Dan offered a *qi shui*, but Mr. Bates just slumped into the couch and shook his head. "Bad times. We Americans have to stick together now."

"Always a good idea to help your fellow countrymen," Dan said. "How's your wife?"

"She couldn't come. Headache. Sick with worry. Didn't sleep. Hasn't eaten all day."

"Worried about leaving?"

"It's Ty. He's been arrested."

"Oh my God. How'd that happen?"

Mr. Bates moaned and wiped beads of sweat off his brow with a handkerchief. "They tell me he joined a student demonstration. When they were confronted by police, he and some others sat in the middle of the street and began some godforsaken Chinese meditation, and the police beat them with truncheons and dragged them off. We don't know where they took him. No one will tell us. We're at wit's end. We don't know what to do." He stared at his hands, wide-eyed.

"What does Wu say?"

"Can't find Wu anywhere."

"I'll find him. Make him cough up Ty." And my money, he thought. "If I have to strangle him with my bare hands." No, Dan thought. Great Buddhist I'm turning out to be. Have to control my anger. Cool it. "The police?"

"Gave us the runaround." Mr. Bates buried his face in his hands.

"US Embassy?"

"Can't get through. And what could they do from Beijing?"

"I'll talk to some students. They must have some idea—"

"The foreign students are all gone," Mr. Bates blurted. "The Australian family, the Canadian . . . all left. Chinese students are afraid to associate with us now. The US Embassy told all Americans to leave as soon as possible, you know. We'd be gone by now if they didn't have Ty. And there are two armies that may fight, and the battleground would be between us and the airport. Armies are already fighting in Beijing. The whole damn country is a tinderbox. Some ignorant peasant-soldier who's been told about foreign devils causing all the trouble might come barging in here with his AK47 and . . . Oh God." He rocked in his seat. "We shouldn't have let Ty . . ."

"Look. I know this police inspector," Dan said. "I'll talk to him. See what I can do." A lot of influence Dan was likely to have with him. He figured he would more likely be the sacrificial lamb than a lifesaver. But when you're clutching at straws . . .

Mr. Bates looked up at Dan with a glimmer of hope and gratitude.

———

Shortly after midnight, Mingyue went with Horse into the railroad yard. They crept through shadows past several boxcars into a truck park and chose a truck at the back of the lot where they were least likely to be noticed. Mingyue opened the door as carefully as possible and cringed at its loud screech. Surely a watchman heard that. He climbed into the driver's seat, sat behind the steering wheel, and put the gears into neutral, holding his foot on the clutch, ready to slam it into gear. Horse opened the hood with another screech and hot-wired the engine to start it. Mingyue's heart beat in his ears.

The engine coughed a few times and died. "Shit!" Horse was loud enough for Mingyue to hear. Mingyue listened. The yard was quiet. The engine coughed again, and Mingyue goosed the gas pedal. It started roughly, threatened to quit, then caught more strongly. Horse slammed the hood shut and leaped into the cab beside Mingyue.

Mingyue shoved the stick into first gear, grinding the gears, then eased the truck forward without lights. The moonlight was enough to steer between the other vehicles but not bright enough to see the potholes. They bounced up and down as much as forward.

Someone shouted at them. Mingyue put on the headlights, jammed into second gear and accelerated. He drove alongside the railroad track until he came to a dirt road and turned on to it. He couldn't see anyone following them in the rearview mirror. When they reached the highway, they turned south and drove across the city to pick up their cohorts.

"We got away," Horse laughed. "We'll . . . have the truck back before sunrise . . . before the police are organized enough to search for it."

Mingyue drove the truck down the dirt alley beside the armory and parked it where Horse told him to. High walls closed in both sides of the road. Behind them on the main road a hundred yards away there was scant traffic, maybe a vehicle every fifteen minutes. Mingyue heard a truck engine come closer and closer, and his stomach muscles tensed. It passed by on the main road, and he relaxed. Ahead, recessed into the wall, was a locked loading gate into the armory. Beyond the end of the wall, the road dwindled to two tractor tracks and went into the fields. Traffic in the alley was unlikely until dawn. If guards heard the truck and were suspicious, they would have to open the locked loading gate or come around the corner from the main gate on the main road. That would take time.

Horse got out of the cab and closed the door cautiously, although the noise echoed down the alley like a shot and signaled for the others to get out of the back of the truck. They were all dressed in black, charcoal smeared on their faces, and wore dark hoods. Mingyue stayed in the cab for a moment longer, the engine idling in case they needed to make a fast getaway. Three men tossed grappling hooks over the wall and scrambled up the knotted ropes attached. Horse and two more men followed them. They sat along the wall like black owls waiting for prey.

Horse signaled, and Mingyue climbed out of the cab and into the back of the truck where he helped another man tie bolt cutters and wrenches to the ropes to be hauled up. Mingyue tensed at the sound of another vehicle and readied himself to leap back into the cab. Headlights shone on the wall at the main street, and Mingyue worried that a vehicle might turn into the alley. The ropes holding the bolt cutters and wrenches dangled silently. The vehicle passed by on the main road, and up the ropes went.

Five minutes went by before the bolt cutters and wrenches were lowered into the truck, and Horse signaled for Mingyue and the eighth man to come up. Mingyue let the engine idle and struggled up, scraping his knuckles on the wall and thinking that he should have worn gloves. When he got to the top, he saw Horse lowering a rope into an open window without bars. One by one, the eight men climbed into the armory; Mingyue went last.

They used flashlights and found themselves in a cavernous room with crates of weapons and ammunition. Each man armed himself with an AK47 and loaded it. They found the inside door to the loading gate.

Horse looked at Mingyue. "When we open the gate. You back in here, and we'll have crates ready to load."

Mingyue climbed back out the window, over the wall, and into the truck.

The loading dock door, a metal roll-up, screeched like it was calling for help.

A shout echoed down the alley. "What are you doing? Stop or I'll shoot."

Mingyue ground into first gear and lurched forward past the gate as it opened, then backed up toward the loading dock. A shot shattered the glass window beside him. He jammed his foot on the brake and ducked onto the seat. A volley of automatic gunfire rang down the alley and bounced off the walls. The night fell still, except for the throb of the engine, which was almost as loud as the pounding of his heart. Mingyue raised his head slowly and looked out the window. He guessed that the gunfire from his companions had scared off the guard for the moment and sat up, easing the truck back to the dock.

"Come help us, Gao," Horse called.

Mingyue helped load crates of automatic weapons, ammunition, and a couple of anti-tank rifles into the truck. He presumed that the guard who had fired was calling for help and would be back soon. Everyone hurried the loading, and no one spoke.

Soldiers appeared at the main road, and someone shouted orders at them.

"On the truck, everyone. Quick!" Horse shouted. "We can go out through the fields. I know the way." He climbed into the cab. Mingyue jammed the truck into low gear and turned into the alley toward the fields.

The rear cab window shattered, and Mingyue heard the thumps of bullets hitting the truck. The men in the back of the truck returned fire.

When they left the alley, Horse said to turn right into a wheat field. They bumped over rows of wheat in low gear, then went down a narrow, muddy, rutted tractor path.

Across the field, they came to another dirt road, bumpy but passable, and went through a small village. Mingyue turned on his headlights. Several more miles of dirt road led them to a paved road.

It was now four a.m., and they appeared to be a normal truckload of workers going to work in a battered truck if one didn't look too closely. Mingyue drove to the cave in the ancient city walls to hide the rest of the weapons.

As they unloaded the crates in the light of their flashlights, Mingyue saw a blue dragon on the back of the hand of one of Ma's men. Identical to Ma's. He watched the other men's hands. All Ma's men had the same blue dragon. He remembered Yingying's warning that only criminals wear tattoos. A gang. Mingyue brooded, not knowing if he had done the right thing. But if they were willing to fight for freedom what did it matter?

They returned the truck to an empty railroad car loading area, just as the sky began to turn red in the east.

Mingyue walked on rubbery legs along the tracks until he and Horse were back to a main road, down which they could get to Horse's apartment to shower and change clothing before they were seen.

"We've done it." Horse, grinned and slapped Mingyue on the back.

Mingyue wasn't sure what they had done.

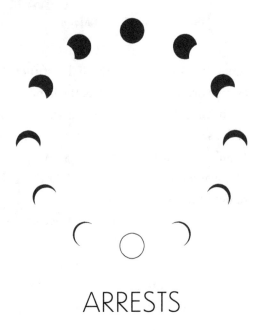

ARRESTS

JUNE 8

YINGYING LAY ON HER DORM ROOM BED STARING at the cracks in the cement ceiling. She had tried to talk to someone in a position of authority in the Jiangsu Army but had been turned away by junior officers at the outposts. No one had been allowed to enter the army's perimeter.

She had tried at eight different places, and at the last one, the guards had threatened to shoot her if she came any closer. Other members of the committee had tried telephones and faxes without success.

Yingying didn't know what else to do.

Sun, a committee member, burst through her open doorway, smiling.

"Did you hear? Someone stole weapons from the armory last night. When the word got out, a large mob of students marched over there and helped themselves. Mortars, anti-tank weapons, everything they would need for a real defense. Our university is now a well-armed camp."

Yingying gasped and sat upright. "What idiot thought up that scheme? And you're happy about it? That could ruin everything I've worked for. We had an ally in the Shaanxi Army. Those weapons belonged to our army. Now they won't trust us anymore. That is just a provocation for both armies to march now." She buried her face in her hands.

"Everything is so confusing." The corners of Sun's mouth drooped. "I don't know what to think. I'm frightened. My friend Bing is so angry that he hopes there will be a civil war, and he's eager to fight in it. He's trying to find out if any of his friends have weapons right now."

"Whom does he want to fight?" Yingying asked. "The army is mostly ignorant peasants who don't understand what's happening and will follow orders blindly. They're not the enemy; the government is. It keeps them ignorant. And fighting won't cure ignorance; it will only harden ignorant opinions."

Sun shrugged her shoulders. "The government denies that seven thousand were killed. They claim that no one died in Tiananmen Square but that many soldiers were killed or wounded by renegade hoodlums."

"That's laughable. Everyone knows they're lying. Voice of America estimates it was three thousand civilians." Yingying pulled at strands of her hair and twisted them around her finger. "I've heard that Deng didn't order the massacre on purpose. His troops panicked, and their officers lost control. But, of course, if Deng admitted that the government didn't have control of its army, he would lose face and appear weak. He would rather be thought a butcher than weak."

"Do you believe he didn't order the massacre?" Sun asked.

"I have more faith in the rumors than in the media. It's controlled by the government. We must presume it's always wrong."

"Well, the rumor that Li Peng was dead was wrong," Sun said. "I heard that a police officer whose son had been killed in the square shot him in the Great Hall of the People, but he was not seriously injured. The policeman was killed."

"How do you know that's not just a rumor too?"

Yingying heard the click of boot heels in the hall and turned to look at the door.

Two policemen entered the room. "Song Yingying?" one of them asked. "Come with us."

The policemen handcuffed Yingying behind her back and pushed her out the door of her dorm and across the lawn to the awaiting police van.

Two dozen students stared at her, but none of them did anything, said anything, made any gesture of support for her or defiance of the police.

"Where are all my comrades when I need them?" she chided them. "Where are all the angry students with weapons? Has all resistance collapsed? Have we been so totally defeated?" The back doors of the van gaped open like the mouth of a devouring dragon.

The policemen lifted her and threw her through the doors, and she crumbled into a heap on the steel floor.

What was it Professor Norton had said about the sign over the entrance to Dante's Hell? She remembered. "Abandon all hope ye who enter here." The policemen slammed the doors shut, and the steel walls echoed her fear. She lay trembling and alone.

So alone.

— ·— —·— —·—

Dan found Ed eating alone in the foreign guests' dining room; Mr. Spock with the Vulcan ears.

"In April, you *already* talked about leaving, and you're still here?" Dan pulled a chair up to his table and sat with him. "I thought you left for the States over a week ago. What are you doing here?"

Ed looked up with the sad eyes of a hound dog whose tail is caught in a steel trap. "You wouldn't believe it. I went to Beijing. Wu took my money and said that a ticket would be waiting for me at the Beijing Hotel. But he lied; they didn't know anything about a ticket for me there. He really screwed me over."

"I believe it," Dan said. "He's the perfect Foreign Affairs Officer. There's no one in Xi'an more capable of making foreigners miserable and getting revenge for colonial occupation. He's got it down to an art."

"I ended up wandering around Tiananmen Square," Ed said. "Saw the Goddess of Democracy and talked to students. The place was a pigsty. Then I stayed at the Beijing Hotel for an outrageous price. After a few hair-raising experiences, when I found all those planes going abroad booked for days, I decided to come back to Xi'an to get my money back from Wu. Couldn't afford to stay in Beijing."

"A bit ironic, isn't it?" Dan laughed. "You were the one most eager to leave all along, and now here you are, practically the last foreigner left at the university. But I want to hear all about your hair-raising experiences." Dan dug into his rice and spicy peanut chicken.

Ed's voice shook as he told his story. On the morning of June 4, he had been on the third floor of the Beijing Hotel and was awakened by shouting, screaming, and gunfire early in the morning. He looked out the window of his room, which overlooked the main street in front of the Hotel, and saw a crowd of people rushing in panic away from the square, which is not far from the Hotel. Moments later, columns of soldiers marched by, toward the square, weapons at the ready. And then there was more gunfire.

Ed had already sent his bags to the airport in hopes of catching a standby flight that morning. He knew he had to get out of the center of town as soon as possible. He dressed and checked out of the hotel without even eating breakfast.

Of course lots of others were checking out in the general pandemonium, and it took a long time. Then there was no transportation available to the airport, and the staff urged him to wait in the hotel, but he went out in front of the hotel to look for a taxi on his own. There were no taxis. People moved up and down the street, some running.

"The street was littered with concrete lane dividers, cement blocks, bricks, bottles, trees, burnt-out truck carcasses," Ed said. "An elderly man grabbed me by the arm and said, '*Laoguai*, get away from here. They'll shoot you. They shoot all foreigners.' That sent a rush of adrenaline up my spine, I can assure you. I believed him and ran away from the hotel as fast as I could."

"Wouldn't it have been safer to stay in the hotel?" Dan asked.

"I don't know." Ed looked sheepish. "Maybe I wasn't thinking straight. But later, I heard that four bystanders in front of the

Beijing Hotel were shot by soldiers. I just wanted to get to the airport. I walked in a mental fog until I reached the American Embassy where lots of Americans were taking refuge."

"Safety at last." Dan smirked. "With their handful of Marine guards to hold off the barbarian hordes like they did during the Boxer Rebellion. Must have felt reassuring."

"Not quite." Ed's eyes looked tired and bloodshot. "A kindly secretary at the Embassy offered to put me up with her and her husband in the foreigners' compound. I was sitting in her living room watching TV when the window two feet behind me shattered and sprayed me with glass, and a couple of bullets bounced off the walls like drunken wasps. I dove into the couch. The husband went to investigate while I curled into a ball and bemoaned my fate. The secretary had just swept the glass when soldiers burst into the room and trashed the apartment. It turned out that soldiers had raked the whole foreigners' compound with machine guns, broken every window, and trashed every apartment, all allegedly because some sniper had fired at them. I figured they just wanted revenge on all foreigners. But they did arrest some Chinese man. No one was hurt."

"It does sound like trashing apartments was a bit excessive if they were just hunting for a sniper," Dan said. "Or at least thorough. Communist-style efficiency."

"After two nervous nights on the secretary's couch, I got a taxi to the airport. Along the way, I heard artillery fire. The taxi driver calmly said that there were tank and artillery exchanges going on as the Thirty-Eighth Army was driving the Twenty-Seventh out of the city. The road was blocked by soldiers a few times, but after a bit more gun-pointing and life-threatening, we got through. I couldn't get a flight home, so I took the first plane to Xi'an."

Dan strode across campus. Perhaps Mr. Bates' fear of some wild-eyed peasant-soldier bursting into the apartment with an AK47 was not so far-fetched. He had to find Wu. Dan promised himself he would be straightforward and firm, but he would control his anger. No threats. Not even the finger. He had to get Ty free.

He entered the Administration Building and went down the hall to Wu's office. The door was ajar. He heard voices. "...dollars to Bangkok? Too dangerous." It was not Wu's high-pitched voice.

"Don't worry," said a deeper voice. "We have that Inspector working with us."

Dan knocked on the door, wondering if it was his dollars going to Bangkok and his Inspector helping. The room became silent. He knocked again and swung the door farther open. He smelled cigarette smoke.

He pushed the door and looked in. Two men stood against the wall, arms crossed, and one sat at the desk smoking. Wu was not there. The man at the desk squinted at Dan. Dan saw the blue dragon on the man's hand as he held up his cigarette to inhale.

"I'm looking for Wu," Dan said in Chinese.

The man at the desk laughed. "So are we." He drew his lip back in a snarl. "He won't have time for you foreigners today. More important things."

Dan stared at the three men. They stared back with narrow threatening squints and sneers.

"Who gave you the authority to decide what is important? You don't look like you know shit." The two standing men bristled, put their hands into breast pockets where they probably had weapons, and looked at the seated one who leaped to his feet and glowered at Dan. Dan switched to scornful English and sneered. "Going to shoot me in the Administration Building? Not much you're likely to do. You're not on your own territory, jerks."

Dan saw that all three men had blue dragon tattoos on their hands. Definitely a gang. Working with Wu and Dan's dollars and maybe the Inspector. He spit on the floor, turned, and walked quickly across campus to his apartment, trying to burn up the adrenaline that flooded his body.

～．～ ～．～ ～．～

Mingyue didn't want to go home and face his father. He strolled aimlessly around the university campus, head down, brooding about the blue dragons all Ma's men wore. A friend stopped him and bragged that students had broken into the armory this morning and taken away weapons.

His friend told of the debates that were raging on campus. Some argued that the students were no match for the army and there would be another massacre. Others argued that the army would not dare to risk a civil war and an even bigger bloodbath than had already occurred. Yet others argued that disaffected factions of the army would side with the students and workers and assure their victory. Mingyue put his fragile faith in the latter position and began to feel that perhaps he had done the right thing after all. It might even be his initiative that would swing the tide and lead to the people's victory.

He was crossing campus toward Yingying's dormitory when one of the female students walked up to him with tears in her eyes.

"Yingying was arrested."

She sobbed and ran back to her dorm. Mingyue stood stunned for a moment, turned, and walked rubbery-legged back toward home. Yingying. Was it his fault?

As he was about to climb the stairs to his apartment, his mother looked out the window and waved like she was trying to warn him. Looking at her, he didn't notice the men approaching. Four policemen surrounded him and grabbed his arms. They forced his wrists behind him and handcuffed him.

How quickly things change into their opposite, Mingyue thought. It's all over. How did they find out so fast? It must have been an informer.

He was ashamed to be pushed into a police van with dozens of students watching. Yingying and his parents would suffer. He sank like a fisherman's sinker into the mud of hopeless despair that his life was over. Slave labor in prison was hardly what one could call life. Prison without Yingying.

His family would lose face now that Deng had won. Surely his quick arrest and lack of student resistance meant that the power struggle was over. Perhaps his father would lose his position. Stealing the weapons had been too little too late. A futile gesture. A kind of suicide. Defiance in the face of destiny. But destiny would not be denied.

The van stopped in front of the building with the big red star that had cracked during the demonstration he had led. He winced. The crack was still there—the crack in the symbol of government power—but the star had not broken. Now it stood as the symbol of his failure as a leader during the riot; of his failure as a hunger striker; his failure to immolate himself; even of his failure to pick a handful of conspirators he could trust not to inform. And if there was an informer, the police must have the weapons he took. Mingyue was sure he had done nothing right and deserved his fate.

The policemen dragged him out of the van and lifted him onto his feet. His legs buckled, and he stumbled and smashed his head on the door of the vehicle. Blood ran into his eyes, and he could taste it on his lips. The policemen laughed and pushed him up the front stairs and into the building. He followed a policeman along a long corridor and down two flights of steps into the bowels of the building. One dim yellow light lit the last corridor.

A guard opened a steel door. After he removed Mingyue's handcuffs, another guard poked Mingyue in the ribs with his submachine gun. Mingyue entered the cell. Its concrete walls perspired dampness, and the room smelled of mold and unbathed bodies. About four feet by six feet, the cell contained a two-foot wide metal shelf hanging down from the wall on rusty chains. On it were a tin cup of water and a chipped porcelain basin that smelled of urine. There was no window.

The steel door screeched, then clanged shut. The lock clicked, and Mingyue heard his heart pound in his chest. The tiny light bulb in the ceiling was barely bright enough for Mingyue to see the five cockroaches crawling in different directions along the edges of the floor.

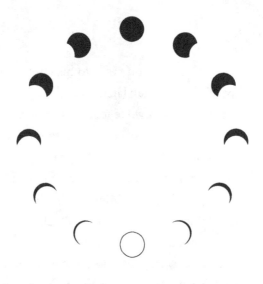

THE BLUE DRAGON

JUNE 8

DAN HAD WAITED FOR HOURS AT THE FRONT DESK at the Xi'an police headquarters. The clerk told him that Inspector Song was very busy, and it was not likely he would be able to see him. Would the Inspector remember him? Surely he wouldn't have forgotten a foreigner he threatened with espionage and hiding a fugitive. A fugitive he knew loved his daughter.

A fugitive who had just been arrested. But why would he bother to see Dan? Dan must just be a thorn in his side when he's got bigger problems to deal with. Well, he would just have to be a very irritating thorn.

Supper hour had passed, and Dan's stomach growled for food, but he did not leave. Finally, the clerk directed him down the hall.

When Dan entered the dimly lighted office, Inspector Song looked up from a file on his desk and frowned.

"I had hoped you would be gone with all the other foreigners by now. You've given me enough trouble." He drew a cigarette from his pocket and lit it. Dan didn't like his red cheek scar and evasive deep-set eyes. Dan despised a corrupt cop.

"Not all the other foreigners," Dan leaned on the desk with both hands and scowled at the Inspector. "You're holding one foreigner. Ty Bates. And I came to do whatever needs to be done to get him released."

"You're way out of your depth here." The Inspector exhaled his smoke slowly. "The whole Bates family gives me a pain." He waved his hand toward a chair, inviting Dan to sit. "Illegal religious missionary activity makes the Chinese government very unhappy."

Dan continued standing, leaning on the desk. The idea of making the Chinese government unhappy after Tiananmen Square didn't bother Dan one bit.

"What makes you think they've done anything illegal? As if there were any laws to break."

The Inspector laughed dryly. "They've given Mr. Wu large amounts of money, thousands of dollars, to bribe government officials to let Chinese students go to American Bible colleges. We've questioned some of the officials and students." He leaned back in his chair and smiled.

"The hypocrites," Dan said. American religious values, he thought. Bribery for Jesus. "So that's why you asked about the Bates when you first came to my apartment . . . and why Wu was so nervous." He slumped into the chair. But was the Inspector just a good actor, acting indignant when he had probably gotten a good cut of that money? Had he somehow been forced to crack down on Wu even though he was in on it? Or was he really honest after all Dan's suspicions?

"You were some help to me when you told about the money Wu withheld from you. That put me on to another aspect of Wu's financial schemes." Then the Inspector squinted at Dan as he took another long drag. Dan watched the cigarette end glow red, then black as the man exhaled a blue cloud. "Wu has been using American dollars for illegal currency exchanges on the black market. We know it but can't prove it, yet. Of course, my investigation has been delayed by political events and other pressing concerns and is not complete." He tapped ash into an ashtray.

"Like arresting students, I suppose. Pressing concerns. The sky is falling. Or at least a red star is wobbling up there." Dan searched for the soul deep in the Inspector's eyes. "I see. You would normally put Ty on a plane for home right away." So much was becoming clear to Dan. The Bates family was bribing Wu. Wu was using the American money, including Dan's, for illegal money exchanges with the men with the blue dragons. But where did the inspector come in to it? "But you're holding him to keep his parents from leaving while you complete your investigation."

One of the Inspector's eyebrows raised slightly. "The Bates family is nothing. They can go home whenever they want. Their son will be sent home after a few months in prison. Good riddance. It's Wu I'm after. I need time to find out whom he's working with." The Inspector jumped up and paced.

Pretty convincing if this was just a cover-up lie. If it was true, the Inspector did not know about the gang and was not the Inspector they were working with. If it was a lie and Dan mentioned the gang, he would be a danger to the Inspector and would probably be thrown in prison immediately for espionage and harboring a fugitive. Wisdom dictated a prudent silence. But then there would be no way to help Ty and Mingyue. Dan's knowledge was all he had to work with. He was hoisted by the horns of his own dilemma. He stewed in silence while the Inspector lit another cigarette. Dan had seldom followed his instinct before, but he had a strong sense of who the Inspector really was. A poet trapped in a practical straitjacket. He gambled.

"Oh shit. Here goes my neck." He braced himself for a counterpunch. "I think I know Wu's partners. Three times I've seen men with blue dragon tattoos on their hands. In Wu's office."

The Inspector leaped to his feet. "The Blue Dragon? Money launderers. Drug runners. Prostitution. A bit of every nasty business. I've been after them for months. Is that who works with Wu? If I knew where to find them I'd tear them to shreds." He smashed the cigarette into the ashtray and ground it brutally. His scarred cheek twitched.

Dan's voice fell. "I may know that too. Perhaps you would consider a bargain. About Ty Bates and Gao Mingyue ..."

Inspector Song and Dan rode in the back seat of the police car with two policemen in front. They drove past the end of the alley where Dan had seen Wu enter the door guarded by the man with the blue dragon. They didn't see anyone down the alley. "Maybe that was just a temporary hangout. But the man guarding the door when I went there couldn't be seen from the street. And that was in the daylight." Dan fell into a gloomy silence. It was after dark, and the alley was not lighted. They drove a hundred yards farther on and parked. The Inspector looked at a map which showed individual buildings.

"That building?" he asked Dan.

"The door was about there." Dan pointed at the map.

"That building has been unused for over a year."

Song instructed his two men to go around the back way to the other end of the building. He walked along the main street, and Dan followed. At the opening of the alleyway, they peered into the darkness. It was like looking into the mouth of a dangerous beast. Song turned on a flashlight. A rat scurried down the street.

"Not good," Song whispered. "A wall blocks the other end. That wasn't on the map. My men will need time to get over it." He turned off the flashlight and lit a cigarette, slowly inhaled and exhaled a few times, and threw it in the gutter. Signaling Dan to follow, he walked slowly into the alley and shone his flashlight on the door. The door opened, and two men stepped out onto the stoop. They had blue dragon tattoos.

Dan heard a movement behind him. He hoped it was the two policemen. Beads of sweat itched on his forehead.

"Looking for something?" one of the men asked. His eyes were dilated, and his face puffed and scarred by combat.

Dan guessed that the man was high on something.

"What do you want?" the man asked again.

"Heroin," the Inspector said.

"Look somewhere else. We don't know you."

"If you did know me, what could you sell me?" the Inspector asked. "I was told you would have lots of stuff. Good stuff from Thailand."

Out of the corner of his eye Dan, saw someone move beside him, and it wasn't a policeman. "Oh shit," Dan whispered to the Inspector, "someone behind us." Two to three, Dan thought, and they all probably knew martial arts. Why did the Inspector taunt them?

"I don't like your insinuation." The scarred man pulled a large switchblade knife from his pocket. He flicked the blade open, and it glittered in the light from inside the door.

Just as the man beside Dan put a beefy arm around his throat, the Inspector kicked the knife, and it clattered down the alley. Dan swung his fist back toward where he hoped his attacker's groin was. He hit the man's thigh and felt the cold barrel of a pistol at his temple.

The Inspector had a gun in his face too. The third man frisked Dan and the Inspector. They took the pistol from the Inspector's chest holster and the identity card from his pocket. Dan wondered where the other two policemen were.

"Police Inspector. The boss will want to see you."

Dan and the Inspector were bound by their wrists behind their backs and dragged into an inner room, bare but for three chairs and illuminated dimly by red lanterns. They were set into back-to-back chairs and tied together at the wrists again. The scar face spoke into a cell phone.

"Yes. A police inspector snooping around at the old warehouse with some foreign devil . . . Song. Don't know him. No one we normally deal with . . . We tied him up . . . Yes, Yes." He turned to the Inspector. "The boss will see you soon."

The men left except for one who sat on guard with a pistol on his lap. The man put the earplugs of a tiny Walkman in his ears, leaned his chair back against the wall, and stared at the two prisoners. Dan's shoulders already ached. His shoulders were pushed forward by the bindings, and with the circulation cut off in his wrists, his hands tingled and felt numb at the fingertips. He wondered if the Inspector's two policemen had been ambushed. He had not heard shots. They wouldn't know where the Inspector had gone. What were they doing? Dan and Song would probably be dead before they found them.

Dan could cut the ropes with the sharpened edge of his belt buckle, but it was in front and the ropes were in back. What if he could slide the buckle around to the back? He gripped the belt in back and pulled so that the whole belt would slide in a circle around his waist. Too much resistance. It didn't budge. He sucked in his belly and pulled harder. The Inspector grunted. The belt moved a fraction of an inch, and the guard leaped to his feet, jerking the earplugs out.

"Don't move."

"My wrists are killing me."

"Don't talk." The guard walked over to Dan and raised his arm in threat. "The next time you move, I'll smash your face." He grinned as if he hoped Dan would give him the excuse. Dan sat still, and the guard went back to his chair and put in his earplugs. He sneered at Dan. After a few moments, he began to read what looked like a comic book.

Dan sucked in his gut again and tugged at his belt as inconspicuously as he could. Holding his numb hands so high strained his shoulder, and it was agony. The Inspector's hands were tied to his. Dan supposed that his every move caused the Inspector pain, too. The Inspector would not know what he was trying to do.

He pulled the belt fractions of an inch at a time. He wasn't sure what he was going to do even if he succeeded. How could they surprise the guard?

The belt caught on a belt loop. He tugged and he couldn't move it. He moved the belt back and tried a second time. It caught again.

Trying not to move his mouth, he muttered, hoping the guard would not hear him. "I can cut the ropes. Help me move my belt to the right . . . your left."

No response. Dan tapped the Inspector's palm and ran his finger across it in the proper direction. "Move my belt." He felt the Inspector's fingers grope his belt and pull. Dan sucked in his gut and pulled, in spite of the bolts of pain in his hands and shoulder. The buckle gave through the loop and moved an inch, jerking his whole body.

The guard pulled his earplugs out, rose slowly from his chair, and strode to Dan's side. He growled. "I said don't move, you long nose foreign devil."

He bashed Dan's cheek with his fist and Dan's chair rocked. The Inspector groaned. Dan tasted blood in his mouth. The guard pulled up the tied hands to inspect the ropes. The shoulder pain made Dan want to howl, but he didn't give the guard the satisfaction.

When the guard returned to his reading, Dan and the Inspector slowly and carefully tugged at the belt until it cut through one loop and came around to the back. The boss could come at any moment, so Dan worked the sharp edge against the Inspector's rope first, hoping not to slash his wrist. Slow work.

He felt one rope give, then another. The Inspector moved his hands and the ropes loosened. He hoped the Inspector was free and sawed at his own binding with numb hands.

The door flew open, and four men entered. One was Wu with a look of terror on his face. Another was the man whose head Dan had smashed. The man looked at Dan with hate in his eyes. The guard ripped the earplugs off his head and stood. One of the men sat in the guard's chair in squat repose and stared at the Inspector.

He was chubby and short but large of presence. He held out a hand with tobacco-stained fingers, palm up, and covered it with a handkerchief.

"Give me his gun." He carefully wiped it with the handkerchief. "We don't want fingerprints."

"No," Wu shrieked in a higher pitch than usual. "I told you . . . no violence." The chubby man sneered. "We have to get rid of them. They know too much."

"Well, take them out of Xi'an to do it," Wu pleaded. "I don't want to be involved. The professor is my . . ."

"You're already involved." The man pointed the pistol at Wu. "You're becoming a nuisance. Do you think we can't do without you? Shut up or we'll bury you too." Wu whimpered and backed against the wall.

The chubby man stood and walked out of Dan's sight. One of his accomplices picked at his teeth with a toothpick. Dan heard the sliding of metal on metal that told him a round was being put into the chamber, and the pistol cocked.

"Inspector Song, you have poked your nose into my business once too often. I know an inspector I can trust to report your death as a suicide."

The rope jerked and tugged at Dan's still-bound hands, taking a chunk of flesh with it. Dan heard the chair behind him scrape and crack. The Inspector had jumped at the fat man. The man with the toothpick groped at his jacket pocket and pulled out a pistol. He was going to shoot the Inspector. They would both be killed if Dan didn't knock the weapon out of the man's hand. He leaned forward, thrust down with his legs, and rose, chair and all. The pistol seemed to explode a foot from Dan's face, and his side stung and burned.

Dan fell to the floor with the ropes biting into his wrists. His shoulder might be broken. He looked up to see the Inspector behind the chubby man, holding the pistol to his temple. The other two men stood pointing their weapons at the Inspector. It was a standoff. Gunfire echoed down the hall.

Dan's head spun as if he were drunk. Warm blood oozed down his side. He remembered a battle in Vietnam—one of his men holding his intestines in his hands as he ran. Gut wounds always led to peritonitis and death. Dan was sure he would die. He gave in to his wooziness, and the world went black.

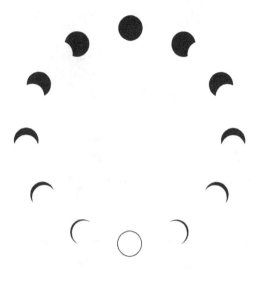

NEW BARGAINS

JUNE 9

THE LIGHT DID NOT GO OFF IN MINGYUE'S CELL. IT was protected by a steel mesh screen. He had no idea how long he had been there. He tried to sleep on the steel shelf but was kept awake by the sense of his own failure and hunger. He had not been fed. It was not at all like a hunger strike if you didn't choose it.

From time to time, a peephole in the steel door opened for a moment. He thought he saw a glimmer of consciousness in the dark hole. Then it closed again and left him alone with his cockroaches.

Finally, the steel door screeched open, and a guard ordered Mingyue to follow him. They climbed three flights of stairs. After several twists of the corridors, they entered an office. To his surprise and disgust, Inspector Song sat behind the desk. The policeman left.

Mingyue heard a gasp to his right and turned toward it. Yingying rushed to him and held his cheeks in her hands. She took a handkerchief from her pocket and dabbed away the dried blood from around his wound. He hadn't realized how much it stung until now as his consciousness emerged once again from the dark recesses of his soul.

"Sit down, both of you," Inspector Song said.

They sat. The Inspector stared at Mingyue. "I know about your little adventures at the armory."

Yingying looked at Mingyue wide-eyed. "You?"

"An informer?" Mingyue sneered at the Inspector.

"Yes, an informer," Song said. He narrowed his eyes and peered at Mingyue. "One of your student friends hopes for a career with the police force. He showed us where the cache of weapons was stored. But they had already been removed."

"Peasants must have found them," Mingyue said. Perhaps Horse had betrayed him. Either way, he had failed again.

"It hardly matters." Song waved dismissively as if he were swatting a fly. "Your caper encouraged a massive raid on the arsenal. There are weapons hidden all over the city now. I worry that they will fall into the hands of criminal gangs, drug dealers like the Blue Dragon."

Mention of the Blue Dragon made Mingyue suck in his breath. So Ma and his friends were criminals; Yingying was right.

The Inspector continued. "If they outgun the police, it will make the task of keeping order and stopping corruption that much more difficult. Do you see what trouble you have caused?" He glared at Mingyue. "But order will be kept."

Mingyue retreated into the silence of the black guilt that ate inside him like acid. Horse was a member of a criminal gang, and he had been used. He stared at his shoes feeling numb.

Yingying spoke meekly. "Deng's faction has won, hasn't it? And you serve Deng and the forces of corruption and repression now."

Song growled. "My job is to preserve order, no matter which faction wins. Meanwhile, I fight corruption as best I can."

Yingying snorted. "And what will you do with us now?"

"You have two choices." Song laced his hands behind his head and leaned back his chair precariously on two legs. "Either you, Mingyue, go to prison for theft, disrupting the public order, and conspiracy to overthrow the government . . . probably a life sentence, though that is not for me to decide . . . or . . ."

Mingyue decided that if Ma had deceived him, he had no reason to be loyal. "Wait. I didn't know my friend Ma was a criminal. Ma and his men had blue dragon tattoos on their hands. I'll show you where he lives."

"He's already been arrested." Song grinned; the first time Mingyue had ever seen him smile. "The Blue Dragon has been beheaded." He pushed some papers on his desk toward them. "Your other choice is that you both go to live with my cousin in Shankuo, a small village in the mountains of Sichuan. Mingyue will change his name, and you two will marry. I have prepared all the necessary documents. I have arranged transportation for you to leave today, and I will notify Mingyue's parents of his situation, though he might not be able ever to see them again in any case."

Mingyue stood stunned, uncomprehending for a moment. He could hear his heartbeats in the silence of the room. Voices echoed in the corridor. Yingying fell against Mingyue's chest and sobbed. He held her and began to grasp the sudden new direction of his life. Agricultural work in a rural village might only be another kind of imprisonment, but it would be with Yingying. He held her tightly and smelled the delicious natural aroma of her hair.

"It would be like prison for you, too," he said to Yingying. "Are you willing?" She held him tighter and nodded.

"I take it that you accept the second option." A sparkle in the Inspector's eyes belied his frown.

<hr />

Dan ate his breakfast of yogurt and coffee in his apartment. The gash in his side hurt, and his ribs ached when he lifted his coffee cup. It was only a flesh wound in his side, a cracked rib, powder burns, split lip, gouged hand, and a dislocated shoulder; not a mortal gut wound after all. What was it, he asked himself, that Tennessee Williams wrote in *Streetcar*? "Desire is the opposite of death." Dan was too Western, not a good Buddhist—too filled with desire to die.

He heard a knock at the door. His side stung under the tape as he walked, his left arm in a sling. He found an envelope outside. It was a letter from Ty. It seemed to be hastily but beautifully scrawled, like some English version of grass characters. He read:

Dear Professor Norton:

We had to leave early this morning—sent home in disgrace, apparently, because of my political activity. My parents are angry at me, but I feel pretty good about it. Thank you. You not only saved me from prison, but it was you who set me on the path to Cold Mountain. As Han-shan said, "The path to Han-shan's place is laughable, a path, but no sign of cart or horse. Converging gorges—hard to trace their twists. Jumbled cliff—unbelievably rugged—And now I've lost the shortcut home. Body asking shadow, how do you keep up?"

The laughter of my joy echoes off those rugged cliffs. My parents would think that my soul is lost, but it is found. Jesus was right that one must leave one's parents to follow the path to God, or whatever name one assigns to that mystery we seek to understand. It is not to deny that their path may lead to God too. There may be many paths up Cold Mountain, and each of us must follow the path most suited to our nature and our state of spiritual development. Some are steep, direct rock climbs, like Zen. Some are longer, switchback trails suitable for the long mule trains of faith—my parents' path—riding with the crowd on the backs of the savior, be he Jesus or Mohammed or Krishna or Amida Buddha. Some, like Mother Teresa and Gandhi, tunnel up through the very heart of the mountain on the tedious path of service. Tantra chooses the helicopter ride, subject to dangerous downdrafts, but it's quick if you survive. My path follows an ice-cold mountain stream up a steep valley.

You have expressed an interest in Qi Gong. Your path will be there when you are ready for it.

Sincerely and gratefully,
Tyson Bates

It seemed to Dan that his path toward Cold Mountain had been a broad spiral around it. The mountain itself was always shrouded in fog, so he could not see it, and Dan got brief glimpses of some shadowy presence but was never sure it was really there, though other people assured him they could see it. The many mule ride salesmen of the established religions he had met all seemed like con artists.

They all had contracts with contradictory small print, and he didn't trust their mules to be more sure-footed than he himself. How fortunate for Ty that he had actually found a path.

Dan heard another knock at the door. It hurt him to walk. It was Gao, slouched and bags under his eyes.

"I heard you went to the hospital last night." Gao's eyes lighted on the arm-sling and tape around Dan's waist. "What happened?"

"Have a seat. Join me for some orange juice and coffee." As Dan poured drinks, he explained what had happened with Inspector Song, Wu, and the Blue Dragon, except that he didn't mention it was part of a bargain for Mingyue. The Inspector would have to explain it to Gao. If the Inspector didn't keep his end of the deal, it would only be raising Gao's hopes to dash them if he mentioned it now. Dan had to keep up the pretense. "Have you heard anything of Mingyue yet?"

Gao had just sat and raised his glass to his lips, but at Dan's words, his hand shook. He put his orange juice down on the table without drinking. "Nothing since my wife saw him arrested. The police won't tell me anything. The only good thing is that I know he wasn't killed in Beijing."

Dan's anger rose. The Inspector was letting him down. But he realized it was early. Perhaps the Inspector hadn't had a chance to make arrangements. Dan called on his Buddha-nature to be patient. His anger cooled. He sat in his armchair and moaned from pain.

"I think of myself while you're hurting." Gao's expression softened.

"It was worth it to catch Wu." Dan squirmed in his chair to find a comfortable position.

"Wu's in prison?" Gao frowned. "It's hard to believe how blind I've been. For twenty years I thought Wu was my friend. He gave me extra money to buy video recorders and things like that in America for my family and for him. Perhaps it was illegal funds. I never questioned. I am so naïve. I didn't know he was a criminal." Gao's voice trailed off, and he seemed to look into a different time and space.

"Well, there is some justice in China after all," Dan laughed dryly. "Wu finally got caught. I'm glad, except I don't know how I'm going to get my money to fly home. That probably got lost in the shuffle. Like they say, 'every good deed is punished.'"

Later that day, Inspector Song arrived. "I honored the agreement to release Ty Bates and am sending Gao Mingyue into safe exile. But there was nothing in our deal to let you off from your crimes. You do not yet have my permission to leave Xi'an. For that, I will require one more service from you."

"Oh shit." Dan's stomach began to secrete large amounts of acid. "What now?"

"When we arrested Wu, we found some of his unused bribe money and a list of six students to be sent to American Bible colleges. Apparently the final payment had not yet been given to the top official who could arrange their departure. Until we have proof that he sent the students and was paid, we cannot arrest him. I want you to make arrangements to send the students and pay the money as Mr. Bates' agent. The Bates family has already left China."

"Jesus." Dan squirmed. "Mr. Bates and Wu won't have mentioned me as in on the plot. I'm not even Christian."

"He won't know or care if you're Christian or just in it for the money." The Inspector paced back and forth like a lynx stalking prey. "Bates worked with the high official's son through Wu. Informers told me that he had passports and visas prepared and air tickets reserved for two days from now. Why wouldn't they believe Mr. Bates would pay you to carry through the deal when he was forced to leave early? The money will speak loudly. We need you to complete the deal so we can catch them in the act."

"You're willing to actually send half a dozen Chinese students to America to catch this guy? He must be a very big fish."

"The students will be arrested in Beijing before they can change planes." Inspector Song grinned. "He is a very high, very powerful, very corrupt official, who hurt many people unjustly during the Cultural Revolution. His son has worked with the Blue Dragon, but we have no proof yet. Yes, I want very much to bring them down."

Something in the Inspector's voice made Dan suspect there was more than just duty or a desire for justice or even career ambition that made him want this man so badly. Perhaps a personal vendetta. And that made it all the less likely that the Inspector would let Dan out of the game.

"So I have to meet the son and give him the money?"

"Half now," Song said. "And half after he gives you copies of the passports, visas, and plane tickets, so we have proof."

Dan wiped the sweat from his forehead. "What if he doesn't trust me? Doesn't believe me?"

"Be convincing." Song smirked. "That or a Chinese prison. I trust you to choose wisely. I want you to phone this number right now and arrange a meeting. We only have two days. By the way, you'll have to take off your arm sling and rib tape."

A voice on the phone told Dan to go, alone, at a certain hour, by a certain route, to the guard shack of a slaughter-house owned by the Army. He was to show the money and would receive further instructions.

Dan walked to the appointed place, arm aching, and counted the money as the guard watched. The guard looked familiar. He might have been one of the men Dan had seen in Wu's office. The hair rose on the back of his neck. Does this blow his cover? But then he realized it might help if the man thought he dealt with Wu. Then again, the man might not have recognized him, since all Westerners look alike to the Chinese. This did suggest that not all the Blue Dragon had been caught. He looked for a tattoo and didn't see one as the man held out his hand with something in it. He was given a slip of paper with a meeting time for the next day and an address. The guard said, "The students will be going through Shanghai and Tokyo, not Beijing. And bring the passport photos."

"Passport photos of the six students?"

The guard nodded.

They didn't have them yet? Dan supposed that they must have a passport counterfeiting operation if they were going to put photos in at the last moment. That could be a problem if the passports were not official. Dan worried about it on the way to meet the Inspector.

An hour later, Dan met the Inspector again. He showed him the slip of paper, but he didn't mention the photos or Shanghai. He had the glimmer of an unformed idea. He loved the irony of it. Was he crazy? Was there enough time?

"Can I see Mingyue before he goes?" Dan asked. "I'd like to say goodbye, after all we've been through together."

"Not a chance." The Inspector laughed. "You'd have to be at the train station right now. His train leaves in fifteen minutes."

⌐⚬⌐ ⌐⚬⌐ ⌐⚬⌐

Mingyue and Yingying sat on the broad concrete plaza in front of the railway station with hundreds of other people, most of them shabby and dirty peasants and workers waiting for trains to the big cities so they could look for jobs. Trains were beginning to run again, but the one to Sichuan was very late. People squatted or lay on the concrete surrounded by sacks and bundles of belongings, eating, talking, or sleeping.

Mingyue felt the irony of his position. He had fought against the corruption of power and special privilege, and here he was the beneficiary of it. But he wondered if it was the same. Deng's son had benefited personally to the harm of others, while Mingyue and Yingying had been struggling for justice and the common good. What harm would the Inspector's help do to others? Mingyue knew the answer: they would be benefiting from protection most other students fighting for the cause wouldn't have. Would it be fair to accept her father's protection, even if it was exile to the country? Would he be foolish not to accept it? He had to speak with Yingying about it.

"Is it right to accept your father's protection?" Mingyue asked. "Isn't that the very favoritism and privilege we were fighting against?"

"I've thought about it," Yingying replied. "You were willing to die for the cause during the hunger strike. And we were both willing to die by immolation. But if we had succeeded, would it have changed anything? We would have been dead and forgotten by everyone but our parents, and the cause would have been defeated anyway. We were in such a hurry to change the world all by ourselves. But it's a big world. We will have to be patient. It may be more effective to stay alive and be willing to struggle for a whole lifetime. It may even be more difficult. Dying may have been too easy."

"It didn't seem easy to me, to leave you." He touched her hand.

She looked at him with drooping eyes clouded by tears. "I am willing to dedicate myself to a lifetime of struggle for freedom and justice," she said. "Let us not be afraid to teach our children what happened, that they may never forget. We would have no children to teach if you went to prison."

Mingyue was not sure he could ever rise out of his depression and disgust at himself and the whole society. Was it even fair to bring children into this ugly world when brutality seemed to win every battle? It seemed too hard. A whole lifetime of struggle that might never succeed. But the world as is was hardly worth living in. Perhaps better the dignity of a struggle that might be doomed to fail than giving in to the certainty of failure if no one tried. Let the struggle be what is important, regardless of its success or failure. The struggle itself could make one noble and make life worth living. If one is born in the mud, one can't help it if one's roots are a bit muddy before one rises out of it like a lotus.

"You're right," he said. He felt her grief and caressed her cheek with a finger to wipe away the tear. He adored her.

Mingyue saw Professor Norton picking his way through the crowd as if searching for someone. He rose to his feet and waved. "Professor Norton, what are you doing here?"

Dan came to him with a big smile and shook his hand. "I had to say goodbye to you and Yingying."

Mingyue pointed at the arm sling. "What happened to you?"

"A minor mishap along life's booby-trapped path." Mingyue frowned, puzzled. "It'll heal. But look, I can get you passports and visas and air tickets and full scholarships to American Bible colleges—well, I can rescue you from the bible colleges when I get home. But you've got to decide right away. I know it's a bit of a shock. You'd have to use false names . . . and ask for asylum as soon as the Chinese government squawked. But think about it."

Mingyue wasn't sure he heard correctly. He saw confusion in Yingying's face. It was a dream come true, but it didn't feel right. He and Yingying looked at each other for a long moment.

"We are among the lucky ones, but there are other students not as lucky as we are." He looked at Yingying and saw her nod. "They will be sent to prison. I know some who would be glad for the chance to escape. But you will have to work fast. The government will be looking for them already."

"Oh, I'll have to work fast all right."

Mingyue and Yingying gave Dan a list of a dozen student leaders who were likely to be desperate enough to take the risk.

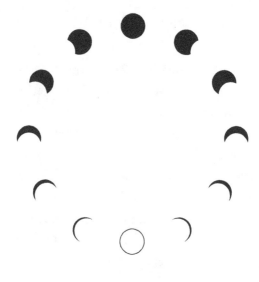

BRIGHT MOON

JUNE 10

WITH FALSE DOCUMENTS AND THE MONEY INSPECTOR Song had given them, Yingying and Mingyue had taken the train west up the Wei river valley to Paoki, then headed south over the Tsinling mountains toward Liangtang in Sichuan.

Mingyue, sunk in gloom, was oblivious of the beautiful mountain scenery.

"Do you think any of those students will actually get to America?" Yingying asked.

"With police looking for them everywhere? Especially at airports? I doubt it."

"We failed," Yingying said. "All our efforts were futile." She slumped back into the train seat.

"It made me sick," Mingyue said. "The useless slaughter, the cruelty. I hated the soldiers. I hated the students' naïveté . . . my own incompetence."

"I hate the corrupt officials," Yingying said. "And they won. I feel so helpless."

"But your father helped us," Mingyue said. "He's not corrupt."

"I hated my father." A tear rolled down her cheek. "But now I don't know what to think. Did he help us because he cared about me? Or did he just need to get me out of the way to save his career?"

"He could have had us both sent to labor camps. That would have been safer for his career. What he did is dangerous." Mingyue touched her hand, and she cried. "I think he really does love you." The reality was beginning to sink into Mingyue's consciousness that he was leaving Xi'an, his family, his friends, his familiar life. "I don't know what to think of my father either. He tried to stop my political activity. But then he joined the big march and supported the students. He risked his own career. Did he change? Or did I just fail to understand him? Now I won't know. I won't see my family again. I'll miss my mother and little brother." They fell into gloomy silence.

The train climbed up a dark mountain valley. Out the window, Mingyue saw that night had fallen. The moon was rising over the mountains, was hidden by clouds, and emerged again. He thought of his name, Bright Moon. The moon had been eclipsed. But an eclipse, however dark and frightening, is temporary. It will pass. Would his eclipse and the eclipse of the Chinese people pass too?

Dan looked at the bright moon as he got out of the taxi. This is loony, he thought. A briefcase of hundred dollar bills. What if they just take them and leave him with nothing? There were supposed to be plain-clothes policemen somewhere here, but Dan didn't see anyone. His only comfort was that stealing from foreigners was a capital offense in China.

He asked at the desk of the elegant Swedish owned Golden Flower Hotel for the room of "Mr. Bao" and was directed to the third floor. He knocked and was told to enter. His hand slipped on the door knob from sweat, and he wiped his hand on his trouser leg and tried again. The dim light in the room revealed three men.

"Search him," one of them said. "Check for wires. We don't want bugs."

A heavy man frisked him.

Dan was sure that a young man in a light blue silk suit was the leader, if for no other reason than the spoiled-child sneer on his face. Dan looked at him. "Mr. Bao?"

"Do you have the money and the photos?" the purported Bao asked.

Dan set the briefcase on a table and opened it. "Half the money. I'll give you the other half when the six students call me from America to prove they are safe."

Dan and Bao glared at each other.

"I don't like to be messed with," Bao hissed. He counted the money on the table and held some bills up to the light. "Maybe we won't . . ."

"All right," Dan said. "Not America. They can call from Tokyo. As long as it's outside of China."

There was a long pause, and Bao scowled at Dan.

"Okay. You just have the students at the airport on time. Here are the visas for good faith. He'll give them the tickets and passports there." Bao gestured toward the heavy man. "But before we give them the tickets and passports, you will have to come into my car with the money. You show me the money, and I'll signal him to hand over the tickets and passports. The students can signal you it's okay. Then you will be my 'guest' while we wait for the phone call. Any funny business, and you're dead. Understand?"

Dan didn't like it that they would be able to take him somewhere and kill him and keep the money. But that might be the best deal he could get for the students. At least they would be on their way. He didn't want policemen at the airport or they might recognize the students. He would have to take the chance. Even Chinese criminals depend on keeping their deals. And he wouldn't tell Song they're not going through Beijing.

He could smell his own flop sweat in the elevator.

HOME

JUNE 12

IT WAS JUST AFTER MIDNIGHT WHEN GAO BAIMA
pounded on Dan's door and burst into his apartment with a packet
of papers in his hand. He collapsed on Dan's couch and moaned.
"My son . . . my son . . ."

Dan sat beside him wanting to put a hand on his shoulder in
spite of the Chinese reluctance to touch.

"Why do I have such a bad son? Riots, hunger-strikes,
immolation, and now this." He choked. "Inspector Song said he
is being sent to the countryside for rehabilitation. Like in the old
days."

Gao buried his face in his hands, and they fell into a gloomy
silence for a while.

"I'm proud of him," Dan said, relieved. "He struggled for justice and freedom. The outcome wasn't in his hands alone. It is doing one's duty to try to make the world better that matters and not the outcome. He wasn't weak but a real leader."

Gao looked at him, mouth agape, as if the possibility of being proud had not occurred to him. "Yes, perhaps I should be proud. But I may never see him again. He's already been sent to Sichuan to work on a farm."

"Not prison, then," Dan said. "I can imagine worse punishments. Perhaps it's really good fortune."

"Yes, perhaps good fortune. You always encourage me." Gao's shoulders relaxed, and he leaned back on the couch. "But I think too much of myself . . . of my son. I came to tell you I've been made the new foreign affairs officer to replace Wu."

"Congratulations." Dan smiled. This was the best news Dan had heard since the six students had called from Tokyo. "You'll be good at it."

"I'd rather teach. I don't know much about the job yet. I did try to arrange a flight for you from Beijing. But there are so many foreigners trying to leave Beijing that it looked like it would be another week. Then someone suggested a different route. I can get you a ticket to Guangzhou at eight in the morning. If I give you dollars, can you get yourself home from there? That American student, Ed, will be going, too."

"Eight a.m. tomorrow . . ." Dan looked at his watch. It was already 1 a.m. "You mean this morning?"

Gao nodded.

"I'll have to pack. No time for goodbyes." Dan smiled. "Of course, no problem."

"Here."

Gao pulled a wad of money and a ticket from the inside of his jacket. "Air ticket to Guangzhou and . . ." He counted out three thousand dollars and a pile of Chinese *Yuan*. "I don't know much about these things. Will that be enough?"

"Where did you get all that?" Dan exclaimed. "That's much more than enough."

"That's what we owe you for the trip here and home, and your last two months' salary."

"But I won't even teach the last month."

"It's not your fault that the university will close early."

Dan felt wealthy and free after so many months of feeling trapped. He could use the *Yuan* to stay in Guangzhou for as long as necessary and for the train to Hong Kong. The dollars would be more than enough to stay in Hong Kong awhile and fly home from there.

"By the way, when I took those documents to Inspector Song for you, he gave back our notes on political events." Gao handed Dan the stack of papers. "He also said something very strange. He looked at the documents and said you tricked him. Then he laughed and said it was all for the best. He not only caught his guy but the penalty for sending student leaders would be even worse than for sending Bible students. I don't know what he meant by that."

Dan smiled. "It's a private joke between us."

Dan got on board the plane ahead of Ed. It tickled his fancy that Ed, who had wanted to leave Xi'an before anyone else had considered it, was the last foreigner from Shaanxi Teachers University to leave. Ed was strangely quiet the whole trip, as if his mind were still back in Xi'an.

Dan half expected the city to be in turmoil when the plane landed in Guangzhou. Dan and Ed took a taxi from the airport through the center of the city to the train station. People were shopping and strolling as if Guangzhou had been unaffected by recent events. Here was where Dan had seen white shirts on men and bell bottom trousers on women in the late seventies when in the rest of China, they had worn Mao suits. Guangzhou was close enough to Hong Kong to get their television programs and be affected by their fashions.

"No," the taxi driver said. "No riots in Guangzhou. Business as usual. A few demonstrations. But most people don't care much what goes on in North China. What they do doesn't affect us much. Everything is peaceful now."

The train ride to Shenzhen through rice paddies plowed by water buffalo, and past subtropical vegetation, soothed Dan's nerves. The ride seemed endless, and the train seemed to crawl. They stopped just at the border. Dan saw dozens of new and half-completed skyscrapers that were sprouting up in the rapidly developing free-trade zone. What a different China this was from Xi'an.

He and Ed had to walk their bags from the train to the border. The border guards were searching a Chinese man's luggage, and Dan tensed. He had the papers in one suitcase. What if his caper with smuggling out students had gotten beyond Inspector Song? What if the police wanted him? His sweat was not just from the tropical heat and carrying bags. He was tempted to turn around and dump the papers in a trash can. There were no trash cans. He steeled his nerves and kept walking.

A guard glanced casually at his passport, stamped it, and waved him through the gate. The train to Hong Kong waited on the other side. Tension he had not known he had carried for months drained from his shoulders. He remembered those movies about refugees

Donald C. Lee

during World War II—the moment of stepping into freedom and not being sure something wasn't going to go horribly wrong, yet. He had been comfortable and enjoyed his year in China, but life was qualitatively different behind the bamboo curtain. Here, his credit cards gave him power to do what he wanted. He felt he had come home.

"I'm going back," Ed said suddenly, startling Dan. There was a tone of finality, of resolution, in his voice.

"What? Right now?"

"When things calm down. For the fall semester maybe. I have a B.A., which is as much as many of the Chinese professors have. I've an English minor, a course in teaching English as a second language, am a native English speaker, and can get around in Chinese. I want to teach English in Xi'an."

"I'll be glad to write you a recommendation to Professor Gao," Dan said. "I guess things are already calming down. I heard that the Twenty-Seventh Army has left Beijing, cleanup has begun, farmer's markets are well stocked, and busses are expected to be moving by tomorrow. Shanghai seems to be the only place where tensions are still at a peak. I suppose that'll be crushed soon, and everything will be back to normal."

"Normal by the standards of a decade ago," Ed said, "not by the standards of freedom we got used to this year."

Dan told Ed what he had read in Gao's latest notes, that over a week ago already, lists of Deng's political enemies had been circulating in Beijing, including Zhao Ziyang and four other members of the Politburo, the military leaders who did not support martial law, including the Defense Minister, a hundred top intellectuals, and now, of course, they were after the top student leaders. All these people would be arrested soon if they had not already gone into hiding, and the purge would filter down to the provincial level. The radio was urging people to turn in student demonstration leaders, free labor union organizers, and martial law violators. People were being arrested in all the provincial cities too.

"It'll be like the Cultural Revolution all over again," Ed said, "when people turned in the innocent against whom they had grudges. It will be a society of fear."

"And you want to go back?"

"They won't have many native English speakers there for a while. They'll need me. And I never felt so alive as I did in China."

They both laughed.

Watching the sampans on the back bay and high-rise apartments of Hong Kong coming into view, Dan thought about the year he had just finished. It had been a terrible year— thousands of students shot and many more lives ruined. The cause of freedom and democracy had been set back in China.

On the other hand, he had seen a blow struck for justice with the arrests of Wu and the Blue Dragon and some corrupt top official whose name he didn't even know. Dan had saved the Inspector's life and sent six student leaders to America. He had played a small part in a small victory against the forces of evil. It was retribution for Vietnam. He had laid some old ghosts to rest. And just because justice had been set back did not mean it would not rise again even stronger. The Romans had lost every battle they fought against Hannibal, until the last one, which won the war. Progress comes in waves, which advance and recede, only to advance farther the next time.

He thought of Yoshiko. She had taught him the Buddhist lesson that one must live in the moment and take what it offers, then let it go. It had been a perfect few days that he could always savor in his memory.

Still, he was glad Gao Baima had given him her address and phone number. After all, the *I Ching* teaches that "perseverance furthers." He remembered all the extra *Yuan* he had which could not be exchanged for dollars. He could give them to Yoshiko, and she would know how to give them to a Chinese Buddhist temple. He would have to call her right away.

In fact, he didn't have to go to the States. Had his brain been so addled by the situation in Xi'an that he couldn't think outside the box? He did not have to teach until August. He could probably get asylum for those Chinese students and get their names back over the phone. Why not go to Japan?

As soon as he got a hotel room, he telephoned her. She said, "Oh, yes, I'd love to see you."

A glow, an excitement grew in his chest. A commitment never to let Yoshiko go.

It had been an unforgettable year. It had been a marvelous year.

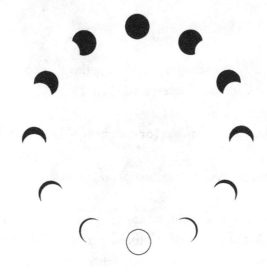

FOR FURTHER DISCUSSION

1. How do you think Dan handled the danger of his situation? Was he naïve? An idealist? Did he have a need for retribution?

2. What were the relationships of Mingyue and Yingying with their fathers? How much did their relationships drive their political actions?

3. What are your thoughts about Inspector Song? Do you think he was secretly sympathetic with the protesters? Was Yingying's judgement of him justified?

4. Was there any character you identified with, sympathized with, liked, or found interesting? Why?

5. How has China changed (or not changed) since 1989?

6. How did you feel during the riot and massacre scenes?

7. There were cultural differences and conflicts between various people in the story, both Chinese and American, often expressed as prejudices. Do you think that several decades of increasing "political correctness" sensitization in the US since then might make such conflict less likely in a similar situation today?

8. Do you think the massacre was intended by the government leaders, or might it have been the result of causes that got out of their control?

9. How do you think Mingyue's character developed throughout the story?

10. Did the book inform you of anything you did not already know about China, and especially about the events before, during, and after the massacre?

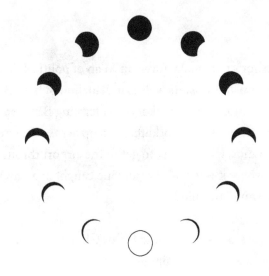

REAL-WORLD INSPIRATION

The descriptions of locations, such as Xi'an, Hua Ching Hot Spring, Louguantai, Dunhuang, and Lanzhou; of Chinese history, like The Tang Dynasty; of life in China during the setting of *Eclipse of the Bright Moon*, such as medical care, worker-boss relations, student housing, the uselessness of credit cards—how it must have changed in the short period since then!—and of the sequence of political events is as true and genuine as Donald C. Lee, as a fallible and limited foreign observer, could make it.

The inspiration of the background events of the protest movement and the massacre, the personal stories, and (often false) rumors of events are all based on a few things:

1. The author's personal witness in Xi'an of political discussions and demonstrations. As well as in Lanzhou of barricades, demonstrations, loudspeakers broadcasting BBC reports in the streets, and seeing forklifts lined up across the street to stop tanks, while trying to get to the airport through streets where it was said that anyone caught in a moving vehicle would be killed.

2. The many stories he was told by his Chinese students and colleagues and other Chinese citizens.

3. What he saw on Chinese TV and heard on BBC radio in Xi'an.

4. A complete record of events in US newspapers and magazines, the articles of which were saved for him in a foot-thick stack by two separate family members.

5. Other information about China was also supplemented by his years of studying and teaching about Marxism and Chinese religion and his studies of Chinese history, literature, philosophy, and politics.

The only exceptions to this are the details of the April riot, the stealing of weapons from the armory, and the shooting of doctors. These were fictionalized events.

Lee even played the role of an "evil westerner" in a major Chinese film, *Terracotta Warrior*, but some of his planned scenes could not be shot because of the political turmoil. China did not have any Western actors and relied on recruiting visiting amateurs for foreign roles. Lee would have included this and other interesting experiences in memoirs, but they would likely have detracted from the dramatic tension in a novel.

There was even inspiration for one of the major plot lines of the novel; the criminal gang. Several months before his departure, Lee was promised to be sent airline tickets that never arrived. He was asked to buy his own tickets and was told he would be reimbursed immediately in American dollars. Since credit cards did not work in China, this was the money he would need to leave China if he had a need to go home early. Lee was assured month after month that he would soon be paid, but he had a vague feeling of being trapped. He suspected that the dollars he was owed were being used illegally on the black market. In the end, he was paid far more than he expected and all was well, but that inspired the idea of "money laundering" which became the first plot line in the novel.

On the other hand, *Eclipse of the Bright Moon* is a work of fiction. Mingyue and Yingying are absolute fictional representatives of all the heroic Chinese protesters, in that they took part in all the major dramatic events of the actual protest movement—a big poster campaign, demonstrations, riots, hunger strikes, self-immolations (or false rumors), and stealing weapons from armories. Inspector Song is the wholly fictional representative of all the government functionaries who—whether they were sympathetic with the protesters or not—were caught between powerful contending forces that could crush them if they made a wrong move.

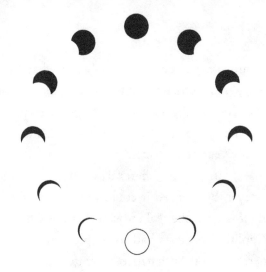

THE AUTHOR'S CONNECTION

Donald C. Lee is currently a professor emeritus of philosophy from the University of New Mexico, and a former Marine Corps officer. In 1988-1989, he was a "foreign expert" in Xi'an, China at Shaanxi Normal University, the university that educates high school teachers and university professors for the northwestern region of China.

There, he taught the history of western civilization and the history of western philosophy, in English, to high school teachers and university professors, and one undergraduate from Inner Mongolia who was recruited for a special program featuring the American professor. Then the Tiananmen Square events happened in the spring of 1989.

Authors are often encouraged to "write what they know." Lee had an experience he wanted to share of life in Communist China during a historically dramatic and significant period of two months. His first inclination was to write a memoir about the whole academic year he had spent there. The novel is a memoir in many senses, for Lee can differentiate what is fact and what is fiction. However, he realized it could not be a memoir for one very important reason: the real individuals from China who took part in the political protests had to be protected from possible government retribution. So, it had to be written as a work of fiction. All of the Chinese characters in the novel that had any political or criminal roles (e.g., Gao and Wu) are partly an amalgam of several people Lee knew and partly fictionalized.

A second reason for writing *Eclipse of the Bright Moon* as a novel rather than a memoir is that Lee's role in the events was as an observer; his actions being so innocuous that they would hardly excite the reader. The American professor, Dan, is in a sense inspired by the author. However, Lee did not receive secret documents, did not hide a fugitive, did not tangle with a criminal gang, did not smuggle student protest leaders out of the country, did not fall in love with a Japanese woman (at least not in that decade of his life), and was not even fluent in Chinese. But he spoke enough to get around.

He did witness several demonstrations, he heard radio and TV reports and the many stories of his Chinese students and colleagues, he was in Dunhuang the night of the massacre and experienced the events of the following three days in Lanzhou as told, except a mob did not emerge from the main bridge and break the window of his van. And he did not cut anyone's arm.

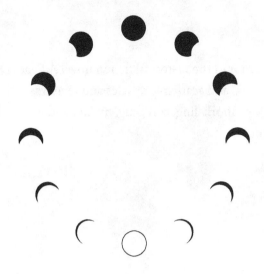

ABOUT THE AUTHOR

Born in San Francisco in 1936, Donald C. Lee received his BA in History and Philosophy at Pomona College. He was a Fulbright Scholar at the University of Tübingen, Germany.

After serving as a Marine Corps Officer in Okinawa and the Philippines and studying French at the University of Geneva, Switzerland, he earned a master's degree in Philosophy at Berkeley—during the Free Speech Movement and anti-war protests—and a Ph.D. in Philosophy at the University of California, San Diego.

He taught Philosophy at the University of New Mexico for twenty-five years and at Shaanxi Teachers University in Xi'an, China, the year ending in the Tiananmen Square massacre in 1989.

He is the author of the historical fiction novel *A Fool's Disciple,* an academic book, and academic articles and reviews.

He enjoys snorkeling, traveling, hiking, and lives in Kirkland, Washington.

If you enjoyed *Eclipse of the Bright Moon*, you might also enjoy *The Wayward Spy* by Susan Ouellette.

When her fiancé, a CIA operative accused of treason, is killed overseas, intelligence analyst Maggie Jenkins smells cover-up and sets out to clear his name, following a trail littered with corruption and deceit, leading straight to a terrorist threat looming where the Russian Mafia, Chechen rebels, Al Qaeda and . . . US government officials meet.

"[A] gripping debut and series launch . . . Ouellette, a former CIA analyst, brings plenty of authenticity to this fast-paced spy thriller. Readers will look forward to Maggie's further adventures."
—Publishers Weekly

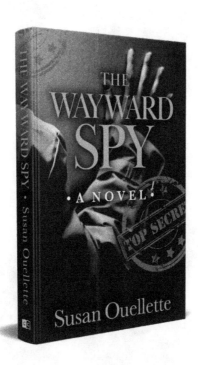

PROLOGUE

TBILISI, GEORGIA

THE ASSASSIN SLID THE GRAY CANVAS BAG ONTO an empty chair to the right. With a final glance at the men seated at the adjacent table, their backs to her, she exited the café's sun-drenched atrium.

Her client had wanted something more dramatic, like a car bomb. But with such short notice, she'd been forced to improvise with the materials on hand. The client wouldn't care. Dead was dead.

After crossing the busy street, she looked over her shoulder. The targets were standing, shaking hands. She was supposed to be further away before dialing the pre-programmed number, but she had to act before they separated. Slipping a hand into her purse, she pulled out the cell phone and hit the number three.

The atrium, a glass-enclosed outdoor dining area at the popular café, exploded into a million tiny shards. A chair flew through the air, landing on the sidewalk in front of the building. Car alarms wailed. Then people.

The American, partially pinned under a mangled metal table, lay still, bleeding profusely from what remained of his right thigh. The other man was motionless, face down on the sidewalk. Crowds gathered on the street as the acrid smoke from the bomb began to dissipate.

When sirens sounded in the distance, the assassin slipped away from the panicked crowd. Under ordinary circumstances, heads turned at the sight of her lithe body, high cheekbones, and striking, olive-colored eyes. Today, she was shrouded in a shabby overcoat, oversized wool hat, and dark sunglasses. The get-up made her feel detached from herself, as if someone else had executed the attack.

The woman turned into the alley where she'd parked hours before. She removed the sunglasses and pulled the cap from her head, unleashing a thick mane of lush, black hair. With a final glance behind her, she smiled. By all measures, it had been a successful morning.

CHAPTER ONE

House Permanent Select Committee on Intelligence
U.S. Capitol Building
November 2003

MAGGIE JENKINS HURRIED ACROSS THE STONE
pavers outside the east front of the U.S. Capitol Building. The autumn wind was especially biting before sunrise. She ducked into
an arched entryway to the left of towering marble stairs, tugged
open the heavy wooden door, and slipped inside just before a sudden gust slammed it shut behind her. She glanced left at a plaque
honoring two Capitol Hill police officers who'd been gunned
down by a madman in that very spot five years earlier. Until the
chaos of September 11, 2001, she couldn't have imagined a more
horrific day on the Hill.

"Morning, miss." The officer's greeting pulled her back to the
present.

"Morning."

She plopped her Kate Spade satchel on the x-ray machine's conveyer belt and passed through the metal detector.

The officer's attention turned to the machine's video screen. "ID, please."

Maggie fished her badge from the pocket of her black trench coat. Getting to work so early meant that it was going to be a long day, but working regular nine-to-five hours hadn't been an option for months.

There'd been one major national security episode after another this year from the U.S. invasion of Iraq to the ongoing manhunt for Saddam Hussein. And besides, the longer she stayed at work, the less time she spent at home. Alone and missing Steve. Three months left on his overseas tour. It felt more like three years.

The officer nodded as Maggie snatched her purse and headed for the Crypt. She paused, savoring the silence in the dimly-lit cavernous room. Soon enough, ringing phones, humming computers, and whirring copy machines would replace the hush.

Her heels clicked across the smooth stone floor as she made her way to the elevator on the far left. Every now and then, wandering tourists would mistake this elevator for a public one. They'd soon discover that it had a sole destination—a rather unremarkable hallway in the attic of the Capitol Building.

Inside the car, Maggie repeatedly punched the up button. A minute later, the old doors groaned open, depositing her forty feet from the entrance to the House Intelligence Committee office. She mumbled a greeting to the night guard, who buzzed her through the main door.

The hearing room directly ahead was dark; she opted for the lit corridor that wound its way around the backside of the windowless space. Uninspiring framed prints of the nation's capital dotted the tan, soundproof, textured walls.

A little further up the hall, her boss Frank Reynolds ducked into his office, shutting the door behind him. *Odd.* He usually wasn't in before 8 a.m. She shrugged and turned into the second office on the left, a small space with worn, government-issue gray carpeting and walls painted to match.

Maggie hung her coat and purse on the coat rack in the corner, slid into her chair, and fired up the Compaq desktop computer. She grabbed a pad of paper and wrote out her to-do list.

- *Finish chairman's briefing book for today's hearing*
- *Ask Agency for latest intel on Putin*
- *Call mom—wedding dress fitting moved to Dec. 4th*

The computer screen brightened from black to green. She logged in, opened the briefing document, and picked up where she'd left off last Friday.

"Could I speak with you a minute?"

She glanced up, then returned her gaze to the monitor. "You're here early, Frank. What's up?"

"Maggie . . ."

She was racing against a deadline. "Can it wait a bit? Have to finish this." The Committee's chairman needed the briefing book ASAP.

"Maggie," repeated Frank. She saved the document and swiveled in her chair. "Sorry—" She paused, startled by the sudden appearance of another man next to him. The CIA's Deputy Director of Operations.

"Warner?" She glanced at the day planner on her desk. Had she forgotten an important meeting?

"Can we talk?" Warner Thompson approached her desk.

He was the CIA's spymaster, a powerful man whose calendar was filled with urgent matters of national security. "What are you doing here? Shouldn't you be in Langley?"

"We need to talk."

She stood, her thighs pressed against the edge of the desk. Warner looked like he hadn't slept. She stared back at him, suddenly aware how odd it was that her fiancé's boss was in her office. "Is everything okay?" A sudden weakness swept over her.

Warner closed his eyes for a moment, as if to collect himself. "I don't know how to say this."

"Say what?" she said as she backed against the chair and sank into it.

Maggie's thoughts occupied two opposing camps engaged in battle. The side that fought hardest was the one insisting Steve was fine. Of course he was. He wasn't in Iraq. Or Afghanistan. He wasn't dodging mortar attacks and suicide bombers. Steve was a spy, a silent soldier, fighting the country's enemies in the shadows, where it was safer. But then there was the other side. The one that knew. She just knew.

Warner knelt beside her. "I'm so, so sorry." His voice cracked. "I came right over as soon as I got the call."

Maggie closed her eyes.

A supersonic slideshow of images flashed through her mind. Steve on his motorcycle. His lopsided grin. The day he proposed. Her wedding dress. News footage of soldiers' flag-draped caskets. The Memorial Wall at CIA Headquarters. All those stars for the CIA's dead.

Not Steve. No star. Not dead. "It's a mistake." She shook her head. "Maybe he's out with an asset and can't report in." Words tumbled from her mouth. "You know how Steve gets when he's in the middle of something big."

"No, Maggie, it's not . . . I'm so sorry."

She looked at Frank. He glanced away.

She fixed her eyes on Warner's. "What are you saying?"

He cleared his throat. "There was an explosion at a café in Tbilisi. We don't know if Steve was the intended target. It could've been mistaken identity or simply being in the wrong place at the wrong time." He took Maggie's hands in his. "Do you understand what I'm saying?"

"Who's we?"

"What?"

She freed her hands and clasped them together. "You said, 'We don't know if Steve was the intended target.' Who's we?"

"The Tbilisi station chief and I."

Her insides constricted, as if a seizure and a heart attack had joined forces against her. "So, the station chief thinks someone killed Steve?" The question sounded absurd. These kinds of things happened to *other* people.

Warner nodded and rubbed his face with trembling hands. "They have his body at the embassy. There was nothing they could do. It was too late."

Maggie heard a moan. When the moan turned into a wail, she realized it was coming from inside of her.

CHAPTER TWO

THE RINGING TELEPHONE STARTLED MAGGIE FROM a fitful nap. Her gaze flitted around, taking in the bedside clock. For a second, she thought she'd slept through the wake. She ignored the phone, rolled onto her side, and stared at the empty half of the bed. Steve's side. Her fingers traced the outline of his pillow, the spot where he'd last kissed her before leaving for his 4 a.m. flight to Tbilisi. "I'll be back. I promise, Maggie," he'd whispered.

For the last eight months, it had been just her in the house, yet she'd never felt truly alone. There'd been calls from Steve. She'd occupied herself working long hours and taking marathon runs on the trail. All helped fill the temporary emptiness until his return. Now, the emptiness was endless.

There was no one, nothing to look forward to, nothing to fill the void.

Kate, her friend from their CIA days together, had offered to stay over for a couple of nights, but then something came up with her husband. Her best friend from college couldn't make the trip from Boston—she was overdue with her second baby. Old high school friends left sympathetic voicemails, but never called back. Everyone was busy. They were married, having babies, leading normal lives. And when you couldn't tell your girlfriends anything true about your future husband, it was much easier to withdraw, to protect Steve, to keep his secrets secret. Other than Kate, none of her friends had a clue what he actually did for a living.

Her head was pounding. She didn't need a mirror to tell her what days of sobbing had done to her face. Her right hand found the damp facecloth on the floor beside the bed. Five minutes of cool moisture probably wouldn't help much, but it was better than nothing. And she had to pull herself together before her parents flew into town.

Her stomach was in turmoil at the thought of seeing Steve's body. The funeral home had assured her that his face was in good condition, and that no one would be able to see the destruction the bomb had wrought on the rest of his body. Maggie let out a guttural scream and threw the facecloth across the room. It landed with an unsatisfying splat against the wall.

Downstairs, the doorbell chimed.

Maggie groaned and dragged herself from the bed. She tugged the black dress from the hanger and slid it over a silk slip and a pair of black stockings.

"Shoes . . . where are my shoes?" The doorbell chimed again as she rifled through a jumble of high heels on the closet floor. "Just a second," she muttered, abandoning the shoes and scampering downstairs.

When she opened the front door, bitter wind greeted her with a slap. Maggie squinted up at her visitor. "You look exhausted, Warner."

Warner shook sleet from an umbrella and wiped his polished wingtips on the sodden welcome mat. "And I feel like hell." His gray-flecked eyes searched her face. "How are you?"

She shivered against the cold. "Hell pretty much sums it up."

"Look, I . . . can we talk for a few minutes?"

Her throat tightened. "Of course. Come in." She was due at the funeral home in an hour. "I have a few minutes." Maggie ushered him into the living room. The soft sage-colored walls felt naked, cold. Assorted frames stood stacked in the corner waiting to be rehung. Their formal engagement photo lay atop the pile. A light film of dust muted her fiery hair and his bright eyes. Steve was supposed to hang the pictures. That was the deal—if she painted the walls, he'd put it all back together when he came home.

In the kitchen, she swallowed the lump in her throat and turned to Warner. "Coffee?" she offered. "We have time. I was going to pick my parents up at Dulles, but their flight was delayed. Snow. So, they'll take a cab directly to the funeral home," she rambled, certain if she stopped talking, she'd collapse in a heap. "They'll be landing soon."

"I'll send a car."

"I should be the one—"

Warner raised his hand. "No. Consider it done."

"Okay." She turned toward the stove. "How about that coffee? Or tea? Herbal? Decaf?" The burner clicked and hissed under the copper kettle.

"Save yourself the trouble. I'm fine." He stared out the window into the darkness. "I have some new information about Steve. It's . . ."

"It's what?"

Warner shook his head. "It can wait."

"What can wait? You obviously came over here to tell me . . . something." She fought to keep from shouting.

"This isn't the best time to talk about it, but I don't want you to hear it from someone else first."

"Hear what?" She hugged her arms around her waist. The fern nestled in the bay window reached out to her, still clinging to life. It was Steve's. All the plants were. Whenever he was overseas, they suffered greatly from her benign neglect.

"Well," he cleared his throat, turning toward her, the pain in his face hardening. "Our people on the ground in Georgia say that Steve was meeting an asset at the café when the bomb went off."

"And?" Maggie snatched pearl earrings off the counter, fumbling to put them on. "That's exactly what you told me three days ago."

"I know," Warner conceded. "But now we have another source confirming the original report."

"Who?"

"I can't tell you that."

She rubbed her forehead and stared at him.

"I don't know, Maggie. None of this makes sense. Steve's tradecraft was exemplary. Normally, he'd never meet an asset in a public place, especially not a Chechen."

A Chechen? She knew Chechnya well from her time as a CIA analyst. A Russian province that bordered Georgia to the northeast, it was home to both radical Muslim terrorists and innocent civilians decimated by two recent wars with Russia.

As far as Maggie knew, Steve's mission was to cultivate ties with Georgia's intelligence agencies and recruit Russian spies who strutted around Georgia as if they owned the place. "Since when has he recruited Chechens?"

Warner pulled a stool up to the granite island. He sat, smoothing the pleat in his crisp, black pants. "That's not really important. It's this new information that has me worried." He folded and unfolded his hands, finally placing them on the counter. "It may be a very serious matter."

Maggie flinched. "What?"

"Steve may have been selling information to Russia . . ."

She stared. Steve was an Eagle Scout, honest to a fault. And he was the most loyal man she'd ever met.

"At this point, it's still just a rumor from this new, unvetted source." Warner shook his head. "But this is Steve we're talking about. He wouldn't get involved with the Russians, not without authorization. I don't know why—"

"Is it true?" she interrupted, her voice barely a whisper.

Warner's brow creased. "I'm not sure."

Maggie's skin burned as if she'd been shocked. "Why won't you tell me who your source is?"

"I told you I can't reveal that. Not even to you." He straightened himself on the stool. "There will be a thorough investigation, and, of course, I will keep you informed of any developments."

His suddenly impersonal tone startled her. "What exactly are you saying, Warner? That I'm supposed to wait for some bureaucrats to decide whether my fiancé was a traitor or not?" She shook her head. "No. You will not shut me out of this process. Clear me into whatever classified programs you have to. I want . . . no, I need to be part of the investigation."

"Even if I could, you're too emotionally involved to handle—"

"Emotionally involved? Really?" Her voice rose over the screech of the kettle. "We were supposed to get married! In April, in case you forgot." She choked on a sob. "There has to be something else going on here. There has to be!"

Warner stood and reached around her to shut off the burner. "I'm in this with you, Maggie. Whatever it takes. We'll find the truth. We will find who killed Steve."

The kettle's whistle gave a final, dying gasp, and the house fell silent for a moment.

Warner checked his watch. "I'm headed to the funeral home. Let me drive you."

"No, I'm okay." She felt gutted, as if her core had been ripped out.

"You shouldn't have to do this alone." He touched her lightly on the arm.

She placed her hand over his and lingered for a moment before pulling away. He was right, she shouldn't be alone, but she was. Because Steve was dead. "I'm . . . no, it'll be fine. I promise not to do anything stupid. No motorcycle."

They smiled.

"That was crazy, Maggie."

"Yeah, Steve was pretty freaked out." He and Warner had been working late one Friday night when she decided to bring them Chinese takeout.

"The look on his face when you pulled up on his precious motorcycle . . ." Warner laughed.

"I know. He . . ." She shook her head. "I wish I'd had a camera." Fresh tears sprang to her eyes.

VISIT US ONLINE FOR
MORE BOOKS TO LIVE IN:
CAMCATBOOKS.COM

FOLLOW US

CamCatBooks   @CamCatBooks   @CamCat_Books

CPSIA information can be obtained
at www.ICGtesting.com
Printed in the USA
LVHW011038110521
687090LV00001B/47